THE ▬▬▬ ▬S

SHEENA KALAYIL

First published June 2025
Published in the UK by
Fly on the Wall Press
56 High Lea Rd
New Mills
Derbyshire
SK22 3DP

www.flyonthewallpress.co.uk
ISBN PBK: 9781915789389
EBOOK: 9781915789396
Copyright Sheena Kalayil © 2025

A CIP Catalogue record for this book is available from the British
Library.

[…]
back then, when I fetched them,
like someone without a homeland,

someone who holds a sail, not his own,
into the wind, not his own
on a body of water, not his own…
Elke Erb
Thema Verfelht

In memory of my father, Mathew Mathai Kalayil

FINDING TOMMY

THE OTHERS

1

It is warm and sunny, mid-June, and four months almost to the day since she first met Armando. That was an evening in February – a bitterly cold evening. Since, they have met nearly every Saturday night at a bar in the centre, in convivial groups. Once for an afternoon barbecue, during which they had half an hour to themselves before being dragged into the mêlée of dancing and drinking – and at which she was introduced to Clara. He had already told her of his daughter, but meeting the small person brimming with personality, with his wide-set eyes but the rest likely inherited from the mother, was a jolt.

She had been determined not to let herself fall for him – too complicated, plenty of fish etcetera – knowing even then that it was futile to sustain such resolve. And if she has fallen in love with him, then she loves him without knowing him, not really. How can she? They have only met once on their own: this a fortnight ago, on a Saturday afternoon when he asked her to help him choose a dress for Clara. That entailed a trip to the city's only department store, on another bright but chillier day, after which they sat in the sun with doughnuts and coffee, talking. He told her of his first post in Berlin when he was so much younger and enthused, starstruck by the big city. She told him of her nomadic childhood, how she had been devastated by her parents' divorce. She had hoped that the afternoon would extend into a trip to the cinema or even dinner. But he said he had plans, plans involving Clara, and although he walked her back to her residence later, he had then left her to catch a bus to one of the new towns north of the centre.

Yet he is not aloof. On the contrary, he is warm and interested, gently chivalrous without being overbearing, but always busy, always otherwise engaged with a formidable array of commitments. A former partner and a small child, alongside a job in a factory, makes for a busy life. The shopping trip spanned only an afternoon; she had felt bereft when he dropped her off. But then arrived this invitation. They are going to the beach, they will have lunch in a restaurant, and Armando has said that he will see her home at night. Which implies that he intends to spend up to twelve hours with her. Whether Clara will always be in tow she has not wished to ask, not daring to appear too eager. But she is eager.

She waits by the magazine stand, just outside the station. He comes striding towards her, Clara in his arms.

'Hello,' he says and bends to kiss her on each cheek – first the right, then the left – so that briefly she catches the scent of his aftershave, before he turns to his daughter.

'Do you remember Lolita?'

The little girl buries her face in her father's neck, but Armando proffers her like an ice-cream – an invitation for her to kiss Clara's cheeks, which are soft, rounded, and scented with peppermint.

'Have you been waiting long?'

She arrived half an hour early but says: 'Oh no.'

'Thanks for coming.'

His eyes crinkle at the corners as he smiles at her, genuinely, as if there was a real possibility she would have refused.

'Thanks for inviting me.'

'Lolita helped me choose this for you, you know,' he says to his daughter, tugging at the hem of the little girl's dress: blue and white, with yellow buttons from the neckline to the waist.

'You look lovely, Clara,' she gushes, and then Armando sets the little girl on her feet and, his eyes sweeping over her, over the red dress it is finally warm enough to wear, says, 'So do you.'

Her heart starts thumping in her chest at his gaze, but she ducks her head and fingers the ribbon in Clara's hair.

'Did your mama do this?'

Clara nods, one hand holding her father's and the other clutching her doll.

'And who's this?'

She shakes the doll's hand, but the little girl only stares back at her, impassively.

'Fufu,' Armando says. Then, 'Lolita is going to be a doctor. She can help us if we get sick.'

At this, shyly, Clara holds up her doll: plastic, beige and blue-eyed, with garish, yellow polyester hair.

'Is Fufu not feeling well?'

She bends down and touches the back of her hand to the doll's forehead.

'No fever,' she says. 'I'll just check her pulse,' and she makes a show of placing her index and middle finger on the plastic wrist and looking at her watch.

'All good. She's probably just a little tired.'

Clara gives her a solemn nod of approval, her eyes shining. And then they stand, the three of them in the sunshine: Lolita and Armando, suddenly awkward, avoiding each other's eyes, smiling down at Clara. Armando looks around.

'She needs the toilet. I'll just take her.'

He says something to Clara, in Portuguese now, and the child pulls at his hand so he stoops down to put his ear next to her mouth, before straightening up.

'She wants you to take her,' he says.

They look at each other.

'Do you mind?'

'Not at all.'

Fufu the doll is passed to Armando for safekeeping. The little girl's hand in hers is soft and tiny and damp. She has little experience with small children, not having grown up in an extended family of young cousins or nieces and nephews. And she is an only child – like Clara. She holds the door open and the child scampers inside.

The restroom is bare but clean, like the city itself, even the country. Bare but clean. The child only needs help climbing up, for then she holds herself upright, gripping the toilet seat without inhibition. A vigorous splashing commences and when she glances at the child, she meets her brown, solemn eyes. She tears off some paper which the child uses, carefully. Then, as she flushes the toilet, Clara runs past her legs and waits expectantly by the sink. Well trained. She lifts the small body, opens the tap and oversees a thorough soaping and rinsing, remembering the clutching hands, and then briefly, instinctively, touches her lips to Clara's head. There is no towel, so they shake their hands dry, Clara now grinning. She pulls open the door again and Clara rushes out to her father.

Again, Armando says something to the little girl in Portuguese, but then in German, for her benefit: 'Did you say thank you to Lolita?'

The child addresses her for the first time in a surprisingly husky voice.

'Danke.'

There is now some relief in Armando's expression: the day has got off to an auspicious start.

'I'll get some tickets.'

He brushes aside her offer to pay, even though she knows that he earns little from the factory. They occupy such different spheres, they may never have met if four months ago she had not been in the common room of her residence at the exact moment when Max, another medical student, came to the door: 'Party over in LK, and we're invited.' She learned then that the laundries and electrical plants and car manufacturers and printing factories, which dominate the otherwise barren landscape in the northern reaches of the city, were largely run by a workforce comprising Angolans and Mozambicans and Cubans. One of these factories – she knows now it was Joachim's – was throwing a farewell party for an Angolan workmate. The party in the warehouse was already in full swing when the convoy of students led by Max arrived, but they were welcomed warmly. Afterwards, on their epic trek back to the historic city centre, having missed the last tram, Max confessed that he had been charged with bringing women, who were vastly outnumbered. And indeed, she had been swirled around the makeshift dance floor by a succession of men, until the one she had noticed – very good-looking, the one who watched her while she was on the floor – asked her if she would dance with him. He did not hold her close, like the others did, and he did not give her instructions, like the others did, but only smiled into her eyes occasionally and, at the end of the song, bowed over her hand. He had hardly spoken. She asked him about the type of music that was playing – marrabenta, he replied, the word rolling off his tongue – and she did not dance again with him. When they were leaving, however, he appeared at her side. He told her that he knew of a bar in the centre, where writers and poets gathered to perform their works. It was shabby, but it had a great atmosphere and there was always something new. Would she like to come one weekend? A few days later, his phone call arrived, along with the invitation to meet the following Saturday evening.

They board the train, to sit side by side, Clara on Armando's lap, and she finds that her arm brushes against his, constantly, with the movement of the train. He asks after her studies as he always does. He is especially interested in her clinical practice, in the patients she has assisted with, but if she asks the same of his work at the printing factory, he always shrugs his shoulders: 'We put the machines to work, that is all.'

The man opposite, his knee hooked over his arm rest, has closed his eyes, but she can see that he is not asleep: his eyelids flutter open occasionally to regard them. Clara leans back against her father's chest, her doll on her lap, humming a tune while brushing its long yellow tresses. Outside, the vista quickly becomes bucolic: flat, green fields and open skies.

'It might be warm enough by now to swim,' he says.

'I remember swimming around this time last year.'

And then she stops. For this time last year, she was still going out with Willy, who is now in Leipzig. Their break-up arrived only a few weeks after their visit to the beach. She can feel the colour rise to her cheeks and she can see that he has noticed.

'I might have been at the beach the same time, then,' he says, smiling. 'But probably not. I would have remembered you.'

She wants to parry back, as flirtatiously as is seemly with the child sitting on his lap, but she can only think to say, 'I wish you had been there,' and she hears that she sounds not light-hearted nor coy, as she wished, but completely sincere. He smiles more widely, the dimple in his chin making a brief appearance.

She tries to look nonchalant, glances out of the window at regular intervals, speaks in a low, neutral voice, tucks her hair occasionally behind her ear, but this is hard to maintain, given that Armando is so close, and given that, while his arm is clasped lightly around Clara's waist, his eyes are mostly on her. As always, when she is near him, she is intensely aware of her body. This is a land where people throw off their clothes at will to worship the sun. She has seen couples on the beach, limbs entwined, half naked, not unlike two snakes mating, and she has seen women walking topless, insouciantly, with sun-burnished breasts bouncing in an abundance of sizes and shapes. The horror she felt at so much flesh on show when she first arrived at age eighteen has evolved, nearly five years on, to an admiration for the abandon, the celebration of the human form with all its varieties and imperfections. Underneath her dress, rather than her usual black one-piece, she is wearing the sky-blue bikini, bought two years ago when she first visited the beach with Willy. She inspected herself in the mirror before leaving her residence this morning and she thought then that she looked well. Now she is not so sure, knowing, at the same time, that she craves to be seen by him.

That first Saturday evening, when she pushed open the door to Sonderbar, her heart was in her mouth in anticipation. The bar is tucked away in the cellar of an old building, and decorated in studied opium den chic, dimly lit by no more than six hanging lightbulbs, cloaked in handmade, red-paper lampshades. A windowless, large, square basement room, with bare wood floorboards, several armchairs and sofas sporting cigarette burns lurking along its dark edges. She had expected only Armando to be there, but he introduced her to Joachim, who was propping up the bar and who had given them all a lift in his car. For there were also his three housemates, and she soon learned that the men always arrived together, even if they did not always leave together.

He has phoned her every week now, arranging a meeting at Sonderbar. He always insists on buying her drink and, after, they discuss, carefully, the writers and poets and their readings, many of which are impenetrable, pessimistic, several of which are hedonistic, bawdy, even crude. While it was Armando who first invited her, and while she arrives for him, his housemates are keen to monopolise her attention, and she is always placed between Tiago and Ronaldo. At least while the performances are taking place. When these are over, it is always Armando who she finds herself talking with and it is always Armando who accompanies her to the residence, before catching a lift with Joachim back to the factory.

Every evening when he bids her goodnight with a kiss, she feels a crushing disappointment that this is on each cheek and not on her lips, and there have been many evenings when she has cried afterwards into her pillow like a teenager, not knowing how much she is imagining, not knowing how to make the first move. But perhaps now he has made the first move, with this day at the beach.

2

They walk along the path, away from the town. The beach stretches for nine miles, a wide expanse of white sand, edged by the clear blue waters of the Baltic Sea. He grew up by the Indian Ocean with its gigantic waves and churning currents, vast and powerful, fringed by palm trees, yet today the sun here is as gloriously bright, the water is as blue.

They walk for at least a mile, absorbing the warm rays. To one side, the path now hugs a wide, flat, grassy area, only two snack-bars in sight. One is still closed; the other, serving kettwurst, has six people crowded around the hatch, four of whom sport the khaki uniforms of border guards. He reminds Lolita that they will have to take Clara back the same distance and so they take off their shoes and drop down from the path onto the soft, deep, sand, warm under their bare feet. Now, away from the path, as if heralding the true nature of today's outing, he presses one hand to the small of Lolita's back, as he points the direction. He has not done this before and it is thrillingly sensuous, to feel the complex lattice of muscles around her spine beneath his fingers.

There is a quiet spot, a cove, beyond which the coast curves around a cluster of rocks, and here they settle with a view of the open water. He throws down the blanket he packed into his bag and takes out Clara's assortment of playthings. There is no one in sight: they have the sand and water to themselves. His daughter is hopping in excitement from foot to foot, pulling at his hand, eager to enter the water, even though the parent-and-child swimming classes at the local pool have not been a success. If he could, he would teach Clara himself, but even if the pool timetable intersected with his working hours, his presence would be scandalous and will cause Petra further embarrassment. At least, that is what she believes. Now he does not challenge his daughter's bravado, only unbuttons

Clara's dress and lifts it over her head.

'I promised Mami if it's too cold we won't swim. We'll try a little bit.'

He looks up at Lolita.

'Will you come in?' he asks, before pulling his shirt over his head, then unzipping and stepping out of his jeans.

He sees that she looks suddenly self-conscious, unsure of where to look, and he understands. From meeting in short bursts, mostly in the dark, bundled up in wools and denims, they are now flinging off their layers in bright sunlight, and parading their bodies to each other. He scoops Clara up with a whoop and jogs away, away from Lolita and down the sand into the water.

The sea is outrageously cold. He keeps a tight hold of his daughter, marvelling, as always, at the hardness and softness of her tiny, wriggling body. Now, in her excitement, she kicks at his ribs and he exaggerates the pain, pretends he will stumble backwards into the water, and she screeches in fear and delight. He splashes some water onto her chest, and she squeals again, clapping her hands against his ears. He tosses his daughter up in the air before catching her, then trailing her feet in the water, her toes funnelling through the waves.

From the corner of his eye, he can see that Lolita has slipped off her jacket, is unbuttoning her dress and he watches as she lets it fall to the sand. He does not watch as she runs towards them and splashes into the water, now swilling around her knees. She gasps and he laughs.

'Can you believe it's so warm outside and the water is still so cold?'

He keeps his gaze trained on her face, but when she bends to dip her hands in the swirling, grey-blue water, he allows his eyes to move swiftly over her body.

'Be a horse! Be a horse!'

Clara is now on his shoulders, pulling at his ears, and he obeys immediately. He charges up the sand with a whinny, Clara yelping with delight.

The dry sand feels luxuriously warm in comparison to the icy water. A nearby circle of rocks forms a perfect shallow pool for

Clara. He takes out the sunhat that Petra has packed for her, ties the straps under her chin, and watches as she runs to the pool.

'Wait for me,' he calls out, but she is immediately intent on a project, squatting on the sand at the water's edge with her plastic spade and a small red bucket.

'Don't go in the water alone,' he calls out again, but she does not respond.

'Filha!'

She looks up now, and his heart turns over at the sight of her heart-shaped face and the frown between her eyebrows.

'Don't go in the water without Papa.'

She nods, impatiently, and resumes her task. How long will it occupy her? He is hoping for a half hour at least, to enable a conversation with Lolita, and with this thought he looks around for her. She has pinned her hair up high on her head to avoid it getting wet, and while she is dipping herself in and out of the shallows, she only once swims a few strokes into the wave. Now she looks up and sees him watching her.

'I can't feel my toes anymore,' she calls out and then wades out of the water.

He bends over, in a pretence of rummaging in his bag, but when she has covered half the distance between them, he gives into temptation. He straightens up and watches her, frankly, his eyes taking her in. He has imagined her many times without her clothes on, but she is truly a vision: the blue triangles of the bikini are single, vivid brushstrokes on the golden-brown canvas of her skin. She has noticed him watching her, and so, to lighten the mood, he collapses on his knees as if in defeat, then falls forwards clutching an imaginary arrow to his heart.

'Papa, what are you doing?'

Clara's voice from the rock pool is high-pitched with disapproval, and clutching her spade, her orange sun hat slightly askew, she makes for a furious, tiny adjudicator.

'Lolita is trying to kill me, that's all,' he says, getting to his feet.

'Pardon?'

'Nada, nada,' he calls out, and Clara frowns and squats down on the sand again.

By now he can see that Lolita has understood his cryptic message even if his daughter hasn't, for she is blushing furiously. He smiles at her, widely, foolishly widely, to hide the fact that he is abashed, mollified by his daughter, the chaperone.

'Sorry,' he says under his breath.

He picks up her towel and hands it to her, averting his eyes as she dries herself vigorously. But then he cannot help watching her, he hopes discreetly, as she unclasps her hair, so it falls in a shiny black pool over her shoulders, before reaching into her bag to pull out a light cotton shawl. It cascades from her hands like a vivid fountain of magenta and turquoise and, dotted with tiny mirrors, shimmers in the sun. She tucks the shawl around her shoulders, modestly, but the soft diaphanous material clings to her body, and only draws attention to her long bare legs. She looks beautiful. He waits for her to sit down on the blanket, demurely pressing her knees together, before he lowers himself next to her and touches the ends of her shawl.

'This is nice.'

'Thank you.'

'It's from India?'

She smiles. 'Yes.'

The breeze is now stiff. The weather is capricious, clouds are scudding across the blue sky from nowhere, casting a shadow over the sand. They watch Clara.

'She notices everything,' he mutters.

'She's very bright.'

'Yes, she is.' He can hear that his voice is full of pride and to avoid sounding boastful, he adds, 'Of course, she gets her brains from Petra.'

Clara's mother, about whom Lolita has received a short biopic – six years Armando's senior and a journalist.

She is smiling, mischievously: 'And her looks.'

He laughs. 'Yes, that too,' he says, even though he knows that Clara bears more resemblance to his second-older sister.

'You must be very proud of her.'

17

'I am. I only wish that I could see more of her.'

At this, he can see her eyes darken, in sympathy or confusion, for he can see also that she does not know how to respond. Only a few minutes ago he was eyeing her up, brazenly, and now he is alluding to his role as a weekend father.

So, he grins at her. 'Tiago wanted to come today.'

She takes to the topic of Armando's wayward friend with obvious relief.

'Did he?'

'He's very jealous I'm with you.'

She laughs. 'Was he even awake when you left the house?'

'He wasn't back from his night out.'

'With whom?'

'I'm not sure. He has a lot of success with women.' He grins. 'But lucky for me, not with you.'

He watches her blush again, but she keeps her chin up, defiantly.

'I'm not his type.'

'I think you are.'

'Well, he's not mine.'

'Again, lucky for me,' he smiles at her.

Unforgettable exchanges, he will replay them later that night. But too brief, fleeting, for when his eyes move over her shoulder to find his daughter, he sees that Clara's two high curly bunches are wobbling in the stiff breeze that is now blowing off the sea and that she is upright, tugging excitedly at something, so intent she has placed one foot against a rock and is using both hands, unaware of the water pooling at her ankles.

He gets to his feet.

'Clara,' he is now half-laughing at her singlemindedness, but as he nears his daughter, he can see more clearly what she is doing and he calls back to Lolita.

'She's found something.'

He tries to prise his daughter's fingers from a strap, attached to a small bag which is caught under a rock. By now, Clara is incensed that her discovery has been taken away from her. He feels her little hands smack at his legs.

'It's mine!'

'Espera,' he replies, firmly, and something in his tone stills her.

Lolita arrives at his side, and he sees her take Clara by the hand. When he finally pulls the bag free, he sees that it is more like a pouch, clipped to a belt. The clip is hanging broken, but the pouch is not misshapen from the water. It is not old; it is nearly new. He opens the zip and glances inside.

'What's wrong?' Lolita asks, for the astonishment must show on his face.

Clara has stopped whining and is staring at her father, as he walks his fingers through the contents. He zips up the pouch and lobs it into the air so that it lands onto their blanket. And then he scans the water around them.

He hears Lolita behind him: 'Armando?'

But he does not answer her, only wades into the waves, towards the cluster of rocks just before the bend, where he can see now that there is something in the water. Something long and dark grey, bumping up and down with the waves, beckoning him and warning him at the same time.

3

She wants to call him back but her voice is gone, and he is wading in deeper and deeper. She simply stares, paralysed, mirrored by the little girl, who has instinctively drawn closer to her. Even from where she is standing, she can see Armando's flesh shrinking in protest at the icy water, but he continues to wade towards the object rooted to its location, like a buoy. But it is not a buoy – now they can see that it is a surfboard. And as she watches, Armando dives under the waves and disappears. Something else bobs up, just once, and then goes down again. Bobs up once again, and then submerges. The surfboard moves, released, Armando reappears, and the other shape, a large shape, rises to the surface. It is the body of a man.

Armando is still struggling, untangling something in the water, finally succeeding so that his arms are suddenly full, clamped around the body. It is a man, in a navy-blue wetsuit. Now Armando looks up for her, at her, and she understands. She tightens her grip on Clara's hand. The child starts squirming, trying to pull away – not so malleable now, stiff and resisting.

'Come, Clara.'

She manages to navigate the little girl back to their blanket.

'Shall we put our dresses back on? It's getting colder now, isn't it?'

She can barely form her words, her lips are numb, even though she is not in the icy water. All the while, it is as if she has eyes on the back of her head. She can visualise Armando escorting the body on the waves, and then carrying it out of the water and laying it on the sand.

'Will you help me with my buttons, and I'll help you with yours?'

She shrugs off the dupatta and pulls her dress on, over her head. The child has one arm around her doll and has quietened. Perhaps she is scared by what is happening behind them, for she does not resist, only touches the fingertips of her free hand to Lolita's dress, ineffectually.

'And now it's your turn.'

She extricates Fufu gently from the child's arms and slips the dress over Clara's head, then restores the doll to her embrace. As she is fastening and counting the buttons out loud, Armando appears at her side to collect his jacket, and she turns around with Clara in time to see him arrange it over the top of the body, eclipsing what is the face. Then he jogs back to them, and she lets the child go. Clara runs over to her father – who is now towelling himself off, pulling on his shirt, his jeans, his teeth all the while chattering – and grips his legs. When he is dressed, she jumps into Armando's arms and buries her face in his neck.

'What is it, Papa?' Her voice is barely audible. 'What did you find in the water?'

'A man who couldn't swim,' he says quietly.

'Can I see him?' She has shut her eyes tightly, even as she asks the question.

'I think it's better if you don't, Clara.'

'Will we take him to hospital?'

He looks over at Lolita. 'Maybe. Let's think for a minute.'

Clara suddenly starts to cry – whether because her father is still shivering from the cold or because she has seen something she should not have – while Armando holds her tight, speaking gently now in Portuguese, soothing her, caressing her back.

She leaves them, crosses over the patch of sand, and kneels next to the body, which is lean and taut in his wet suit. It is the corpse of a fit young man. Automatically, she checks for his pulse on his wrist, just as she had done with the doll Fufu, and he might as well be a plastic mannequin, for he is stone cold, stone dead. She lifts the jacket and sees mottled indigo skin in places, porcelain white in others, a charcoal bruise on the forehead, and eyelids half-closed over startlingly blue eyes. She passes her fingertips over the eyelids, and she drops the jacket to touch his stiff, cold wrist again. Around it there is a bracelet, like that more commonly seen on a teenage girl, which she unclasps so that it lies in her palm. It is a collection of blank and lettered beads, which spell out a name: Tommy. She is about to lift the jacket from his face again, as if to ascertain that when he was alive he suited his name, when she hears voices approaching.

She gets to her feet, slipping the bracelet into the pocket in her dress and then Armando is suddenly behind her, gripping her elbow. He takes her hand and pulls her closer to him, away from the body, just as a small crowd gathers around them. They are four men, dressed in the khaki clothing of border guards, all agitated, sweating as if the day were not turning much cooler than its promising start. One brushes unceremoniously past Armando to bend over the body, and one asks him, brusquely, for his papers. When Armando, still shivering beside her, does not answer immediately, the guard barks his demand.

'Die Papiere!'

'In my jacket,' Armando says, and he points to the figure on the sand.

The guard squatting by the body removes a plastic wallet from the inside pocket of the jacket, from which he extracts the papers to inspect, and it is obvious that he is giving them more attention than necessary, buying time while thinking what to do. To her side she sees that the surfboard, now untethered, has washed onto the beach a few metres further away and she watches as another guard hurries forward to retrieve it. It looks incongruous in his arms – he is plump, pale-faced, not like the young man stretched out on the sand, the water now lapping at his feet.

Now the first guard, the leader of the pack, straightens up, holding the plastic wallet like a menu in a restaurant, before he passes it to the youngest of the quartet, who springs into action, withdraws a notebook from a pocket, then stands alert, pen at the ready.

The leader addresses Armando: 'Why did you bring him here?'

'Sorry?'

'Why did you bring him here?' his index finger moving up and down like a drill, pointing at the sand.

'Because,' Armando is speaking slowly, 'because I didn't want to leave him in the water.'

'You could have called us.'

'I didn't know you were here.'

A silence follows, as if this were a rebuke. The second guard takes his own jacket off and deftly swaps it with Armando's. Then he pats and presses, pushing his hands into each pocket, withdrawing the contents, which are not many: a plastic card from the factory passed over to the younger colleague with the notebook, a hair band matching those that are already in Clara's hair, a box of matches and a packet of cigarettes, and then from the inside pocket, a trail of small square shiny packets. This is held up for everyone to see. A set of unopened condoms, available everywhere, which she knows are distributed monthly at the factory where Armando works, but the guards nod grimly. Beside her she can feel that Armando has stiffened, and then she feels his fingers squeeze her hand, tentatively. She squeezes his hand back.

'When did you get here?'

'A couple of hours ago.'

'By train?'

'Yes.'

'Why did you come here? Isn't it better with the little girl,' Das Kleine Mädchen, 'to be nearer the town?'

'We wanted somewhere quiet.'

The man fingers the packet of condoms, his eyes flickering between them, suggestively.

'Somewhere quiet.'

All the while, the fourth guard is gathering their things – Clara's bucket and spade, the blanket, Armando's towel, and making a pile next to the rest of their belongings. Then he calls out. He is holding up the pouch with the broken clasp, which he throws in the air to the leader who catches it, opens the zip and then closes it.

The man rotates slowly to face Armando: 'You found this?'

'Yes.'

'But you didn't tell us.'

'I forgot it was there.'

'You forgot,' shaking his head. 'Were you going to keep it?'

'No.'

'Did you look inside?'

'No.'

The man holds his eyes. 'Were you waiting for him?'

'Who?'

His foot points to the body. 'This.'

'No.'

'You don't know him?'

'No.'

'Then how did you know he was there?'

'We saw the board,' Armando says, and now he points at the pair of binoculars hanging off the guard's belt, 'And if you were using those you would have seen it too.'

There is silence, and she finds she is holding her breath. When she glances at him, she sees that Armando is gazing at the guard with an affected innocence, but that his eyes are cool. Clara, in his arms, is staring open-mouthed at proceedings, attuned to the nuances of her father's tone and hence to the undercurrent of antipathy. Before them all, the guard's face whitens.

Then, with a chilling note of warning, 'Vorsichtig.'

For the first time, the youngest, the one with the notebook, breaks his silence and addresses Lolita.

'Are you the mother?'

But before she can reply, Armando interrupts, hurriedly, his voice laden with anxiety, 'No, no she's not. I invited her today.' He might as well have said: leave her out of this.

The youngest guard nods, not unpleasantly, while the second guard makes the same demand to Lolita as he had with Armando, his voice still tart, but not a bark: 'Identification.'

'In my bag,' she says.

The plump, pale guard near their pile of belongings tosses the bag to her and she extracts the plastic wallet and hands it over to the youngest guard.

'Ah,' his face breaks into a smile. 'You're from India?'

'Yes.'

'You speak good German,' a compliment that has not been extended to Armando, who speaks far better than her.

'Thank you.'

'You know, my cousin designs the posters for many Indian films,' he continues, while he scribbles in his notebook. Then the card is handed to the second guard, then to the leader, then back to her, like a game of pass the parcel.

She tucks it back into her bag and clears her throat. 'Oh right.'

'Yes, yes. Beautiful posters. Beautiful films. Singing and dancing,' the young guard is laughing. 'You're studying medicine?'

'Yes.'

'That's good. Good.'

Now the first guard, the leader, the one who interrogated Armando, says, tetchily: 'Enough.'

Again, silence falls. The inquisition she has been subjected to has been jovial rather than menacing, but she finds her palms are damp.

When the leader speaks again, it is to Armando. 'You must tell no one.' And then, 'Do you understand?'

She watches as Armando nods, slowly, his eyes fixed on the guard.

'Do you understand?'

'Yes.'

'And her?' He doesn't look at Lolita, only flicks his fingers at her.

'Yes,' Armando says. 'She understands.'

Behind them, the murmur of the waves and the squawk of a seagull can be heard, but only as a background to the silence – even Clara has not uttered a sound. And then the border guard breaks the stare and says, dismissively, 'You can go.'

Armando takes her elbow, and they move to their pile of belongings, gather them in their arms and climb up the beach to the path. She feels his hand pressing into the small of her back, but more insistently than before. On the path, miraculously, there is still no one. No small crowd, no bystanders, either because they had indeed found a private haven, or the exact opposite: that what has happened has been noted and a blind eye has been turned. Armando wipes the sand off Clara's feet, before slipping on her socks and shoes.

The rest of the day is lost. It is hours earlier than they had envisaged. They have not had lunch; they have barely spoken to each other. They make their way back to the train station along the road, now weaving their way through the shoppers and walkers who are enjoying the warm sunshine, mostly in silence, except when Clara, finally, finds her voice, and whines that she is tired. At this Armando lifts her onto his shoulders, and for this and perhaps for the spectacle they always make, he receives some pointed looks. From the great height, the child starts babbling, pointing out what she can see, before she suddenly cries out, her short legs banging against his collarbones, startling her father.

'Fufu! Fufu!'

'What is it? What is it?'

Armando's voice is hassled as she has never heard before. She notices that he is holding the doll upside down by the legs, so she takes it from him, smooths its hair and places it on her own shoulder. Clara gives her a small, grateful smile through her tears.

They board a train, and Armando takes out a sandwich from his bag, which he gives his daughter. Their earlier, flirtatious mood has dissolved into a mute obedience – they were told to return to the city and that is what they are doing. As well as the tight ball in her stomach when she thinks of the dead body, the men passing their ID cards back and forth, she also feels a weight of disappointment: that a day she has so looked forward to, all the hours she expected to spend with Armando, have been taken away from her.

But then Armando speaks to her in a low voice.

'I will drop Clara back at Petra's, and then we can talk.'

A curtailed day with his daughter is a sacrifice, she knows.

'Are you sure?'

'It will be better for Clara, in case they want to talk to me again.'

'Do you think they will?'

'I'll call Joachim when we get back.'

Then he lifts his hand, the one that is not resting on Clara's back, and she thinks he is about to take hers, but the child looks around suddenly and his hand drops back to his side.

*

She waits in a shadow at the top of the stairwell, and watches as Petra comes to the door, her hair wrapped in a towel. Clara is fast asleep in her father's arms, her face pressed against his shoulder and with the rubbery neck of a very young child, this is at an awkward angle. Her parents talk at length. They are no longer a couple, but there is something undeniably intimate between them. An evident trace remains of all the moments they have shared, of the type she has never shared with Armando. She shifts on her feet, troubled by her prurient imagining of the coupling between Armando and Petra which has resulted in Clara.

She turns her back on the small family, takes a few steps down the stairs, but within seconds, her curiosity gets the better of her and she climbs back up to watch them again. Petra's lips are moving. Armando reaches out to touch the mother of his child on the shoulder, and then swiftly on her elbow. Up then down, a gentle caress. Petra stretches out her arms and the child is passed from one parent to the other. At this, Clara awakens, her face puffy from sleep, one cheek scarlet. The door closes.

But Armando does not turn away immediately. Perhaps he is picturing a different life, one in which he walks through the threshold as a husband and sits at the table with his family. When he finally heads towards the stairwell, she runs lightly down to the bottom and steps outsides. She waits for him where he had left her, in the square outside the block of flats.

He draws up to her and smiles, touches her elbow as he had Petra's.

'So.'

'So.'

'Shall we find somewhere we can talk?'

She nods.

'Are you hungry?'

'Not yet.'

He insists they take the bus back into the centre, even though he will have a longer return journey to the factory. They sit side-by-side as on the train, and now he holds her hand, but she finds she cannot enjoy the touch or the sentiment, feels too constrained to lean against his shoulder, even though her head is heavy with fatigue. And Armando, too, is tense beside her, quiet, perhaps rehashing the conversation with Petra, lamenting the hours lost with Clara. In the centre, they avoid Sonderbar, where they would be most welcome, and she knows this is because he does not wish for their conversation to be interrupted. Instead, they choose a bland, beige bar, opposite a business hotel around the corner from her residence. On their arrival, he asks the bartender if he can make a call to Joachim, while she takes their drinks to a table.

She watches him speaking on the phone. When he hangs up, he talks to the bartender, and hands over some money.

'I've ordered two macaroni cheese,' he says as he sits down at the table. 'Or do you want something else?'

She shakes her head. They clink their beer glasses together.

'What did you say to Joachim?'

'I asked him to call the bar if anyone comes asking for me.'

They sip their beers in silence. When he puts his glass down, she asks, 'Will Clara be all right?'

'I don't know how much she understood. I'll call Petra later.'

He never refers to Petra as 'Clara's mother', he always uses her name which on his tongue becomes more rhotic, as if he savours the sound and which only cements her suspicions that there is still a residual love, a still-existing bond. But then he reaches forward to brush a strand of hair away from her face. The touch of his fingers against her cheek makes her mouth instantly dry.

'I'm sorry the day changed so much,' he says.

'I'm sorry you don't have the evening with Clara.'

He smiles. 'Well, it's nice to have the evening with you.'

Tears suddenly flood into her eyes.

'Hey…'

'I'm tired, that's all,' she says.

'It's a reaction,' he says.

He means a reaction to finding the body of the young man and perhaps he is right. But she is ashamed, for she knows it is also a reaction to the view she was recently afforded. The child in the father's arms, the intense look on Petra's face, the constant conversation between the parents. The plates of food arrive on the bar and he rises to retrieve them. They are two unpretty blobs of yellow. She watches as he generously squirts tomato ketchup over his plate before offering the bottle to her. She shakes her head.

'What was in the pouch, Armando?'

He takes a few seconds to answer her, digging his fork into the wobbly mass before he speaks.

'Money.'

She stares. 'You mean?'

'Deutschmarks.'

'How would he have got them?' she whispers.

'You can buy them if you know where to ask.'

'Why did he have money on him?'

He glances up at her, but then shrugs, saying nothing.

'What do you think happened?' she asks.

He does not answer immediately. He chews his mouthful slowly before swallowing.

'Who knows? Maybe it was too cold in the water?'

A heart attack, hypothermia. He looked young and fit but an unknown, underlying condition might be tested in the waters of the Baltic Sea.

'Didn't a friend realise he was in trouble?'

'Maybe he was alone. Maybe it was night-time and dark.'

'He would have been a good swimmer.'

'The rope to his board was twisted around something,' Armando says. 'And the board was lodged in a rock so holding him down below the surface.'

'Why would he go out on his own in the dark with all that money?'

He looks up at her again then lays down his fork.

'He was trying to get to Denmark, Lolita,' he says, quietly.

'He was trying to get to Denmark?' she repeats, incredulous.

'To get to the West,' he says. 'It's only forty kilometres or so. That's not far for a good swimmer, and he could paddle on his board.'

She stares at him, and he gives her a brief, grim smile. She has yet to taste her meal and feels her head swim of a sudden. She feels his fingers clasp her wrist.

'Eat, Lolita.' He might use the same voice with Clara.

When she scoops a spoonful into her mouth, the sharpness and saltiness rush through her like a blood transfusion. She realises she is ravenous, and she empties her plate in seconds. When she looks up, she sees that he too has pushed his plate aside and that he is watching her, sipping his beer slowly.

'Did you tell Petra?'

'Yes.'

'What did she think?'

He hesitates. 'She said it was unfortunate the border guards came, that they make things...' He says something which she doesn't understand and seeing this, he searches for another expression, and she wishes, strongly, that they did not need to converse in German. 'They complicate things.'

They fall silent, and then she asks, 'Do many people try to get across to Denmark?'

'I don't know. But I think some do, yes.'

'Why?'

He smiles ruefully, his eyes crinkling at the edges.

'For you and me this might be paradise, Lolita. For them no.'

'Do you think this is paradise, Armando?'

'I know that if I had not come here, I might be dead.'

He grins then, to temper his words.

She looks around. There are perhaps twenty people in the bar, and those under thirty are wearing snow-washed denim, the uniform of youth. The women have teased, permed curls, and nearly all sport blue eyeliner. Some of the men have moustaches, none have beards. There are some older men drinking on their own, and at another table, there are three men playing cards. In short, the patrons of the bar in this beige hotel are a fair representation of the local population.

She looks back at Armando. 'I think he was called Tommy.'

She pulls out the bracelet from her pocket and lays it on the table. Armando's eyes lock into hers.

'This was on his wrist.'

'Why did you take it?'

'I don't know.'

He is uncomfortable, perhaps even horrified, but he says nothing.

'Will they tell his family?' Her voice is soft.

'Yes. I'm sure,' he says.

'How can you be sure?'

He shakes his head. Then, reluctantly, 'No. No, I can't be sure.'

'Should we try and find them?'

There is a man on the other table watching them, and she picks up the bracelet and slides it back into her pocket. When she glances back at the man, he is watching the television in the corner of the bar.

Armando's lips are pressed together, and he is shaking his head, firmly.

'No, Lolita. No. We tell no one about this. We leave this now.'

'You told Petra.'

He looks taken aback. 'Because of Clara.'

Again, a reminder of that bond. The jealousy which started bubbling as she watched Armando and Petra at the front door bursts its banks and floods her, with as much heat as the desire she was feeling seconds previously. She realises she is shaking, trembling. He stands up suddenly, and swivels himself round to her side, puts his arm around her and pulls her to him. The man at the next table is watching them again, his eyes on them even as he lifts his glass to his lips.

'Come.'

Armando half-lifts her off her feet with one arm and with his other hand he gathers their beers. He leads her past the bar, past the bartender who is watching them blankly, and rather than finding a quieter place as she expected, he places the beers on a table just underneath the television, where they will have to lean into each other, thigh against thigh, press their lips to each other's ears, to be heard. Whereas previously she would have relished such a tête-à-tête, all the joy has been erased.

'He may not be a local,' he is saying now. She can smell his skin, her face is only inches away from his strong neck and chest, but now she only stares at him, dully. 'He could be from anywhere.'

'But it's likely that he is?'

'No reason, Lolita.'

'Why don't you care?'

His eyes widen at the harsh tone of her voice.

'I do care.'

She is unsure why the words are dropping from her mouth, but they are: 'What if his family is waiting and waiting to hear from him?'

'They will tell the family, Lolita.'

'You don't know that. You don't know anything.'

She is surprised herself at the anger in her voice, but she holds his eyes, stubbornly.

He says: 'We can do nothing for him now.'

'But for his family?'

'We don't know if he has any family, Lolita. We know nothing about him.'

'We know he's called Tommy.'

There is a shadow now in his gaze, of compassion perhaps, but when he leans forward to speak in her ear, it is not to relent.

He says: 'We have to think as well about ourselves.'

'I don't understand what can happen to us.'

'Maybe nothing will happen to you. But I'm not a medical student. They can replace me easily.'

She feels a flutter of pity, but pushes it aside, tries to scoff. What he is saying, she knows. But she is angry that he is laying it out so baldly, and she is angry that everything he does revolves around the love he has for his daughter.

'We can tell no one about this, what we found.'

'You mean who we found.'

'Yes, sorry. I meant who.'

'If you feel this way, then why didn't you just leave him in the water?' Her voice is like a whip.

He is staring at her and then he lifts his hands up as if in defeat, but to her surprise he cups her face between his palms. He leans forward and she wonders if he is going to seal their secrecy with a kiss on the mouth. But instead, he kisses her forehead, as if she were a child, even Clara, and this makes her suddenly even more angry. She stiffens and he moves back in surprise.

'I must get back,' she says, without looking at him.

'Lolita.'

She stands up and picks up her jacket, leaving her unfinished beer on the table. She hears him hurrying after her, and on the street, as she is slipping her arms through her jacket, she feels his hands briefly straighten her collar.

They walk in silence for many minutes. When she glances to the side, she sees he has pushed his hands into the pockets of his jeans, but that he does not look relaxed in any way. There is a tension in his shoulders and the set of his mouth, and she feels sorry, suddenly, for her harsh tone. But she hardens her heart against him, just as she realises that they have been speaking to each other with an intimacy they did not have before. They have spent hours alone now, shared a dinner, touched each other: all in wondering what to do about a dead man they do not know.

When they turn onto the street on which her residence stands, he speaks: 'I do care, Lolita. I'm just afraid that if I get involved, I will get in trouble.'

She stops walking and looks up at him. He looks young under the streetlight, and he is. Even if he is five years older than her, he is only twenty-eight. And now he looks young and confused by her behaviour, which makes her only more irritated.

'People aren't supposed to be afraid in paradise, Armando.'

'That's true,' he tries to smile.

A gaggle of students suddenly rounds the corner, and they wait until the group has staggered into the residence.

'You think I'm a coward.' His tone is light but she can see that he is serious.

'I didn't say that,' she mutters, not looking at him.

'No,' he says, 'you didn't say that.'

She raises her head. His expression breaks her heart and she opens her mouth to take everything back, but before she can speak, he steps forward, into her, and kisses her. His full lips press against hers for many, many beats, and she is lost in the feel of him.

His hand is on the small of her back and then it is on her waist and she feels his thumb briefly press through the thin material of her dress against her pelvic bone. But there is sorrow in the kiss, an apology, or even uncertainty that it will ever happen again. And then he breaks off, abruptly, as her eyes are still closed and walks away, down the street.

She spins around violently, races up the path to the entrance and launches herself up the stairs at such a speed that in seconds she has reached the top of the flight. And then, just as violently, she reels around and clatters down, throws open the door and charges out onto the street, where she bangs her nose against a dark shape, as hard as a lamppost.

Her eyes fill with tears from the pain. She tries to peer around the shape in front of her for any sign of Armando, but a body is blocking her vision, already blurred by the tears.

'Are you alright?'

She nods, swipes at her eyes. Armando has disappeared into the night.

'Are you sure?'

Through her tears, he swims into her vision, and she can see that he is of her age, and his green eyes are full of concern.

She pulls away from his grasp.

'I'm fine.'

His hands drop to his sides, and he opens his mouth to speak but she has already turned away. She is being rude – she has not apologised nor thanked the stranger for his kindness. But she cares for nothing, now that she has learned that she is capable of being cruel, and above all, that she is capable of being cruel to Armando.

4

He knocks softly on Joachim's door and hears the scrape of a chair. His boss's face appears at the window, then the front door is opened. Joachim is wearing a maroon-coloured dressing-gown over grey pyjamas and with his shaggy black hair and spectacles, looks less like a company director of a printing factory and more like a schoolteacher.

'Armando.'

'It's late. Sorry to disturb you.'

'Is everything okay?'

'I wonder if I can call Petra.'

Joachim opens the door wider. 'Come in.'

There is classical music playing in the background, not loudly, but Joachim turns it down. The room is not warm, but not cold, and there is a hint of cinnamon in the air, which lends a cosy, old-maidenish feel. The television is not switched on, and he can see that Joachim has been sitting at his dining table, with a stack of books. He is a cultured, curious, knowledgeable man, and unusual. A man who, at his own expense, has repurposed a property so that his workers are not crowded in large dormitories like schoolboys, but in smaller cohorts of four, with their own kitchen and bathroom: an arrangement which allows a semblance of normal life. It was Joachim who introduced them all to Sonderbar. Most of the men never went back, only he did, and then – following his account of the many good-looking women frequenting the readings – his housemates.

He has been inside his boss's house many times; he knows he is Joachim's favourite. He has read most of the books on Joachim's shelf, even – after telling him about the girl he danced with – a copy of Nabokov's Lolita. He met Petra through Joachim, when his boss agreed for the intrepid investigative journalist to interview some of the city's migrant workers for a report that only made copy after being ruthlessly redacted. Yet in the five years that he has known Joachim, he has never seen him with a woman, aside from the sister visiting from Berlin. The man appears to live a monastic life.

Now Joachim discreetly leaves the room, and he dials Petra's number. She answers after three rings, her voice sleepy.

'Did I wake you?' he asks.

'Yes.'

'Sorry. I just wanted to know how Clara was.'

'She's sleeping.'

'With you?'

'No. She wanted Fufu, that's all.'

'Did she say anything?'

'Only that you tried to teach someone to swim.'

He hears her sigh.

'How much did she see?'

He takes a breath. 'Quite a lot.' Then, 'Or maybe not as much as I think.'

'I hope she doesn't have nightmares.'

'Yes.'

'Did anyone ask for you back there?'

'Joachim hasn't mentioned anything.'

'Those guards will probably not include you in their report, Armando. It makes them look bad they didn't find the body themselves.'

'It's true.'

'They might have taken your names just to warn you off.'

'Yes.'

Petra sounds calm, and what she is saying makes sense, but she does not know of the argument he has had with Lolita. He hears her shifting, most probably looking at the clock, and sighing again, and then she says: 'Clara told me that apparently this Lolita helped you buy her dress.'

'Uh...'

'And that Lolita helped her put it back on.'

He says nothing.

'But the buttons were not done right.'

He laughs. 'I didn't notice.'

'Of course you didn't. And neither did Lolita.'

Every time she says the name, he feels like a character in a play, standing between the two women in his life, each stationed at opposing ends of a stage. Then he shakes himself. Lolita is not a woman in his life. Not yet.

'Is she the medical student you mentioned?'

'Yes.'

'If Clara asks me about her, what should I say, Armando?'

'She's a friend, that's all.'

'I didn't know she was coming to the beach.'

'No, sorry, it was a last-minute decision,' he lies.

'Are you sleeping with her?'

'No.'

'But you want to, don't you?'

He says nothing.

'You've never introduced Clara to any of your other women, Armando.'

He bristles. 'You make it sound like I have a harem, Petra.'

'You know what I mean. This is different. Now Clara has met her and is talking about her and telling me that this Lolita helped you choose a dress for her.'

He remains silent.

'And will you go back to India with her? When she finishes her studies?'

'Petra…'

'Don't lie to me, Armando. I don't care who you are sleeping with, but if it's going to affect my child, then I have a right to know.'

He feels his face grow warm.

'Yes, you're right. But she's a friend. Nothing more.' His stomach contracts, even saying the words.

'I'm going back to sleep.'

'Okay, I—'

She has hung up.

He winces. He should have told her that Lolita was joining them today, but he resents the taunt: 'your other women.' He has not led a celibate life since he broke up with Petra, since the unplanned blessing that is Clara. While he has not had, nor wished for, prolific success, he was his most reckless during the months after Clara was born, Petra's parents building up a barrier and encouraging him to wash his hands of the affair, even of his child. He picked up women to mask the emptiness he was feeling. But when Petra stood up for him, when Clara was six months old, perhaps convinced finally by his persistence of his sincerity, and then when the Saturday visits became a routine, he found that he had grown up, lost his appetite for such liaisons. The packet of condoms, plucked from his jacket pocket and held up between thumb and index finger: he had forgotten they were there, so little use has he had of them of late, which makes Petra's taunt even more unfair. The last occasion was a full year ago, a moment of weakness, following a hurtful argument with Petra, an evening which he remembers now with another wince.

He is still gripping the handset. He depresses the switch and dials the common room of the students' residence, but only allows it to ring twice. Lolita is not unworldly, but she has an elegance and purity about her which makes him ashamed to remember the other women. And she is braver than many he knows, probably braver than him. It was clear that what she learned of him today displeased her. He should, perhaps, not try to see her again until the dust that they have kicked up has settled. But why, then, would he part from her with a kiss?

Joachim re-enters the room, a tray holding a vodka bottle and glasses in his hands.

'Is Clara well?'

'She's fine. We took her to the beach.'

Joachim knows much about his life, including his delicate relationship with Petra. He knows, as well, of the separate, opposing tug of Lolita Devi. Now, as he watches Joachim set the tray down on a side table, he remembers how she looked earlier in the day, the breeze ruffling her hair, checking for a pulse on the blue-white corpse of the young man. Joachim pours a generous shot into each glass and hands one to him.

'Prost.'

He downs the vodka in one gulp, but it does not give him the usual rush. When he looks up, he meets Joachim's concerned gaze, and he has a strong urge to tell him everything. But it would be selfish. This is the man, the friend, who drove him to Petra's parents' house after she had given birth to Clara, so he could see his daughter for the first time without the humiliation of arriving on the doorstep, just off the tram like a stranger. Who talked with the parents in the living room, as if he were a relative of Armando's rather than his boss, while, in Petra's old bedroom, he held his baby daughter for the first time – a morsel of honey-coloured, sweet-smelling perfection. A miniscule yet fully formed, warm human being. Petra's face was pink with emotion on seeing his tears of happiness and wonder.

'And how is Lolita?' his friend asks.

When he tries and fails to speak, his friend grips his shoulder, then says, humbly: 'I'm no expert with women. But no problem is insurmountable, Armando. A wall is only there to be climbed over.'

It is interesting that he uses such a metaphor so glibly.

Joachim is watching him, and while he knows his friend will not press, he feels that he needs to reciprocate.

'I think it's hard for Lolita,' he says, 'that I have Clara. No girl her age wants to be the wicked stepmother.'

'Did Clara make a fuss?'

'No, the opposite. She likes Lolita. But it's not romantic to be invited to spend a day with a small child, is it?'

Joachim smiles.

'No, not very romantic. Not in the conventional sense at least,' he says. 'But from what I know of Lolita, a bigger mistake is not to be authentic. She is the type of girl who does not want to be underestimated.'

He says nothing.

'She likes you,' Joachim is now speaking gently. 'It's easy to see that. More than likes, Armando. She is probably in love with you and what man would not like to have a girl such as Lolita to be in love with him?'

It is sheer conjecture on his friend's part, but it sparks a flash of hope in his chest. Joachim is lifting the bottle to replenish their glasses, but he holds his hand up.

'I must go. Thank you for the phone call.'

Joachim says, 'Don't go yet. Sit for a little bit?'

He must be lonely, on some level. But Joachim also senses his reluctance, and so places the bottle back down on the table, speaks as solicitously as a woman: 'Another time. You must be tired.'

He leaves Joachim's house and walks across the cobbled esplanade towards the buildings lined up in silhouette, on the right of the giant warehouse. In the dark, the aspect is of a collection of stables set around a courtyard. In the light of day, the impression is swiftly dispelled to show three sides of a square made by brick-built former offices, re-modelled to house the twenty men in six separate flats. Joachim's office is simply a partitioned area of the factory, while the band of women who deal with orders and accounts work from a separate building, in fact a former stable, a ten-minute walk back towards the town, nestled in the woods to the west.

The hallway of the flat is dark when he enters, but that is because they are in the kitchen, door closed, with music softly playing. He glances at his watch. It is past midnight. He wishes simply to wash and go to bed, but he pushes open the kitchen door to see bottles of beer on the table, and that they are laying cards: Gilberto, Tiago and Ronaldo.

'Ah, he returns,' says Gilberto, the cigarette in his mouth bobbing up and down like a referee's whistle. 'Is she still a virgin after tonight?'

He does not disabuse them of their assumption, only laughs along with the others and moves to the sink. He pours himself a glass of water, which he drains as the laughter continues, before helping himself to a piece of grilled chicken from the pan, noting that the marinade is not as good as his, a detail which pleases him. He is proud of his culinary skills, which are much appreciated by his housemates.

Gilberto holds up his beer.

'We're celebrating Ronaldinho's birthday.'

He clinks his glass with their bottles. They were all much amused that when Ronaldo last visited his family in Mozambique, he had impregnated the daughter of a neighbour, and now has a two-year-old child in situ and a promise to marry the girl on his return to uphold.

'Parabens,' he says to Ronaldo, who shrugs and looks pleased.

'So tell us. How is the beautiful Lolita?' This from Tiago.

'Still beautiful.'

'You went to the beach?'

He nods.

'Did you do it on the sand?'

'Clara was with us.'

'Friend, you think she likes to go to the beach with another woman's child? You need to take her out on her own, make her feel special, give her something to remember. If you don't, she will find someone else.'

'I'm afraid, Tiago, that someone will never be you.'

Tiago darkens with embarrassment, as the others hoot with laughter, and he can make his exit. Of late, he finds the endless bonhomie tiresome, and he prefers to spend more and more time alone. But he could have done worse. None are political zealots, nor layabouts, all try to maintain a tidy household. The three are his brothers, his comrades-in-arms.

He showers quickly, the tang of sea water infusing the steam. When he lies down on his bed, he finds that he is trembling, even though the night is not cool. He pulls the covers higher up his chest, stares into the dark. He can hear the others now pushing back chairs, calling it a night. Tiago opens the door, lumbers across the room to fall into his bed and promptly begins to snore, contentedly.

This is something else that sets him apart. For them, life here is but a procession of days of drinking and merriment and scant responsibility. They believe in the promise made by their government of a secure future of comfort awaiting them back home – unequivocally, uncritically. Why can't he, Armando, be similarly carefree? It can't be fatherhood alone, because he is by no means the only father among them. Does he love his child more? He cannot allow himself such arrogance. It might be that it is they who are the more prepared, knowing that, with stealth, an inevitable fate awaits them, and all the time which could have been spent light-hearted and untroubled is not time that can be regained.

He was fourteen when the war of independence from Portugal was won, and his country is still at war, with itself. He had a sister and a brother, who both died well before their time, far away from home. He has lived through war but, other than his father, then lying peacefully in a coffin, he has never seen a dead body. Of the consequences of violence or landmines or poverty, he has seen plenty. The amputees, hare lips, glaucoma, boils on shaven heads. But to hold close to his own a body which is uncorrupted, yet stripped of vitality, this is a new experience. Lolita would have seen more cadavers through her medical training, but even her face was bleached of colour when she bent down to take the young man's wrist between her fingers.

He tries to focus his thoughts now on Lolita and how she looked on the beach, rising from the water like a black-haired Venus, sitting next to him with her bare legs so close to his fingers, and his heart does that familiar somersault in his chest. From months of watching, biding his time, to thinking when is the right time? To leaping forwards, eyes closed, to clutch at whatever future he can conjure up, but landing instead – now his stomach tightens – on a disastrous end to the day.

Tiago, in the bed adjacent, snuffles loudly, thrashes in the bedclothes and then flips over. He turns himself over the opposite way, to face the wall on his side of the room and wait for sleep.

5

She dreams that she is lying on the sand entwined with a body of a man, which is first Armando and then Tommy, who is surveying her with his cool, blue eyes. His lips begin to move in soundless speech, when she wakes abruptly. She leaves the bed and opens the door to the corridor. After padding down to the shared bathroom block and using the toilet, she returns to her bedroom. The residence is a repurposed historic building, with a palatial central staircase, high ceilings throughout and ornate hanging lamps, wrought-iron bannisters and balustrades. The bedrooms which line the passageways, however, are narrow, fitted with cheap blue carpet, furnished with a single bed, a washbasin, a desk and a wardrobe. Hers has been home for nearly five years, even if it is more functional than homely. The largest wall, the one above her desk, is patterned with diagrams and mnemonics to help her remember the details of the human body —each sinew and blood vessel and bone — or the chemical structures of various enzymes and hormones. But the other wall holds a poster of Rajamalai, the mountain that towers behind her mother's house, under whose gaze she spent her adolescence, dreaming of her future.

At the washbasin in the corner, she splashes her face with water. Few will surface from their rooms for some hours: the residence only comes to life well after midday on Sundays. She chews on a now-stale bread roll, and instead of dressing and opening her books, leans her pillow against the wall and sits at the head of her bed. The window looks on to the trees in the small square below. If she turns right out on the street and carries on to the end of the block, she reaches a large park with a maze of paths lined by linden trees. The university does not stray far from the park, with both the main university building and the principal hall of residence standing to the east, each presiding over their own patch of green. A narrow press of streets opens up into a large, cobbled square, with the town hall. From a once pretty, brightly painted, affluent trading post, the town is now faded and grown reluctantly into a city, in places incoherent, formed by a patchwork of planning initiatives. Only the mediaeval centre, a compact gridwork of streets hemmed in at the eastern edge by the sweep of the river, offers a glimpse of its former wealth. If she turns left out of the entrance, a ten-minute brisk walk takes her to the swimming baths, housed in the last of the historic buildings on this side of the city. A few streets north of the swimming baths is the hospital complex, a quartet of modern buildings, stark and austere, but a confident marriage of concrete and glass, and beautiful in their way.

Now she finds herself excavating the depths of her dream from earlier: what did it feel like to lie with Armando? On the beach, he had stood before her, nearly unclothed. Tall and strong, with a smooth and hairless torso, narrow hips and broad shoulders. He had tossed his daughter into the air with careless confidence, he had plucked a man from the sea, adroitly. She had seen his eyes on her body, and he had kissed her. She turns away from the window, at the same time as she hears her neighbours congregate in the hallway. One bangs on her door. Does she have any aspirin? Is she coming with them to the laundry room in the basement?

She is listless through the day when she should be revising for an exam, staring blankly at her notes, doodling endless circles within circles. Tommy. A soft, childish name. On a whim, she leaves her room and descends the staircase to the post room on the ground floor. The porter who has a cabin near the entrance suddenly appears at her side.

'Fraülein,' he says, nodding his greeting.

The pigeonhole marked with her name is empty, but she hovers, pretending to be searching for something in her pockets.

'You have no post, Fraülein,' the man says, but he sounds helpful rather than suspicious.

'Yes, I know, I just…' she digs in one pocket furiously, her brow creased. Fortunately, he does not find her charade particularly exciting, and leaves.

She searches the name labels on the pigeonholes and finds two Tommys. In each pigeonhole she leaves a note: *I have a message for you, Room C12, Lolita.* Someone knocks on her door a few hours later, a curly-headed blond answering to Tommy, who is cheerful and good-natured when she fakes an error on her part. When no one else appears – and she does not leave her room for hours in case she misses the second Tommy – she creeps downstairs to the post-room and finds that the note in the other pigeonhole is no longer there. Perhaps the Tommy has picked it up and decided to throw it away. Or perhaps someone, even the porter, has been stationed to monitor the traffic to the post room. Why did she leave her name and room number? Now she feels her skin grow cold at her impulsiveness. And of course, now she notes that there are six other nametags sporting the initial 'T'. She leaves another, unnecessary, note in the second pigeonhole – *Sorry, I made a mistake! Ignore my previous message* – and runs back upstairs.

In the large common room on the first floor, furnished with threadbare sofas, a warped table-tennis table and a random collection of stools and wooden chairs, she finds a slip of paper pinned to the corkboard with her name in capital letters. She reads the note: Armando called, no message. Normally they arrange to meet up before saying goodbye, but last night things went awry.

Armando called. He is a doting father, which she should admire, for she herself has wallowed in her parents' uncomplicated love and warmth and openness. Both are alumni of the Peoples' Friendship University in Moscow, where Sushilla Jacob trained as a doctor and Romesh Devi as an engineer. Their own experiences led her parents to encourage her to apply for a scholarship to the Deutsche Demokratische Republik, the DDR, rather than submit to the exorbitant fees, and bribes, required to gain admission in Bombay. She is proud of her parents. She is the child of a love marriage between two people from diagonally opposite ends of India, the north-east and the south-west. Different religions, different languages, different classes – a marriage which defied convention and social norms. If there is anything in her upbringing that makes her the person she is now, it is this hybridity. Knowing this, however – that the essence of who she is derives from her parents – only convinces her that she is less complete than either of them. By the age she is now, each was an advocate for social justice. In contrast, she – content and peaceable, blessed with good looks and enough brains – lacks their depth, their drive. Is this why she is clinging to the idea of helping Tommy, or Tommy's family? To, somehow, recreate her parents' imagined response? Her heart aches. Now she regrets everything she said to Armando, her unbending petition for a man she never knew, when the man she does know, the man she loves, was making a plea.

She tucks the slip into her pocket, not sure she will call, not sure what she can say or what she understands from their disrupted day, before trudging back to her room. She finds she is exhausted and turns in early, on an empty stomach, and then sleeps through her alarm the following morning, which means she arrives for her placement on the casualty ward with a minute to spare. The consultant in charge says nothing as she joins the semi-circle of her colleagues, already gathered for their morning de-brief. She slips into a space between Maria and Beate; the latter flashes her a sympathetic grin. When she falters over an eighty-year-old patient – whose blinking, avid, blue eyes only remind her of the young, dead man – Hans Lütwiler interrupts her peremptorily and commands another medical student to take over. He has a reputation for excoriating rebukes, usually delivered in public for maximum humiliation, but he refrains on this occasion, which leaves her anxious. When will the punishment arrive?

It arrives when they break for lunch, after she has finished half a bowl of cloyingly sweet green soup, which leaves an unpleasant film on her tongue. Jürgen informs her that she has been summoned to the office of the Facharzt, which is in a different building, across the forecourt. She takes the stairs down from the canteen, and then out into the fresh air. But it does not feel fresh – rather, it is muggy, with a strong odour of exhaust fumes blowing in from the ring road further north. Hans Lütwiler is at his desk when she knocks on his door. To her chagrin, her eyes fill with tears as he begins his assessment of her poor performance, which might explain why he picks up his chair and places it next to hers, so that they are on the same side of the desk. It is then that she notices the door is closed behind them and that he is smiling. He wears his fair hair long and he is a tall, handsome man in his late thirties, a

Viking type. His grey eyes look darker than usual, and she realises he is not wearing his glasses and that he has a smell: a musky smell not unlike aftershave gone sour, as if he has become too hot and is perspiring through his shirt. All this she notices while he expresses his great sympathy for her: she must be homesick, she is studying in a foreign language, an extraordinary feat, and he would happily offer her extra tuition. For this, his apartment is at her disposal. Now his hand – a manicured, elegant hand – is moving towards her, and she realises that it is aiming to settle on her forearm or even her thigh. The image of the young man flashes before her – with his slack, blue lips, his soft, sagging skin, the seaweed blocking one nostril – and a wave of nausea overcomes her. She vomits into the space between her feet and Hans Lütwiler's feet – vomits, by the look of it, most of the green soup.

Afterwards, she remembers how Hans Lütwiler sprang to his feet, crying out an oath, knocking over his chair. How the worn beige carpet was much improved by being decorated with a virulent splash of green. Hans Lütwiler had opened the door and shouted out for the cleaner, pushing a cart at the end of the corridor. A truculent, middle-aged woman had arrived with a roll of blue paper towels and soap in a spray bottle.

'I'm sorry,' she had said, but he was dabbing furiously at his shoes and so she slipped out of the office and left the building. Leaving behind her Hans Lütwiler and his bright red face, and the image of the young man with seaweed in his nose.

6

Through a fortunate turn of events, on Tuesday, Joachim gives them the afternoon off. They have discovered a nest of mice, and the pest control company offers a slot that very day. The men are asked to report back by six in the evening to finish off their jobs. They leave the factory floor while Joachim is visible in his office, on his phone, running his hands anxiously through his hair.

He should offer to stay and help Joachim but decides to take advantage of the fortuitous break to visit Clara. The others are planning a football game followed by an early dinner at a bar in the village, but he catches a tram and then a bus to Petra's street. At the end stands the kindergarten, an incentive for the young families the town's planners had hoped to attract to the area. The town is one of many built after the war to accommodate the city's rising population, and Reutershagen is one of the nicest. However, Petra complains of the lack of atmosphere, and of her commute to the newspaper offices, overlooking the river at the eastern edge of the centre. This takes at least half an hour, sometimes even an hour on an overcrowded tram, too long for her. He knows that Petra would prefer to be closer to the centre where she grew up and which, despite the bombardment during the war, has retained some of its historic charm. Yet neither does she wish to live with her parents, and her restlessness does mean that the Saturdays when Armando has Clara for the day are now a valuable part of her routine, a day to herself. He knows as well that, even though she adores Clara, she feels her career has been impeded by motherhood. She works hard and she is ambitious.

He has never arrived unannounced at the kindergarten, and his last visit was nearly two years ago, so it is not surprising that the woman who answers the bell eyes him suspiciously. If he were asking after any other child, he is sure that she would have closed the door on his face but given that Clara is the only Afro-German child under their supervision, when he introduces himself as her father, she only hesitates. 'She's not here.'

'Didn't Frau Micke drop her off?'

The woman shakes her head.

'Did she phone in?'

He waits but she appears reluctant to supply any information. It is possible that Petra is ill, it is possible that Clara is ill, or upset, suffering now from nightmares. He has made the decision to go and knock on Petra's door, when the woman speaks up.

'She's with her grandparents. Frau Micke called this morning to tell us.'

The parents' house is just south of the town square, convenient for Petra to drop the little girl off before going to work.

'Thank you,' he says and in relief, smiles into her eyes. She smiles back, and self-consciously touches her hair.

'There is no need to worry,' she says.

'Yes, thank you. Enjoy the nice weather,' he says, cranking up his smile a few watts, in gratitude, and she pats at her dress, gives a little laugh.

'Yes, thank you. And you.'

He sees a tram approaching the stop outside the kindergarten and breaks into a run, lunging through the doors just in time. He chooses to stand, avoiding the free seat next to an old lady, who is staring at him in disgust. He hangs on to the strap, stares out of the window. It might be that Clara is at her grandparents' because she has become upset by what happened at the beach, or it might be that Petra has plans after work. Either way, he is not party to these discussions, he is simply a weekend presence in their lives. If he thinks too long on the matter, he gets a slow burn in his chest, at the distance placed between him and his daughter. But would he want to be living in Petra's house, as Petra's man?

Alice Micke, Petra's mother, an attractive woman in her late fifties, answers the door. She is the same age as his own mother but looks twenty years younger. Still slim, slimmer than Petra, with hair carefully cut into a flattering, feathery bob and make up discreetly done. She wears a cream sweater over fitted blue trousers, silver jewellery. She quickly hides her surprise at seeing

Armando and greets him courteously, as always. He does not kiss her on arrival, neither will he do so on leaving. He does not shake her hand. They are not a tactile family. When he first met them, he attempted to kiss Petra's mother on the cheeks in greeting, Mozambican style, and they had bumped heads awkwardly.

Now she tells him immediately that Clara is at the park with Opa, they've only just gone. No, the child is not unwell, only that Petra is having dinner with them this evening, and because she needs to meet a deadline, it was easier to leave Clara with them in the morning rather than rush back to collect her from the kindergarten. She speaks quickly, and she appears slightly nervous. He realises that it is very unlikely that Petra will have given a full disclosure of events from the weekend to her parents, and that his sudden appearance is disconcerting for her mother.

'You're not working?'

'The factory closed this afternoon.'

Her mother smiles, almost shyly. 'It's nice to have Clara to ourselves, without Petra telling us what we should or shouldn't do.'

Perhaps she is worried that he will claim Clara for the day, depriving the grandparents of this precious opportunity. He should be grateful that the Mickes guard their time with the child so jealously. They wanted Petra to have an abortion – now they dote on Clara.

'Yes, I understand. I need to be back for six. I was just taking a chance.'

Now that the plans for their day are no longer under threat, Alice Micke visibly relaxes and opens the door wider.

'Would you like some tea?'

He accepts: such invitations are rare and even more momentous given that Petra's mother is alone in the house. She has always appeared slightly scared in his presence, but today she leads him through to the kitchen in a familiar fashion. He has risen over the years in her estimation, for he knows that they had all – all of Petra's family – expected him to abscond or ignore his responsibilities as Clara's father. His intention of giving part of his salary to Petra had flabbergasted them. Anyway, Petra refused. He suspects not only out of altruism, or an acknowledgement of his modest income – it is another way of cementing herself as Clara's sole provider. Now anything he buys for Clara is a gift, as one would receive from an uncle rather than a father.

'We were talking, actually,' Alice Micke is saying. 'We would like to host Clara's birthday party this year.'

This celebration has been held in Petra's apartment until now, usually a small affair, with her parents and sister, and a few friends. For Clara's second and third birthdays, Petra allowed him to bring along Joachim and Gilberto.

'We have the garden, and we can invite as many people as we wish,' Alice Micke says, and then she smiles, lowering her eyelashes. 'Petra has finally agreed.'

Perhaps Petra has considered that the four years of rejecting her parents' offers is sufficient punishment for their appeals for a termination of her pregnancy. The parents have a nice house and the garden is spacious. He can imagine a party on their large lawn would be much enjoyed by his daughter.

'We can invite four friends from nursery, and of course you can bring your two friends.' She must mean Joachim and Gilberto. 'It will be a good opportunity.'

Hadn't she said as many people as they wished? Such a declaration is at odds with the family's habit of counting – two of this, two of that, like Noah's ark – which he has never liked. But he brushes aside this irritation.

'Thank you. I look forward to it.'

'And I will make the cake this year, something else Petra is letting me do, finally.'

She laughs self-consciously, and he smiles in response. It is her way of affecting intimacy, he can see.

'What shall I bring?'

'Oh nothing, nothing.' Now her cheeks are pink. 'Aside from two friends, of course.'

She offers him some of her home-made bread spread with butter and jam, and he has two cups of tea while she speaks of the garden. Sitting at her table, he realises that she has watched him grow like his own mother has not. And, leaving the house, knowing that

Alice Micke will stand by the window to watch his departure, he feels an unbearable sadness. He has very little idea of what the day-to-day life of his child is like, and he has even less sway over how it is conducted. Petra did not even want him to speak in Portuguese to Clara, the language of the coloniser – Petra's words – although it has been reimagined on independence as a language of unity for all the different tribes. But he stood firm, even though it is not what he uses with his own mother. How will Clara communicate with her other grandmother if, when, they finally meet?

He has still an hour and a half before he needs to report back at the factory and, factoring in the return journey, he has at least forty-five minutes of free time. He follows his feet, as if his heart has nothing to do with this. The Mickes' house sits on the southern fringes of the centre, and he cuts back into the town, and then bypasses the leafy park to his left to take one of the newer roads which lead directly to the hospital complex. He has only been inside the hospital once before, despite living in this city for five years, to accompany a workmate who had collapsed in the middle of the factory. Now he stands in front of the desk in the casualty reception for at least ten minutes before the woman who is sitting in front of him, who is studiously cutting a piece of paper into sixteen pieces, looks up. Something he has learned about this country: there is no reward to be gained from interrupting an individual undertaking a bureaucratic and utterly useless task. She stares at him, the pair of scissors in her hand still open, like a crocodile's mouth.

'I've come to see Lolita Devi, one of the medical students.'

Her eyes move once, up and down. Then, 'A medical student.'

'Yes.'

'This is the casualty department.'

'Yes.'

'For accidents and emergencies.'

'Yes. Sorry. But I really need to talk to her. It's a kind of emergency.'

He grins at her then, apologetically, humbly, channelling as much charm as he can into his gaze.

'Could you find out if she is on a break? If she's busy, I'll leave.'

There will be very few occasions when the woman before him can wield such unchallenged authority, other than when sitting at this desk. He holds her eyes, blocking any expression from his face which might be read as sarcasm or impudence. Finally, she sighs, her brow furrowed in impatience. But he has played his hand well, for she puts the pair of scissors down and places the pieces of paper one of top of each other, while he grits his teeth. She lifts the handset of the telephone in front of her. When he does not move, she shoos him away, so he retreats some paces away from her desk.

The department is not busy, just like the whole country never feels busy. A small, bored population, looked after by the State, few accidents or crimes or mishaps to propel its populace to the hospital. The woman raps her knuckles loudly on her desk: a novel way of drawing his attention.

'Wait there,' she points to a bench. 'She'll come in fifteen minutes.'

He gives her a bow. 'Thank you very much.'

In less than fifteen minutes, Lolita pushes through the swing doors leading from the triage zone. Her eyes scan the waiting room, before alighting on him. He gets to his feet, his heart suddenly thudding, and watches as she strides towards him. She has a stethoscope tucked into the top of a short white coat. Underneath this, she is wearing a cream blouse tucked into a slim pair of dark grey trousers. She looks clever and competent, and she is approaching him at some speed.

'Has something happened?' The concern in her voice lends him some hope.

'No, don't worry. Joachim has mice, so I have some time off.' He grins, for the third time that day summoning all his charm. 'And I just wanted to see you.'

She looks at him, not saying anything. Now that she has been reassured of no calamity, he senses a change, a cooling down, and for the first time since he met her those months ago, he is not sure that she is pleased to see him.

He forces himself to continue: 'I wondered if we could talk?'

She continues to look on at him. But then she says, 'Let me see what I can do.'

He watches her push back through the doors, her ponytail swinging, and spends an anxious five minutes, heart thumping, feeling like a teenager on his first date before she comes out again, her white coat replaced by a short jacket, the same jacket she was wearing at the beach.

'I have about half an hour.'

They leave, the eyes of the receptionist following them all the way through the waiting area and onto the large forecourt in front of the hospital. There is a small square of grass with benches and an empty fountain in the far corner and they walk towards it.

He wants to take her hand, but they are both jammed into the pockets of her jacket and so he says, instead: 'It's nice to see you.'

She does not respond in kind, and he feels his skin tightening when she says, 'I'm sorry I was so awful to you.'

He feels a surge of relief and tenderness. 'You have nothing to be sorry about.' He touches her elbow, and she glances up at him. She looks miserable.

'How is Clara?'

'Good. She's with her grandparents. I've come from their house.'

'Is she staying with them because of what happened?'

'No, I don't think so. Petra and Clara are having dinner there tonight.'

They walk along the edge of the grass square and find a bench, facing out onto the street.

'Would you prefer to go and get a coffee somewhere?'

She shakes her head. 'I don't have time. Beate is doing me a huge favour.'

They sit down and she sits close to him, so that her thigh is pressed against his and he sees this as a good sign, and so he crosses one arm over his body to clasp her upper arm. It is slender in his hand, and he runs his thumb tentatively along the muscle.

'You feel nice,' he says, risking a smile.

Her lips curl upwards in response, but briefly, and neither does she look bashful as she might have done a few days ago. Something has changed between them. They have accelerated to a point further along than he might have imagined, or even hoped, when he invited her to the beach. But has it come at some expense? Whatever, something has changed, and as if to acknowledge this as well as capitalise on it, he impulsively touches her lower lip with his thumb. She doesn't move away, and so he traces the shape of her mouth, then her eyebrows, strokes her cheek. But her hands are jammed in her pockets, and while he can see that her pupils are dilated and her lips are moist, that she is trying to regulate her breathing, she still says nothing.

He drops his hand. 'You're angry with me.'

She shakes her head, slowly. 'No. I'm not.'

'Then you're disappointed in me,' he tries to smile as he says this, but his cheeks are stiff.

She shakes her head again.

'Speak to me, Lolita.'

'Why did we have to find him?' she whispers.

She means the boy, the dead boy.

'I don't know.'

'I wish we never had.'

'I know.'

'I didn't like them. I didn't like those border guards. What will they do with him?'

The words are tumbling out, and he sees she has stopped herself from uttering the name: Tommy.

'I don't know,' he repeats.

'I've never felt so, I don't know,' she searches for a word, 'so foreign.'

He smiles slightly and shrugs.

'But we are,' he says.

'I hated seeing the way they treated you.'

He says nothing. Perhaps she had expected him to be bolder. Less docile, less compliant. What can he say? She is right that he did not wish to antagonise the guards. He is beginning to realise that he has a much better understanding of this country, his adopted home for the last ten years, than she.

'Do we just pretend we never found him?'

It is not a scathing rebuke. He can see that it is a genuine question.

He says, tentatively, 'We might have to, Lolita.'

She is silent, for a long time, and then she looks up and meets his eyes.

And so he says: 'If they send me back, who knows if I will ever see Clara again?'

He has spoken from the heart, put into words a fear that has been circulating inside him since his daughter was born. She looks away now and nods, her hands still in the pockets of her jacket – she has not touched him once.

'I understand,' she says, but she doesn't, he can see that.

He forces himself to speak: 'That bracelet...'

'I've thrown it away,' she says, quickly.

He is surprised by the wave of relief which engulfs him.

'Thank you.'

She shrugs her shoulders. They sit in silence now. She stretches a foot, twists an ankle to the right and then left, and when she speaks again, it is not to revert to the extraordinary discovery from their visit to the beach, but instead to ask: 'How long were you and Petra together?'

She is not looking at him, but at her foot.

'Two months maybe?'

'How did you meet?'

'She came to the factory to interview us. Joachim arranged it.'

'And you started seeing each other?'

Perhaps she wants to know if it was as convoluted then as it is now to conduct a relationship. It wasn't. Without Clara, time seemed endless and elastic.

'Yes. But then we broke up. And I hadn't seen her for weeks, when she came by one evening,' he says. 'To tell me she was pregnant.'

She is silent. Then she looks at him.

'You didn't want to get married, Armando?'

He shakes his head slowly.

'Why not?'

'Petra was worried that she would find it difficult to get work if we did. That's not why she told me she was pregnant. She just wanted me to know that the baby was mine.'

He smiles, weakly, but she does not smile back.

'To be honest,' he continues, 'I think Petra prefers it this way. She's very independent.'

'Are you still in love with her? With Petra?'

Her eyes are large and dark and solemn.

'No.'

'When did you stop loving her?'

'I'm not sure,' he says slowly, 'that I was ever in love with her.'

She does not gasp in dismay or disdain, but her expression dims. Petra's fortitude will not be a surprise, but the bare details of the affair might be. Perhaps she has witnessed his devotion to his daughter and imagined that this meant a devotion to Petra, which never existed. As he describes it, even to his ears, the relationship appears too lukewarm and mechanical to have produced such a beloved child as Clara. Now her lower lip trembles and he resists the urge to touch it again.

'But,' he continues, to complete the story, 'she'll always be Clara's mother.'

'Yes, you're right. She will.'

He leans forward so that he can feel her eyelashes brush against his lips, and they are wet with tears. But she doesn't lift her face to him, offer him her mouth and her hands are still jammed into her jacket pockets. She seems to be searching for something to say. But then she appears to give up, gets to her feet.

'I should get back.'

They have at least fifteen minutes to spare, but he sees that she is crying, and so he does not press her. They retrace their tracks to the hospital entrance, which looks as quiet and as unused as before. She is sniffing quietly, wiping away her tears and he feels helpless. But she stops at the entrance, and vaguely leans towards him.

'Will I see you on Saturday?' he asks. 'Will you come to Sonderbar?'

'I don't know. I start on nights at some point.'

They stand together, suddenly like strangers.

'Please, Lolita,' he is begging now. 'Please don't be angry with me.'

'I'm not angry, Armando.'

'Please understand.'

Now, finally, one hand comes out of her pocket and she lays a palm against his cheek, briefly.

'I understand.'

She looks weary, but she is not moving away, only standing so close that he can smell the scent of her skin. She lifts her hand again, touches his cheek again, and then rests it on his chest, and he finds his voice: 'Can I kiss you?'

The words have fallen out of his mouth, when he should have simply taken her in his arms. For he is scared now, not sure that she will not shove him away, something that would hurt like hell and from which he does not feel he could recover. But to his utter joy, she lifts her face and so he instinctively puts his mouth on hers. She parts her lips so that their tongues meet. She steps in and he steps in, so that they are now closer than they have ever been before. He can feel her small, firm breasts through the thin material of her blouse, and he slides his hands under her jacket, so he can feel every shaft of her ribs and each notch of her vertebrae.

The release is immense, he finds he is close to tears, and it takes a monumental effort not to cry like an infant into her mouth. He has no reason to cry, anyway, for the way her hands are gripping the back of his neck, the way she is kissing him, everything about their embrace only confirms that all he has hoped for, all he wants of Lolita Devi, need not remain in the realms of a dream but might well belong to a not-too-distant reality.

7

She has the morning free – no lectures, no shift in the hospital – and it is market day. Once a month, visitors pour in from surrounding villages, filling the town square. In the crowd, she is jostled – 'Entschuldigung, Fraülein' – even shoved if she stands too long in one place, for these are hard-boiled, persistent bargain-hunters. But she does not mind. She lingers, wafts and muses and, that which makes her unpopular, seldom buys.

At a music stall, she browses through the boxes of cassettes, hoping to find a gift for Armando. Most are pirate copies of well-known bands from the West, but she finds a compilation of Georgian folk music, which she had bought for herself recently and really enjoyed. She does not know, however, if he owns a cassette player: she has never seen his flat. It might be spartan, barely furnished, or it might be, given that four men live in it, a complete mess. The time is approaching – she can sense it – when they will spend a night together, even if that exact location is still undetermined. They have crossed over a threshold, and now in each other's presence, the desire they feel is electric, clearly mutual. It is a wondrous, expansive, beautiful thing to be in love with Armando Dos Santos. The sun is warm and sensuous on her bare arms and she languishes in a reverie of tangled limbs, of the feel of his hard, muscled body, of how he would move, until a young man in grease-stained overalls, who is standing near her, speaks: 'Beautiful day, isn't it?' She tears herself from her daydream, smiles her agreement, and his face breaks into a wide, gratified, grin. He looks vaguely familiar, and he is on the verge of saying something, when the stall owner growls at her: 'Are you going to buy anything or are you just taking up space?'

She pays for her selection, and as she makes her way back towards the park, she bumps into Aditya and Prem, two engineering students from Bihar, on their way to visit Prakash, a journalist for

Janayugom, who works from and lives in an office-studio leased from the Reisebüro. Prakash is a protégé of Banaji – an attaché from the Communist Party and her mother's childhood friend – who lives in a new town on the fringes of the city. Along with Banaji's wife, Shanti, the six of them form a small community. She cannot easily turn down their invitation, and so she accompanies the boys to see Prakash, who has only just risen and is unshaven and hairy-chested in a white singlet and mundu. After accepting an over-sweetened, milky cup of tea, served in a disturbingly scummy cup, and spending a half hour listening to prophecies on how the upcoming India-Pakistan cricket tour will play out, she can take her leave with good reason, for her father is calling her.

Spontaneous contact with her parents is impossible: if she wishes to speak to either, they need to pre-arrange a day and time for a telephone call. Because these phone calls are costly, because they are beset with delays and static and echoes, they are not frequent and she and her mother communicate as well through weekly letters.

When her parents separated, when she was fourteen, her idyllic childhood became no less loving, but peripatetic. Her grandfather, a judge on the Supreme Court of Kerala state, bought Sushilla an old tea-planters' cottage near Munnar, a hill-town in the Western Ghats, from where she opened a clinic. Romesh Devi remained in Imphal, which meant that every school holiday heralded a days-long train journey across the country to Manipur to stay with him. She never wonders if her father is lonely – he has a paramour, a woman from Sweden who has made her home in India and who runs a yoga centre from the bungalow they cohabit. But sometimes she wonders if her mother is lonely, for she has lived alone for nearly a decade. She knows her exciting, passionate mother is neither prudish nor straitlaced, and therefore might have a private life unknown to her daughter – and she herself has been reticent. She had told Sushilla of Willy, but not that they were having sex. More inexplicably, she has not mentioned Armando. Uncomfortable, troubling, to analyse this glaring omission. There was a game she played as a teenager, when she wrote the name of a crush from school on a piece of paper and then folded it as many times as was feasible, before throwing it in the river near their bungalow. Has she changed at all?

She arrives back at the residence in time to mount the stairs to the telephone bay on the second floor for the allotted time. The telephone in the booth rings minutes later. She suspects that this call will be something related to Elisabet, the Swedish girlfriend, and she is thinking of how she will react to the news, even before her father announces the news: they are getting married, for it is getting harder and harder for Elisabet to renew her visas. Romesh Devi is trying to downplay any talk of love and romance, and so she interrupts him: 'That's great, Baba.'

'Oh thanks, darling,' his voice is suffused with relief. 'It won't change much, day to day.'

'I'm very happy for you.'

The wedding will be a small affair, in India, and both the bride and the groom want their adult children to attend. But Elisabet's daughter, some years older than Lolita, married and pregnant with her first child – and ironically the closest kind-of-relative geographically, living in Malmö – has a window of opportunity before she enters the third trimester. This detail fixes the possible wedding date to December, and this is the thrust of her father's call. The flights to India are exorbitantly expensive. She has only gone back home three times in the last four years, and these visits have become more difficult to arrange now that she has started her clinical studies. Attending her father's wedding will reduce her time with her mother, in the mountains, to a week at most.

'I'll talk to her, Baba.'

'Oh thank you, darling.'

'I'm sure she'll understand.'

'She's been very gracious about our plans, but she misses you terribly, I know. We all do. Of course, she's invited as well. She'd be most welcome.'

She promises to pass on this invitation, even though she knows her mother will not leave her clinic. The conversation ends with father and daughter sending their love to each other across the wire, across the oceans. Back in her bedroom, she opens the drawer of her desk to find her writing paper, and the stack of letters she has received from her mother. The last letter is at the top, and the sight of the familiar slanted hand, provokes an intense longing, a warm ache in her chest. The dried petals of a hibiscus flower fall out of the envelope, as she unfolds the sheets of paper and lies down on her bed to savour her mother's words again: *You know how I dismiss Matthu's worries about the wood pile? How I love seeing it, thinking of the winter nights when we light a fire. Well, we did find a snake there! A majestic cobra which Matthu managed to trick into a sack before we called the rangers.*

She picks up her pen and begins a letter to her mother: Darling Mummy. As always, the words flow easily. She writes about the wedding and makes some suggestions for the logistics. She writes about the weather, her placement in the casualty department. Then her pen hovers over the paper, and she remembers the way the youngest border guard, the one who collected all their personal details, had held his pen above his notebook in a similar fashion, while the body lay on the sand.

Should she tell her mother about the dead young man they had found? But she would be breaking the trust Armando has placed in her. She could, instead, write about him, Armando. *Mummy, I have met the most wonderful man. He is kind and intelligent and, by the way, very handsome. I think about him all the time and I think I want to spend the rest of my life with him.*

She adds a few more sentences to the letter before signing off, but makes no mention of Armando, nor of the dead boy, Tommy. She leaves the residence and walks down to the corner of the street.

It is quiet, a pleasant evening in a small city in the DDR. Thousands of miles away, her mother will be falling asleep in her bedroom, the windows wide open, a breeze blowing through the light curtains. The rains will have soaked the ground during the day and the night sky will be clear until the next cluster of monsoon clouds gather. She kisses the letter as if it were her mother's cheek, before dropping it into the post box.

8

He should stop there. He has kissed her, felt her body pressed against his. He has the taste and smell of her to permeate his dreams. But the feelings he has had since that first dance, the familiarity yet otherness of her, the curiosity which switched to admiration before long, and then wonder that she could be all things – beautiful and compassionate and brave – flood into him, drown him, drown out any sensible thought or unselfish motive, so that he feels ten years younger and taken over by events. By his first true love? It took him months to suggest that afternoon shopping trip to buy Clara's dress. Only a fortnight after to invite her to the beach. Two days later to visit her at the hospital. His caution, his reticence is evaporating. His heart is filled instead with happiness, anticipation.

His eagerness has been somewhat curtailed by circumstance. Over the last month, he has only seen her twice as she is working night shifts. But today, as he arrives at Petra's to collect Clara, as he scoops up his daughter high, as she squeals in delight, he is also thinking forward to the evening when he will see Lolita. She has let him know that she will be coming to Sonderbar.

As if his daughter's thoughts are in tandem with his, she asks, 'Is Lolita coming with us?'

This question arrives as her mother is handing over a small bag with supplies – sun hat, a bottle of water, and Fufu – and Petra slows down a fraction, her eyes regarding him coolly as he tugs at one of Clara's bunches.

'No, it will just be you, me, and the animals.'

They are going to the zoo, because Petra hates zoos and would never take Clara, and because he is running out of ideas for how to occupy his daughter's attention.

'I'll be out this evening,' Petra says, 'so you'll see my mum later.'

She rarely goes out, and he is curious about her plans, but he keeps silent. Clara pulls his ear.

'Can we go, Papa?'

Petra reaches up to kiss Clara and then to his surprise, he feels her lips briefly brush against his cheek. It is a white flag, a truce perhaps. She smiles at him as she waves them goodbye, and then he feels guilty because he has not told her about Lolita, about how he is letting something grow, or even nurturing something.

Once, maybe now six or seven months ago, Petra had invited him in when he was dropping Clara back and they had sat at her kitchen table, like a family, to eat dinner. He had felt so happy that he was taken unawares when, after the meal and while they were doing the washing up, Clara out of earshot, Petra had asked him: 'Is this how you see the future, Armando?' He knows it was not out of spite. She meant: where is your ambition? Is this life – the life of a factory worker, a father who sees their child once a week – is this enough for you? She said once that his mind as well as his land had been colonised, that he accepted things too easily. He had been stung by the sentiment, but he had not retorted: you can talk. We waged a war against the Portuguese, but here, however much you grumble, you carry on. Only a few take things into their own hands.

With this thought, the vision appears before him like a spectre – the young man, the boy with the blue-white skin who he had pulled from the sea. Someone who had taken things into his own hands and died. He had hoped the memory was long buried.

'Papa?'

Clara is tugging at his hand. The bus is approaching the stop. He gathers up his daughter, kisses her cheek while she wriggles in his arms happily. She is bubbly and chatty and as always when it is just the two of them, he speaks to her in Portuguese. When she responds in kind – and this is happening more and more often – his heart leaps with love. As he finds a seat for them halfway down the bus, he wonders why Petra has not spoken of a new man: she had dived into a relationship with him with alacrity, but now he sees that it is not her usual way. Perhaps her engagement this evening is of a romantic nature. And how would he feel if Petra brought someone into her life? He would be jealous: not over Petra, but Clara. The thought of another man making her breakfast, tucking her into bed at night, actions he has had the privilege of doing perhaps five times over the last four years makes the blood rush suddenly into his head, fills his ears with a roaring sound. He looks at Clara, who has climbed onto his lap and is seeing to Fufu's toilette.

'Clara,' he says. 'Does Mami have a special friend?'

It is a ridiculous question, too vague, but with the perception of the very young, his daughter says immediately, 'Do you mean Bruno?'

'Who is Bruno?'

'Mami's friend.'

'Have you met him?'

She nods, her eyes still on Fufu.

'Where did you meet him?'

'At Oma and Opa's.'

So, this Bruno has been introduced already to the Mickes, who will of course be over the moon if Petra settles down with a nice German man.

'Do you like him?'

His daughter shrugs, then puts Fufu down on the empty seat next to them, pivots on his lap so she is facing him, wraps her arms around his neck and kisses one cheek and then the other.

He smiles. 'What is that for?'

'That's how you say hello with Lolita, but not with Mami.'

He manages to maintain his smile, but before he can think of something to say, Clara asks, 'Will we see Lolita again?'

'Do you want to?'

His daughter nods.

'Then maybe we can arrange to meet her one day.'

He cannot tell his daughter that he is seeing her that night, for fear she will relay the information to Petra. He sets her down on the empty seat.

'Will we go to the beach with her again?'

He looks at Clara who is now not looking at him, but smoothing Fufu's hair.

'We'll see.'

'Can she come now?'

'No, she's working.'

'In the hospital?'

'Yes.'

'Can we go to the hospital?'

'I think she'll be really busy. She won't be able to talk to us.'

'Fufu has a tummy ache.'

'Maybe she needs an ice cream, to make her feel a bit better.'

Clara nods, gravely, and he suppresses a smile. They descend from the bus hand-in-hand. He last took Clara to the zoo a year ago, and while not much has changed, this visit is not a success. In one of the cages there is a morose zebra, and Clara becomes upset: for surely it is lonely. Where are its friends? Perhaps she sees herself in that lonely zebra, as an only child. Even the reminder of an ice-cream and then the ice-cream itself fails to lift his daughter's mood. She is cranky through the rest of the day and later, when he hands her over to her grandmother, he mentions that she has been off-colour and might be coming down with something. But with a painful disloyalty, Clara suddenly brightens, bounds into the apartment happily, giving him only a cursory farewell.

'She looks fine to me,' Alice Micke says, smiling widely, and then as if sensing that her comment might be seen as unkind, adds quickly, 'I suppose it was a little hot today for the zoo.'

He is deflated, surprised by how hurt he is, and Petra's mother seems to feel she has said the wrong thing, for she continues: 'You know what children are like.'

He doesn't, not really, and Alice Micke speaks again into the silence: 'Don't forget the birthday party. You can bring two friends.'

It is kind of her to remind him, although he had not forgotten, and it is more than a month away, ample time for many reminders, especially over his strict quota of friends. He bids her goodbye and catches a shuddering tram back to Lütten Klein, staring out of the window during the journey, vaguely disturbed by how the day has unfolded. Back at the flat, as he is showering, he tries to wash away his anxiety. But the feeling of an impending change in fortunes, of the day not quite having had its say, continues as the four men pile into Joachim's car and they drive into the centre to Sonderbar.

But when she pushes open the door to the bar, when he sees her look around and meet his eyes, the way her face lights up, everything is forgotten, and an almost painful happiness rushes through his veins. He waits, with heart hammering in his chest, as each of the other three – Gilberto, Ronaldo, and Tiago – greet her, until finally she is standing before him. He bends down, risking a hand pressed to the flare of her hip, while he kisses each cheek, breathing in the scent of her hair. His hand has not gone unnoticed by Gilberto, who raises his eyebrows and twists his mouth into a sideways grin – nor by Lolita, who does not move away, but who blushes slightly. He orders her drink at the bar and brings it back to the table. As if they have all noted the new territorial, possessive air he radiates, the men now leave Lolita on the end so he can slide into the chair next to her.

'How are you?'

'I'm okay.'

'It's nice to see you.'

'It's nice to see you.'

They have parted from each other with a kiss four times now, and as if she can read his thoughts, she gives him a life-affirming, beautiful smile.

'How was Clara today?' she asks.

'I took her to the zoo.'

'She must have loved that.'

He smiles, but he does not tell her: it was all wrong. Perhaps he should have, because now he has not been transparent, even deceitful, and he feels a flutter in his chest. He tries to ignore it.

'When you've had your drink,' he whispers, 'shall we take a walk?'

It is now their routine, to stroll through the evening streets, holding hands, looking up at the night sky, and at some point, sharing a kiss. It is a pretence that he needs to ask her first. She nods, flashes him another smile. So easy, so fluid, so normal has it become to arrange a night-time stroll with Lolita Devi, an opportunity to have her all to himself as he had only imagined previously. But something unsettling has lingered, taken root, the vestiges of the anxiety or dread from earlier – a sense of foreboding that one day his daughter may no longer enjoy his company, even that Lolita may forever be a reminder to his daughter of the day at the beach. He glances at Lolita who is studiously listening to the orange-haired young woman reading a poem, while standing on one foot like a stork. He trusts that she has put the dead boy out of her mind, but how can he know for sure?

Because his thoughts have been disjointed, troubled, he finds that he has finished his drink more quickly than usual, and when he orders another one, it is not a beer but a shot of vodka, which – strangely, something else to add to this ominous day – goes straight to his head. He watches her from the bar. Her gaze is on the performance and the light is stroking her face and neck. When the crowd applauds, when the compere announces that was the last reading, they both look at each other.

'We're just getting some air,' he says to Tiago, who nods without making any salacious comment, on his best behaviour in front of Lolita.

'How was your week?' she asks.

But out in the night air, on the street, he has no desire to relate which machines he cleaned and fixed, no desire to stroll aimlessly, or peer into empty shop windows. In fact, he finds he has little inclination to talk: he has an overpowering hunger to be alone with her. For a second, he even wonders whether Joachim has left his car unlocked, but dismisses that tawdry vision from his head. He takes her hand and leads her away from their usual route, down some steps where he remembers there is a courtyard. It is quiet and dark. Their footsteps echo against the walls around them. There is a faint smell of urine mixed with tobacco, but Lolita does not complain, only allows herself to be led. He has no idea what the time is, but it must be late, because there is no one around.

Perhaps it is the moonlight, that last shot of vodka, the feeling of being in their own private space, but he cannot stand it any longer. He pulls her to him for a kiss, a kiss which becomes long and exploratory, and then more urgent, his erection pressing blatantly against her. For the first time, his hands truly roam: he feels her nipples stiffen under his fingers. His thighs are edging her thighs apart. He is on fire, lost to time, lost to where they are. But he feels her suddenly jerk away, and then she is pulling down her dress, and he moves his hand away from where it has found itself, between her legs.

Her gaze is over his shoulder, and he turns around, to see a trio of people standing some metres away. They were most likely passing through the courtyard on their way to the town square, but are now staring. One is Petra, one a man, whose hand is on her arm, and the last is a woman clutching her hand to her chest. The two he does not recognise look supremely uncomfortable; Petra alone looks serene.

He has never, he realises almost with disinterest, crossed paths on evenings or weekends with Petra. They keep different schedules, frequent different haunts. Except for tonight. For whatever reason, he had assumed she would be going to the theatre, but she will have been attending a work event, for the warehouse which houses the newspaper's offices is, really, only a stone's throw away from where he has brought Lolita. She is wearing heels and a close-fitting tomato-coloured dress, and she looks well. She is watching him, her hands to her sides, but her face shows no sign of distress. She mutters something and the man seems to object, but then he nods and leads the other woman away, into the dark. Lolita has moved some paces away from his side, and then he hears her mumble a goodbye. Before he can say anything, she has darted across the courtyard and is running up the steps. He wishes to run after her, but he is compelled to stay where he is.

'Petra.'

She only looks on at him with that calm, unhurried expression.

'I'm sorry,' he decides to say.

She grins then – and it is an awful sight – and she takes a step forward and he sees that he has truly hurt her. Whether with his lies, or by the spectacle with Lolita – she is hurt and angry.

'You lied to me.'

He feels his stomach clench, but he steels himself and moves closer to her. He touches her elbow, briefly.

'Petra…'

'Remember, Armando. Clara is my daughter. Whatever you are doing, wherever you end up, I'm the one who will be taking care of her.'

She turns away then, but he catches hold of her wrist.

'I'm her father.'

'Let go of me.'

'I'm her father,' he repeats.

But she says nothing, only stares at him so coldly that he releases her, and he sees with some shame that he has left the imprint of his fingers on the flesh of her wrist. But she does not rub herself or draw attention to this, only purses her lips and then she leaves him, her heels tapping against the cobbles. He hears her footsteps pause as she must have caught up with her friends, and then they fade into the night.

He takes the steps two at a time, crosses the street, into the town square. There is no sign of her; she must be running as well. He sprints through the park and only on the road in front of her residence does he catch a glimpse of her: catches sight of her stricken face, her glistening eyes, just in front of the large entrance door.

'Lolita!'

She stops, her hand still raised to the door.

'Lolita. Can we talk?'

She stares at him dumbly, and when she opens her mouth, her voice is so low, so muffled with tears, he can only just hear her.

'There's no point.'

'I'm sorry,' he says.

'For what?'

'For…' he clutches for the right words – I don't know what I was thinking, I shouldn't have touched you – cannot find them, and says instead: 'I'll talk to Petra tomorrow. She'll be fine.'

She shakes her head.

'Can I call you tomorrow? Please, Lolita.'

She says: 'I just need some time.'

And then the large entrance door opens, and two young men spill out, laughing, swerving around her, shielding her from his view. When they move away from the path, he sees that she is gone. He starts walking, his feet are heavy. There is no sign now of Petra and her companions. Was that Bruno? The men say nothing when he re-enters the bar, perhaps his face tells them enough.

Later, he sits at the back of Joachim's car, his friends' conversation an indecipherable hum, Lolita's words ringing in his ears. She wants time, when he feels that time is the last thing he has. Events seem to be hurtling towards him and time is speeding up, propelling him to a future that he cannot see. One where he cannot be certain that he has Clara, one where he is even less certain that he has Lolita.

RAINBOW DDR

9

It is weeks before he sees her again. Loitering near the residence on Karl Marx Strasse hadn't worked – he did not catch sight of her and was unable to figure out her hours. His job at the garage has not helped, given that he reports for work at seven in the morning. He has written about her, charging out of the university residence, her hair flying behind her. That night, he had taken a different route home having, unusually, gone for a drink after work. It was fate that he was walking down that street at that time. He remembers everything – that she was wearing a red dress which ended mid-thigh, a dark jacket with the collar turned up and tennis shoes. Her small gold hoop earrings, and long black eyelashes. He has seen women like her, dark women, when his grandfather took him to France, that summer when he turned seventeen. Moroccans, Lebanese. And even darker: Senegalese, Ivorians. Here, however, he feels starved of any connection with the outside world, and the girl he has seen is definitely from the outside world. She has floated into this monochrome landscape from a land that bursts with colour.

He takes to hanging around the main university building, which only fills him with envy of the students wandering under its high-vaulted ceilings, or gathering on the grass verge in front of the columns and arches, unaware of their very good fortune. Every day, after he leaves the garage, he loops westwards to the residence where she collided with him, collided with his world, he likes to think, then crosses through the park to this main building. The presence of a university in this city dates from the fifteenth century, but the building with which he is now familiar – and its neo-Renaissance grandeur – was erected in the nineteenth. He meanders on its grounds as if he belongs – an unlikely student, however, in his overalls and work boots – absorbing the atmosphere while looking out for the girl. He is frustrated that he cannot find her in this small city, by no means teeming with people. What on earth has brought her to this shithole? His visits become less frequent, and he has resigned himself to never setting eyes on her again, when one day, weeks later, he sees her walking some way ahead of him in the park, under the linden trees now in full leaf. She is heading for the flea market in the town square.

The triumph he feels is that of a predator, and he stalks her just as if she were his prey, keeping a close enough distance so she will not drop out of his sight. There is a lyricism to her gait, and when she arrives in the market, she quickly becomes engrossed in the cassette selection, all of which leads him to believe that she must be a music scholar, which in turn explains why he has been unable to find her: the entrance of the music department is on the south-facing side of the university building, which he has neglected to patrol.

As if to celebrate this happy event, the town is at its prettiest, with the Rathaus a baroque pink and white wedding cake waiting to melt in the sunshine. On either side, the tall and thin gabled townhouses, in faded yellows and blues and pinks, are tightly stacked like books on a shelf. These bear ornaments and filigrees and curlicues. Hard to believe that a few streets away is the giant department store, a slab of blank, grey concrete punctuated with windows as narrow as staples. He stands as near to the girl as is polite, rejoicing at this re-encounter, hoping she will look up so he can catch her eye. She is dressed in jeans and a light grey t-shirt, and she has her hair twisted into a bun at the nape of her neck, so he can see her face, the exotic shape of her eyes, her high cheekbones and pillowy lips. But she does not look up, only sifts dreamily through endless cassette boxes. Finally, he attempts an anodyne comment on the weather, for which she rewards him with an incandescent smile. Then she hands an empty case to the stall holder, who rummages through his stash to find its cassette. She speaks in correct German, but she has an accent. When she is leaving, her eyes flash at him, again without recognition, and then away.

'Ja?'

The man in front of him is bulky and broad-faced and he has not been polite to the girl, and so he speaks roughly to him in turn.

'Which cassette did she buy?'

The man stares at him, chewing on something.

'The girl before me. Which cassette did she buy?' His tone is urgent now, she is walking further and further away.

'Why didn't you look for yourself?'

'Why can't you just tell me?'

'You want to buy something, or you just want information?'

'Jesus, tell me. I'm not asking for your blood type, am I?'

'Why do you want my blood type?'

The man is obtuse and grey and unappetising, as are all the men in this godforsaken backwater. Even the women are dowdy frumps. But he cannot then, through honesty, stop from correcting himself – Trudy, the secretary from the garages, with whom he is sleeping, is beautiful, and he remembers then that he had said he would meet her later.

He gives up, catches sight of the girl turning down a side street. He trots after her, then falls behind at a safe distance. She is a quick walker, light-footed. Her hair shines in the sun. And then two figures detach themselves from where they have been lounging, their hair as black and shiny as hers. One calls out something and the girl stops. They are two young men of his age, who greet her with easy familiarity, in a language he cannot recognise. They place her between them, and all three fall into step. He feels suddenly, irreversibly excluded, and he turns off abruptly, and stumbles down the street, seething with jealousy, for many minutes and many hundreds of yards, before he realises that he will now not know her destination and will forever have to rely on coincidence. He dashes back to the corner, but there is no one, save one old lady wearing an old fur coat. He has lost her.

He meets up with Trudy as they arranged, and because her parents are out, they retreat immediately to her bedroom, where they peel off each other's clothes efficiently. After, he nuzzles her neck and strokes her back, just as he remembers the other girl, with her wavy black hair and quick, light feet.

'Are you coming with me?'

Trudy belongs to a choir, run by her mother's company. She has a good singing voice, but the choir's repertoire is antiquated and dull and he has spent far too many evenings waiting for her outside, to walk her back to her parents' house. Now he looks at her and he sees that she has asked him not because she wants him to accompany her, but because she doesn't. Perhaps she has found someone else. He isn't surprised: Trudy is blonde and leggy and turns many heads. What surprises him is how little he cares. He will never be a good writer if he cannot truly feel a gamut of emotions. He tells Trudy he is busy, and she only smiles and kisses him affectionately on the mouth. They get dressed and although he has toyed with the idea, he does not wait at the corner to see if she leaves her parents' house alone, but heads home.

He lives with his grandfather, in a spacious apartment on the ground floor of an old house across the bridge. This side of the city retains some of its genteel charm from centuries previous and the small gate at the end of his grandfather's garden opens onto the promenade along the river, lined with old gas streetlamps. While his parents' apartment in East Berlin was never cramped – his sister Lili, three years older, has been living with her boyfriend for years – his grandfather's apartment is much larger. The bedroom he has occupied for the last year has ample space for a desk, facing out to the river. It is this desk which has lured him away from Berlin. Although he did not need much persuading: he has always been close to his grandfather, Rainer, as he calls him.

Unlike in Berlin where he spent at least two hours commuting to work every day on dirty, stifling trains, leaving him bad-tempered and chafing against the monotony of his work, here the garage is a thirty-minute walk away and his working day extends only until three in the afternoon. That leaves him hours to sit down at his typewriter before dinner with Rainer, after which he reads through his earlier attempts. He has sometimes torn up pages and pages, although of late, as he has become happier with what he produces, he has tended to file them away in a drawer. Aside from the occasional evening out with the other mechanics – he very much appreciates Philip's sardonic humour – and his semi-regular coition with Trudy, he has little social life. He has surprised himself by his dedication and his monk-like existence: although, do monks have semi-regular coition?

The attempt at a story he wrote about the girl with the long black hair was one he tore up into pieces not much more than five centimetres square. He has seen her twice now, but he does not see her again, until a few weeks later. Philip loses his grip on a drum, and his reflex is to deflect this from crashing onto the car they are repairing. In doing so, the drum bangs his cheek and something flies into his eye. Philip manages to extricate a seed of encrusted grease and dust, but he cannot open his eye for the pain and the tears, and his cheekbone wields a gash which bleeds through the sticking plaster. The foreman relents, making a big show of his leniency, and sends him off to the hospital.

He has been waiting for some minutes when she appears. Now she is wearing a white coat, a doctor's coat, and his heart stops as she approaches him with a clipboard and calls his name.

'Theo Becker?'

He gets to his feet, one eye streaming with tears and still only half-open, his head spinning, and in his surprise at this stroke of luck, he staggers towards her. She jumps forward instantly to meet him and takes his arm, sending an electric current through his body.

'Can you walk?'

'Yes. Thank you. I just, uh, tripped. I'm fine. I can walk.'

She believes he is half-concussed, rather than giddy from the sheer joy of finding her again, for she holds onto him while she leads him through a set of double doors into a wide area with rows of beds. She gestures for him to sit on one of the beds, then walks a pale blue curtain around them, cocooning them in a makeshift cubicle. But the curtain is parted immediately and a tall man, also in a white coat, enters, glances at him and then, in a completely normal but abnormal fashion, puts his hand on the girl's shoulder.

'What do we have here?'

She speaks quietly. 'Possible trauma to the eye.'

The man looks at him briefly, his eyes running over his overalls before addressing the girl.

'You can handle this, Lolita?'

'Yes.'

He squeezes her shoulder and makes to leave, before pirouetting on his heel as if he cannot separate himself from her.

'Call me if you need me.'

She only nods, but there is a slight flush to her cheeks. They are alone again, and she makes some notes on a clipboard.

'Let me take a look.'

His heart is in his mouth and now he is grateful for his injury, because she is leaning close, gently prising away the sticking plaster. Her face is inches from his and where else can he legitimately look but down her throat into the neckline of the blouse she is wearing. There is a fine gold necklace nestling in the hollow of her throat, and beyond that he can see the swells of her breasts enclosed in a white cotton brassiere and he feels a twitch in his groin. She pats her fingers around his eye, pulls down the eyelid. She appears not to hear his heart, pounding in his chest.

'What happened?'

He tells her and she asks, 'Do you have the object with you?'

'No.'

'Do you have a headache?'

'No.'

'Can you follow my finger please?'

She holds up her index finger and tracks it to one side and then the other, up and down, then she straightens up, so that the coat parts and he has a glimpse of the narrow waist of her trousers. He forces his eyes to meet hers, and they are dark and serious, and showing no sign that she is in any way impressed by his proximity.

'There is a slight abrasion to your cornea. I can give you some drops to speed up the recovery. And there is still some grit around the eyelid, which is why it's so uncomfortable, but I'll clean it.' She touches her finger to his cheekbone. 'You have a nasty cut here, but you won't need stitches. I'll clean this as well, but it will sting, just to warn you.'

Then, in a heart-stopping moment, she looks at him, directly, and smiles.

'Are you brave?'

'Are you a doctor?'

She is still smiling. 'You don't trust me?'

'Of course, but—'

'I can call a nurse if you prefer,' she nods in the direction of the world outside the curtain.

'No, I want you. I mean,' he gulps, 'thank you.'

She pulls forward a tall tray set on wheels, carrying instruments and cotton wool and liquids in bottles, so that it sits alongside them. She dabs at his cut with cotton wool. She is concentrating, and he can tell that she is trying to avoid fanning him with her breath.

He clears his throat.

'Your name is Lolita?'

'No, I haven't.'

'Sorry?'

'No, I've not read the book,' she says, deadpan.

'Actually,' he confesses, 'I haven't either.'

She shrugs her shoulders.

'I'm Theo.'

'I know.'

'Yes...of course.'

She continues to work, in silence.

'Where are you from?'

She doesn't look at him. 'I'll give you three guesses,' she says.

'India?'

'Right first time.'

'How long have you been here?'

'Nearly five years.'

'And you came here to study?'

She nods.

'You speak German very well.'

'Thanks, so do you.'

He has been reprimanded.

'I'm sorry,' he says. 'Maybe you think I am rude.'

He feels a sting on his cheek bone, and he flinches involuntarily, but she makes no comment. Then she says, 'You speak German like one of my professors and she is from East Berlin.'

'Yes, I'm also from East Berlin.'

'Why are you here?'

'I came here to live with my grandfather.'

She leans back now as if to view her handiwork.

'Do you like it here?' he asks.

'I do, yes.'

'It's not boring for you?'

She glances at him. 'No, I don't find it boring. Do you?'

He feels a frisson of pleasure. She is interested in him. He enjoys the feel of her eyes on him, and so he takes his time, and he looks back at her, steadily. He has had his fair share of girls falling for him, citing a certain poetic look he has, and so he is quietly confident she will be thinking the same.

'Sometimes.'

'Well,' she says, 'maybe it is, compared to Berlin.'

Now he thinks he must sound like a snob.

'No, I meant,' he flounders, 'I meant, it's a bit…it's not like living in the West.'

She regards him with her large dark eyes. The tube of ointment remains in her hand, and she appears to have forgotten it, before she seems to come to and replaces the lid and sets it down. He sees then that her fingers are hovering over the other items laid out on the instrument tray, hovering not resting, not deciding on one thing. She is thinking of saying something and when she speaks, her voice is soft:

'How do you know life is any better on the other side?'

The same doctor from before, the tall fair-haired man, suddenly reappears. There is little space and hence he is standing very close to the girl, so close his arm is pressing against hers. He catches the odour of stale coffee, while the man mimics the girl's actions: peering into his face, holding an index finger up, pulling at his eyelid.

'So?'

The man straightens up and then once again rests his hand on the girl's shoulder. She does not move away, but he can see she has trouble meeting the man's eyes. Her voice as she recounts her assessment is low.

When she has finished, the man says: 'Yes, correct.'

Then he turns to Theo, smiling, his hand still on the girl's, Lolita's, shoulder, like she is a lamppost, or a stack of books, or his favourite pet. It is a large hand, and it is not closed; rather, it is splayed so that each finger fans out, pressing on a different part of the girl's shoulder, so that it is easy to imagine it, the hand, splayed over her breast, or over her thigh. He feels something rise up inside him.

'You are not seriously wounded, soldier,' the man is saying in a jocular tone, just as Theo feels his hand lifting itself of its own accord, from where it was resting on his knee, to clamp itself around the man's elegant wrist. His hand picks the man's hand off the girl's shoulder in a definite, deft movement and places it next to the man's side.

There is a pin-drop silence. There is no noise even from outside the curtain, as if the whole area is waiting with bated breath to see what will happen next. His eyes lock into the tall, fair-haired man's, in his white coat, a pair of glasses tucked into a pocket, a red stain appearing on his already pink cheeks. No one says anything. The girl, Lolita, is not looking at the man, but staring at him, Theo. He can feel her eyes on him, even if he is not looking now at her, but instead at the man at her side, whose gaze he is holding, and who is becoming redder and redder.

'Would you please leave us, Fraülein Devi? I'll take over here.'

The girl leaves immediately, the blue curtain swishing closed behind him.

Now they are alone, and he can feel his heart beating in his chest, and a dry taste in his mouth.

'You shouldn't touch her like that,' he says.

The man reddens even more, but there is something else in his eyes, which are boring now into his.

'So now you come here,' he says, his voice barely a whisper.

'What?'

'Did Herr Blick send you? Or was it Major Neuberg?'

He stares. There is the hint of tears now in the man's eyes.

'What do you know about life,' he glances at the clipboard, 'Theo Becker?'

'I think—'

'My wife left me. She left me, not only the DDR. I couldn't keep her here. Leave me in peace.' And then he takes two paces backwards, so that the blue curtain envelops him like a shroud, and he speaks in a disturbingly heartier voice. 'All finished here.'

The man parts the curtains and waits for him to get to his feet. Then the man walks back towards the outside world beyond the double doors, and he follows in his wake, glancing around. There is no sign of her. As he enters the waiting area, he stops.

'I'm not who you think I am,' he says, but the man walks away without a word.

The woman behind the reception desk is watching him with a scowl, and she narrows her eyes as he approaches. He hopes he has caught her last name well enough.

'Can I see Fraülein Devi again?'

The woman stares at him, impassively. Then a slot appears between her lips, a millimetre wide and no more, and through which she says: 'Why?'

'She said she'd give me some eye drops, but I think she forgot. She was, uh,' he clears his throat, 'called away.'

'I'll get a nurse.'

'Could I see Fraülein Devi?' He knows he sounds desperate. 'Please?'

She lets out a long sigh, raises her eyebrows so high they scrape at her hairline, then picks up the phone. She covers the mouthpiece and jerks her head, so he moves away, lifting his hand in gratitude.

She comes out of the double doors a few minutes later, looking much younger suddenly, her face bruised, her expression uncertain. He smiles as she walks over, but this time she does not reciprocate. She is holding a small plastic medicine bottle in her hand, which she hands over to him. 'Here you are.'

'Will you be in trouble?' he asks, in a low voice.

She colours slightly.

'Will he make things difficult for you?'

She holds his eyes, then shakes her head, almost imperceptibly. 'I don't think so.' Then, 'I think he's really lonely.'

He feels – and he is surprised by his reaction – annoyed by what he hears. Better that she is upset and distressed and thereby accepts his chivalry with gratitude. He hears himself speaking and he hears that his voice has a petulant, sullen tone.

'You should not forgive him too easily.'

She glances at him – she has heard the tone – and shakes her head. 'No. It's not that,' but she does not elaborate, only takes a step away from him.

'You don't recognise me.'

She looks up then in surprise, before she shakes her head, slowly.

'You were in a hurry. I think you hurt,' he touches his own, 'your nose.'

He sees a flicker in her expression.

'I remember now.'

'I wanted to ask your name then,' he continues, babbling like an idiot. 'But you rushed off. Then I saw you at the market, the other day. At the cassette stall.'

A wariness enters her eyes, and so he continues quickly, to reassure her, 'It was a nice surprise to see you again. And this,' he gestures around him, 'is a nice coincidence.'

Now she looks like she wishes to make a quick exit. He kicks himself: she will think he is a voyeur and she is noticeably withdrawing from him. Desperation makes him bold.

'Can I see you again?'

Her eyes widen in surprise. Suddenly, there is a commotion on the other side of the large room. He is running out of time, and so, as if neither can hear the cacophony in the background, he asks: 'Can I see you?'

She ignores him again but, after a moment's hesitation, extends her hand. He takes it. It is small and cool, and her palms are dry. They shake hands, up and down. She tries then to retract her hand but he holds on, only for a second, but enough to elicit a smile. As she leaves him, her lips are still in a smile, but her eyes are dark and sad. She does not look back as the doors swing shut behind her, and he stares at these for a long time before he realises that there is nothing else he can do but leave.

*

After inspecting the wound on his cheek, his grandfather instructs him to make some coffee to bring out into the garden, where he is tending his roses. One of the perks of his grandfather's adventures in his youth are the many contacts in the West he still enjoys. Hence, his consistent supply of excellent coffee and chocolates sent by friends in packages to his old research institute that somehow, while clearly opened for inspection, have always been released onwards. Carrying the tray into the garden, he finds Rainer lying on the grass, on the slope from the kitchen door to the rose bushes and tulips, propped up on his elbows, and so he does the same, stretching his legs and arms out under the sunshine, and tells him about the Indian girl he met at the hospital, and the doctor who thought he was an informant for the Stasi.

His grandfather will appreciate this sting in the tail, for it was Theo's refusal to be recruited that has led to the downward spiral his life has taken. He was an excellent student at school, a shoo-in for the chosen few. But he was called one day into the headmaster's office where, sitting on a chair to one side, was a man wearing a grey suit, steel-rimmed glasses and a tie which was badly knotted. That he remembers such details, even that the man was wearing one sock inside out, only validates what his headmaster told him, obviously uncomfortable but beholden to praise Theo Becker's acumen, his powers of observation and his natural ability to gain the confidence of others. Qualities, it appeared, that were useful to the State. Clearly, the man sitting next to the headmaster's desk, who said nothing but only gazed at Theo, was from the Stasi. And despite the disinterest of his gaze, he was interested. Nothing was made explicit: he was not yet seventeen, but he understood. When the headmaster offered him extra tuition for the school-leaving exams, he declined, claiming that his weekend job playing assistant in his father's architecture practice left him little free time. In truth, he had no wish to engage in the Stasi's puerile, cruel treatment of those they took against – deflated tyres, broken pot plants, shaved pets, pornographic photos left lying around in people's homes or offices.

That night, he overheard a heated exchange between his parents, his mother exhorting his father to contact the school, even beg any intervention such as they could make from Rainer, to ensure that Theo's future was not in jeopardy. But in the end, neither parent decided to risk further attention to the family, and when he was not chosen for the Abitur, they bore his anger and ranting stoically, his mother only later leaving fliers for the People's Colleges in his bedroom. Rainer took him that summer to France, to visit his old comrades from his war days, as if to give solace to his grief, as if to help him forgive his country. And if anyone could bring him round to accepting this disappointment as a blip rather than a death-sentence, it was his beloved grandfather.

Rainer is seventy-four years old, and a dyed-in-the-wool, card-carrying hero. He had left Germany aged twenty-three, just before the war, when life was already near-unbearable for Jewish families. He had gone to France where, under Nazi occupation, he joined the Résistance. There he married Elise, the daughter of his old neighbours also displaced from Berlin, and Theo's father was born. After the war, the family reinstalled themselves in Germany, in Dusseldorf. The fact that Theo's father was born in France and then lived in West Germany has always lent him a certain cachet. He feels that Marc has been speckled in some indefinable way with stardust, some of which he hopes has brushed off onto him as well, by dint of being his son. His father could have grown up in West Germany, married there, had his children there. But it was not to be, for both Rainer and Elise Becker became disillusioned in the West. Once, his grandmother had revealed that they had been outraged with the role that former Nazis maintained in society. Not considering themselves Communists, they nevertheless decided to join the great socialist experiment in the East. And so, the family moved from Dusseldorf back to East Berlin.

This journey in reverse to so many others was the making of the Becker family. In the East, his grandfather was celebrated as a war-hero and, with no inconvenient past allegiances, became a respected chemist and later head of the academy. Because of his voluntary relinquishment of a life in the West, his loyalty was rarely questioned. Even after the Wall was erected, Rainer was allowed to travel. Over his working life his grandfather, therefore, had opportunities to leave aplenty – yet he truly did not wish for it. After Elise died – ten years ago now – his grandfather moved up north to be nearer the sea.

Now Rainer rather obviously brushes past the reminder of Theo's Stasi encounter and instead, steers their conversation to the girl from India.

'It is a country I would like to know better,' his grandfather is saying. 'When she came to visit that first time, Indira Gandhi, I was part of the delegation to show her around Berlin.'

He does not recognise the name, and his grandfather touches his arm in a mild rebuke.

'She was the Prime Minister, of India, Theo. You remember old Heinz?'

He has a vague recollection of a wiry old man, and so he nods.

'Well, Heinz used to work for Filmfabrik Wolfen. One of their main clients is the Indian film industry. They buy their colour film from us, you know.'

He hadn't known.

'It was because Heinz and I collaborated on some projects that I was also invited to meet the Prime Minister. An impressive woman. Small, but strong. I remember when she was assassinated, we mourned her death. She was a true friend of the DDR.'

Now he remembers. The headteacher had been emotional on breaking the news, and they had lowered the flag to half-mast, all marks of sorrow and respect rarely afforded to citizens themselves. He will never understand his country.

'So, this girl. She's studying medicine?'

'Yes.'

'She will speak English, Theo. You might be able to get lessons from her. Maybe you could teach her Russian in exchange.'

He knows his grandfather is teasing him, but he can only hear himself saying, grumpily: 'Why would she want to learn Russian?'

Now Rainer is laughing.

'Is she pretty?'

'Very.'

'What's her name?'

'Lolita.'

'God help us!'

'It suits her.'

His grandfather sips his coffee, his eyes still dancing with amusement.

'Did you ask her out?'

'I did.'

'And?'

'She ignored me.'

Rainer laughs.

'I have to say I like the sound of this Lolita,' then pats him reassuringly on the arm. 'You have many talents. I'm sure you'll manage to convince her.'

It is true that he has significantly more in his armoury now – most notably, her name. In the morning, he phones the garage to say he will be delayed, fabricating a problem with his grandfather's plumbing. He packs his overalls into a bag and dons corduroy trousers and a collared shirt, Italian-made, a gift from one of his father's Libyan clients. He is confident that he will pass for a university student, and a bookish, well-mannered one at that. Despite the last five years of working as a cog in the great DDR machine, the veneer which comes from a relatively pampered upbringing – with parents in well-paid jobs, living in a milieu of photographers and designers and theatre directors – has remained intact.

He is familiar enough now with the student residence on Karl Marx Strasse. He waits near the entrance and when the door opens to let out a trio of girls, he holds it open for them and then slips inside. There is a grand central staircase, which he quickly alights, but on the first floor he sees row upon row of anonymous brown doors. He wonders whether to ask the woman washing the floor with a mop and bucket, but she has a piercing, unwelcoming stare. He descends the stairs and returns to the entrance. To one side, there is a cabin with a glass window, behind which he can see a man in a porter's uniform. He knocks on the window and waits for the porter to slide it open, reluctantly.

'Uh, I wonder if I can see Lolita Devi?'

'She left half an hour ago.'

'For the hospital?'

'For the hospital?' The porter mocks his voice and accent. 'No, not there.'

'Do you know where?'

'Am I her secretary?'

'No,' he takes a breath. 'I'm sorry, sir.' He plunges his hand into his bag and retrieves a notebook. 'She left this behind yesterday. I wanted to return it because we have an exam tomorrow.'

The porter raises his eyebrows, and he sees behind the man two bottles of vodka and three packets of cigarettes, a commercial enterprise, no doubt, related to the paper tacked to the wall: 'Keine Besucher nach 22.00 Uhr'.

He turns away, preparing to return with an appropriate bribe when the man speaks.

'Swimming pool.'

'Huh?'

'Swimming pool.'

The window is slid shut with a bang.

Not bad, not bad for a morning's work. He is particularly chirpy at the garage; the foreman eyes him suspiciously. When he clocks out, he visits the swimming baths near the residence, a grand building with Grecian columns. The young woman on the reception desk ignores him disdainfully when he asks – does an Indian girl come here? He goes back the next day and there is a man on the desk, who winks lasciviously at Theo's question and who shares his thoughts on women from the Orient. They are taught from an early age how to prioritise a man's pleasure, in the kitchen and in the bedroom. They will give whatever you ask for, they have been trained for everything. They never argue, always obey, and they remove all the hair from their bodies. He tolerates the man until finally he receives the information that he needs.

Yes, the girl comes regularly, and usually on Tuesdays. And so, the following Tuesday morning, that is where he is.

10

Her placement in casualty ends that week. There will now follow two weeks of classes and an exam before she begins the next in obstetrics. She has handed in her report, attended lectures, helped Beate move into an apartment with her boyfriend, accompanied Banaji's wife, Shanti, on a shopping trip, and invested in a better pair of boots for the upcoming winter. To all eyes, therefore, she has carried on as normal. But inside: she bears a constant ache in her heart, her veins feel dry of any blood, her throat is permanently parched. The whole world speaks to her in a muffled voice. Her whole being yearns for him, even though it is abundantly clear that he is beholden to Petra. Best to pretend that they had never breached the barrier of a platonic friendship and dabbled in something more. Best to pretend, in fact, that night, that surrender, never happened.

And yet she cannot forget, cannot pretend that she did not learn something about him which in equal parts scares her and excites her. He had presented himself as he truly is: an adult male, with an intense physicality beneath the gentleness, the playfulness. Those moments they shared: where would it have ended? And what if their first act of love had taken place on a street filled with the stench of spilled beer and stale urine? She cannot stop herself from diving into a dark, deep pool of shame and self-pity. The memory of Petra's appearance along with two others, strangers all to her, and witnesses all to what she was doing, even now makes her feel sick.

Although he called once and left a message, she has not called back. Since that evening, on the two occasions she has slunk back to Sonderbar – through whatever compulsion, for whatever reason – she has resumed her spot in between the other men, who have been uncharacteristically silent on this change, and she has only seen Armando once. Then they had made stilted conversation, both treating each other with extreme politeness and formality.

And he had left early, claiming that he needed to oversee something at the factory, even though Joachim remained at the bar. Their relationship – if it can be called that, if it could ever have been called that – has been stunted, stopped in its tracks.

She walks briskly, determinedly, in the early morning fresh air. If she keeps herself busy, she can delay the moment later in the day when time stops, a thunderclap sounds, the heavens open and all her longing for Armando rains down, drenching her. She has started swimming again, after a hiatus of a few months. As a child in Imphal, her father took her to the campus pool. In the south, she swam in the river near their bungalow. She was not the only girl in the water, but the only one in a swimming costume, and this attracted much attention, hence Matthu, her mother's housekeeper, always accompanied her. Now, humming uselessly to herself, she runs up the steep flight of steps leading to the entrance of the swimming baths. The pool inside is large, clean, organised and costs a pittance.

She finishes her lengths and is climbing out when she notices that someone is standing to one side. When she steps off the ladder, he does not step on but says, 'Lolita,' and so she looks at him. It is the patient with the minor trauma to his eye. The nice-looking young man, who had lifted Hans Lütwiler's hand off her shoulder.

'It's Theo, if you remember?'

She nods, self-conscious in her costume and white swimming cap.

'Uh,' he swallows, 'you're leaving?'

'Yes.'

'Can I meet you outside?'

His hair is bone dry, and so is, from her quick glance, his body. 'Aren't you going to swim?'

'No,' he says. 'No, I've just realised I've forgotten something. I'll come another day.' And then he grins, sheepishly, as if hearing his own weak explanation.

'Can I meet you outside?' he repeats.

He has nice green eyes, and he is clearly keen, but is waiting respectfully for her response.

She nods, slowly. 'Okay.'

He grins more widely. 'Thank you. Don't rush.'

When she glances back, she sees he has already left the pool area, most likely to ensure that he is ready before her. And sure enough, when she comes out, she sees he is waiting at the bottom. She descends the steps, slowly.

'Hi.'

'Hi, Lolita.'

'How's the eye?'

'Oh, fine. Great. I used those drops, as you said.'

'This is quite a coincidence.'

He nods, vigorously. 'Yes, isn't it? But I'm very pleased to see you again.'

His tone is nonchalant, but his efforts are so obvious that she finds a laugh bubbling in her throat, which she manages to quell. He notices and once again grins sheepishly.

'Can I invite you for a coffee?'

'I have a class at nine o'clock.'

'We can go there,' he points to a diner across the road, which she knows well. 'I won't take much of your time.'

He orders a coffee and pastry each and insists on paying, even though she produces the coupons she receives as a student. The man who serves them at the counter, who is well-used to her coupons, regards this act of gallantry suspiciously. They take a seat at a table by the window, and he leans his elbows on the table. His whole demeanour exudes an irrepressible joy, which is refreshing, even infectious. For the first time in weeks, she feels the balloon of gloom that has engulfed her deflate slightly, as if from a tiny puncture. She sips her coffee.

'Didn't you say you worked in a garage?'

'Yes,' he says, 'I do. Not today, though.'

It is mid-week, surely a working day.

'How did you find me?'

He looks startled.

'I didn't—'

'Come on.'

'I went to the student residence,' he says, and he is blushing, 'and asked after you. They told me you came swimming.'

'I see.'

He is squirming in his seat.

'I just want to get to know you a bit better.'

'Why?'

'Because…' he looks around the diner as if trying to find the correct answer, runs his hand through his hair, 'because…'

'Because you're bored?'

He shakes his head. 'No, not bored. Intrigued.'

'Because I'm Indian?'

'Because you're beautiful.' And then he blushes again.

It is a nice compliment, and sincerely spoken, and she is surprised that it pleases her. He looks awkward, runs his hand through his hair again, then says: 'Please don't worry, Lolita. I'm not a creep.'

She responds with a moue, but she is enjoying herself, can hear the hiss of the gloom as it escapes from that balloon. She bites into her pastry, brushes some flakes from her chin, taking the opportunity of his averted gaze to inspect him. He has nice hands and the stubble on his cheeks is a darker brown than the hair on his head.

'Where does your grandfather live?' she asks.

He looks up gratefully at the turn of the conversation, and gestures towards the east. 'On the other side of the river.'

'Why are you living with your grandfather? Does he need looking after?'

He laughs, genuinely.

'Oh no. No, he doesn't need looking after.'

'Then why?'

'I think my family wanted me to be as far away from the Wall as possible.'

It is a bold admission, and he appears to sense her consternation at his reply, because he adds, quickly: 'I wanted to come as well. I don't have to work long hours here, not like in Berlin. And that means I have more time and space to write.'

'You're a writer?'

'I wouldn't say that, not yet. But yes, that's my dream.'

She sips her coffee. He is munching happily on his pastry.

'What kind of things do you write?'

Now he looks abashed, but he says: 'I'm working on a novel. I've written some short stories as well.'

'But you also work in a garage.'

'Yes.' He grins. 'I'm a good mechanic. But it wasn't my choice. I wanted to go to university, but they wouldn't give me a place.'

She knows that entry is limited, but she would wager the young man before her would be a good candidate.

'Do you know why?' she decides to ask.

'I turned down an offer to work for the State,' he says. 'I don't want to be part of all that. I suppose it was their way of showing their displeasure.'

His tone is offhand, but she has touched a nerve. There is no arrogance, however, only an honesty, a directness to his responses, even though he has spoken softly. He has shared with her that his ethos of life is at odds with his government's, which is no small thing to admit to a stranger. She knows it is not easy for these people to trust others. If Armando has adopted any local habit, it is this extreme caution or, further along the spectrum, paranoia.

'Well,' she says, 'I think you were brave to turn them down.'

'Do you?' He looks astounded.

'You had your principles. And you've paid a price for them.'

'It could have been worse,' he says, but she can see that he is gratified by what she has said.

She raises her coffee cup as if in a toast.

'I think you have some good material there for your novel, Theo.'

He laughs. 'I never thought of it in that way.'

He places the rest of his pastry whole in his mouth, chewing happily, smiling at her as if they have overcome an obstacle, passed on to safer ground.

'Do you know Sonderbar?'

He shakes his head, still chewing.

'It's in a basement on Kleinestrasse, on the other side of Centrum,' she says. 'They have open nights for writers and poets. Maybe you should go there and read out some of your work.'

He takes some time before he swallows and looks bashful, does not assent. Rather, he changes the subject: 'Do you have days off?'

'I do.'

'Could I take you to the seaside? It will be warm enough to swim now.'

His words stop her – hadn't Armando said the same thing? Her skin grows cold. The dead body they found in the sea might once have been a personable, vital young man like the one before her. And why has he gone to such lengths to find her? His eyes on her are green, not blue, not like Tommy's. But what if he is Tommy's brother? A cousin? There is a resemblance, isn't there? They have the same build; they might be the same height. He might have been at the beach himself, seen what had happened, followed them back to the city.

She looks around, the diner is empty. The man who served them has now moved into the back room. They are alone, as far as she can tell.

'Were you there?'

'Sorry?'

She loses her nerve, picks up her cup but finds it empty. There is a clatter from the back room, a tray falling to the floor, as if to remind her that their server is likely to reappear, and she will lose her chance.

'Lolita—?'

She hears herself asking, as casually as she can but her voice sounds tight: 'Have you ever thought of swimming across the sea, to Denmark?'

Her question falls into silence and he stares at her, appalled.

Finally, he speaks. 'No.' Then shakes his head. 'No, I haven't.'

'Could you swim the distance?' she whispers.

'In a swimming pool, maybe. It's different in the sea, though. I don't know if I could do that.'

She nods, bites her lip. She can feel his eyes on her but cannot meet them.

'There were these two guys what, maybe three years ago?' he is speaking quietly. 'It was a big story on West German radio, because they used surfboards with handmade sails attached. The sea was rough, and they became separated. One managed to make it to Møn and the other was picked up by a Danish fishing boat.'

She says: 'And what if they hadn't made it?'

'They'd have gone to prison, for sure. Five years at least.'

His responses are open, guileless. If he is acting, then he has a talent. A wave of disappointment rolls over and away from her, along with the last vestige of doubt that he might know of Tommy.

'Some people do it,' he says, 'but they are usually the ones who have no other choice.'

'And do you have a choice, Theo?' She feels ashamed for asking him, but she cannot stop herself.

'I thought about it once. Not swimming across, not that. That's madness. But my grandfather took me to France some years back, and I had to come home on the train, alone. I remember when the train left the station in Paris, I wondered whether I should get off at the first stop and just stay.'

He stops there, smiles nervously, runs his hand through his hair.

'But I was young, only seventeen,' he says. 'And I knew my grandfather would be really disappointed with me. And it would have made things difficult for my family.'

He shrugs his shoulders, self-consciously.

'Do you regret it?' she whispers.

'Yes, sometimes,' he grins, but his eyes are solemn. 'But I'll find my own way to live in the West.'

She gulps, taken aback by the surge of compassion and admiration that has rushed through her, for the young man in front of her.

'Can I ask why you're interested in swimming to Denmark, Lolita?'

He is smiling, tentatively. His eyes are warm and open, and she feels another rush, not of compassion but of loneliness: for she has been lonely. The desire to share the story is overpowering. She has obeyed Armando's instructions and has spoken to no one of it, not even her mother. And while normally she might have exercised more restraint, the circumstances – the young man's candour, his easy-going, warm presence – seem to unlock her tongue.

She begins: 'We were at the beach a few weeks ago...' But then something causes her to backpedal, as if she feels Armando's hand on her shoulder, and she performs a verbal sleight of hand and continues: 'And we saw the border guards recover the body of a man from the water...'

Her words peter out and Theo makes no attempt to fill the silence that follows. In fact, he appears dumbstruck. The news of a dead compatriot, even if it transpires that it is not a relative or a friend, would naturally upset him.

Yet when he finally speaks it is only to say: 'We?'

'Me and my friend, Armando,' she says and can then feel herself blushing.

The silence is now thick and expectant.

'Armando,' he repeats. 'That's a strange name for a German.'

'He's from Mozambique.'

'Mozambique?' From the way he says it, she is not sure he knows where it is.

She says: 'He works in a printing factory in Lütten Klein. He was the one who told me about Sonderbar, actually.'

A shadow flits across his eyes.

He says, his tone light: 'He's your boyfriend?'

'No, no. He's not my boyfriend.'

The silence extends, her cheeks are still warm.

'Sorry,' she says. 'Maybe I shouldn't have mentioned it. Forget I said anything.'

She means the dead body, but she realises that he might assume that she means Armando. The server bustles back to the counter, whistling through his teeth, and she glances at the watch on her wrist.

'I need to get going.'

'I'll walk you to the hospital.'

'No, no,' she stands up, shrugging into her jacket. 'No, finish your coffee. Thanks.'

And before he can get to his feet, she has flung herself across the small diner, through the door. The enormity of what she has done, the fact that she has half-broken the promise she made to Armando to a relative stranger – that she believed, even if for a few minutes, that he might be connected with the discovery in the sea – all of this clashes somewhere in the pit of her stomach, alongside a pang of pleasure, from the certainty that he is watching her hasty departure. She does not look back as she crosses the street, even though she can feel his eyes following her every step of the way.

11

At the garage, Trudy is ignoring him, and he wonders if he has forgotten a promise or a rendezvous. But over lunch one day, he sees her flirting with Lothar, and he thinks: oh well.

Philip nudges him and nods his head in their direction, at Trudy throwing her head back in a cackle while Lothar looks at her, wolf-like, ready to pounce.

'What do you make of that?'

'Nothing.'

'It doesn't bother you?'

'No. I don't blame her. I've been rubbish.'

'Spoken like a man whose candle burns for another maiden.'

Philip's grandparents are Russian on one side, which might account for his romantic flair with language. Indeed, his friend's words are apt: for he has spent every day since meeting Lolita in a state of excitement. He is convinced that he likes everything about her. Her smile, the faint hairs between her eyebrows. How she had said: good material there for your novel, Theo. She is a foreigner, but she fits into the city seamlessly. His own experience of the world is miniature in comparison.

The following Tuesday, the foreman at the garage grunts when he phones in an excuse: another burst pipe in the bathroom. That last time, she had galloped off, with sudden haste. He still has no phone number to call, but he knows a good deal about her now. Where she lives, and how she spends her time. That she has been to the beach. With this Armando.

But she is not there when he arrives at the swimming pool and he has to wait until ten minutes to the hour before he sees her coming out of the changing room. Her skin is a palette of golds and a hint of ochre near her knees and elbows. He tries not to inspect her body overtly, but even in the cold water of the pool he feels another throb in his groin.

She has not seen him. She looks preoccupied, tucking a wavy strand of hair into the lip of her cap as she nears the pool's edge. She climbs down the ladder, entering the lane beside his and begins a breaststroke, her head bobbing up and down purposefully. She does not raise her eyes to see him treading water in anticipation of a wave and a smile – only when she stops at the opposite end to take a breath does he have a chance. He ducks under the rope separating the lanes to hear a shout from the lifeguard, which he ignores.

'Lolita?'

Her head whips around in surprise.

'Hi.'

'Hi.'

The water is clinging to her eyelashes and eyebrows which are very dark, very black against her skin.

'Can I see you afterwards?' He is speaking rapidly, for in the corner of his vision he sees the flat poolside shoes of the lifeguard approaching.

'I've got to be at the hospital as soon as I finish today.'

'Okay.'

'Hey!'

She pushes off. The lifeguard is semaphoring angrily and so he dives under and when he surfaces, he hears the man shouting after him: 'No crossing the lanes!'

She is intent on swimming and so he continues himself, and he is just finishing a lap of butterfly when he sees her holding onto the wall, waiting for him.

She says: 'You're so good.'

The admiration in her voice floods him with excitement. He manages a modest smile, executes a perfect tumble-roll and cleaves through the water with added vim and vigour, alternating front crawl, his favourite stroke, with butterfly, his most impressive, hoping she is watching him, offering a prayer of gratitude to the Pioneers. But when he looks up, he sees that she is climbing out, her buttock cheeks winking at him, before she grabs a towel and wraps it around her waist. Her route back to the changing rooms entails passing him.

'Lolita!'

She stops.

'Will you, uh, will you please wait for me outside?'

She dabs at her face with her towel, then nods. His heart soars as he catapults himself out of the water. He showers and dresses in record time, so quickly that he is waiting alone for many minutes outside before she reappears. She has towel-dried her hair, and it lies loose around her shoulders. She looks glowing and fresh-faced and clean and lovely. He watches her descend the steps towards him, slowly.

'Hi,' he says.

'Hi,' she replies.

'It's nice to see you again.'

She tilts her head, noncommittal.

'Can I walk with you to the hospital?'

She nods, glancing up at him briefly.

'I hope I didn't offend you the last time,' he says.

She shakes her head. 'You didn't, Theo.'

The use of his first name sends a shiver down his spine. He clutches for the next thing to say but can alight on nothing, wordsmith that he is.

She speaks, into the silence: 'I didn't know you were such a good swimmer.'

'Yes. Listen,' he sounds impatient, he knows, but the hospital buildings are already in sight. 'Can I see you tonight?'

'I'm having dinner with some friends.'

'Oh.'

They walk on, now he is disconsolate, and within minutes they have arrived on the forecourt of the hospital.

He says: 'Can I have a phone number? So I can call you?' Impulsively, he reaches forward and touches the ends of her hair. 'Please, Lolita.'

She does not shrug off his touch, but neither does she seem to have noticed it. He shifts from foot to foot, disheartened.

'This dinner,' she says, suddenly. 'Do you want to come?' Then smiles at his surprise. 'If you like Indian food?'

'Uh,' he hesitates, then confesses. 'I've never had Indian food. I don't know much about it.'

'Then it will be a good way to learn.' She is laughing for some reason, but she sobers up on seeing his confusion. 'There's a guy here who hosts a dinner for us every couple of months,' and as if reading his thoughts, she adds, 'By us, I mean me and two other students. They won't mind you coming.'

So not the Armando person.

'Are you sure?'

'Yes.'

'Well, if you're sure.'

'I'll phone ahead,' she says. 'It might be boring for you though.'

'Where will it be?'

She gestures westwards. 'Over in Connewitz. I normally take the bus.'

'Let me pick you up,' he says. 'I'll borrow my grandfather's car.'

She smiles. 'Okay.'

They part then. When she has entered the building, he punches the air in glee. Impossible to be any good at the garage, but he puts in an appearance and agrees to work some extra hours to compensate for his grandfather's fantasy plumbing issues, watching the clock obsessively. Finally, he can leave. Her words, every word she has spoken, beat in time with his feet as he half-runs back home. He finds his grandfather in his garden.

'Can I borrow the car?' he shouts out, without waiting to hear the answer. He runs the shower hot first and then freezing cold, and while he is dressing, Rainer enters the bedroom, chuckling, holding in his hand a bouquet of flowers from the garden.

'The Indian girl?' he asks, mildly.

'Can I take the car?'

'You can,' his voice has a smile. 'And you can take these as well.' He lays the flowers down on the bed.

She is waiting outside the residence, wearing jeans and a soft sleeveless top that he would describe as Indian in nature, from its cut and embroidery. Her long hair is arranged in a style his sister would describe as half up and half down, and she wears long, dangly earrings and jangly bangles. He reminds himself that she has not dressed solely for his benefit, as he springs out of the car, and runs around to open the passenger door for her, before reaching into the back seat to produce the bouquet of flowers. Her eyes light up and she appears touched and happy, and he makes a good effort at appearing unfazed by the fact that he is escorting her to a dinner party, months after first bumping into her and believing that he would never see her again.

Their destination is a fifteen-minute drive out of the centre. On the way, she explains that Banaji, the host, is a friend of her mother and has lived in the DDR for twenty years. It is his wife Shanti who is cooking the dinner. Also present will be Prakash, a journalist, and with these three she will speak her mother's language, Malayalam. But the two other students who are attending, Aditya and Prem, are both from the north of India, and with them, she will speak Hindi. That there is more than one Indian language is news to him, but he only nods sagely. On arriving at the new town, they climb the stairs to the third floor of the apartment block, where even from the corridor, he can hear a babble of overlapping, lilting voices.

The room is sparsely furnished but dense with aromas that he does not recognise. There is a dining table, and a sofa fashioned from a single bed with a coverlet and cushions. A television stands in pride of place, next to a bookshelf, stacked with books. The old Communist, Banaji, immediately engages him in fluent but nearly indecipherable German, the accent is so thick and unfamiliar.

'Come, drink my friend,' the younger man, Prakash, shoves a bottle of beer into his hand.

The woman, Shanti, barely visible in a cloud of steam, is tending to various pots in the kitchen. Lolita is moving with familiarity around the older woman, stacking plates and gathering glasses.

'Where are you from?'

He blinks. 'Sorry?'

The man Prakash is smiling at him. 'Where are you from?'

'East Berlin.'

'Ah, Berlin.' He sweeps his arm across the room and pronounces: 'Der soziale Fortschritt Kann an der sozialen Position des weiblichen Geschlechts gemessen warden.'

Then, 'You know who I'm quoting, I'm sure?'

'Uh, Marx.'

'Exactly. What do you think of our Little India then?' pointing at Shanti toiling away at the pots, Lolita at her side, 'the position of our women is not great, is it?'

'Let him be,' Lolita says, carrying a column of plates which she sets on the dining table. Shanti offers him a bowl of snacks, smiling and saying something which is clearly an invitation. He selects a small, breaded cake which he bites into, obediently. A searing heat erupts on his tongue and the men who have been watching from the living room burst out laughing at his coughing fit. Shanti hands him a glass of water, her face pinched in apology, which he gulps down, desperately. He catches sight of Lolita biting her lip.

The table is not even large enough for four and after filling their plates Lolita and the two other students sit cross-legged on the rug in the centre of the living room. But as he moves to follow them, the woman, Shanti, stands up and gestures to her seat at the table.

'Oh no,' he says.

Banaji barks something at his wife. But she does not sit down as he has expected the husband to have ordered. Instead, she goes back into the kitchen before reappearing holding aloft a spoon.

'For you,' Prakash says, his mouth full, and there is another burst of laughter. And then he notices that no one is using cutlery, but are moulding neat balls of rice and chicken with their fingers.

He sits next to Lolita, and sees the slim one, Aditya, watching him, expectantly, a smirk on his smooth, dark face, which riles. So, he accepts the challenge, spoons the rice and sauce into his mouth and swallows, then waits a few seconds before a fire blazes down his throat. He can feel the blood rush to his face, and sweat droplets break out on his forehead. Again, there is much laughter, another glass of water is poured for him, but Lolita does not participate in the torrent of ministrations: she must realise that he is tiring of the hilarity. At least, after this initiation rite, he is forgotten. Now no one addresses him – there is no more German spoken.

He manages, manfully, to finish his meal. Lolita gets to her feet first, to gather plates, the men handing these to her imperiously, without looking at her, without breaking the flow of their conversation. She rests a hand on Shanti's shoulder when the woman begins to rise.

'Theo will help me,' she says, in German. He recognises his cue and gets to his feet with alacrity. They move together to the kitchen.

'Do you mind?' she whispers.

'No, not at all.'

'We can leave after this.'

She runs the water into the sink, and as she soaps and rinses the plates, she smiles at him occasionally, and he delights at the domesticity of their activity. At one point she whispers again: 'Have you recovered?'

He whispers back: 'I thought I was going to die.'

She laughs. 'You won't die. You did very well.'

'They are nice people.'

'They all like you.'

'Do they like Armando?'

She smiles, even though he notes that a shadow passes through her eyes.

'They've never met him,' she says.

'Oh right.'

'He has a daughter, Clara. He spends most of his free time with her.'

'Oh.'

'And,' she says, 'I'm not sure they would like him as much as they like you.'

'Why?'

'Because,' she says, emptying the sink now and scrubbing the draining board. 'A man like him would be a step too far.'

She doesn't elaborate, so he is left to surmise himself. Because he is African? Works in a factory? A German mechanic is not a much better prospect, surely. She takes the tea-towel from his hands and hangs it over a cupboard door to dry.

'Shall we?'

They re-enter the living room, where the men are having a heated discussion. Lolita bends down to speak in Shanti's ear and the woman says something to him, smiling.

'She says you must come again.'

'Please tell her thank you for having me.'

Some words are exchanged between the two, before Shanti embraces Lolita in farewell. Aditya looks up, still smirking, but no one else takes any note as Lolita leads him to the front door. It closes behind them with a quiet click.

'You don't mind we didn't stay for dessert?'

In fact, he is thoroughly enjoying being part of her escape.

'No, not at all.'

'It will give you instant diabetes, anyway.'

She skips down the stairs like a gazelle, as if newly liberated and once outside, in the darkening gloom, she breathes deeply, as if coming up for air. Compared to the humid, close atmosphere of the apartment, the air indeed smells sweet. She walks towards the car without any prompting, and he realises the evening is drawing to a close, and his heart begins to sink.

'Uh, would you like to go for a drink?'

'I have a really early start tomorrow, sorry.'

'A quick drive then?'

She looks up at him. While her eyes are a deep shade of brown, each has a light orange trim around the pupil. She nods.

'Okay.'

'Have you seen the windmills?' he asks.

'No.'

They drive along the streets which are silent now, holding barely any traffic, and then on the road that hugs the coast, which is empty. She doesn't talk. She has her face turned to the window, which she has opened, so that her hair is blowing back. Without her seeing, he lifts one hand from the steering wheel and holds it up so strands of her hair briefly caress his palm. His heart is full, but she is silent and, if he is not mistaken, she is thinking of something else, or someone else. The two windmills loom ahead of them – with chipped paint but retaining their imposing dignity, one sea-green, the other deep pink – separated by a field full of wildflowers in vivid blues and pearly whites, unblemished and untouched over the hundreds of years since the windmills were first erected.

'It's beautiful,' she breathes and then turns and smiles at him, but even then, he can see that her eyes are sad.

He makes a circle around the windmills, and then re-joins the road back to the city, and he can see her watching the windmills disappear from view in the wing mirror. At the residence, he parks in front of an entrance, ignoring the disapproving look of a passing elderly woman, and runs around to open the door for her. When she climbs out, she has the bouquet of flowers in her hand. She tucks some hair behind her ear.

'Thank you. For the flowers and for the drive.'

Her voice is low.

'Can I see you at the weekend?' he blurts out.

She hesitates, then says: 'I was thinking of going to Sonderbar on Saturday. Do you remember I told you about it?' She looks up at him: 'Why don't you come, Theo? You could read some of your writing.'

His heart skips a beat – either because she has said his name or at her suggestion.

'You should come. You never know. You might even find that things are more interesting on this side of the Wall than you thought.'

She is smiling now, in better spirits finally, and so he smiles back at her, into her eyes.

'Well, meeting you has certainly proved that already.'

'Armando told me about it,' she continues, and he feels the smile drop from his face. 'He goes there with his friends.'

There is a silence.

'They're all writers?'

'No, they're like me. We just listen.'

'They're German?'

'No, they're like me,' she repeats, still smiling. 'We're foreigners.'

And when he doesn't say anything, she continues, 'They were all brought over from Mozambique to work in a factory in Lütten

Klein.'

He says, humbly: 'I had no idea.'

'You don't seem to know much about how international socialism works then, Theo.'

She is being playful now, which is nice to see, but the drip-feed of information about this Armando person only lends weight to his assumption that the man is a rival.

To lance the boil, he asks: 'Does he have a girlfriend?'

'No, I don't think so.' She stops smiling and there is a short silence.

'But I told you he has a daughter,' she adds. 'The mother is German. They're not together anymore.'

Then she holds out her hand. He takes it.

'Will you come?'

'Yes. Yes, I will.'

'We can meet here at eight?'

'Yes.'

'Good night.'

'Good night.'

He has kept hold of her hand, but finally he lets go, and she starts walking towards the entrance door.

'Will Armando be there on Saturday?' he calls out to her.

She stops.

'Yes,' she calls back. Then, 'I'd like you to meet him. You'll like him.'

And as she passes through the large entrance doors, he thinks: I'm not sure I will.

12

She extended the invitation on a whim, but over the following days she realises that arriving at Sonderbar with Theo may be misconstrued by Armando. But what is there to misconstrue? She enjoys Theo's company: uncomplicated and refreshing. And why should she assume that his presence will in any way affect Armando, who has not tried to reignite whatever had been ignited before that awful evening? He and Petra will have consolidated their existing arrangement. That is not her business, just as who she makes friends with is not his.

Yet she is trepidatious when Theo meets her outside the residence. They are less relaxed with each other than previously. She knows she is nervous about introducing him to the men. He might be nervous about this as well or about reading out his work, or both: certainly, as they walk through the city, he pats the inside of his jacket several times, where he says he has stashed some of his writing.

On arrival at the bar, she finds the men at their usual table, and they give her their customary smiles. Armando is not with them. She feels a swoop of disappointment, until she sees that he is standing at the bar with Joachim and has not yet noticed her entrance. Now there is a change to the men's expressions as they watch her approach, for they have taken note of Theo. But they rise as one to greet her, taking turns to kiss her on both cheeks.

'This is Theo,' she says.

There is a brief silence, and then Tiago holds out his hand.

'Freundschaft,' he says, before quickly glancing over to Armando, as if in apology or even as a distress signal. But Armando has yet to notice their arrival. Theo shakes hands with each man as they say their names and then he throws her a look: one name is missing. As they take their seats, she sees Theo search the room. It is not difficult to identify Armando, who is still talking to Joachim, and it is uncomfortable to watch Theo's eyes run over him, clearly sizing him up. At that moment, Armando looks over, his face lighting up briefly on catching sight of her, before his eyes rest on Theo standing at her side, his expression instantly becoming blank. He says something to Joachim, who raises his glass in greeting, with a tentative smile. Then Armando is approaching, with three bottles of beer dangling from the fingers of one hand.

'Hello, Lolita.'

Her name when he says it sounds, as always, voluptuous, but she has little time to analyse his reaction otherwise, because she can feel his lips brush each of her cheeks before he pushes a bottle into her hand. He hands the other to Theo, who looks suddenly so much younger and non-plussed.

'Oh, thanks...'

'This is Theo,' she says. 'He's a writer.'

She can hear her voice sounding enthusiastic and excited, the false notes, and she is aware that Theo is staring at Armando, the bottle of beer looking incongruous in his hand somehow, before he says: 'It's nice to meet you. Lolita has told me a lot about you.'

Armando's teeth flash in a grin.

'She hasn't told me anything about you,' he says.

'Yeah,' Theo looks uncomfortable now. 'No, we've only met recently, not long—'

But Armando has turned away already, and her heart sinks and she feels a stab of pain. She follows his movements as he moves to another table but not to sit down at, for he is only picking up a chair, which he now places next to Theo, even though there was space enough to squeeze in next to her. Now Theo is sitting between them, as if a recalcitrant child. The men on her one side ask after her and she tries to respond, while on her other side sit Theo and Armando, who are not talking to each other, not even looking at each other. Finally, after some minutes, Theo extracts some sheets of paper stapled together from the inside of his jacket.

He has said that he has not yet decided what he will read and now he repeats that, and she tries to smile and nod, and then he touches her elbow briefly before getting to his feet, saying that he will ask if he can be added to the list of performers for the evening, and again she nods and smiles, all the while aware that Armando is gazing ahead, pressing the bottle of beer to his lips, gulping, wiping his mouth, pressing it back, never looking at her. They both stare straight ahead, to watch Theo talking to the owner of the bar, without saying a word to each other and she feels cold and small and miserable.

This was an outright, irreconcilable mistake. Perhaps, on some level, she wished to hurt him, remind him that she has been patient and understanding, that she cannot be expected to wait for him. But she is willing and able to wait for him, for he is all she wants. Yet she cannot reach across and take his hand, she can think of nothing to say and only sits, feeling the bar of the chair pressing against her back, the cold wetness of the beer bottle seeping onto her thigh, and nothing else. Armando is angry, and he is angry with her. He has never acted so cold, been so silent with her.

Theo returns and falls into his seat with a nervous smile on his lips.

'Yes, he says I can read tonight,' he tells her, glancing at Armando, who does not acknowledge him.

'That's great.'

'I've never done this before. Never in Berlin.' He is speaking quickly, excited, tense, his whole body emanating a nervous energy.

'You'll be great.'

'It's a really cool place.' He is looking around: at the prints on the walls, the cushions and hangings, the many people dressed in tie-dye, and batik and homespun clothes. 'I would never have thought it existed in this shitty city,' he grins at her, and she tries to smile back.

The microphone is set up and the first writer bounces up. There is usually a theme – a malaise with living under an authoritarian regime – and the man with a long, black beard and tatty, red scarf around his neck is exemplary, as is the next act, and the next, and the next. Beside her she sees that Theo is perspiring in his jacket, the beer that Armando bought for him has been drunk and his bottle is now empty. When the compere calls his name – 'Theo Becker!' – he gets to his feet, turning once to meet her eyes, before bounding up to the microphone. Then he stands, straight-backed, in his dark green corduroy jacket, his hair shining under the spotlight, looks once at the audience and then at his notes, and begins to read. The story is about a man who realises, as his girlfriend is brushing her hair in the morning, that he no longer loves her.

He reads in a clear, direct way and she is transfixed, for it is excellent. His simple, spare sentences ring out with a subtle depth. The language takes on a beauty she has not recognised before and he has infused himself in the words, so that she feels that what he has written could only exist in German and only be read by him. When he finishes, however, there is silence, before sporadic, half-hearted applause. Perhaps for the denizens of Sonderbar, a writer should be an agitator, a commentator on the many problems in their environs. Theo's story is too much of an inner life, doubts of the self, and too adept, too polished, compared to the histrionics of the previous speakers. He lopes back to the group. She squeezes his arm.

'That was so good.'

He smiles back, weakly. He looks exhausted. And then he leans forward, and he is resting his damp forehead against hers.

'Thank you,' he says, and she feels that he is trembling, and she instinctively touches her hand against his chest, where she is sure she can feel his heartbeat. He grabs this hand and presses it to his mouth, then his damp cheek, and when he releases it and moves away from her, he is still smiling, and she sees as well, over his shoulder that Armando has a pulse working in his jaw, and that he has probably witnessed the brief intimacy. But before she can say anything, although she has nothing to say, really, the next writer is already in full flow, booming out a treatise about the interior border separating the East from the West.

This is the last performance: the readings end, music starts playing over the speakers, and tables are rearranged so that the makeshift stage is no more. She herself gets to her feet, before she realises that Armando is standing in front of both her and Theo.

When he speaks, it is to Theo: 'Is she real? The woman?'

'Not really,' he hesitates, glances at Lolita. 'She's based on, uh, my ex-girlfriend.'

'She had beautiful red hair?' Armando is smiling.

'She was a brunette.'

'But the woman in your story has red hair.'

'I suppose,' Theo hesitates, 'I suppose I needed to make her a different person in some ways.'

'That's what you do? You start with something real and then create something different?'

She had not expected such an interrogation, and she wonders if this is a way that Armando can show her that he is interested in other things, aside from her. But he appears genuinely absorbed in Theo.

'How do you know when to diverge from the truth?'

She has seen him in this mode before. They have between them often divulged their impressions of the other readings, and he is better read than she is. But she has not been so ignored and while what she should do is walk away, leave the two men, she finds she is riveted, as is Theo, who seems spellbound, his mouth partly open. He appears unsure of what Armando is trying to say, and as if sensing this, Armando gathers himself. He shrugs, as if shaking off his loquacity, and then extends his hand. Theo takes it, his jaw now noticeably dropping.

'I am not an educated man,' Armando says. 'But you were the best. In fact, the best I've ever heard. I wish you success.'

She feels a flood of envy at the generosity that Armando is extending to Theo. What about me? She wants to speak so that he will look at her, but she cannot, and he is already moving away, walking towards the bar where she sees him join Joachim again, who raises his glass again, to toast Theo.

The rest of the evening passes as if in slow motion, with the sound turned down. Tiago corrals Theo for a deep discussion, she makes conversation with the two other men who appear shell-shocked, out of their depth with the palpable tension in the air. Armando remains at the bar with Joachim. He is hurt. She has hurt him, and she did not need to assume that he is unaware of what might have prompted her distance over the last weeks. He is only too aware of what he can and cannot offer her, of his obligations, of the limitations imposed by others, as well as by themselves, on what they can share.

Finally, enough time elapses so she can suggest that they leave. The three Mozambicans shake Theo's hand, reiterate their admiration of his work, kiss her affectionately. But from his position at the bar, Armando only lifts his beer bottle in farewell – as if any good will on his part has been exhausted. As if it is inevitable, perfectly normal, that it will be Theo, not him, walking her back to the residence. They climb the stairs from the basement to the street. It should be a pleasant – even jubilant – end to the evening, but she cannot speak, cannot make conversation, and after many minutes, finally, Theo breaks the silence: 'Armando seems like a nice guy.'

'Yes.'

'But it looks like,' he pauses, 'something happened between you?'

'Yes.'

He stops walking, catches her elbow so that she is forced to face him.

'Can I ask what happened?'

She cannot confess to that night: Armando's hands on her body, under her dress, and the expression on Petra's face. She has tried too hard to bury that memory, that shame, to give it away so easily. It is not where it started, anyway. It was when Armando pulled the body out of the sea that he also pulled a djinn from a bottle, a malicious spirit which let her believe they had a chance, but which has sullied every moment they have spent together since.

She says: 'When I told you about our visit to the beach, I didn't tell you everything. We found the body, not the border guards.'

He is staring at her.

'When was this?'

'Months ago, now. In June.'

'How did you find it?'

She closes her eyes, re-enacts the scene. There is a terrible pleasure in unleashing the images from that day. The scenes which play before her are velvety and rich: the sea is oily, and more vividly blue than it was, the body longer and leaner with a face which is unblemished and porcelain-pure, not mottled in places. The two of them are larger than life, looming like giants in the landscape, while the little girl scurries between them, the director of the play.

'Clara was playing in a rock pool, and she found a bag. I think Armando knew then what that could mean, that someone was in the water. Because he looked around and spotted this surfboard floating in the waves, but not coming in. Something was holding it down.'

She opens her eyes and sees that Theo is still standing in front of her.

'Armando went into the water and found the man. He was all tangled up with the rope from his board, so Armando untangled him. But he was already dead and he was young. He was our age, I would say. Blond hair, blue eyes.'

The streetlamp above throws a harsh, yellow light, and she knows that he will be able to see that her eyes are dry, parched even, but that he may not be able to see how empty and dull she feels inside.

'The border guards arrived then and told us to tell no one. They made us leave and they took over.'

He continues to stare. No matter how simply she has related the tale, he will understand its magnitude. Why not tell him, now, everything?

She says: 'He was called Tommy.'

She dips her hand into her bag and draws out the string of beads. He holds his hand out and she curls the bracelet onto his palm.

'I took it off him,' she says. 'He had it on his wrist.'

'They let you?'

'Before they came. Before the border guards came.'

'Does Armando know?'

'He thinks I've thrown it away. He told me not to tell anyone about it.'

But she is telling Theo.

When he says nothing, she continues: 'I wonder whether I should find his family. They may not know what happened to him.'

He is weighing the bracelet in his palm, even if it weighs almost nothing. His mind might be sluggish, still intoxicated by the euphoria of reading his work. But now she needs him and so she waits, hungry for his complicity. She wants him to say, leave this with me. I'll make some enquiries. We'll figure this out, don't worry.

But instead, he says, 'Lolita, you can do nothing for him.'

She tries to swallow, but it is impossible. There is a large, dry, prickly mass at the back of her throat: a composite of all the hurt and despair and torment she is feeling. He will be thinking that the tears that are gathering will be spilled because of the dead boy. But they are as much for Armando, for the coldness from him today.

'His family probably already know,' Theo continues, quietly. 'Someone might have been expecting him in Denmark, someone who would let them know he never made it.'

He is only telling her what she knows already. It is now August. If the boy had any family, they would now have heard that his exploit came to a sorry end. This is a story that has been playing in her head, off and on, in the weeks since it happened. But it is a story that has moved on now. She looks down, sees her feet, Theo's feet, and then she can feel him pulling her closer and she feels herself melt into him. The tears well up, and she lets them soak into his corduroy jacket. He holds her gently, for many moments and then she hears his voice in her ear: 'Try and forget this, Lolita.'

She steps away from him.

'That's what Armando said.'

He still has the bracelet in his hand but then he holds it out to her. She takes it and drops it back into her bag. She never expected him to say anything different, and as if he too is aware that the rendition of this story is only an avenue to another, he asks: 'You disagreed? You and Armando?'

She wipes her nose with the back of her hand and nods. 'Yes.'

'But that's not the reason why things are strange between you.'

'No, that's not the reason.'

'Then what is it?'

She takes some time, for she realises she owes her honesty to this strange young man, who has appeared suddenly in her life.

'I think,' she says slowly, 'we both realised that it's hopeless between us.'

The tone of her voice echoes her words, for she herself can hear the hopelessness. And now? She has shared with Theo a secret she only had with Armando. She has placed both onto an equal footing, and this might have been her intention, all along.

He takes a hand in each of his, and then kisses her on each cheek – first the right, then the left – as if he has learned the custom from the African men in the bar. Then he drops her hands, and takes a few steps back, without saying anything. She walks to the entrance of the residence, opens the big door and lets it close behind her.

13

He knows his rival now, for that is indeed what Armando is. And quite a rival: taller and stronger, like a dark-skinned Greek god. Handsome, with wide set eyes and cut-glass cheekbones. Against such a man, he himself appears a boy. Although, he is not without depth, he has suffered his fair share. He is a child of the goddamn DDR, after all. Yes, Armando is a significant rival, but one who can be challenged. He feels a tweak of shame, for the man had been magnanimous in his compliments, and genuinely self-deprecating. I am not an educated man, he had said, even though he had shown himself to be perceptive, and a linguist.

He longs to see her again, but it will be more than a week, at least. On Thursday night, his grandfather picks him up after work in his Trabant, and they set off for Berlin. On arriving in Friedrichshain, he receives a warm welcome. He has loving parents. They met and married and had their children young, and they are still youthful. And both have found outlets for their passions: his mother is an actress and his father an architect. His sister Lili has also found her niche, as a dedicated research scientist now working at the university, taking after Rainer. It is only he, Theo, the black sheep, the writer-mechanic, who has truly been swallowed up into the grey, grimy belly of the State. Only he was forced to attend night classes, after work, to complete the Abitur. Only he attracted the attentions of the Stasi.

He is pleased that Lili is attending the family dinner that evening, and not long after, his friend Hugo arrives. He hasn't seen Hugo for nearly a year. He has lived in self-imposed exile, distancing himself from his former life: both his idyllic childhood, when he believed that everyone lived as his parents did, and his early adulthood when he was sucked into the arduous, bleak realities of the DDR. Now he and Hugo sit in the shared garden of the apartment block, while Hugo smokes a cigarette, and they catch up on each other's lives.

Hugo is still dating the girl he met at photography college, Marina, and they plan to move into their own flat. He finds he is telling Hugo about Trudy – and how it fizzled out – but he does not elaborate on the arrival on the scene of Lolita Devi, not wishing to tempt fate by talking of her, not when his thoughts are replete from their last encounter. Yet he tells his friend about Sonderbar and how he had read out – for the very first time, to a room full of strangers, mostly – the words he had composed, crossed out, re-formulated, and – omitting the exchange with Armando – that the audience had been largely unimpressed.

At this Hugo laughs, and laughs even louder when he describes the polemic he should have written. But he realises he is sharing this with his old friend not in mockery, but because the existence of Sonderbar has, he will admit, humbled him. It is a locus for dissent and as such the bar will be monitored by the Stasi. There will be informants in the crowd, smiling and mingling like Judases, noting which are the most belligerent contributors. It is not hidden, other than being below ground level in a basement: Centrum, the city's department store, is only a few metres away, the Rathaus a mere ten-minute walk away. True, ten, twenty years ago, it would have been shut down: late state socialism is more indulgent. But, even so, reading out loud a critique of the State is a bold rebellion, and it is more than he has ever done.

'Remember when we thought we should do whatever we could,' he says, pointing his finger in the right direction, 'to get over there?'

Hugo nods and taps his ash into his coffee cup.

'What happened to us?' he asks, and his friend understands immediately what he means.

'We've not changed, Theo.'

He says nothing as Hugo drags on his cigarette and then continues: 'You still want it, don't you?'

He does want it. But what is 'it' exactly? The story he has told Lolita, when he contemplated absconding from the train in France, is well-worn: he related it to all his friends on his return, and to many, many since. Only a couple of years previous, he and Hugo plotted, in all seriousness, to target and seduce an Austrian tourist apiece, and marry their way to the West. Now his friend is happily ensconced with Marina. Is that what happens to everyone in the end? A dumb acceptance, a grudging contentment?

They leave his parents early the next day. There will be the wedding of a second cousin to attend on their return, but before that, he and his grandfather will be spending a night in Prague. He has not travelled much, something which the past weeks and his new acquaintances have shown up. Paris with Rainer, now five years ago, and of course Czechoslovakia, as soon as the open border policy between the two countries was arranged. They went back and forth, for camping trips, city escapes, even to attend the opera, nearly every year during his childhood: joining a convoy of Dederonski families, in their trusty Ladas or Trabants. This time he is accompanying his grandfather to a reunion of Rainer's old war friends. At the last, in Paris, there had been an American son-in-law, Stephen Radowski, a writer who made conversation with him in fluent German, which also had the quirk of sounding quintessentially American. He had revealed at age seventeen to this American stranger his own putative ambitions. Now he intends to pass on some of his work to the man, for who knows what might then happen?

He takes the wheel. They have a quick stop at a roadside stall in Dresden and then take to the road again. When they cross the border into Czechoslovakia, the landscape changes and the roads become better. The small villages and towns that they drive through seem to be more vividly coloured, gayer than those they have left behind in the DDR and he wonders if it is proof of what he has always maintained: that life is greyer and blander in his homeland than anywhere else.

They enter the outer limits of Prague and find their way to the address. They will be staying in the hills overlooking the city, in the apartment of a friend. The apartment is in a handsome old mustard-coloured building with dark green windowpanes. The friend is Judit, a woman in her late sixties, who has the surname Temple, because her late husband was an Englishman, and who shakes his hand firmly before pulling him down to kiss his cheek.

'Mais, qu'il est beau, Rainer ! Tu n'as jamais dit…'

She is fluent in French, which is thus the language of the evening, and which he does not speak, but which he understands well enough. The contingent from France is already there, having flown in earlier in the morning. But the gathering of war comrades is incomplete, only Gérard and Octave have made the journey, the rest now too old to travel, and in their midst Rainer is noticeably more sprightly.

For dinner that evening, Judit has prepared a Hungarian goulash. They sit around the long, hardwood dining table positioned opposite tall windows thrown open to the square below. As the meal progresses and her former job as a chemist at a Budapest research institute becomes evident, so does the possibility that she is a more than a friend to Rainer. He manoeuvres himself into a seat next to the American son-in-law, Stephen, who is, thankfully, eager to practise his German – 'I never get to speak it day to day!' – and who is gratifyingly eager to read his writing – 'Damn straight I'll read your work!' On being handed the brown envelope in which lies the story of the woman with red hair, the man begins to leaf through the sheaf of papers, right there at the table. He gulps his wine, trying not to watch, and then the American claps him on the back: 'I'll see what I can do, kid!'

That is enough excitement for one evening, but then Stephen Radowski drops a bombshell. Between mouthfuls of the goulash, he reveals that the fence dividing Hungary and Austria has been de-electrified, has been for a few months now. He freezes, speechless, with his spoon halfway to his mouth. And there is more: the party had planned to meet in Budapest, but Rainer was refused an exit visa. The American speculates that the two are not unconnected, for the authorities must have suspected Rainer's grandson – that is, Theo – of being a flight risk.

This news is momentous. He looks across the table at Rainer, who is in deep conversation with Octave.

'Je te jure, je te jure, c'était le même mec qu'il y avait quatre ans…'

The American begins to chatter, sensing Theo's bemusement. He forces himself to respond, but his head is spinning. Rainer's plans have never before been thwarted by the authorities. The American is most probably correct: it is because of him, Theo, the refusenik.

As they have been speaking, the party is breaking up. The others are staying at the hotel at the bottom of the hill and they begin to take their leave, arranging to reconvene late morning. At the door, Stephen Radowski is preoccupied with helping old Octave into his overcoat. As they are leaving, he suddenly loses his nerve, opens his mouth to call the man back, retract the envelope from where it is tucked into the American's armpit. But then Judit places a hand on his arm, and he hears the door click behind them. They have gone, his writing along with them.

'Je peux te donner les clés.'

He can make out that Judit is suggesting that he takes in the lights of the city and that she will give him an extra set of keys, so he can let himself in whenever he returns. Rainer appears engrossed in the view from the window and offers only a perfunctory grunt of approval. He folds the map that Judit is proffering him into his jacket pocket, and takes the stairs down to the ground floor and out into the night air. It is a warm, balmy night, perfect to explore the city of Prague, which he is familiar enough with. There are several bars and brightly-lit, well-stocked shops with colourful displays, and he can hear snatches of French and German and English, as if to underscore the cosmopolitan ambience. On a less salubrious avenue off the main drag, when he hears the thump of music, he turns into a doorway. The man on the door regards his Marks der DDR disparagingly, then pockets them and nods him in. The music is deafening. On the floor, people are gyrating with Central European abandon. Eventually he joins them, led to the dancefloor by an attractive girl in a clinging minidress.

And on that dancefloor, hemmed in by strangers, he wonders: do they know? Will someone sidle up to him, 'I'll take you, we can climb across the border now', and if this happens, will he take the risk? But nothing happens, and he feels no disappointment. Hugo had said: we've not changed, Theo. But has he, in fact, changed? Has Lolita changed him? She has set his insides in a turbulent spin of some permanence, so that for the first time in his life he was reluctant to leave the DDR. The last few weeks, it has felt like he is walking through a house with many rooms, and in each room, he is witness to a different story. A dead body is pulled from the sea. A party of Indians congregate to speak in tongues and eat with their fingers. A writer reads to an audience who gaze back at him, agog. In another room, he sees himself with Lolita, lying on a bed in each other's arms, she is stroking his face. This room, he has not visited, not yet. He enjoys watching the girl who has dragged him onto the dance floor, even the fleeting touch of her body, but he is also unmoved, for she is not Lolita.

The apartment is in darkness when he gets back, a bed has been made up for him on the sofa in the living room. He falls onto the sofa and, as he closes his eyes, for some reason he thinks of Armando and that strange comment the man had made: I wish you success.

*

In the morning, Rainer musses his hair, makes a show of being surprised to see him sitting at the breakfast table, pretends to look for signs of a female companion hiding somewhere, while Judit, displaying an ease with Rainer and his antics, ignores his grandfather and only quizzes him on the sights that he had seen. Their farewell after breakfast is sombre, and tender, and Rainer is quiet as they drive away from the hills, leaving the city behind. He wishes to interrogate his grandfather, but it is only when he feels that an appropriate time has elapsed that he speaks: 'Stephen told me. He told me you applied for a travel visa to Budapest for both of us and that you were refused.'

Rainer knots his eyebrows, shrugs his shoulders.

'Yes.'

'Because of me?'

'I don't know, Theo. It's possible.'

'Because of the border fence to Austria?'

He is keeping an eye on the road, but he is also watching his grandfather.

'Maybe.'

'So you knew the news about the fence? You knew it was de-electrified?'

Rainer nods.

'Why didn't you tell me?'

Rainer does not answer immediately, then speaks slowly: 'I wasn't sure what to do. Even your parents hadn't heard about it.'

'People will start finding out soon enough, Rainer.'

'Yes.'

The road passes under them, and he glances at Rainer to see that his grandfather is watching him, with a steady gaze.

'You weren't tempted, Theo?'

'Not for long.'

'It crossed your mind?'

'It did.'

'But?'

'I want to do things my way. And I want to see Lolita again.'

'Really? It's that simple?'

'It's that simple.'

Rainer gives a short laugh, like a bark.

'Will I meet her?'

'I'd like you to.'

'She can come for dinner, maybe?'

'That would be nice, thank you.'

But he doesn't tease him further, and for this reason, and by the set of his grandfather's jaw, he can see that Rainer is still tense. Rainer, with his full head of white hair, still-black eyebrows. And he feels that love and awe for him that he has felt all his life. Rainer, who returned to a country that had rejected and persecuted him, in the conviction that he could make it better, that it was his home. Rainer, who still exudes a boyish excitement, who has seen the worst of human nature, and still believes in humanity.

He says: 'I met some people through Lolita. Did you know that there is a group of Mozambicans working in a factory in Lütten Klein?'

Rainer raises his eyebrows. 'All over the country.'

'Isn't it strange? To bring people from Africa to do our lousy jobs?'

'They might be very grateful to be here.'

'Because life in the DDR is so fucking fantastic?'

Now Rainer grimaces, and shuffles in his seat. 'Because their country is at war, a civil war that has dragged on for years now.'

'Come on, Rainer.'

'Well,' his grandfather gives a vague wave of his hands. 'Think what you like, but a job is a job, Theo. They get paid and they are safe.'

'Why can't they work in Lütten Klein but live wherever they want?'

His grandfather only sighs and looks out of the window.

'You know why not, Rainer. Say it. Because the good citizens of our country wouldn't stand for it. All men are equal, except the ones we don't like.'

His grandfather knows him too well to launch a denial, and as well, Rainer, of all people, is all too aware of the feelings of a large proportion of their countrymen.

Instead, his grandfather asks: 'How did Lolita meet them?'

He racks his brains: this is something she has not told him.

'I don't know,' he says, finally. 'But I do know that she's very good friends with one of them. I met him the other night. This guy called Armando.'

'And where did you meet him?'

'At a bar in town. I went there with Lolita.'

'He is not imprisoned in the factory, then. He is free to enjoy himself of an evening.'

He glances at Rainer, who only gives him a modest smile.

'I suppose.'

'Would you like to invite him for dinner with your Lolita as well?'

'No, we don't need to,' he replies, too quickly, and Rainer bursts out laughing.

Now his grandfather is looking more relaxed, back on familiar territory, and he finds himself speaking of his rival, Armando: about the daughter Clara who has a German mother, about the evening at Sonderbar and the compliments the man had made on his writing. But when he tells Rainer about the visit to the seaside,

126

about how Armando had pulled a republikflüchtling out from the sea, and how Lolita had shown him the cheap bracelet – Tommy – his grandfather stops smiling and falls silent. He looks to his side at Rainer, who has now closed his eyes as if to block out those very images, block out any reminder of the unpleasant, rotten core of his beloved DDR. The story has cast a pall over them, but as they pass the sign which shows they are nearing the Czechoslovakian border, his grandfather stirs again.

'What were you and Stephen conspiring over?'

'My future literary career.'

Rainer raises his eyebrows.

'He's taken one of my short stories.'

And it is a brusque, ugly reminder of their reality, when Rainer asks, urgently: 'What is it about?'

He looks at his grandfather.

'Not the work of a dissident, don't worry.'

His grandfather scowls. 'I didn't mean that.'

'Well,' he pauses as he overtakes a green Lada, the first car they have seen for nearly an hour, 'there is no mention of the DDR. It's all about what goes on in someone's head.'

'It sounds fascinating.'

'Mm.'

Rainer is trying to row them back to their usual jesting, but it is a difficult trick to perform today on this car journey and there is a decided unease between them now. They fall silent again, and he thinks Rainer has, in fact, fallen asleep, but with eyes still closed, his grandfather reaches out and lays a hand on his forearm.

'It's better you tell no one what you told me, Theo. About the boy they found.'

'I know.'

There is a short queue for the border post just ahead. The tarmac is like a blue snake winding ahead of them. Or something more benign. Like a blue ribbon at the end of which he knows he will find Lolita who – it is painfully obvious – is in love with Armando. How quickly can one love another? No idea. But this he knows: he is twenty-two years old, with completed Abitur and a vigorous beating heart, warm blood in his veins. He has passion and talent, and he has a thirst for life. He has seen nothing of the world yet: it awaits him. Of late, his eyes have been opened to so many things, not least that life is but made of chance.

They will be back in Berlin in good time, to join the preparations for his cousin's wedding. They will be back in the DDR. If he had disappeared into the night in Prague, and found a means to travel to Hungary, would he have leap-frogged over the fence into Austria? It is not that he has become risk-averse, or even that he is more philosophical about his lot. It is possible that the frustration at being penned in, a frustration he was riven with only a couple of years ago, is evolving into a willingness to wait for change to arrive and – something he will not voice aloud – a relief that others will bear the brunt of enabling it.

14

Hans Lütwiler has not been seen for days, ostensibly on sick leave, but rumours are rife: the word on the street is that he has left the country. After that incident in casualty, he avoided her, appearing diminished and forlorn. His final report on her performance had been fair, neither overly critical nor overly complimentary. Now she learns that his wife defected some years ago, and his career stalled in consequence.

One day, Professor Caroline Scholz calls a meeting with her, which, bewilderingly, takes place on the staircase of the medical building. Here the professor quickly becomes tearful. She needs to know what happened between Dr Lütwiler and Lolita's patient. The one who insulted Hans, the one who must have contacted the authorities about Hans – this might have proved the last straw for her much-loved colleague. Caroline Scholz has been asked to write a report on Hans Lütwiler, and this must tally with the patient's file. What had he said to Hans? What did Hans do? It dawns on her after some minutes that Professor Scholz is talking about Theo. He moved Dr Lütwiler's hand, she says. His hand? The professor squints at her, uncomprehending. It was on my shoulder, and he took it off my shoulder and then Dr Lütwiler told me to leave. Caroline Scholz's face is red now, her eyes are dry, and she nods her dismissal.

She flees. But the whole exchange is troubling and leaves her feeling shaky. Theo had said: you shouldn't forgive him too easily. Had he reported Hans Lütwiler? Would he have gone that far? She should feel, perhaps, disgust for Hans Lütwiler. But she finds she is feeling sorrier than ever for him, and for Caroline Scholz, and for this sad, sad, country she has found herself in.

These are strange days. The hospital is understaffed, and the clinicians who supervise the students are less amenable to ad hoc demonstrations of procedures. Sometimes she feels overwhelmed, living thousands of miles away from her parents. She misses switching between English and Malayalam and Hindi as she does back home – here she is limited to German alone and sometimes she finds that the language grates. Sometimes she is unsure why she is where she is, doing what she does. At one point, she had dreamed of becoming a teacher rather than a doctor, and she can easily imagine this life now: closing the door on the classroom at the end of the day, bidding goodbye to the pupils, riding a bicycle to a house with a garden to tend to. Sometimes she seriously doubts she has what it takes to complete her medical training.

But she continues attending the few lectures that remain, taking her exams one by one, assisting with the patients on the wards, ignoring the sensation that they are, all of them, on the cusp of something unknown, something that will change them forever.

*

It is a hot and sticky day, but there are probably only a few more weeks, possibly days, before a chill creeps into the evenings, before the leaves start to turn, then fall. The inevitability of the seasons is still a cause for some wonder. Now the autumn looms ahead, with a tranche of important exams and two placements to pass. She leaves the residence before anyone on her floor has materialised from their bedrooms. She rarely travels to the outer reaches of the city, and before long the tram has left the criss-cross of streets she knows so well and is trundling through unfamiliar territory.

The man sitting next to her taps her on the shoulder, interrupting her thoughts and she starts in surprise.

'Sorry,' he smiles, revealing tobacco-stained teeth, his breath reeking of alcohol. 'Do you have a light?'

She feels his hand stroking her arm. She gets to her feet and moves to another seat. The older woman to her side gives her an encouraging pat on the knee, and mutters: 'Disgraceful. Too many of these men, nowadays. Drinking too much. Upsetting young women.'

In fact, she has had more unwanted attention on the streets of Bombay and Delhi, but she smiles at the woman, who continues to tut at intervals, the man swaying, silent now, in his seat. There are fewer people in the carriage, they are nearing the end of the line.

It is a Saturday, and she needs to catch him before he leaves to pick up Clara. She hopes that she will find his flat, which she has never visited. She could knock on Joachim's door and ask for directions, but he may not be in or – the clock above the post office tells her that it is half past eight in the morning – even awake. It is anyway pleasant to sit and watch the outside world, and she feels calmed by both the scenery and the soothing motion, until she realises that the journey is taking longer than she expected: perhaps there are more stops on a weekend. Finally, however, she sees that it is drawing up to the crossroads, where she recognises a bottle shop on one corner and a butcher on another, and she dings the bell to signal that she is getting off.

But when she descends, she is unsure which road will lead her to the track connecting the small village to the open country, where the factory complex is a blot on the landscape. She has only visited the factory once, for that afternoon barbecue, months ago now. She goes into the butcher's and waits in a queue until she reaches the counter. No, she doesn't want a cut of meat or sausage, only directions to the printing factory. Why does she want to go there? The butcher looks suspicious, as if he is beholden to warn her of the accompanying dangers. There are men from Africa, with no wives or children. Only men. I have an appointment with Joachim Bechtel, she says, his face clears, and he points her the way.

From leaving the small village, the walk is long and straight, and the factory buildings are in sight for a long time. At least the single track ensures that if Armando is making his way in the opposite direction, she will see him. And what then? What will she say? I'm sorry I brought a friend last week to Sonderbar? I'm sorry we haven't talked for ages. I know you're angry with me. But what if he were not angry, what if she had simply misinterpreted his behaviour? That night, when she had run away, she had told him: I need more time. Time for what? She sees now that her behaviour has been confusing, and what message will this broadcast – her surprise appearance at the factory?

But she forces herself to put one foot in front of the other, and she forces herself to continue her journey, until finally she is passing the administrators' block on her left. The sun is high and she feels a sheen of perspiration on her forehead. She removes her jacket and tucks it into her cloth shoulder bag, and passes through the gates of the factory which are standing open. Joachim's car is parked just inside, and his house is on the right. She is now in the middle of the courtyard, the warehouse and factory floor ahead of her.

There are only about five men congregated in this courtyard, wearing overalls, ready for work. All are smoking, and all turn and watch her approach. She feels her face grow hot as she approaches the closest group, who are taking long, slow drags from their cigarettes, while observing her in unblinking, unfettered fashion.

'Good morning,' she says, cringing inwardly at her politeness. 'Could you tell me which flat Armando Dos Santos lives in?'

Three pairs of eyes regard her silently. One man removes the cigarette from his mouth but says nothing. She is not sure she should offer her hand, none of the men do so, and so she hooks one hand onto the strap of her shoulder bag and pushes the other into the pocket of her denim skirt, which only makes the man lower his gaze. He lets his eyes travel slowly down and up the length of her bare legs.

'You don't recognise me,' he says, unsmiling, but using the same words that Theo had used a few weeks ago. 'We met at the despedida a few months ago. I am Paulo.'

'Yes, of course,' she says although she has no recollection of the man.

'You want to see Armando?'

'Yes.'

'Lucky Armando.'

'Lolita!'

The man narrows his eyes and glances over her shoulder, and she looks back to see Joachim, on the other end of the courtyard, walking briskly towards them, in a white collared shirt and black jeans. The men around her do not move.

'Lolita,' Joachim says, again, as he draws up to her, then to the men: 'You can go now.'

'Yes, boss.'

The voice is sarcastic, but the speaker, Paulo, stubs out his cigarette under his boots, and the three move away, unhurriedly. She sees them join the other two who have been watching and then all five saunter into the factory. Joachim takes her elbow, waits until the men have disappeared before speaking again.

'What are you doing here?'

He looks surprised and concerned, which only makes her more embarrassed to say, 'I just wanted to see Armando.'

He looks on at her, the expression on his face not changing, keeping his hold of her elbow. Finally, he says: 'He won't be in. He's usually gone by now on a Saturday. You know he goes to see Clara?'

Her face is now, she is sure, bright red.

'Yes, I hoped to catch him before he left.'

Joachim glances at his watch. 'It's nearly half past ten,' he says.

She is floored: how did the time pass so quickly? She is certainly unused to traversing the city, has certainly underestimated how long the journey would take.

'I'm sorry,' she says. 'Sorry to bother you.'

Joachim has not let go of her elbow, as if he fears she will break free and run around the complex, tearing at her hair.

'No, it's no bother. It's nice to see you,' but he has yet to smile a welcome. 'Would you like some tea? Or coffee?' He gestures to his house. 'I have to go into town to get some supplies, so I can give you a lift back.'

She nods, and he drops his hand, ushers her across the courtyard, but they have only gone a few paces before he stops.

'That's their flat up there,' he is pointing to the building to their right, a nondescript, brick box. She can see that the windows on the floor above are open.

'I'll just ring the bell to make sure he's not in,' and she watches as he walks quickly to the front door to the side of which are two doorbells. He presses one, then shading his eyes from the sun, watches the window on the first floor. There is no movement, no response.

'As I thought,' he says, when he draws abreast of her. 'Armando will have gone, and the others are on their shift.'

She is deflated. The day stretches ahead, a day that she should be spending at least partly readying herself for the upcoming tests, doing her laundry, batch cooking. But a day she knows she will now spend agonising over what was said, not said.

Joachim opens the door to his house and stands aside to allow her to enter.

She accepts a cup of tea, asks as well to use the bathroom, which is full of displays of shells and stones and dried flowers. Aside from Banaji's, she has not entered a home in the last five years and Joachim's is charming. She catches a glimpse of the living room, full of books and pictures and cushions and lamps. She finds him in the kitchen, pouring her tea from a large teapot.

'You have a lovely house.'

Joachim looks pleased.

'I like it,' he says. 'At times it would be nice not to be so close to work, but I like the space. And the view.'

He gestures to the window. From the kitchen, the view is of the nearby woods and open land: hard to believe there is a factory on the other side, outside the front door. He offers her a plate of biscuits, cradling his own mug of tea. He has kind eyes, and he is attractive in a grizzled, gentle, shabby way, with his thick, dark hair. He is well into his thirties, he might be close to forty, and he has the air of man who has travelled all corners of the globe, even though she knows that he has not.

'How are your studies going?'

She is surprised when she answers, honestly, 'I'm finding it hard to be motivated at the moment.'

He smiles at this.

'You need to make sure you don't burn out, I imagine.'

She sips her tea.

'Sometimes I worry I don't have what it takes.'

He smiles again. His eyes are gentle, and she sees them move over her quickly.

'You have many qualities that will stand you in good stead,' he says, but he does not list these. 'And I have never studied medicine, but I know that it must be hard. I'm sure you will make an excellent doctor, Lolita.'

She tries to think of a bright response but can only smile back at him, weakly.

He seems to be thinking. 'We had an order a few years ago you might find interesting. Wait, let me see if I can find a sample.'

He leaves the kitchen and when he reappears, he is holding a large book in his hand.

'An order from India. I think three years ago?'

It is a biology textbook, in English. She fingers the pages, takes in the diagrams of the digestive tract, the reproductive system, the passages describing respiration.

'For many years, we also printed the posters for the film industry. I wish I had kept some of them to show you.'

She looks up and sees that he is smiling, nothing else. He is not sending her a message through a code, to remind her of the boy they found in the sea, Tommy. He is trying to make conversation, make her feel welcome. She lets the textbook fall shut, and Joachim must feel that he is gaining no purchase, for he sets his mug in the sink.

'I'll just get my things and then I can give you a lift. Please make yourself at home.'

She feels sorry for him now. He might have expected her to be a better conversationalist, rather than as quiet as a frightened rabbit. She remains in the kitchen while she hears him moving around the house, and then he appears at the door again.

'Shall we?'

He unlocks the passenger door for her and when he gets behind the wheel, he tells her he can drop her off at her residence. She does not want him to know what she has planned in those minutes she was left alone in the kitchen, and so she agrees. They leave the flat, barren outpost and soon they are passing the butcher at the crossroads. The man is standing outside, in his blue apron, smoking a cigarette, and he waves to them, a broad, knowing smile on his face, which makes Joachim clear his throat uncomfortably.

She would rather stare out of the window, but she makes an effort to talk with the kind man beside her. She asks after his mother, who she knows lives alone, and they laugh over the mice that plagued the factory. But neither mentions Sonderbar, which would be a natural topic of conversation, and by this omission, she knows that Armando has spoken about Theo. Or perhaps it was obvious enough to Joachim that Theo's appearance is the reason for her impromptu visit. When he drops her on the street outside the residence, she waves him off, waits for his car to turn the corner and then crosses the road to walk through the park towards the town centre. From there, she will catch a bus to Reutershagen.

The need to see him is immense. The chances that she will be able to find Armando and Clara by wandering the streets around Petra's flat are not insignificant, if Armando has not prepared an outing for his daughter. Of course, by the same reasoning, the chances that she will cross paths with Petra in the same environs are just as high. But she will take the risk: there is no point in attempting to focus on her books and run her errands without seeing Armando.

The tram and bus stop are on a junction, and at the other end of the street is the boys' residence. The bus stop is directly in front of the university's sports centre, which she knows they regularly visit. Today is not a day she wishes to come across either, but she ends up waiting long enough for the bus that she spies them, with two lanky blonds, all with kit bags over their shoulders. They catch sight of her and approach, to gather in a semi-circle around her, the two she does not know freely looking her up and down. She notes with a sinking feeling that Prem has an eager glint in his eye: he has memorised the intricate transport network of the city, and he will assume she is on her way to visit Banaji and Shanti. And, sure enough, after introductions are made, he pipes up: 'Didi, aap kaun si bas chahte hain?'

'Mujhe jana hai…' she points vaguely northwards.

'Because you know on Saturdays it's better to get the Line 6 to Connewitz,' and he points to the tram stop in the middle of the junction, 'and change at Leninplatz to the E10 bus.'

'Oh right.'

'Only three minutes transfer time, but it's very reliable. You can save twenty, twenty-five minutes.'

Behind him Aditya, who is grinning from ear to ear, winks, and she takes her cue and switches from Hindi to German, to address the two she does not know, 'Are you on your way somewhere?'

'Badminton game,' one of them says, his eyes still devouring her.

'Or take the Line 6 to Mannenstrasse,' Prem is saying, blinking rapidly with excitement, 'and change to the E12.'

'Yaar,' Aditya claps him on the shoulder, and leading him away, throws over his shoulder, 'Aapka din shubh ho, Didi.'

'Enjoy your game,' she calls out and watches as they enter the sport centre, just as she sees the bus to Reutershagen roll around the corner.

By the time she descends from the bus, the day has reached the zenith of its heat. The sky is covered with thin, white clouds tinged with ochre, as if they are parched by the sun. The most obvious place to start would be the children's playground, a few blocks away from Petra's flat, and as if in validation of her quest, she sees them immediately, a father and daughter who look like none of the three or four families in the playground. Her heart contracts at the sight of them.

They are walking hand-in-hand, moving from the seesaw to the swings, when she sees Clara stop. She notices everything, he had said. Now the little girl is tugging her father's hand and pointing. She watches as Armando first stoops down to his daughter and then looks across. He unrolls his frame, slowly, to his full height, and her heart is suddenly in her throat. She lifts her hand in a tentative wave, and he lifts his, slowly. She crosses the road, and then she is standing in front of them. Clara is clutching the omnipresent doll to her chest and is a vision of suppressed excitement in her white vest and frilly shorts. She squats down in front of the child.

'Hello Clara, hello Fufu.'

Clara holds up her face and Lolita glances at Armando who is watching her – his eyes not angry, no, taken aback perhaps – before kissing the little girl on each plump, slightly sticky cheek.

'It's nice to see you,' she says.

'And to see Papa,' Clara points to her father as if in command. She straightens up and tries to smile, and then he is kissing her on each cheek. The smell and feel of him, so close, so warm, after a torturous week of anguish, after all these weeks of distance, is delicious, but all too brief.

'Hello, Lolita.'

'Hello.' She can hear that she sounds breathless.

'This is a nice surprise,' he says.

'I'm sorry to interrupt your time with Clara.'

'No, it's no interruption.'

'I hoped I might find you round here,' she says.

'You were looking for us?'

He still looks taken aback, unsure of what to do. Clara pulls at his leg, and he bends down, so his daughter's lips move against his ear. But he does not translate, only says something in Portuguese, and when she tugs at his leg, in German, 'I will ask her later.'

'Can I ask her now, Papa?' in her familiar husky voice. 'Please?'

He hesitates, then nods.

Clara turns to her instantly, her eyes shining.

'Will you come to my birthday party?'

She looks at Armando, who shrugs, then says to his daughter, 'Lolita may like to bring her friend as well.'

'Who is her friend?'

'Someone called Theo.'

This news does not seem to please Clara, who frowns slightly.

'Is Theo a boy?'

'Yes, he's a boy,' his eyes holding hers, then, relenting, to his daughter, 'No, he's an adult, Clara.'

Clara mulls over this information, then addresses Lolita, solemnly, with an air of great generosity and much sacrifice. 'You can bring your friend Theo to my party.'

She decides to say: 'That's very kind of you Clara, but I'm not sure he will be able to come.'

'Lolita will let us know in good time,' Armando says. 'She needs to ask her friend if he is free. He's a very clever, very busy person.'

He is grinning now at her and it is wonderful to see his glorious, wide smile, and to feel his eyes on her, and it appears he cannot stop looking at her.

'Having fun?' she asks.

'A lot.'

Clara is watching her father with some disdain. She lets go of his hand and runs to the set of swings, where one has just been vacated. Now Armando jogs after Clara but throws a backward glance at Lolita first. Is it an invitation to follow him? She does so, arriving by his side as he is lifting Clara up onto the seat of the swing.

'Hold tight,' he says, and then pulls the swing back to a point high in its arc to suspend his daughter, while she squeals in anticipation. He lets the swing go and she skips to the other side so she can meet the child's feet and push her back. Clara chirps with pleasure, looking adorable and they push the little girl to and fro for some minutes. But she has arrived not only to court the child: she needs to speak with him. So, she circles back and takes up position by his side. He says nothing, appears focused on pushing his daughter on the swing. Now the earlier light-hearted mood has evaporated, now neither of them seem to be able to meet the other's eye, and when he finally speaks, his voice is low.

'Where is Theo?' he asks.

'He's gone away for a few days.'

'Ah.'

But then he says nothing more.

She waits until Clara is sailing again in the air.

'I don't want you to think that there's anything between us.'

'You mean, not yet. Because it's clear that boy wants something between you.'

She is not sure how to respond, but then he speaks again: 'What I mean to say,' his voice is low, 'is that he's a nice person and it was interesting to meet him.'

'I want to do it alone!' Clara shouts, propitiously, and so they both drop back, move further away to the edge of the playground and are now standing together, unencumbered. He pushes his hands into the pockets of his jeans.

'How did you meet him?'

'He came to casualty.'

It is not the full story, that will be clear to him. It is the first time in a long time that when they have been talking alone, his hands are not on her person, somewhere, and she finds herself willing at least one hand to leave his pocket. But nothing happens.

'You look very nice.'

He has spoken softly, and she glances at him to meet his eyes.

'I feel very hot.'

'It suits you,' he says and smiles, but then looks away, and they both watch his daughter, who is now kicking her legs a little less energetically. Their time alone will not be infinite.

'I went to the factory this morning,' she says, 'but I got there after you had already left.'

His eyes widen in surprise.

'Joachim gave me a lift back into town.'

She seems to have rendered him speechless. Now she delivers the line she has prepared, even using a dictionary to find the right word in German, which she hopes he will understand.

'I just want you to know that it wasn't malicious,' she says. 'Bringing Theo.'

And he understands perfectly, demonstrating once again his command of the language.

'Did I say it was?'

'No, no you didn't.'

They fall silent, and then he speaks: 'That evening...'

She swallows, waits for him to continue.

He says: 'I want to say, Lolita, that it was not the way I wanted things to be,' but then he stops.

She asks: 'Has it caused you a lot of trouble?'

'With Petra?'

'Yes, with Petra.'

He takes some time to answer, he seems to be choosing his words carefully.

'Not a lot. But yes, a little.'

'How?'

'Petra is worried that Clara might get confused.'

She has not told him the full story of Theo, and she is sure he is not telling her the full story now. She has no right to demand one, but after a few moments, she finds she is speaking again.

'If I hadn't met Clara, Petra wouldn't mind?'

He does not answer that. She is no longer sure why she felt she had to see Armando so urgently, when she has no solution or plan of action, and when he is so clearly stymied, unable to proceed without dispensation from Petra. She feels angry with the woman she has never met, but then quickly feels ashamed: for she is not a mother.

'I don't think it's just about Clara,' he says finally.

'It's about me?'

'It's about how I feel about you.'

The words are nectar, his eyes are on her and are dark with longing. Finally, he removes one hand from the pocket of his jeans, and she feels it curl very briefly around the back of her neck, and she feels his thumb stroke her collarbone. Her heart dives into her stomach, but before she can respond, his hand has moved away. It was a touch that lasted seconds, a touch that Clara has not witnessed.

'But it's complicated,' he says. 'It shouldn't be, but it is. And it's not fair for you.'

Clara jumps off the swing and begins hurtling towards them.

'I understand,' she is speaking quickly. 'I mean, I just wanted to see you, as a friend.'

As soon as she says the words, she wishes she had not, for now he may think that she does not feel the same yearning. But there is no time to explain, the child is drawing up.

She says: 'I'll go now. I don't want to make things difficult for you.'

Clara will relay this surprise visit to her mother and may even relay the invitation that was extended to her birthday party. Now she cannot wait to remove herself from his closeness. She can feel tears gathering and she has no wish to cry again in front of him. So, she waves at them, breezily.

'Bye, Clara!'

She runs across the road and down to the corner, climbs into a bus which is just pulling in, without checking its destination. All she wants is to get away. She moves down the length of the bus, then looks out the window. She waves again and Clara lifts her hand in response, but Armando does not.

15

His sojourn in Prague and then the wedding in Berlin means that he has shifts to make up for Philip and Lothar, who have covered his absence at the garage. While he does not mind the extra work, he finds when working alone that he misses their company, something which surprises him. It might be that he wished to share the news he has procured of the de-electrified fence, but the few days that elapse when he is on his own in the workshop serve as a cooling chamber and he makes no mention.

He eats his mid-morning sandwich while chatting to Trudy, who is remarkably sanguine and forgiving over his shabby behaviour towards her. But without further distractions, he manages to finish work punctually every day, after which he finds himself rushing back to the apartment, desperate to return to his creation, to sit at his desk and tap for hours at the typewriter. He dines with Rainer, who indulges his taciturnity, then dashes back to his bedroom, re-reads his work, tearing up, re-wording, re-phrasing into the night.

Lolita is, of course, an exception to this routine. Soon after his return to the city, he calls the residence and leaves a message. When she phones back, he is ecstatic: she might be answering his call, but it is the first time she has initiated a conversation and, the result of the call, a rendezvous. He arrives at this, their first since that night at Sonderbar, with a picnic basket stocked with a bottle of Czech wine, bread and cheese and pickled peppers, and a selection of miniature pastries from his cousin's wedding breakfast, wrapped in a patterned cloth. Part of him wonders whether when he sees her, he will think: oh well. But he doesn't. Instead, when she comes out of the residence and walks towards him, he feels his heart start thudding in his chest, and his tongue feels suddenly over-large for his mouth. She has not dressed up for the occasion – she is in jeans and the light-grey t-shirt he remembers, her face is free of make-up, and her hair is pulled back loosely into a bun – but she looks ravishing.

When she reaches him, he stands in front of her for some moments, his gaze is frank, and she is not unaware of his admiration, for she smiles bashfully, her lashes fluttering against her cheeks. He leans down, spying a hint of the thin gold necklace against the nape of her neck, and kisses her on both cheeks.

'Hello, Theo.'

'Hello, Lolita.'

'Did you have a nice trip?'

'I did,' he says. 'But it's nice to be back.'

'Really?' She is smiling widely now.

'Yes, really. And it's especially nice to see you again.'

He holds out his arm, and she takes it, steps closer to him, so that momentarily her breast brushes against his forearm. He escorts her down the street to where he has parked Rainer's car.

'I thought we could go for a drive. It's just such a nice day, and we won't have many of these.'

'You're right.'

He points through the window to the basket in the backseat. 'I've brought us a picnic, and some things from the wedding.'

'That's so sweet of you.'

She cannot meet his eyes, but she looks pleased.

'Shall we?'

She climbs into the passenger seat without any hesitation, without any knowledge of their destination, which heartens him, and they drive off. He has already decided on a visit to a lake, a twenty-minute drive away.

'Have you been very busy at the hospital?' he says.

'It's pretty intense,' she replies, and then gives him a shy smile. 'I really do also need to study for this exam I have the day after tomorrow. I'll have to get back for five, if that's okay, Theo.'

His heart sinks: he had hoped they would spend the whole day together.

'I'll make sure you get back.'

They drive south beyond the ring road, and the countryside looks, he admits, rather fetching.

'Do you remember that doctor?' she asks suddenly. 'The one who...'

'Yes.'

He glances at her. She is staring out of her window.

'Apparently, his wife left the country some years ago and he had a lot of trouble from the authorities because of it.'

'I know.'

From the corner of his eye, he can see her head swivel sharply towards him.

'How do you know?'

'He told me.' He shrugs. 'When we were alone.' He glances at her again. 'I hope he hasn't caused you any problems?'

'Oh no. No, it's not that,' she says.

He returns his attention to the road, and then hears her add, softly: 'He's gone away, that's all.'

He wonders whether she has heard any rumours, of the de-electrified fence, whether she is seeking some kind of confirmation from him, but he does not give any, and she only continues to look at the passing fields. When they arrive at the lake, they find scores of other picnickers, with baskets and bottles just like he has prepared.

'We Germans can never be original,' he mutters, as he spreads out the blanket he has brought. He waits for her to stretch out on it, before he throws himself down next to her. 'We all do the same things as each other, like sheep.'

She laughs. 'I don't mind being a sheep today.'

They clink the plastic cups he has brought for the wine, and he is pleased that she eats heartily, complimenting his choices. There are several young families with small children, and he observes her surveying them.

'How's it going?' he says. 'I mean, with your studies. Apart from this exam that I will make sure you study for.'

She looks down, plays with a knobble of wool on the blanket. 'I'm having a crisis of confidence, to be honest.'

'Well, you're the best doctor I've ever had,' he says but her lips only twitch in response.

'When I was little, I remember I thought that being a doctor meant that I'd be saving lives every day,' she says. 'Maybe because I remember my mother dragging me out with her on night calls, or maybe things are always more heightened in India. But it's not like that. In fact, sometimes I wonder whether all I can do is to make sure not to make a mistake.' She shakes herself then, tries to smile. 'You must tell me all about Prague.'

He can see she is in a low mood, and that she does not wish to dwell on her studies, and so he obliges. He tells her about Rainer's reunion, the mysterious Judit, even about the American, Stephen Radowski, who has taken his work away with him.

'It would be wonderful if he can get it published, wouldn't it?' Her eyes are lit up.

He can feel his cheeks becoming warm. 'It would, yes. I suppose.'

She is smiling at him now, and she seems to be waiting for him to elaborate. He pulls out a blade of grass and begins to tear it in half, and half again, not unlike how he has torn many pages of his writing, including the attempt about Lolita.

'I don't know how it works, not really,' he says. 'But I've always imagined that if I lived in the West, one day I'd get a phone call from a publisher. Herr Becker, we loved your work, we'd love to see more.'

He has imitated a theatrical, flamboyant West Berliner and Lolita laughs, but he can see that she can see he is serious.

'Well, maybe it's actually going to happen, Theo,' she says.

'Maybe.'

He had been surprised how much he revealed of himself at their first meeting in the café, when minutes after sitting down he was bleating on to her about the lost Abitur and his literary ambitions – she seems to sweep away his defences, make him garrulous – and he surprises himself again by telling her now what he has only thought to himself: 'Stephen might be my chance at a break.'

She says nothing, but her eyes soften. He chucks the pieces of grass onto the ground and wipes his palm against his shirt. Lolita is still watching him.

'Aren't there any magazines over here you could send something to?'

'There might be, I've not really tried to find any. It's hard to know if they're not connected, you know, and whether they would force me to change things and...' He sounds lame, he can hear it, but she interrupts him.

'Well then,' she is holding out her plastic cup to him. 'Here's to your man in the West.'

He grins and touches his own cup to hers. Her large eyes are fixed on him, and yes, she does look excited at the prospect of his dreams being realised. And it is possible, he thinks, that she has missed him, this last week and a half.

He asks: 'Have you seen Armando recently?'

Her expression dims slightly.

'Yes, I met him and Clara last Saturday.' Then she smiles. 'We have an invitation. To her birthday party.'

He splutters on his wine. 'Birthday party?'

'Yes.' She is laughing at his reaction and she looks relaxed suddenly and radiant in the sunshine. 'She invited me and she said I could bring a friend. It was Armando who suggested you,' and then she stops, and he knows that the man suggested more than that.

He scrambles around in his head: 'I suppose I should get her a birthday present.'

'We could give her one together, if you like. I was going to get her some pastels and colouring-in books. She's very fond of drawing.'

'How old is she?'

'She's turning four.'

Lolita is munching on a piece of cheese, watching him.

'Would you like to come?'

'Would you like me to?'

She blushes. 'Yes.'

'Then of course.'

He delivers her back to the residence for her revision session, and when they part, she raises herself on tiptoes to kiss his cheek. The next time they meet, he takes her to the cinema, and on another evening for a drink. He is courting her, biding his time, so that she can feel comfortable, so that she can sweep aside any residual hope of Armando. It is on dropping her back after their last rendezvous that he says goodbye with a kiss on her lips. She does not respond, not properly, but neither does she turn her face away.

DIE WENDE

16

There is news circulating in Joachim's factory of a young Mozambican, found dead in a canal in a city fifty miles to the south. While the authorities claim he slipped and fell into the water while drunk, rumours of the bruising to his face suggest that he was attacked, lost consciousness and thus drowned. In a country where crime, at least violent crime, is rarely heard of, this news is deeply unsettling. The men confer. Where they are, they face little hostility, for now at least. The four housemates cite Sonderbar and the welcome they all enjoy there. The rest counter that one bar, and the mitigating presence of Joachim, does not constitute a welcome. Most have found their own entertainment near the factory, where the trade of the Africans and Cubans has been tolerated. But the news of the young man whose family will hear of his passing from thousands of miles away, who will grieve without knowing the full circumstances of his death, who could have been one of them, disturbs the equilibrium they have all taken for granted.

He wishes not to be party to such discussions, just as he has always avoided spirited political debates, but it is impossible to extricate himself from these without seriously offending his comrades. Yet, if he was feeling distant and disconnected from them a few months ago, now he is feeling more so. While they are preoccupied by the underlying seam of resentment towards them, he cannot stop thinking about Lolita. He misses her desperately. He was upended when she arrived at Sonderbar with the German boy and he was upended again when she arrived at the playground unannounced. He should not have let her leave in such a rush, he should have been braver, perhaps even taken her to meet Petra. Now Petra will be introduced to her at Clara's birthday party. Theo's presence at Lolita's side might well lubricate the event, but he dreads seeing them together.

He arrives to collect Clara on a rainy Saturday and Petra's mood, when she greets him dully at the door, matches the grey clouds and insipid drizzle. Then, glancing behind him at the rain, she opens the door wider.

'Do you want to come in for a bit?'

Since that evening, when she had seen him and Lolita, Petra has been different: softer, gentler with him. Perhaps, on reflection, she views the display she had witnessed as evidence of how he is treated some way between a child and adult, and, with no place of his own, forced to touch a woman in shadowy corners. Or perhaps, in the conversation which had followed a week after, when he arrived to pick up Clara, his declaration that Clara would forever be his priority has cast him, in her eyes, in a new light. Whatever, he knows that Petra is not vindictive, not callous, and neither is she a fool. However much she might be tempted to reduce his visits as punishment for his obfuscation about his feelings for Lolita, she is also aware of his merits as an involved father.

She has always taken charge, but she has, concurrently, always treated him as an equal. Once, she arranged a long weekend in Prague, where she introduced them both as Dederonskis, using the nickname Czechoslovaks used for East Germans. He had not thought he had any right to be called an East German, and he remembers feeling warmed by her words. A few weeks after their sojourn in Prague, she became embroiled in a big story, and he tired of her. Not long after, she announced that she was pregnant.

Now they sit at the table in her kitchen-dining-living room. She pours him a coffee while Clara scampers to her bedroom to continue her elaborate role-play, the territory of an only child. They hear her talking to the imaginary cast of characters and exchange an uneasy smile across the table. She looks tired and, because he knows she will not take offence, he comments on it.

'Yes, I'm exhausted.' She leans back, blowing out her puffed cheeks so her fringe rises and falls. 'I've been working really hard on this report, met the deadline, but now Karl wants to cut it down and won't even commit to publishing it.'

'What was it about?'

'That new building project, on the other side of the Connewitz. I worked on it for months.'

'That's disappointing.'

'It's really good, so I can't understand it.'

'Maybe in a few weeks he might change his mind?'

'It doesn't work like that.'

'Yes, of course. Sorry...'

'No, I didn't mean to sound like that.'

She pushes her fringe away from her face. The hairstyle is new and short, and he doesn't much like it, and neither does she, for she tugs at the fringe, saying, 'This was a mistake.'

He smiles.

'What do you think? Honestly.'

'I prefer your hair longer.'

'I know. I should never have listened to my hairdresser.'

He reaches across and squeezes her elbow. 'Hair grows, remember?'

'Mine takes ages.'

'You look good,' he says. 'Don't worry.'

'I look like I'm in drag.'

He bursts out laughing and she grins along with him.

'But thanks for saying.'

'You really don't look that bad.'

'Yeah, well...'

Petra has always had a very charming smile, and now grinning at him, she looks years younger. Wouldn't it be easier, he thinks, if they were a real family? It might be true that her career would be affected if she married a Mozambican contract worker, but might her reasoning be masking something else? It appears that the friend Bruno is just that – a friend. He works at the same newspaper; he has a son the same age as Clara who lives with the mother in East Berlin. They have common interests, and he is good company – but nothing more. She had offered this information after only a tentative question on his part, and again he wonders at how their own entanglement happened so quickly, so smoothly. He does not like to dwell on this, but she might have been in love with him while he was a young fool, up for a new sexual experience. She might still be in love with him, but her pride prevents her from any exposition. She would balk at the humiliation of her feelings being unrequited.

She clears away their coffee cups and as the rain has abated, he takes this as a signal that he should leave. When he gets to his feet, she gives him a tired smile which becomes wider as Clara clumps into the room, Fufu clutched to her chest.

'Are we going now?' his daughter asks.

She has spoken in Portuguese, and he glances at Petra, but she does not look annoyed: every boundary is softening. As they are walking in the direction of the playground, his daughter continues in Portuguese.

'Lolita vem à minha festinha?'

The subject of Lolita coming to her birthday party, along with her mysterious friend Theo, is now one for which Clara seems to have an unquenchable curiosity. Like father like daughter.

'Sim.'

'Ela vai comer o bolo de aniversário?'

'Cláro.'

This news seems to require some mulling over, and he takes the opportunity to ask after her week at the kindergarten, which is excellent. The childcare available is the jewel in this socialist state's crown. Petra has often said that the options available to her, to have a child and continue her career, has been the one aspect of her country she is most proud of. Her relatives from Munich, when they visit, are full of stories of the cost of juggling careers as parents. Petra does not, however, acknowledge that one other convenience is that there is only one career in play – he does not enter the equation.

This week at the kindergarten, they have practised writing and reading and there was a visit from a puppeteer, which Clara describes at length. It is in these conversations that his daughter also inadvertently reveals details of Petra's life: whether she had a meeting in the evening, what they ate, which corresponds to how tired Petra is.

Today is a day like the many, many others he has spent with his daughter, after Petra had stood up for him to her parents. At first these visits were hour-long walks with the baby in the pram, although by then Clara was already eight months old, sitting up unaided. He would take her out of the pram, gingerly, sit on a bench with her on his lap. On warm sunny days, he would put her on a blanket on the grass, and when she started crawling, these moments were his excuse to roll around and play with her, allow her to clamber over him. The feeling of her small hands and the weight of her miniature body was so joyful his heart felt like it would burst. He behaved like a child himself: frolicking, play-acting, becoming a lion, an elephant, and her favourite, the horse, amusing her as he had never been by his own parents. It seemed to come to him naturally, here in the DDR. She started walking at thirteen months, which meant she could then wear boots and coats and the playground that was a twenty-minute walk, toddle-time, from Petra's flat became the perennial destination. By eighteen months, he was taking her out for either the whole morning or soon after her post-lunch nap for the whole afternoon. Then she was two years old, then three, and the visits have become longer. Now he has lunch with Clara and brings her back in the evening. And all the while his daughter is growing, so from week to week he can see a change, her personality – strong-willed, stubborn, but with a strong compassionate streak, curious, demanding – becoming more and more evident. Of course he sees Petra in her, but also his second-older sister, who has a heart-shaped face like Clara, and who left Maputo as a late teenager to work as a cleaner in South Africa. He can imagine Clara making a similar decision at an older age, leaving behind Petra and himself to embark on her journey in life. But how can he imagine Clara at that age and not imagine where he will be? And how long will his daughter be happy to spend her Saturday with her father in a routine that will soon, inevitably, become dull? And how old will Clara be when she realises her father is a low-paid, low-skilled worker whose presence is tolerated, but not especially welcomed, in the country of her birth?

An hour or more in the playground will take them to lunch at the restaurant nearby, where Clara will lay out her colouring pencils and crayons on the table and produce a picture he will take away with him. Then there is another walk or another visit to the playground. He has bought a small bicycle with stabilisers for her birthday: he enlisted both Petra's approval and Joachim's advice for this, and the bike is ready for collection from Centrum. This will add variety to their time together, as he can teach her how to pedal around the playground but, more worryingly, Petra has mentioned that there are ballet classes she wishes Clara to attend after she turns four, which take place on Saturday. He could drop his daughter at the venue, but it would also mean that his time with her will be an hour and a half shorter.

The rain starts falling again, a proper shower, interrupting his train of thoughts, and he runs with Clara in his arms towards the nearby bus shelter. He takes a few minutes to notice that there is a woman standing in the shelter, a middle-aged woman with a square face and reddish curly hair who is staring at them, whose eyes flit between him and Clara. She opens her mouth, and he knows what she is going to say and he does not want Clara to hear a word and so he gathers his daughter up and moves out into the rain.

'...with our women.'

'Why are we going back into the rain, Papa?'

He presses Clara close. 'Let's stand under the tree instead, there's more space.'

A memory from his childhood: the many posters and campaigns warning of the dangers of sheltering under a tree in a storm. Cuidado com os raios! But there is no lightning and there are also several other buildings and poles which will serve as lightning-conductors and he feels a fleeting sadness over how different his daughter's childhood is from his.

He has set her on her feet, and she is fussing with Fufu. Her lovely honey-coloured face, the roundness of her cheeks and the dark brown eyelashes: could there be anything more beautiful? There are many like Clara in Mozambique, evidence of relations with the Portuguese, or Arab traders even earlier. Yet the society is not immune from prejudice, and his own family has its own share of bigots. Once Clara had asked him in a small voice: will Avó like me? When he had responded that his mother, his sprawling family, would love her, she had asked: will they like Mami, even if she is not African? He remembers his response had been to twirl her like a baton, while she yelped in delight, as if that was the best salvo to her worries. Now he picks her up and grips her, aching with love.

'What is it, Papa?'

'You know I love you, don't you, filha?'

'Cláro,' she says in the same tone he used earlier and his heart soars.

When the rain stops, they make their way to the restaurant, where the young waitress gives them a particularly warm welcome, as if she knows it is exactly the right day for confirmation that they are not universally unwanted. They sit at the table of Clara's choice and learn that the restaurant is now offering soups for lunch. A hot broth is welcome after the rain, and he watches Clara sitting ramrod straight, using her spoon meticulously. When her bowl is empty, she descends from the table to watch the fish in the tank in the corner and the young waitress comes up to clear the table.

'Would you like some dessert?'

She has a pretty smile and again he feels a surge of gratitude for her warmth.

'What do you have?'

She grins. 'We have a really good chocolate cake today.' Then whispers: 'You might have noticed that we have a new chef.'

'Sounds good, thank you.'

'Two pieces?'

'Just one please.'

Petra doesn't like Clara having too many treats and he has been reprimanded for indulging her sweet tooth. His daughter, as if a hound scenting blood, scurries back to the table and climbs onto her father's lap as the waitress returns.

'Here you are. I've brought you two forks.'

'What do you say, Clara?'

'Thank you.'

'Bitte,' the young woman is smiling prettily again.

'This is for you, filha,' he cuts the cake with the edge of his fork, 'and this is for Papa.'

'Your piece is much smaller, Papa.'

He kisses the top of her head. 'Don't tell Mami.'

'I want you to have some more,' and she holds her fork above her slice like a sword. But he can see she is already caving in.

'No, I want you to have the bigger piece, filha.'

She pretends to struggle with this, gives a sigh and he stifles a laugh. It is pleasant to watch her demolish her cake in minutes. Then she moves back to her chair on the opposite end of the table and he watches his daughter as she arranges her colouring pencils in sets depending on their shade, like an artist gathering her tools. Maybe she will be an artist when she grows up. Maybe he will visit her exhibitions, as an old man: this is my father, she will say.

'What are you going to draw?' he asks.

'A picture for Mami.'

Perhaps his daughter has intuited her mother's gloomy mood. His own mood is somehow low, and he watches his daughter, with furrowed brow, draw a swing with herself on it. He finds himself holding his breath. Will she draw her father on one end and Lolita on the other? He cannot dissuade her from doing so and he will have to explain to Petra later, if she asks.

*

He wishes to stretch his legs before returning to the factory, so after he drops Clara back with Petra, he walks the long way to a different tram stop. The streets in this new town hold less charm than the city centre. The trees are still young, and in a country of mature forests and woodlands made of giant oaks and conifers, these saplings are dwarfed by the colourless concrete boxes, each with identikit facades, set in a regimentally ordered grid of streets. He has never been to West Germany, but he has always imagined there would be more inventiveness in the rebuilding of a razed, empty, post-war canvas. Pictures he has seen of Frankfurt or Bonn show crowded, snaking streets, lined with shop window after shop window offering luminous, varied displays. A consumer society, the type to disparage, but which most people he knows here crave. And this city is particularly austere, even compared to East Berlin, where he and his comrades had their initiation to the country. At least in Alexanderplatz they could find tropical fruit and vegetables and condiments, to remind them of home. Once they had bought three bottles of Portuguese vinho verde along with five tins of sardines in olive oil, and with music blaring from a cassette player, had enjoyed an evening of revelry in their dour dormitory.

At first, the DDR was a playground for him: a place of unremittingly hard work, yes, but where he received a salary and had opportunities to travel and buy clothes and beer and cigarettes and go to parties to meet girls. He had escaped the danger of war, but also, the crushing boredom exacted by war: water shortages or power outages and interrupted schooling. But Clara has been the pivotal change to his life, his before and after. Now he has a daughter, he is no longer tethered to his home country. His priorities are less about taking care of siblings with whom he has not lived for ten years – who are, aside from one sister, older than him. Not even, God forgive him, his widowed mother, who has four sons, and only needs one, surely, to look after her. José, the eldest now that Alberto died in the mines in South Africa, works for the Ministry of Agriculture, as much as this Ministry is operating amidst a civil war, and he is close at hand. Now he, Armando, has a daughter who he loves ferociously, but who he sees for a paltry half day a week.

A car which was idling on the side of the road, a blue Trabant, now draws up and cruises alongside him, at a slow enough pace so that it accompanies him for many metres, and the peculiarity of this situation brings him out of his reveries. When he looks to the side, he can only see himself reflected in the windows, and the shadow of a man in the driving seat. He slows down to a saunter so that the engine stutters, before the car makes a sudden U-turn and speeds off. Few people in this new town seem to resent his weekly appearance, but perhaps even that is changing. He looks behind and sees no sign of the blue Trabant, only a handful of people walking.

He boards the tram, finds a seat near a window and rests his elbow on the ledge, his chin on his hand. Lately, he has spent his Saturday evenings reading, working through the books that Joachim has more recently acquired, or accompanying some of the men to the bar in the village, which is rudimentary, unfriendly and without the ambience of Sonderbar. But he wishes to avoid seeing

Lolita with Theo, even though his housemates have said that the pair have not reappeared. They will next meet, all three, at Clara's birthday party, the following weekend.

He had hoped that the past few weeks of absence would cure him of Lolita. They haven't. He had hoped that the love he has for his daughter would somehow eclipse the other love he is feeling, diminish the yearning. It hasn't. The tram shudders to a stop and he descends, to trudge down the long straight road to the factory, disconsolate, any warmth or optimism that had sparked from the joy he always feels after seeing his child, all expended, extinguished. Instead, he feels bereft for a girl he never had, jealous over a relationship he has no idea is developing. He expects someone to erupt from the gloom around him, brandishing a knife: a fitting end to a strange day. But he arrives at the factory gates unscathed, and a heady aroma of meat and fish and potatoes and rice emanates from the flats and mingles in the courtyard. The evening is colder than it has been for some days, but it is early for everyone to have retired to their separate flats. Normally after work, the men congregate in the courtyard, and there might even be a game of football just outside the entrance gates, but today all is quiet.

When he passes Joachim's house, he sees him sitting in the window. Joachim has been gracious about not receiving an invitation to Clara's birthday party this year – he was only pleased that Petra's parents will be hosting, a sign of a détente in a previously cool relationship. Now he raises his hand in a passing greeting, but Joachim stands up and gestures for him to come to the door. He is tired and is not in the mood for conversation, but he waits and before long Joachim opens the door.

'Do you have time for a quick cigarette?'

'Yes.'

'Let's go for a walk.'

It is not a common invitation, for normally he would be invited inside the house, which holds the familiar smell of cinnamon, and which is comfortably warm, but his friend pulls on a jacket and comes out. Joachim lights a cigarette and then holds out the pack. The administrator's block is dark, and he is wondering whether they will walk back down the road leading to the village, when Joachim opens the gate leading to the woods. The fallen leaves crunch beneath their feet, and it is nearly pitch black, but before they enter its depths, Joachim stops and leans against a tree trunk. The streetlamp throws enough light so he can see his friend's face: unshaven, his hair a shaggy black mop.

'How was Clara?'

The usual start to a conversation, but this taking place in the woods is not usual. His friend continues in the same gentle way, with discreet queries as to how the day progressed, archetypal Joachim, but there is something else tonight. An invitation for a moonlit stroll is a precursor for something else.

He asks: 'What is it?'

'For some time now,' Joachim says, 'I've been getting these. They come through the door which means someone comes into the compound,' and he pulls out some papers from his pocket. 'After the first one, I started keeping an eye out and I've seen a blue car parked further down the road, on occasion. I've not seen anyone come to our compound, but I'm not always looking, of course. But today one went through the door of your flat. Gilberto showed it to me. Word will get around now, among the other men, and so that's why I'm telling you.'

He takes the papers. The weak glow from the streetlamp offers just enough light for him to read.

'They're not pleasant,' Joachim grimaces.

Each is a letter made from cut-out magazine titles, in the style of a ransom note, to disguise the handwriting of the writer. Although the people who are writing them clearly do not need to disguise their identities, nor the purpose of these missives: these are clearly intimidation letters from the Stasi. They question Joachim's fondness, or predilection, for the black men in his warehouse; they question whether Joachim is aware of what they are involved in. Two of the letters name him, Armando Dos Santos, as an enemy of the State, who engages in activities that undermine the integrity of the country that has welcomed him. Such acts of ingratitude mean that he and his friends should be sent home. The letters are chilling in their childishness, in their casual menace, but he feels hot with fear.

'Which one went to the flat?'

Joachim taps one which spells out his name, and it is correctly spelled, before saying: 'I have no intention of sending you home.'

'Can they make you?'

'They will need to get approval first from the Ministry.'

His heart is hammering in his chest. Petra's thwarted report, the blue Trabant earlier. Neither are coincidence — rather, both are part of an orchestrated campaign. He had felt before that time was accelerating, in connection with a possible, now hopeless, relationship with Lolita. It appears he was mistaken. It is his ejection from the country which is growing closer.

'Don't worry,' Joachim repeats. 'They want to scare me and they want to scare you.'

'Well, it's working.'

He throws the letters into the air and they fan out and flutter like birds, and then he watches as Joachim waits for them to land on the ground, then bends heavily, picking each carefully and replacing them in his jacket pocket. He makes no move to help, he finds he is paralysed, can barely lift his hand to place the cigarette between his lips. He lets the cigarette fall from his fingers to the ground, momentarily hoping it will cause the dry leaves to burst into flames, which will engulf him and all the poisonous surroundings, but he presses his shoe onto the glowing tip and crushes it beneath his sole.

'Did something happen?'

Joachim is standing in front of him, the papers now out of sight.

'Yes. But months ago.'

'When?'

'June.'

'And?'

'Nothing.' he says. 'Nothing. I was worried at the time but when nothing happened, I thought it was the end.'

The need to tell Joachim the story is overwhelming. He might even be able to ward off any overtures from the driver of the car from earlier, from the menace with which it prowled alongside him. But he resists. The man standing before him has been a true friend, a mentor, a brother. Joachim has so far, despite the generosity of his actions, remained removed from acts of intimidation. It will be unforgivable if because of him, Armando, that changes.

'What did Gilberto and the others say?'

Joachim shakes his head. 'They were worried. It's only natural. I explained to them as I am to you now that your contracts to work here have been arranged by the Ministry.'

'Has it happened before?'

'What do you mean?'

'Have we,' he means all the men, all over the country, and he knows Joachim will understand this, 'have we ever been sent away for being enemies of the State?'

'I've not heard of it.'

Joachim lights another cigarette, which is unusual: he rarely chain smokes. So, he is nervous and troubled despite his demeanour.

'Do you want to tell me what happened?'

'I do. But I won't.'

He sees Joachim's teeth flash in a smile.

'Was Lolita with you?'

'Why do you ask?'

'I just wondered if that's why you've not been seeing her.'

He says nothing, and Joachim does not press him. They stand together not speaking, and then he asks: 'Why has it started now, Joachim? After so many months?'

His friend is silent for a long time.

'I don't know,' he says, finally. 'But you might find that you know the answer to that already.'

He contemplates those words. Joachim finishes his cigarette, then stubs it out against the sole of his shoe, and then picks up this and the other ends, including the one he had discarded, always careful, always considerate.

He asks him: 'What do we do?'

'We do nothing. We wait and see what happens.'

'What shall I tell Gilberto and the others?'

'That you have no idea what is going on.'

'They won't believe me.'

'Then tell them to come and see me if they have any problem with it.'

Joachim starts walking back to the gate, and so he follows him. He will admit that he had never thought that his friend could be so brave. His gentleness, his old-maidenish habits, tender concern: all hide a steeliness. For while they might well forcibly remove Armando, and he will then be removed from the situation, this is his friend's home. A home Joachim loves, where he belongs and from where he has no easy exit.

17

He is picking Lolita up in fifteen minutes and so he checks the table in the kitchen-diner, laid with a white cloth, heavy cutlery, the folded napkins. There are late roses from the garden in a vase, and the whole room has been brushed and tidied. Rainer is at the stove, in an apron, tending to the large pot – a chicken casserole, French-style. A much less exotic offering than the rich spicy food he had eaten at the old Communist's dinner party, only weeks ago, but before he had Lolita in his life. The wine is cooling in the fridge. There are Swiss chocolates as well, from Rainer's stash, for after.

'Don't be late,' his grandfather says.

'I'm off.'

'And don't crash the car. I want to meet this girl.'

It is only a half-hour walk to her residence, but he is taking the car and he might suggest an evening drive. What he hopes for, however, is that Rainer makes good on his promise to visit some friends after dinner, so that he and Lolita can have the apartment to themselves.

Now he pulls up at the residence and waits until he sees the large door open. He watches her approach. Her hair is loose and she is wearing the long dangly earrings she wore to Banaji's dinner. This is what he can see of her. It is a cold day in late September, but she seems to be excessively wrapped up in long, dark brown coat and a thick woollen fuchsia scarf. He gets out of the car and waits for her to draw up. He kisses her on the lips in greeting, only a peck, but one which still sends a shiver of anticipation through him.

'You look lovely,' he says.

'Thank you.' She tugs at the collar of his shirt, a dark grey Italian affair from his father's collection. 'You look smart.'

'I thought I'd dress for the occasion.'

'Is it an occasion?'

'Rainer is dying to meet you.'

'I'm nervous now,' she laughs.

'No need to be.'

She pulls out a deep, round tin from her shoulder bag. 'I had no idea what to bring. I'm rubbish at buying wine. So I made some cakes.' She lifts the lid and he sees a dozen pale yellow cupcakes dusted with icing sugar.

'Wow.'

'I'm a terrible baker, I'll warn you.'

'Shush.'

With his finger, he touches her lips. They are soft and, unusually, tinted for said occasion, a detail which fills him with a sense of promise. The gesture he has made is old-fashioned, even cheesy, but there is something about their courtship which makes him behave as he has never before.

When they get into the car, when he tries and fails to catch a glimpse of her legs, just inches away from his hand on the gear stick, but hidden by the long dark coat, he tries not to breathe in her scent for fear it will drive him insane. He is excited even before they have arrived for his grandfather's dinner: how will he manage over the next couple of hours? They take the ring road to skirt the old town centre, and before long are pulling into the tree-lined street on the other side of the river, at the end of which stands the large old house, divided into generous apartments.

She hangs up her coat in the hallway, unwraps her scarf, unzips her boots, with each action revealing a little more of herself – so he can exercise those qualities of observation so admired by the Stasi in his now habitual scrutiny of Lolita Devi, so he can file away the details of her slender neck, the shape of her buttocks where they stretch her short denim skirt, her lovely legs in dark woollen tights. She is wearing a soft blue jumper, but from the way it moulds itself around her breasts, she is not wearing much underneath, at least.

Rainer takes her hand and looks into Lolita's eyes for some time. Then, showing off his enviable charm, he places one palm against his chest as if in a swoon, before raising her hand to his lips.

She is blushing and Rainer is grinning: triumphant, suave.

He tugs at her elbow, 'Remember me?'

She laughs but does not look at him.

When she produces the cupcakes, Rainer exclaims, like some old European count: 'Ah les madeleines, my favourite.' Then, 'Come, Lolita. Have a glass of wine. We are having for dinner another favourite of mine, chicken casserole à la Normande. You know I spent much of my youth in France?'

And so the conversation as they partake of the meal – as his grandfather points to the ingredients of home-made apple cider and slices of apple – turns to the formative years Rainer spent in France, before, during, and after occupation, when he was the age of Lolita and Theo now. At the table, his grandfather treats Lolita as a fellow émigré, learning about life in a country not their own, in a different language ('Tell me, do you ever dream in German?'), who counts that country as a second home, even if it is vastly different in culture and ideology ('You will find you have some German habits, just as I have some inadvisable French habits.'). Lolita, he can see, is fascinated by his grandfather, which is not surprising. Yet Rainer, while replete with incomparable tales of jeopardy and tragedy and comedy, as always, is just as adept at prising stories from his audience, so that Lolita relates much of her early life, of the uncommon marriage between her unconventional, bohemian parents, her childhood spent traversing the subcontinent. She is clearly close to her mother ('Sushilla! But both of you have the most melodious names!') and it is of her that she mostly talks. When she does speak of her father, she mentions the wedding which she will be attending at the end of the year.

'You will be escaping from us for a while,' Rainer says.

'Will you be going away for long?' he asks at the exact same time, which for some reason provokes laughter from Rainer and Lolita.

'A couple of weeks at the most,' she says, eventually.

'I'd love to visit India,' Rainer breathes.

'I'd love to visit France,' Lolita sighs.

'Ah, perhaps I can take you one day, ma chérie…'

'If you get a permit to travel, if they allow you,' he interjects, and to his annoyance, they both burst out laughing again.

'Theo thinks life is a bed of roses in the West,' says Rainer, behind his hand, in a stage-whisper to Lolita.

'Well, at least I could go wherever I wanted, whenever I wanted, without begging for fucking permission.'

Rainer raises his eyebrows at his vituperative tone, and he gulps.

'Sorry.'

She is looking uncomfortable now, but says quietly: 'Well, you'd both be very welcome to come and stay with us in India. My mother has a lovely house in the mountains.'

Finally, after the meal, Rainer announces that he will be paying a friend a visit and he feels a tremor of anticipation. But at the last minute, Rainer offers to show Lolita his garden, and the outdoor lighting he has installed. He watches, seething, as on go the hat, the gloves, the enormous scarf, the knee-length wool coat, the boots, all of which he intends to remove. He remains in the kitchen, ostensibly doing the washing up but anxiously peering through the window into the dark of the garden where, courtesy of Rainer's celebrated lights, he can see that his grandfather has made her laugh. They are still laughing together when the back door re-opens and they clomp into the kitchen, stamping their boots on the doormat.

'I'll help with the washing up,' Lolita says.

'I've done it.'

He might sound terse, because they exchange a glance and a knowing smile: Rainer and Lolita, conspirators.

But Rainer does continue by saying: 'I won't come in. I'll go out the back gate.'

Then he turns to Lolita, takes her hand and kisses it.

'La belle mademoiselle.'

'Christ's sake, Rainer,' he snarls.

His grandfather laughs and so does Lolita, and he folds the tea towel away, petulantly. But then Rainer pats his arm, and gives them a salute, 'Have a good evening, children.'

The back door clicks shut, and they are alone.

She sits down at the kitchen table before he can direct her to the living room, or, as he hopes will be their destination, his bedroom.

'Do you want some more wine?'

She nods, shyly, and he replenishes her glass.

'That was a lovely dinner,' she says. 'Your grandfather is adorable.'

'He obviously thinks you are wonderful,' he says. 'And I'm not surprised.'

'You're like contemporaries, the two of you,' she says. 'Not like grandfather and grandson.'

'I think he prefers not to think of his age, to be honest.'

'Is he close with your dad?'

'Maybe not as much. I suppose it was always a bit more tense. It's a generational thing.'

'What do you mean?'

'When my dad was younger, I wouldn't say that he was ashamed about Rainer, far from it.' He pauses, gathering his thoughts. 'It's just that many of his own friends couldn't be so proud of their fathers.'

'Because of what happened during the war?'

'All those Nazis didn't just disappear in a puff of smoke. A lot of them were the mothers and fathers of my parents' generation.'

She presses her lips and then raises her wineglass to her lips.

'When did your grandmother die?'

'Ten years ago.'

'He must miss her.'

He nods, remembering Judit and how Rainer had spent the night in her bedroom. Perhaps they had both known each other when their spouses were present and were now rekindling a latent or ignored spark. Then he shakes himself: he shouldn't waste a minute. He decides to be bold.

'I'll show you my room,' and she stands up obediently and follows him out of the kitchen-diner.

His bedroom is at the end of the hallway, and as they pass the coat stand, he asks: 'Shall I hang your coat up?'

'No, thank you.'

Thus, when they enter his bedroom — with its bay window looking onto the back green, the streetlights and firs along the riverbank, with all his mess tidied away, save for his guitar and writing materials on his desk – she is wrapped up as if on an Arctic expedition, wearing all her clothes like armour. The only flesh visible is her face, lovely as it is, and her hands, elegant as they are. She makes a beeline for the windowsill, where she perches, her chin invisible among the folds of the gigantic woollen scarf, her arms folded across her chest.

'Do you play?' she asks nodding at the guitar.

'A little. I'm out of practice.'

He is unsure where to sit. At the desk? He can pull his chair closer to her. But that may lend a formal air to what he hopes will become a carnal act. He decides to drop down in a casual way on his bed, to lean against the wall with his legs outstretched, and he notices that her cheeks are slightly flushed. So, she is not unaware of his intentions. Or perhaps she is overheating in her layers.

She points to his bookshelf: 'You have a lot of books.'

'I have more back home in Berlin.' He decides to add: 'I'll take you some time. My parents would be happy to have you.'

She sips her wine and straightens her shoulders and for a second he thinks she will shrug off her coat, but she doesn't.

'I can hang your coat up on my door,' he says.

'No, thank you,' she repeats.

'I can barely see you under all those clothes,' and he cannot avoid a sulky tone.

She gives a little laugh, but makes no move, only says: 'Is this where you write?'

There is a typewriter on the desk, surrounded by piles of paper and so it is not the most perceptive comment, but he nods.

'Yes.'

'Will you read me something?'

'Something I've written?'

'Yes. I've only heard you read the once.'

She is cradling the wineglass in her hands, as if it were a mug of hot chocolate. He remembers what he wrote about how she had charged out of the student residence and slammed against him, that very first night. He has since written two more pieces. They are not part of a story, more like a way of remembering their interactions, his impressions of her, as they become more substantial, fuller, vibrant. He has not kept either of them.

When he does not respond, she does not appear to be offended by what may be a rebuff. Instead, she turns to look out the window and he takes the moment to observe her, to decide on what strategy, what plan of attack: he wants her so badly he can barely speak.

'Lolita,' he says. 'Will you take off your coat?'

'Why?'

'I want to see you.'

'You're seeing me now.'

'I want to see more of you.'

She clears her throat.

'Shall we go for a walk along the river?'

He says: 'Okay. Later.'

She turns her head again and looks out of the window.

'Can you please take your coat off?'

He does not expect it, but she shrugs her coat off, her eyes still on the river outside, slides her arms through its sleeves, and then, unbidden, unwinds the giant scarf – once, twice – so he can see the slender column of her neck. She lays the scarf to one side on the windowsill. Now she looks at him. She says nothing, however, only picks up the wineglass again and takes a sip of wine.

'Take something else off.'

Her wine glass is now empty, but still in her hands. She opens her mouth to say something, but then closes it. He pulls off his shirt, over his head.

'Your turn.'

She grins – at least she grins – but then she presses the wineglass to her mouth, against her lips.

'You'll get cold.'

'I won't. I'm burning up.'

Now she laughs, but he sees her eyes move quickly over him: there is still a flush to her cheeks. He leans back on the wall, which feels cool against his bare skin. He can barely breathe, but he does not break his gaze, only watches her quietly. Her shoulders shake in silent laughter, but her cheeks are conspicuously red now.

'Theo, I'm not going to take off my clothes.'

'Okay.'

'You can put your shirt back on.'

'I'm only going to take it off again.'

'Are you?'

'Yes, I am.'

'Don't be so sure of yourself,' she is shaking her head, but there is a quiver to her lips which belies the flippant tone.

'I'm not sure of anything when it comes to you, Lolita.'

He is completely sincere, he can hear it himself and so can she, because she stops smiling. She slowly places her wine glass on the windowsill, and folds her hands in her lap, her eyes on her fingers, as if she were knitting another gigantic scarf to wrap herself in. But then she looks up and he sees her bite her lip, and there is something new in her eyes: an invitation of some kind or a plea.

He vaults off the bed, covers the floor in a couple of bounds, and she herself is rising to her feet. But not to fend him off, for she allows him to reach for her, allows him to lift her jumper off over her head, so her hair spills down over her face, over her bare shoulders, over the straps of her white cotton brassiere. This he unclips as he presses his mouth on hers, his tongue finding her tongue, and he tries to slow himself down, tries to be gentle, but he knows he is being more urgent, more persistent than he should be, desperate now.

He does not go down on her first, as he has imagined doing. He does not find the right place to touch her between her legs, as he has also imagined doing. He moves her clumsily across the room, his hands gripping bare flesh, makes it to the bed but not into the bed. In the end, he is half-kneeling on the floor. He has a wondrous view of her, naked, her thighs spread apart, her hair fanning out on the bed. Yet her eyes are closed, and her face is turned away from him as if she is imagining someone else: Armando of course, he thinks, briefly. But other than that sole intrusion, it is all a roaring sound in his head, he can feel the sweat drip down his chest as if they are in the tropics. Then he plunges into darkness as if diving off a cliff, plunges into beautifully cold, fresh, black water.

'Theo?'

He is surfacing now, coming up for air. He opens his eyes.

'Theo can I just...' she is trying to push him off. He has collapsed onto her and his elbow is digging into her thigh. He quickly rolls off.

'Sorry.'

'It's okay.'

She wriggles on the bed to disengage herself from the twisted quilt. He takes hold of her hips, tries to bury his face where her legs meet, but he feels her hand twisting in his hair, pulling him up higher. Her cheeks are bright red again.

'No, don't...'

'But you didn't...'

'Don't worry...'

Their faces are now level. He pulls the pillow lower down so they can rest their heads. He strokes her hip.

'I'm sorry. It will be better next time.'

'Stop, Theo.' And then, gloriously, she touches his lips with her fingers then brushes them against his cheek. 'It's just nice to be held.'

He wraps his arms around her, pulls her close, revelling in the silkiness, the smoothness of her, but when he kisses her, he tastes the saltiness and sees the tears, tracking across her cheeks, dribbling into her hair.

'Are you okay?'

She nods, but when she tries to speak, she only makes a squawk, like a wounded bird, a sound which makes them both laugh and his skin tingles at the feel of her shaking against him. He traces the tracks on her cheeks.

'Lolita.'

She is smiling, but the tears are still rolling down, and she swipes at them.

'Are you okay?' he repeats.

'Yes,' she croaks.

'I've wanted to make love to you for so long. That's why...'

'Theo,' she touches his lips again. 'Stop.'

She leans forward and her hair falls on his face as she presses her lips to his. He pulls her even closer, his palm caressing the small of her back, he is sure he can feel her heart beating. They lie like this, her warm breath tickling his ear.

'Can I use the bathroom?' she whispers.

He releases her, and watches as she rises from the bed, holding one arm across her breasts. He reaches behind him to feel for his shirt, which is lying crumpled against the wall and throws it to her.

'Here.'

'Thanks.'

And suddenly her arms are lifting upwards so he can see her body arching, those luscious dark nipples, her navel, the neat triangle of dark hair, the muscle in her thigh, and then she is covered by his shirt. She skips across the room and out the door, her long legs flashing, and he takes advantage of her absence to remove the condom, which he is amazed he had the presence of mind to put on. The drawer of his desk is still open, the box he had scrabbled for still visible, and so he rolls off the bed, gets to his feet and closes it. Outside, the lights lining the river break up his reflection in the window, but he can still make out his bare shoulders and chest, still make out that his penis is standing at half-mast now.

She takes a long time in the bathroom, so long that in the interim his penis deflates, and he grows cold. He is not sure whether to get under the covers, decides not to, instead pulls on his trunks and finds a t-shirt in his wardrobe. Finally, he pads down the hall and taps on the bathroom door.

'Lolita?'

It opens slowly. Her eyes are dry now, but he can see she has been crying. She looks beautiful in his dark grey shirt, all tousled hair and soft mouth and bare legs.

'Come.'

He takes her hand and leads her back to his bedroom. But when they enter, she says, 'I should be going.'

Her words fall into silence. He turns to face her; she does not quite meet his eyes.

'Stay,' he says. 'Stay the night. Rainer won't mind. He'd love to see you at breakfast.'

He tries to smile but his heart is aching. She tries to smile as well, but it is clearly a colossal effort. She looks like a little girl doing her best to be brave.

'No, I won't. But thank you.'

He steps away. It is not cold between them, not that. Rather, it is confused, as if they had not just shared that act of intimacy but are still politely circling around each other.

'Do you want to see the river, before you go?'

She smiles, genuinely now. 'Yes, please.'

He drops her hand and picks up his trousers from the floor.

'I'll let you get dressed.'

He goes to the kitchen from where he can hear her moving around his room, collecting her clothes. He pulls on his trousers, stares outside the window. He hears her arrive behind him and he turns around. She is back in her blue jumper and skirt, her coat and scarf are over her arm. He pushes his hands into his pockets and tries to give her his most winning smile.

'You look beautiful,' he says.

She smiles back, but he can see it is still an effort. Then she stops smiling, bites her lip again, but there is no invitation now in her eyes, no plea.

'I'm sorry, Theo.'

Her voice is low and even and her eyes are large and dark and filled with something: not desire for him.

'I understand,' he says, even though every cell of his body screams the opposite.

'I don't know what it is,' she says.

I do, he thinks. Fucking Armando. But he says: 'Don't worry about it.'

'It's been a while,' she is whispering, 'it's a bit overwhelming.'

'Yes,' he says. 'I have that effect on women.'

She laughs, and there is a grateful flicker her eyes. Then she stops, and her voice when she speaks trembles, a detail he finds some comfort in.

'Have I spoiled everything?'

'No,' he moves forward and takes her hands in his. 'Not at all. You can't get rid of me that easily. If we've gone too fast, if...' he struggles to find the exact words, 'we can take it slow, Lolita. I'm sorry if I rushed you into anything.'

Before she can answer, before he will have to hear any response, he lets go of her hands and busies himself with slipping on his jacket, tying his boot laces.

They talk of inconsequential things on their walk along the river, which is unbearably romantic, a light fog softening the harshness of the streetlamps, passing only the occasional dog walker, and two drunken men. It is a magical walk during which she does not wear the gigantic scarf – and at one point she takes his arm and leans her head briefly against his shoulder. Now that she is out of his bedroom, she seems lighter suddenly, happier, more confident. And when he drops her back at the residence, prepared not to touch her at all in farewell, it is she who leans forward so her face is an inch away from his and it is she who lays her palm against his cheek.

'You're a good person, Theo,' she whispers.

'Am I?'

'Yes, you are. I'm lucky to know you.'

Tell me one thing, Lolita, he wants to say. Is there any hope? Do I have any chance?

But instead, he says, 'I'm the lucky one.'

She kisses him on the lips, a soft kiss, more than a peck but not much more, yet which holds a hint of promise, and which still sends that sharp stab of desire through him. But the kiss does not quite lift his mood. He hears Rainer open the door later that night, well after midnight, and pause in the hallway where he will see no extra coat hanging up, no extra pair of boots. And in the morning, he is grateful that his grandfather does not tease, only says: 'A lovely girl. You must invite her again.'

18

The atmosphere in the flat is torrid. At night he starts grinding his teeth, a habit from his younger years, when his father was taken away by the Portuguese, only to return five months later, gaunt and silent. He stops smoking: his customary morning cigarette only makes him feel nauseous. All the men have now heard of the anonymous letters to Joachim, but few regard the threats made as anything other than a threat to them all. If Armando has been singled out, then it is only a matter of time before another becomes the next target. Most of the men no longer leave the environs of the factory.

One morning, on an early visit to the woods – a routine he has doggedly maintained – he sees that the blue Trabant is parked on the road, close to the administrator's building. When he leaves the woods a half hour later, the car is still there. The window has been rolled down, even though it is a chilly day, and he glimpses a man sitting behind the steering wheel, wearing a tracksuit jacket with yellow stripes down the arms, smoking a cigarette, slowly, thoughtfully. He forces himself to continue as normal to the factory compound, pushes the side gate open and walks into the yard and rounds the corner, then doubles back, bent low, hugging the perimeter, to the corrugated fence outside the warehouse. He presses his eye to a gap between the slats. The man has thrown out his cigarette and is making notes in a notebook. He watches, holding his breath, until the man tosses the notebook onto the seat beside him and turns on the engine of the Trabant. The car arcs back towards the village. He is still holding his breath, when something drops behind him, and he instinctively kicks his leg out backwards. His heel catches soft flesh and there is an aggrieved howl from some defenceless animal, which skitters onto the fence above his head and then over, out of sight. He looks around, no witnesses to his loss of control. He is ashamed to have hurt an innocent creature, just as he feels a cold finger of fear touch his heart. Clara.

He gets through the week somehow, and on Saturday he is relieved to be leaving the factory complex with a mind to be back only much later at night. For, after the garden party he has been invited to stay for dinner at Petra's parents' house, when Clara will open her gifts, the first ever invitation of its kind. Joachim has already offered to drive him to Centrum where the bicycle for Clara awaits, and in the car his friend hands him a box wrapped in shiny pink paper: a birthday gift from Joachim and his elderly mother, and he is touched as always at his friend's thoughtfulness.

As they drive into the city, he tugs at the collar of his shirt, checks again that he has shaved cleanly in the wing mirror. He spent much longer than usual this morning deciding what to wear, opting finally for a long-sleeved, grey shirt, a present from Petra in the early days. Not only does it have the right level of formality for this birthday party, but it will please Petra.

'Don't worry,' Joachim says, grinning. 'I can guarantee that Clara will have the best-looking father at the party.'

'I just hope she likes the bike.'

He has told Joachim about the other guests, and the special invitations extended to Lolita and Theo.

'And give my regards to Lolita,' Joachim says, reading his mind.

'I wish I hadn't let Clara invite them now,' he blurts out. 'I'm not sure it's a good idea.'

'Armando, it will be fine.'

'I haven't seen her for weeks and I don't want to see her now.'

'You don't mean that,' Joachim is laughing.

'Not when she'll be with that boy.'

'It's your own fault they're coming by the sound of it.'

'It was a joke. I didn't think she'd take me seriously.' He sounds pathetic now.

Joachim is still laughing, but not unsympathetically.

'He's probably got her into bed…'

'That's none of your business now, Armando.'

Joachim's voice is soft but stern. His friend is right. He should have better used the five months' head-start which he instead squandered, uselessly. She will have already surmised his feelings, but perhaps only the lust. Not the rest, not the other deep longing: the sensation of being incomplete and only completed by Lolita. He had never said: I'll talk with Petra. I'll change my day with Clara. I'll find a way we can be alone together. Now the jealousy sears through him, as he is sitting in the car on the way to his daughter's birthday party. He has no claim over Lolita, none at all. She is young, she will forget him. She has moved on.

Beside him, Joachim taps at the steering wheel, as if choosing his words carefully.

'Look on this as an opportunity to make Lolita happy, because I'm sure she was really happy to be invited.'

He is right, his friend. Her voice on the phone, when he called to confirm the details, was warm and excited. He had been admirably restrained, limiting their conversation to the arrangements for the party, refusing the temptation to extract more details about the blossoming liaison with the boy, Theo.

On arrival at the department store, he declines Joachim's offer to wait to escort him to the party: he wishes to arrive alone this time, the bicycle in his hands. At the collection counter, he sees that there are two bows in bright orange with trailing pink ribbons tied to the handlebars.

'You said it was a birthday present,' the shop assistant says, her lip-sticked mouth stretched wide. 'I hope you don't mind, but I took the liberty.'

He feels a lump in his throat at this unexpected act of kindness, at odds with the burgeoning hostility from the local population and he wonders at how sentimental he is becoming.

'That is very kind of you,' he says.

'I think your little girl will be very pleased,' the woman purrs.

'Truly, thank you very much.' He takes her hand impulsively and presses it. 'Thank you.'

She is blushing to the roots of her hair. 'My absolute pleasure. Please do pass by another day. And bring your daughter.'

He leaves the department store, certain that the woman and her kindness are a sign of a successful day ahead. It is chilly, but the sky is clear and there is hardly any breeze. He turns down the cobbled street, garnering some looks from passers-by for the small, red bike tucked under his arm, but he ignores them. He is consumed by a feeling of pride, that he will be the giver of this gift which cost a small fortune: this shiny, brand-new, bright red bike with pink ribbons fluttering from its handlebars.

'Is this yours?'

The voice is confident and amused. He turns around to see a man, of middle age and average height, with a tanned face and blue eyes. There is a lit cigarette in one hand, and a black wallet in another. It is not his, but he nevertheless instinctively feels in his pocket.

'No, I have mine here.'

'Are you sure?' The man is grinning. 'It's not yours?'

The man has opened the wallet and, like a magician, is displaying the notes, in a fan. Even from where he is standing, he can see that these are Deutschmarks, totalling at least a hundred, and he feels the back of his neck prickle.

'No, thank you for asking. But it's not mine.'

The man nods, pushes the notes back into the wallet, and flips it closed with one hand, with practised grace. 'I think I know you,' he says now, pointing with his nicotine-stained middle finger, and it is clear now that he is the driver of the blue Trabant. The man is still grinning, showing his very straight but not-quite-white teeth.

He takes a step away, and shakes his head, forcing himself to smile back. 'I don't think—'

'It's Tommy, isn't it?'

Es ist Tommy, nicht wahr?

He feels the smile drop from his face, so quickly that he tries to replace it, which only makes the man grin wider, like a shark.

'No.'

He tries to move away now, but the man puts his hand on his forearm, dropping ash from the cigarette onto his wrist.

'Sorry,' the man now brushes the ash away with his fingers, smooth and cool to touch.

'I think you've made a mistake,' he decides to say.

'Yes, yes,' the man clamps the cigarette between his teeth and claps Armando on the shoulder. 'Yes, my mistake.'

THE OTHERS

He grips the bike tighter, turns around and walks off, willing himself not to look back, willing himself to put one foot in front of the other, until he reaches the Mickes' street. Then he stops, to stand, paralysed. There are no cars parked. There is nothing untoward in sight. There is only a pair of pink balloons tied to the heavy knocker on the Mickes' front door. The man has not followed him, but he will know where he is headed. They know everything.

He is already late. Petra had asked him to arrive before the other guests: he presumed this was a consideration on her part, to avoid him knocking on the door like a stranger in front of Clara's friends' families. Now he sees a couple, a little girl between them, march up to the door purposefully, while he, the father, loiters on the pavement. They knock, the door opens, they enter. He looks around again: there is no sign of the man or the blue Trabant. With a monumental effort, he forces himself to walk to the door and knock, as the previous couple did, to greet Petra's father and enter the house which is busy like he has never seen it.

The main events of the party will not take place inside but in the garden, a decision which is borderline inhospitable, given the chilly weather. Perhaps Alice Micke has capitulated to her fears over the rug in her living room becoming soiled with fizzy drinks and crushed cake crumbs. But she has been blessed with a sunny day, and the rays do hold enough residual warmth so that the guests can comfortably mill in the very long garden at the back of the house. At the very bottom he can see a puppeteer is setting up. There is a table to one side on which paper cups and plates of sandwiches have been laid out. Petra's father is explaining that the family gathering after this short party will be held in the living room: he sounds apologetic for his wife's fastidiousness. The bicycle is carried upstairs to be unveiled in the evening, and he walks through the glass door separating the kitchen from the garden. He can count four small children apart from Clara, and, standing around in various clusters there are eight adult strangers, and all the members of Petra's family who live in this city. There is no sign, yet, of Lolita and Theo.

His heart has at least slowed down to a normal rhythm. He sees Clara standing in a semi-circle with her friends, while Alice Micke conducts a game. His daughter looks anxious, as if she too is unsure about the buzz in the atmosphere, and his heart breaks. She is wearing a frothy, light pink affair, and she is smaller, he notices, than the other children, who appear burly and solid beside her. He has rarely seen her with her contemporaries, he realises, and next to them she is small-boned and delicate, like his sister at this age. And unlike the inquisitive, assertive, strong-minded Clara he is well-acquainted with, today she is quiet and timid, her large brown eyes taking in everything, while her playmates jump up and down, shouting answers in response to Alice Micke. He sees Petra approaching, looking harried. She is wearing her tomato-coloured dress, which clashes with the new highlights in her hair. Her younger sister, Jessica, is taking photographs, and he instinctively places an arm around Petra's shoulders, and she does not push it away. They both smile as the shutter clicks.

'Fantastic!' Jessica shouts. 'You both look fantastic!'

He removes his arm and sees that Petra is staring at him. She asks under her breath, impatient rather than solicitous: 'What's the matter?'

'Nothing, I—'

'You look like you've seen a ghost.'

'No, I—'

'Just pretend at least that you're having fun, God's sake.'

'I—'

But she has rushed off.

Now the puppeteer is ready and as the show begins, he sees that Lolita and Theo have arrived, and that Jessica is taking their photo. The present Lolita has brought is pressed against her chest. They have observed the formality of the invitation, for Theo is wearing his smart corduroy jacket and Lolita is wearing a long-sleeved, flowing elegant dress with a deep v-neckline he has not seen before, made from some soft material with an Indian-print. Theo puts his arm around Lolita, around her waist, as they both grin self-consciously for the camera, and then Jessica is chattering to them, fingering Lolita's dress in admiration. He turns away to watch the puppeteer and Clara. Petra has tied her hair in the usual high bunches, but he knows that his sisters would have braided and beaded it for her birthday and his throat tightens.

'Are you Armando?' the man next to him is holding out his hand. 'Simon. Sofia's dad.'

They shake hands. He eyes the small group of children. There is one little girl with a broad face like the man Simon, and who, unlike the other children obediently sitting cross-legged on the rug, is on her feet, berating the puppeteer.

'She's like my wife,' the man mutters under his breath. 'Always wants to be boss.'

He is not sure if he is expected to laugh, but thankfully the man turns away. He glances back, to see that both Theo and Lolita have a glass in their hands, and are in conversation with Alice Micke, who is clearly taken by them. At that moment, Lolita looks across and catches his eye. She smiles, tentatively, and he feels a stab of pain. He does not feel ready to talk to them, but Lolita is watching him expectantly and so he begins to walk over.

The distance is not long, but it allows him a good view of her, to absorb how lovely she is, in that dress. Alice Micke is talking avidly to Theo, who keeps looking over to gauge his progress towards them, while Lolita is steadily watching him approach. Alice Micke leaves them, finally, and trips up to meet him halfway, her face shining.

'What a charming couple. Where did you meet Theo?'

He does not correct her: at least Petra has not forewarned her parents.

'At a bar in town.'

'You know that his mother is the actress, Anke Potente? Richard and I saw her in a production of The Cherry Orchard in Friedrichshain some years ago. I can't believe I have her son in my garden!'

'I didn't know,' he manages to say.

'Didn't you? Theo tells me they live just opposite the very theatre where we saw the play. On Botzowstrasse.'

He knows East Berlin well and he knows that street and the theatre. It is a pleasant, cultural area, bound by one of the largest parks in the city.

'And his girlfriend! That dress! She's utterly charming.'

'Yes.'

'I'm so pleased you invited them. Make sure they help themselves to some food.'

You mean they are allowed one sandwich each, he thinks, unkindly, as she skips off. He swallows and looks back at the beautiful couple. The boy has his hand behind her, and is smiling, slyly, his brown hair falling onto his forehead, his lips pressed close to her ear, unaware that Lolita's large, dark eyes are fixed elsewhere. There is something arresting in the tableau: Lolita looking directly at him, beseeching empathy or clemency; Theo taking his chance, whispering a betrayal which will seal his claim on her. And as he has this thought, suddenly, he knows.

It floods into him like lava, this knowledge, and with it arrives a white-hot anger, so strong that the image before him disintegrates and he fears he will fall to the ground. But he doesn't. The chatter continues around him, the puppeteer's zany dialogue rattles on behind him. His feet take him back to where he had been standing minutes earlier. He only glances back once to meet Lolita's gaze, her face crumpled in disappointment and confusion, but he turns his back to her. Across the garden, Petra is talking to her sister, to all intents little interested in the arrival of the infamous Lolita. Clara is now sucking her thumb, which he knows she is normally only allowed to do at bedtime: Petra will be vexed by this public display. He wants to charge into the group of children, swoop his daughter up into his arms, and, knocking every chair and table over, run from the house. But he doesn't.

Finally, as the puppeteer is reaching his finale, he looks back and he sees his opportunity. Lolita is speaking with one of the other mothers and Theo is walking towards the house, carrying the two glasses, now empty. He skirts the limits of the gathering, quickly. As he approaches the kitchen door, he sees Theo at the sink, where he is rinsing the two glasses, courteously, then drying his hands on a towel, and then appearing at the doorway. He intercepts the boy. Theo looks startled at his sudden appearance.

'Armando. Hey. Hi…'

He says nothing, only moves to the side of the house where there is a narrow alley leading to the street at the front and Theo seems to understand and follows. At the edge of the house, he stops and waits for the boy to draw up, slowly, his expression bewildered.

He begins without preamble: 'I know Lolita told you about the body we found. She did, didn't she?'

Theo nods, and his shoulders relax somewhat: perhaps he had expected an interrogation over their relationship.

'The border guards told us to leave. They wanted it to look like they had found the body. It makes sense, doesn't it?'

'Uh...yes. It does.'

'Because if we found it, it means that they weren't doing their job properly. They won't have mentioned us in their report. Do you agree?'

'I guess. Why—?'

'Did you tell anyone else?'

'Sorry?'

'Did you tell anyone else?'

'Tell anyone else what?'

He takes a breath. He is finding it harder than he expected to separate the jealousy he has – pure cold jealousy that this boy in front of him is probably sleeping with Lolita – from the very real necessity of extracting information.

Theo has noticed his agitation, for he asks: 'Armando, are you all right?'

'Did you tell anyone else that we found the boy?'

Theo remains still.

'Did you tell anyone his name?'

The boy's expression is now guarded, and this makes him speak through clenched teeth.

'Today, before I got here, a man came up to me on the street and asked me if I was Tommy. But the boy's name was not Tommy. Lolita doesn't know, but I saw an ID card in his pouch. He was called Stefan. Stefan Müller. The Stasi will know that. So how did they find out about the name Tommy?'

Theo whitens, he takes a step back, and bumps against the opposite wall of the alley. He covers his mouth briefly with the palm of his hand, drops it.

'Rainer...'

He waits.

'Who is he?'

'Uh...'

'Rainer. Who is he?'

'No one,' Theo is now bright red, he is shaking his head. 'He's no one. I promise. I'm sorry.'

He turns away then and starts walking back. He hears Theo behind him call his name, but he doesn't stop, and then there is a hand on his arm.

'Armando, wait—'

'If I lose Clara,' he says, not breaking his stride, but Theo is trotting abreast of him. 'If I lose her because of you, because of this Rainer, I'll kill you. I'll kill both of you.'

Theo drops back and he emerges from the alley into the garden. Petra comes up to him, a frown creasing her forehead.

'Where have you been? We're ready for the cake.'

'Yes.'

'You have to light the candles, remember?'

'Yes.'

He goes into the kitchen where the cake, Alice Micke's triumph, is displayed proudly on a stand. He knows he has been given a great honour to carry the cake, with candles lit, into the garden. He looks through the back door and his eyes seem to find Lolita, watching him, a concerned look on her face, which breaks into an encouraging smile. She looks beautiful, and his heart aches. Theo is drawing up to her side, his face white as a sheet, and he does not put an arm around her shoulders as before.

He looks down and reads the lettering in red icing against the background of pink icing. He tries to light a match, but his hands are trembling and it does not catch and he wants to throw the box down and smash his fist into the cake.

'Let me.'

Petra's father has a sonorous voice. He enters the kitchen, gently takes the box of matches from his hand and the four candles are lit within seconds in swift, deft movements. He feels a hand on his shoulder, and he looks at Richard Micke beside him in surprise. The man is looking at him, kindly.

'An emotional time. Birthdays.'

'Yes.'

They hold the gaze. But he will not help me, he thinks. If I cannot keep Clara, if I have to leave this country, no one will help me, and I will lose Lolita as well. He blinks back the tears that have arrived behind his eyes, which he can do successfully under the guise of concentrating, while he carries the cake towards the table in the garden.

Everyone is singing loudly and out of key. He catches Petra's eye and finds he wants to pull her head to his chest. Then he sees the blur of an elegant dress and has a deep, primeval desire to bury his face in Lolita's neck. But most of all, as he approaches Clara with her two high bunches and frothy pink dress, most of all he wants to hold his daughter tight in his arms, her cheek pressed against his forever.

19

Rainer is not at home when he gets back, but it is not late. The birthday party had come to a natural end when the youngest guests became fretful and their parents escorted them home. It had been an afternoon when, making a mockery of his legendary observational skills, he watched no one aside from Armando, before and after their exchange. And certainly, after the exchange he devoured the man like he would a lover. He barely laid his eyes on Lolita. When the other children and their parents had left, she pulled at his sleeve, 'I think we should go.'

She looked unhappy. Armando had not spoken to her. He felt sorry for her but was unable to articulate everything he understood, everything he had learned. He nodded, still unable to speak, his mind still clogged. The formalities of taking their leave from the grandparents and mother, and Clara, who held her arms up to Lolita, occupied him for some moments. Only afterwards did he realise that it was Armando who was walking them out, leading them from the garden through the kitchen, down the hallway, as if he were the host, and he noticed that Lolita was ill at ease, unsettled by the man's earlier froideur.

So, the three of them trooped like a row of ducks through the house, Lolita in the middle, and Armando did not bid them goodbye at the front door but stepped out himself, walked ahead down the short path and then waited for them on the street. Lolita's face was flushed at this odd behaviour, his own body felt cold. They gathered in a triangle, Armando at the apex.

'Thanks for inviting us,' Lolita said, but Armando had simply nodded, brusquely.

He had wondered what to say, but in the end all he could do was stretch out his hand, and the man took it, contrary to what he had expected. They had shaken hands and Armando had looked him in the eye. There was no anger visible now, just a cold hardness.

'Uh thanks, it was nice.' He sounded young and his voice faltered, and Armando had only nodded again, curtly, then turned to Lolita, who was starting to speak.

'Yes, I really enjoyed...'

But he slid a hand behind her neck, interrupting her speech, and kissed her full on the lips. The pose was a classic, deeply romantic – her head tilted back, his mouth pressing down on her – and it seemed to last for an age. When Armando had finally released her – for it was he who broke the embrace, not she – he simply strode back to the front door, left ajar, and shut it behind him.

He had no idea what to say, only pushed his hands into the pockets of his trousers. He did not know where to look: the street, the lines of the tram ahead, the cobbles that patterned this part of the city. When he finally raised his eyes to Lolita, he saw she was watching him.

'Why did he do that?' she asked.

He shrugged his shoulders.

'What happened?'

'What do you mean?'

'You looked like you were arguing earlier. What was it about?'

'Nothing.'

'Tell me, Theo.'

'We were talking about you.'

She looked on at him, and he had little idea how convinced she was. While they were walking away, however, he saw her quickly press her fingers to her lips, not to wipe away the kiss, but as if in shock, or to savour the touch.

The only saving grace was that she had already indicated she would be busy that evening, perhaps anticipating the need for a night alone as solace. She had given him a peck when they parted, but he could only think of it as a sop, that the same lips had been kissed by Armando. For once glad to be leaving Lolita, he had headed for the river, the bridge, which would take him back to Rainer's apartment.

But Rainer is not at home when he arrives, and so he waits, at the table in the kitchen, and it is so silent that for the first time in the fourteen months he has lived with his grandfather he hears the kitchen clock ticking like a bomb. He thinks: this is a story that is happening in countless homes in the DDR, why should it be so surprising? He thinks: he will believe he is protecting me, that is what he is going to say. Rather he informs than a stranger. He thinks: all those years in goddamn France. Was he ever betrayed?

And, he thinks, opening the fridge, taking out a jar and spearing a piece of pickled cauliflower with a fork: I have never known a black man, not really, and certainly not one from Africa. When he and Hugo used to hover near the tourists at the Wall, he had on occasion seen a black person. Once one had spoken to him, in English, and then, when Theo had stared at him blankly, in German: 'You live round here?'

'Yes.'

'I used to live not far from here.'

'Oh.'

'In the American zone of course,' and the man had smiled, friendly and relaxed in his red t-shirt and blue jeans, baseball cap, exuding Western joie-de-vivre, exuding off-duty military, US style.

The shadows gather but he does not move, so that he is sitting in the dark when he hears the key turn in the front door and Rainer enters, a bag of kindling in his hands. His grandfather switches on the hall light and spies him sitting at the table.

'Oh, you're here,' he says, but he does not exclaim: why are you in the dark? Has something happened? He realises that he will never, ever fully appreciate the depths of the man who is his grandfather. He can feel, already, that Rainer knows exactly what is raging through him.

'You told them.'

Rainer does not react, only comes into the kitchen, turns on the lamps, sets the kindling in the basket by the door. He stands at the sink and washes his hands.

'Who is it? Who do you report to?'

'It's not like that, Theo.'

He is drying his hands on the old towel that hangs off the sink.

'Then what is it like?'

Rainer says nothing.

'How long have you been informing on me?'

His grandfather winces – at least he has shown some emotion – but then he says: 'It's better it's me and not someone else, don't you think?'

'How long, Rainer?'

'Not as long as you might have decided, sitting in the dark.' Then he sighs. 'But when you went to Sonderbar, you attracted some attention. I had a call afterwards.'

He scoffs: 'I don't believe you.'

'They wanted to know if you were becoming more hostile. They saw you speaking with Lolita afterwards. They saw you comforting her. That's how they described it to me.'

He slams his hands down on the table.

'You didn't have to tell them what she told me!'

'No, I didn't. But what should I have said?'

'That she's homesick?' His voice is almost a sob. 'That she's worried about her fucking exams? Christ's sake, Rainer!'

'You don't know who else she has spoken to, Theo. And if they found out what happened from someone else, they would assume you had lied and that will only make them more interested in you.'

'You should have told me! You should have told them to speak to me!'

'You've suffered enough, son.'

He cannot stop the tears that flood into his eyes, and he is ashamed that these tears are not for Armando, but for himself. He has never believed his family truly appreciates how difficult it has been for him, the only one to have been plucked from the sheltered, warm, cultured lifestyle that they enjoy. He has envied his friends for years, embarking on careers in science labs and offices and studios while his future was hijacked. He alone had to study at night-school for the Abitur, has applied every year for a place at university without success. He alone has written thousands of words without knowing where and how his journey will end.

Outside the windows, it is pitch black until the lights along the river are suddenly switched on. He looks up and sees that now his grandfather is sitting opposite him, not looking at him, his face turned away and his legs outstretched under the table. And is there not a tiny bit of relief inside him, a tiny bit of gratitude that Rainer has shouldered something, he is not sure what, on his behalf? Yet it would have been easier if Rainer had carried on with a great pretence: I don't know what you're talking about. Now they are both agents in the subterfuge.

'But they've left Lolita alone. It's Armando they are following.'

'Yes.'

'Why?'

'She has a friend here.'

Banaji.

'But Armando has no such friends.'

'No.'

'You can sacrifice him, Rainer? It's that easy?'

His grandfather holds his eyes but says nothing.

'Your wonderful DDR. Is it really worth it?'

'It's about you, Theo. Nothing else.'

He feels now a flood of relief, of gratitude, but he says: 'I don't believe you, Rainer. I don't believe anything you say any more.'

His grandfather smiles: a thin, sad smile.

'I know that when I returned, I was called a hero.' Rainer's voice is low and even. 'But you see, Theo, I never saw myself as a hero. I'm simply a scientist who determines the balance of risk, calculates probabilities. So, when we were in France, I evaluated the risk of doing something against the risk of doing nothing. The probability of being caught and then punished for being a Jew while I was doing something was not dissimilar to hiding out and then some desperate collaborator uncovering me. I would still be punished as a Jew. So why not, then, do something rather than hide? I distributed flyers, Theo. I didn't handle a gun, but distributing flyers and spreading information carried as much risk, the same punishment, so why did I need a gun? And then with your father as a small child, another baby on the way, and darling Elise. Impossible to calculate, with all the variables that family life throws at you, impossible to calculate the probability that we would be happier as a family, that I would be a better father, a better husband if we remained in the West. One of us could fall ill, one of us could die, your grandmother could have an affair! Who could say what happens in other families would not happen in ours? So why not, then, live in a country which followed a philosophy I believed in? In the end, we were happy here, at least as far as I, as a man, could tell. I believe I made your grandmother happy. But I was never naïve. The probability that the philosophy of the DDR would harden and become corrupted was the same as for the philosophy, if there is any, in the West. This is how it was with your friend, Lolita's friend, Armando. The same calculations. The balance of risk and of probabilities.'

It is a long speech and at the end of it, when he says nothing, Rainer gets to his feet: 'I'm going to bed.'

He stays alone at the kitchen table, unable to move. Or should he force himself to stand up, pack his bags? Instead, he goes outside into the back garden, into the black night. He should pull out all his grandfather's precious seedlings, trample all the autumn roses: a vengeful destruction of a back garden would serve as a fitting end to the plotline. He goes back inside the house and finds a vodka bottle, pours himself a shot, downs it, but then thirsts for a glass of red wine. A full-bodied, blood-red wine with smoky undertones: a better match for deceit and betrayal than cold, colourless vodka. There is a bottle on the counter already open from the previous night and he takes this with him outside into the garden. It is a clear night. He sits on the damp grass and looks up at the sky, at the constellations. He thinks: a facile, pseudo-cathartic revenge on the rose bushes will never feature in my novels.

He gulps the wine, wipes his mouth with the back of his hand. What has he learned tonight? Rainer is as baffling as ever. He is not sure whether his grandfather feels any remorse or shame that he has used somebody as a decoy to protect him, Theo. The lights are on in Rainer's bedroom, and his silhouette can be seen moving around as he readies himself for bed. Is he imagining it or are his grandfather's movements slower tonight, more deliberate, more like those of an old man?

He turns his face away to focus on the river ahead. He contemplates walking along it, throwing the bottle into it, throwing himself into it, but instead he goes back into the kitchen and finds some ham in the fridge, and a fruit yoghurt, and bread, and some more pickled cauliflower. He makes himself a plate, which he takes outside again, determined to chill himself to the bone, and there he eats and drinks, alternating a mouthful of food with a swig of wine. The light is still on in Rainer's bedroom, but there is no sign of a silhouette now. He must be lying down in his bed.

He goes back into the house, draining the bottle of wine as he walks, deposits it and the empty plate in the kitchen sink and walks down the hall. There is no light coming now from under Rainer's door, but without knocking he pushes it open.

'Rainer?'

He stumbles into the room, his eyes adjusting to the gloom. Rainer is lying on his side, one arm under his head, wearing the old white t-shirt he sleeps in. He looks older and frailer and smaller lying down, but his eyes are bright and they are trained on him.

'Theo.'

'What did you mean?'

His grandfather only looks up at him with his bright eyes.

'It didn't make sense. Why give me the long speech about balance of risk and probability? What the fuck has that got to do with Armando?'

His grandfather slowly raises himself on one elbow: 'That change you want, Theo, that change is coming.'

'Don't talk in riddles, Rainer.'

Now his grandfather shrugs.

'For two weeks now, there have been protests in Leipzig, we will start hearing of them soon. Thousands of people, protesting against SED, demanding the borders be opened. There is talk that Honecker will resign within weeks, if not days.'

It feels now like his head is rotating on a spit, ready to be roasted. He blinks, swallows, tries to speak, but only manages to open and close his mouth like a goldfish, making no sound.

'You see the DDR as a place of rules and restrictions, Theo. But it's also a place of safety, where no one is hungry. SED has been like a mother hen, sitting on its eggs. But if we take away that hen, all we have are the eggs, and it's only when you break an eggshell, that you see if it's bad inside or not.'

He stares at his grandfather, completely confounded.

Then Rainer says: 'What your friend Armando most likely needs to fear will not be the Stasi.'

The way he says it makes him ask: 'What do you mean?'

'You think,' now Rainer smiles tiredly, 'you think that if SED falls, if the DDR fails, that it will come at no expense. But everything comes at a price, Theo.' He lays back on the bed, heavily. 'Someone will pay. Nothing comes for free.'

He stands there for some moments, swaying slightly and he realises that he is, finally, drunk, as befits the events of this evening. He has no idea what to do, so he lurches backwards towards the door.

'Goodnight.'

'Goodnight, son.'

*

Rainer keeps a low profile, and he finds that it is, in fact, easy to carry on living with his grandfather. He also finds that it is true, what Rainer had said: everything is changing. He starts listening to a West German radio station on his transistor, something he had stopped doing a few years back. There has been a steady exodus already of his compatriots through Hungary into Austria, all through the summer, but there is now a demand for change at home. The protests in Leipzig are now being replicated in most cities. Honecker does resign, but this does not satisfy, and the protests continue. Few are reported on DDR television, but on West German stations, there is footage of protesters being dragged and beaten by police, although more often lines and lines of policemen are shown standing by, looking perplexed and uncertain.

One day, he tells the foreman at the garage that he is not coming back.

'The plumbing in your grandfather's house?' the foreman asks, drily, revealing an acumen he never afforded the man.

Lothar and Philip decide to stay on, but they join him for a celebratory beer, to toast his new-found liberation. He feels more affection for them, on taking his leave, than he had expected and promises to keep in touch. As he walks back through the town square to the old bridge leading to the other side of the river, he thinks about how he might solicit a publisher, even success in the West. Herr Becker, we'd love to see more of your work. He reaches Rainer's apartment, opens the door to his bedroom, with its desk and the typewriter, and he thinks: this is it.

When he next meets Lolita, straight off a shift at the hospital, mid-afternoon, he drives her out of the city to the beach. He does not know for sure that she has not returned since that day in June, but he feels that she needs to return. They walk along the sand, a bitter wind blowing, so he can legitimately put his arm around her, and she nestles into his coat. They walk for miles, starting in the dusk and on and on while it becomes dark. He tells her about his new routine without the garage and the feeling of a new lease of life; she tells him about her new placement in obstetrics. The wind becomes icy. Their eyes are watering and noses are running by now: it has grown too cold to be out in the elements, and they turn around and walk back on the sand towards the town. Neither mentions the body: he does not tell her of his real name, Stefan Müller. They do not mention Armando, either, and the strange birthday party. But the wind, the cold, the constant sound of waves rising and crashing on the sand and receding, as if the sea is chanting its blessing, all of this he hopes will exorcise the memories that Lolita has about both the dead boy and Armando.

They eat dinner in a shabby restaurant with sticky plastic tables: an oily but delicious meal of fried fish and potatoes. Afterwards in the car, before they leave the beach, the sea roaring in the dark before them, he kisses her. She lets him touch her body under her clothes, and when she holds him, briefly, he nearly explodes beneath the touch of her fingers. But then she breaks away, and so he retracts his hands from inside her brassiere. He craves to see her naked again, to make love to her again. He asks her to come back with him to Rainer's and stay the night, but she refuses. He does not persist and after he has dropped her off at the residence, he sits in the car for some minutes with his head resting on the steering wheel, trying to drag himself back to a normal heartbeat. When he calls her the next day and leaves a message to call him back, she does, and on the phone, she repeats what she has said before: she is lucky to know him.

At the end of October, just weeks after that birthday party, there is news that all the prisoners who the Stasi had imprisoned have been released. In effect, the Ministry of State Security is dissolving before their eyes. He borrows Rainer's car and drives to the outskirts of the city to the barren landscape where the factory is situated. He drives along the track, which Lolita has described well enough to him, and then waits, the engine idling, the woods to one side, dark and menacing, outside the factory gates. He turns off the engine and places a hand on the door, ready to open it, to leave the car, to stand in front of the gates. He feels certain that Armando will at that moment amble into the courtyard, spy him standing in the fading light and stroll over to him, so that he can relay his message: I'm sorry for any part I played in your fear, but you should not be afraid anymore. The old borders are crumbling, the vice is loosening, and I am not sure why we should be living through this exact moment in history, but I know that history is being written.

But no one comes out. He can hear some owls in the woods, and the wind rustles ominously in the dark and he loses his nerve. He switches on the ignition, turns the car around and drives away.

20

The letters to Joachim still arrive, the blue Trabant still follows him, but it is clear this is the work of a person who is deranged, not right in the head: a lone, crazy wolf. The Ministry of State Security is facing scrutiny of its activities over the last decades, but perhaps even when its downfall is imminent, for its most evangelical proponents, their sadism has become a compulsion. The news arrives of an amnesty for all inmates of the local prison, most of whom will have been incarcerated for being enemies of the State. There is a very real chance of the government collapsing and the threat from the Stasi, so present, so real, only weeks earlier, has now been replaced by something else: the fear of the unknown.

Some weeks ago, Petra moved back into her parents' house, with Clara. She has been spending long hours at the newspaper; it is all-hands-on-deck covering the protests. Many journalists are now selling their eyewitness accounts to Western media outlets, he knows that Petra is one of them. Last week she left to station herself in Berlin and a few days ago, he received a telephone call from her, telling him her parents have requested that he visits Clara at their house, where they will ensure he spends as much time with Clara as he wishes: he is invited to have lunch and dinner with them. For they are too concerned about the rise in resentment against contract workers to let him and Clara roam the streets. In the centre some days earlier, there had been ugly scenes when some contract workers were refused entry into Centrum, the same store from which he had bought Clara's bike, just weeks earlier. He wonders if that shop assistant, with her flirtatious smile, is among those who are now barricading their doors.

Joachim holds a meeting in the courtyard. It appears that the contracts from Romania and Bulgaria have been suspended, only those with Nigeria remain. Because of this slow-down, Joachim charges him with a maintenance project, the type of which they normally only undertake every two years. The two teenagers are also tasked with helping him, but they are even more insolent and indolent than usual. Most of the time, he finds he is working alone. The other men have different jobs, outside: repairing the roof of the administrators' block and the gutters of the accommodations, replacing some of the windows. It is November and the nights are bitterly cold, but the snow has not yet arrived and so the work is manageable.

Since Clara's birthday party, he has barely spoken to his housemates. In the evenings, Gilberto remains in the bedroom he shares with Ronaldo, glued to the radio tuned into a West German channel. He still plays football regularly with Tiago, Ronaldo and some of the other men, but they do not talk much before and after the game. Alongside the work Joachim has assigned them, these regular football games, and evenings spent catching up with the news of events, the days pass quickly and few, except for him, notice that they barely leave the factory compound.

One morning, he is oiling one of the machines, when Joachim, still in his pyjamas and dressing-gown, comes to find him. His friend beckons him, and then walks back to his house, and so he downs his tools and meets him at the front door.

'Lolita is on the phone. She wants to talk to you.'

It has been weeks since he last spoke to her, not since Clara's birthday party. He glances at Joachim: he looks hungover, and his eyes are bloodshot. The living room looks unused, untidier than usual. It does not hold the scent of cinnamon but rather, and this fills him with unease, the air is stale. He has neglected his friend, he has been wallowing in his own worries, so absorbed in himself that he has not shown Joachim the same friendship he has always received.

'How are you?' he asks.

'Fine,' Joachim replies, but his words sound slight slurred. 'Give her my hellos.'

The handset is lying on the telephone table. He picks it up.

'Hello?'

'Armando?'

Her voice rushes into him, into his bloodstream: the cadences, the accent. He will never love anyone like he does Lolita. This thought, this acceptance nearly takes the strength from his legs. It is a thing of wonder that he remains standing.

'Hello, Lolita.'

'I'm sorry to interrupt you like this. Did Joachim mind?'

'No, I don't think so.'

'Oh good. He didn't sound himself.'

'No,' he glances back, but there is no sign of Joachim and he can hear the sound of water boiling from the kitchen. 'No, I think he's tired or something. All the news, you know.'

'I know.' Then, 'And how have you been?'

He clutches the phone, diving into her voice.

'Fine.'

'And Clara?'

'She's fine. Thank you for the present, she's been using the pastels every day.'

'Oh that's so nice. I'd love to see some of her artwork.'

'Yes.' Is that a hint? Does she want an invitation? He is not sure, and so he says: 'She's staying with Petra's parents.'

'Is Petra okay?'

'Yes, she's fine, just busy. She's been based in Berlin for some time. Reporting on all the protests.'

'It's strange, isn't it,' she is speaking softly now. 'Only months ago, remember, we found that young guy...'

He is stunned she is mentioning this, and he can think of nothing to say, just as he realises that he was correct in assuming that Theo would not explain their argument.

'Do you remember, Armando?'

He clears his throat. 'Of course.'

'I wonder why,' she hesitates, 'why he didn't wait.'

He waits for her to continue, but she doesn't.

'Things have happened so fast,' he says, eventually.

'You're right. It's been so chaotic at the hospital. Half of our professors seem to have left the DDR already.'

'Joachim's lost most of his contracts, we have hardly any work to do.'

'You remember my mother's old friend, Banaji?'

'I do.'

'He had a dinner for us last week, for me and Aditya and Prem. He might have to go back to India at some point to wait things out, it was very complicated what he was saying. But he also said that contract workers are in a difficult position now. Have you been okay, all of you?'

'So far nothing too serious has happened.'

'So they're true? These stories of attacks and stuff?'

Her voice is full of concern.

'What about you and the boys?' he says in response. 'I hope you haven't had any difficulties.'

'No, we haven't,' she says. 'We've just been carrying on.'

The two others are engineering students, he knows. He remembers that day after they had found the body: he had told her that she was different, being a medical student. He hadn't known then how correct he would be proved.

'I hope you've been okay, Armando.' Her voice is still etched with worry.

'I'm fine. Only that,' he gulps, as if for air or courage, and does not allow himself to divert from what he needs to say: 'Only that I miss you.'

She is silent for a long time, and he can hear her breathing, softly.

Then she says, her voice low: 'I miss you too.'

'But I'm sure Theo has been keeping you company,' he decides to say, in as jocular tone as possible.

She does not respond immediately.

'Yes, we've been seeing each other.'

'Ah,' he tries to laugh, but even though he knew it all already, he feels like punching the wall in front of him. Lucky boy, he should say. It was clear as day that was going to happen. Well, you gave me a chance, kind of, and I didn't take it. But he says none of this, only hangs onto the phone, slouching now, pressing his knuckles to his forehead, paralysed into adolescence.

'Armando?'

'I'm here.'

'Was everything all right at Clara's birthday party? We didn't really get a chance to talk.'

He closes his eyes. It was such a long, long time ago now. He had wasted all his energies that afternoon on anger at the boy, consumed by a purported betrayal, the importance of which has now evaporated into a nothingness.

He says: 'I'm sorry, I know I wasn't very polite.'

'Oh, it's not about being polite.'

'I was jealous,' he says. 'I found it hard to see you with Theo.' She is silent.

'But it's all my own fault,' he says. 'It's not yours.'

'What do you mean that it's your fault?'

'I don't know,' he says, miserably.

They fall silent again and he wonders if he has said enough, if it is now clear that he has been suffering these last few weeks, that he wants her to be his.

But when she speaks again, it is to say: 'I've phoned because we're going to Berlin. I have a few days off. I'm meeting Theo in a few minutes, and we're taking the train down. He wants to see the protests for himself. We're staying with his parents.'

He can think of nothing to say.

'I just wanted to hear your voice,' she says, softly now, 'before we left.'

'Are you not coming back?'

She laughs, but it is forced, and there might even be a hint of tears in her voice.

'No, of course, I am. I've got a shift on Saturday.' She pauses. 'I've been working quite a lot. There are so few doctors, so many seem to have left the country. I feel, I don't know, useful.'

He stirs himself. 'That's great.'

'But I have the next couple of days off,' she says, 'So I'm going down with Theo. I just wanted to talk to you first, I don't know why.'

When he does not respond, she says, and her voice is stronger now: 'Well, I'd better be going.'

'Yes,' he manages to say.

'I wish we could have...' her voice peters out.

'Yes,' he says, although he cannot know what she wanted to say.

'I'll call you when we get back.' Then, 'Shall I?'

'Yes.'

'Maybe we could meet for a coffee or something? I could come up there.'

'It may not be safe to come here,' he says.

'Oh…okay.'

'So—'

The line clicks dead and he is left with the dialling tone sounding in his ear. He hangs up the phone and turns around to see Joachim standing in the doorway.

'Everything okay?'

He nods, but he cannot move and he finds it difficult to speak.

'Do you want a drink?'

It's half past nine o'clock in the morning. He hopes that his boss, his friend, means a coffee, but he notes that Joachim has gravitated towards the cabinet where the vodka bottles are stowed.

'No. Thank you.'

Joachim smiles, tiredly, and moves aside to let him pass out the front door.

'Come by later,' Joachim says, as he walks out.

He nods, unable to give his friend solace, and he makes it nearly all the way across the courtyard before he pivots and sprints back to Joachim's house. He bangs on the front door, and Joachim might have gone to the bathroom or upstairs, because it is many minutes before he comes to the door, still in his pyjamas.

He asks: 'Can I please have a couple of days off? You can take it off my wages and those boys can finish the machine. I've done most of it anyway.' Then he swallows. 'I want to go to Berlin, Joachim. I'll be back tomorrow, or maybe Saturday.'

His friend stares at him.

'Lolita is going to Berlin with the boy.' He can hear the urgency in his voice. 'With Theo.'

Joachim is still staring.

'I want to go too. I'll find them.'

'In Berlin?'

'Yes.'

'Armando, you forget that Berlin is a big city.'

'I know where his parents live. I know the street.'

There are many questions to be asked, but as is typical, Joachim only nods, and then catches his shirt as he is turning away.

'Do you have money?'

'Enough.'

'Wait, Armando. A few minutes won't make a difference. I'll give you an address. You'll need somewhere to stay the night.'

He watches as Joachim walks to the desk in the hall and finds a pen and a piece of paper.

'My cousin. She lives in Treptow. She has lots of space, so she won't mind you staying.'

He does not take the paper.

'She lives alone?'

'Yes.'

'Joachim, I can't just turn up and expect her to let me sleep over.'

'You can. I'll phone her.'

When he still does not take the paper, Joachim laughs, and it is good to see his friend laughing, his face bright with something, perhaps even joy that he, Armando, is finally waking up.

'Take it Armando. You won't scare her. Martha has bigger balls than either of us.'

He takes the paper and glances at the phone number, at the address and then at Joachim, who is still smiling, who looks more like his normal self, although his hair is shaggier than normal, uncombed.

'What will you do today?' he blurts out.

'I have the pleasure of seeing my mother later,' his friend says, drily.

'Look after yourself, Joachim.' His throat is suddenly tight.

His friend only chuckles quietly, then closes the door. He should knock on the door again and they should share a cigarette, walk to the woods and discuss Joachim's options, his visions for what will come next after whatever is going to come manifests. They could even discuss the pros and cons of what Armando is going to do, not least the immensity of the task of finding Lolita and Theo in a city as big as Berlin, which will be more crowded than normal, given the large protests of late. But he needs to change out of his overalls and leave as soon as he can, otherwise everything will be harder. If he is as quick as he can be, they will still have a two-hour lead on him.

It is a Thursday, and he has very rarely over the last five years left the factory grounds on a Thursday. Once when Joachim took him to see Clara who had chickenpox, and another time when Ricardo, one of the Cubans, was leaving and everyone went to a restaurant in the centre at his request – he had fallen in, unrequited, love with the waitress. Now, he walks out of the gates not long after ten o'clock in the morning. Joachim is at his window and gives him a wave. He had not told him that his money is depleting. He decides he will take the tram into the centre to walk south and then – what success will hinge on – hitch a lift. In the past, he has tried to do so with Gilberto and Ronaldo, without luck, but on his own he might have more of a chance. He boards a tram, which is empty save for one other old man, who gazes at him through rheumy eyes. The tram hurtles through the streets into the city, but he pays little attention to this unexpected velocity. The streets are quiet, as if the whole county is holding its breath, waiting for the next round of protests to erupt. The tram jerks to a stop in the centre and he disembarks, and he thinks: she is just a few streets away, with Oma and Opa.

But he tries to place his daughter out of his mind. This time, this time he will allow Lolita to engulf him, his thoughts. The sound of her voice, vividly painting an image of what she will be doing with Theo, has galvanised him into action, and he is finally coming out of his stupor, his self-pity. How could he have allowed things to reach this stage? All his fears, that ridiculous Stasi man, have melted away and another fear is rearing its head – that for circumstances or constraints, real or imagined, but none of them unknown in history, that he never took his own destiny in his hands, never acted on this true feeling of love that he has for the girl, Lolita. That if he does not act, does not grab at any opportunity he might have, he will forever regret it, die a bitter old man, never knowing the answer to 'what if...?'

He crosses through the town square and somehow everything does feel different, less warm: fewer people, but more eyes on him. But he ignores it all and marches on, his head high, his shoulders back, towards the junction of roads orbiting the centre. Now the landscape is ugly and flat. The cars rush by and he finds a spot on which to stand. It is a fool's errand, he knows. He would be better off walking the whole way to Berlin. But he holds out his thumb, his head filling with images of Lolita from the last months, and these images possess him, blind him, so that he does not notice a car has stopped a few metres in front of him and has needed to sound its horn to attract his attention. He runs towards it, glancing at his watch: twenty minutes. He has been standing by the side of the road for only twenty minutes, and because he has been dreaming of her, he might have missed this miraculous chance of a lift.

It is a green Lada, and the man behind the steering wheel has a beard, greying in parts.

'How far do you want to go, cowboy?'

'Uh...' he is momentarily taken aback. 'Berlin?'

'Not as far as Africa then?'

He does not have the patience for this, but he recognises his extraordinary luck so far and time is ticking by. The man is laughing at his own joke, but he is also clearing some space from the passenger seat, throwing a bag that was resting there to the back seat, so he asks:

'Are you going to Berlin?'

'All the way, my friend. All the way.'

And then, when he hesitates, the man says, 'You seriously don't think anyone else is going to stop for you, do you? They're more likely to put you in a zoo.' Then he tosses aside an empty cigarette packet and dusts the passenger seat with his hand. 'Get in. I'd like the company.'

He opens the door and slides into the passenger seat.

'Put your bag on the back seat. Make yourself comfortable.'

'Thank you.'

The man grunts, pulls out and within seconds changes to fourth gear, his engine revving loudly.

Then, 'My great-grandfather is buried in Africa. You are from Africa?'

'Yes.'

'Maybe you've been to the war cemetery. He's buried in Cameroon somewhere.'

He realises that it is a question, for the man is flicking his eyes from the road to him, the road to him.

'I'm from Mozambique.'

'It's far away?'

Thousands of miles, he wants to say, on opposite sides of the continent.

'Yes.'

'He's buried in Limbe,' the man says. 'Of course, I never knew my great-grandfather.'

He is grinning now.

'I'm Dirke,' he says.

'Armando.'

'That's a nice name.'

'Thank you.'

'French?'

'Portuguese.'

'Ah Portuguese. Where did you say you were from?'

'Mozambique.'

'Ah, I see,' he grins again for some reason, wolfishly. 'You know Berlin?'

'Yes.'

'Why are you going there?'

Again, the man is glancing from road to him, road to him. The drive could take three hours, or – he glances at the speedometer – two-and-a-half hours, and the man has given him a chance, however slight, at success.

'I want to see someone.'

'Someone?' He is still grinning. 'A woman?'

'Yes.'

'I'm not surprised. You're a good-looking guy.'

'Uh...thank you.'

'I'll be driving back up from Berlin in a few days.'

'Okay.'

'If you want a lift back, Armando, after you see your woman.'

'That's very kind of you.'

'Listen, open that,' and he points to the leather bag at his feet. When he unzips it, he sees among the folded t-shirts, a collection of bottles of Pilsator.

'Open one for me,' the man, Dirke, says. 'And have one yourself.'

He slides his hand into the bag and feels the cold touch of a bottle opener. He opens the bottle and passes it to the man, who takes a long swig, then places the bottle between his thighs.

'You don't want a beer?'

'No, thank you.'

'You're worried?' He taps his hand, on the ring on his finger. 'My wife. She'll kill me if I drink too much. I'll be careful.'

And, true to his word, despite the two bottles of beer the man drinks, the car never wavers from the road. Before long, they pass Teterow, and Dirke is still talking.

He stops himself from looking at his watch every few minutes. He has managed to leave the city and be on his way earlier than he had ever hoped: the gods are most definitely smiling down on him. He will need them to continue smiling if he is to have a chance to tell her everything, something he should have done many, many months earlier. What he cannot dare to contemplate is the possibility that he has misunderstood her, her voice and intentions, misunderstood everything that has happened between them over the last months, misunderstood the girl, Lolita, so catastrophically that she will not share his happiness when he finds her.

21

The epic scale of the protests, with images showing thousands blocking the streets, filling the squares, chanting in unison, move him as much as they terrify the authorities. He is astounded by his compatriots: such passion, such ferocity, such resolve. He watches the weekly spectacles from afar, but these begin to reel him in. A few days after a large protest in Alexanderplatz, he decides to travel down. He calls his parents, who remain sanguine on hearing that he has not worked at the garage for weeks. He does not tell them about Rainer, and about what he discovered. He does not mention Armando, and Clara's birthday party. All those anxieties and agonies seem already to belong to a sepia-tinted past, all have become relics of antiquity, within weeks. The speed of change is cruel, exposing the way they have all lived their lives as a sham.

When he invites Lolita to come with him, she asks: 'Will I meet the woman?'

'Which woman?'

'The woman with the beautiful red hair. Or rather the brunette. The one in your story.'

He blinks in surprise.

'You remember that?'

'I loved the story. Will I meet her?'

'No. No, I don't think so.'

'Where is she?'

'She's in Berlin somewhere,' he says.

'What does she do?'

'She worked in a pharmacy.'

'How did you meet her?'

'Are you really that interested?'

'I'm trying to imagine what you were like in Berlin, Theo. I didn't know you then.'

He doesn't understand exactly what she means, but he tells her: 'She's my friend's aunt.'

'Aunt!'

'Young aunt, but yes,' he clears his throat. 'She was twenty-nine.'

Lolita is laughing by now, her hand clapped to her mouth. He pulls her close.

'I must have a thing for older women,' he says, before kissing her. 'Seeing that you are a whole seven months older than me.'

He can do that now: kiss her at will, pull her so close that her body presses against his, touch her face and hair and lips. But that is as intimate as they have been since that wondrous occasion in his bedroom. Although – was it wondrous? He has obsessed over the details: he should have kissed her for longer, he should have moved her to the bed first, before taking off her clothes, he should have prioritised her pleasure before penetrating her. He should have told her, perhaps, that he is in love with her.

The plans to go to Berlin swiftly fall into place and he finds that along with his toothbrush, he is packing the manuscript he has been working on. It numbers nearly two hundred pages already and fits the large brown envelope snugly. On the day of departure, Rainer is quiet but affectionate, as he has been all these days, and gives him a paper bag to send him on his way, filled with bread and cheese, and slices of fruit cake. He leaves the apartment in the chill of the morning, the river glittering under the pale sunlight. He walks over the old bridge, and then into the town square. There is a perky, jaunty feel to the city, as if it has spruced itself up just as he is leaving it. The Rathaus is bathed in a rose-pink light, the remnants of last night's frost coating it like a dusting of icing sugar. The sunlight catches the peaks of the pink and blue and yellow townhouses, so that they stand like giant candles. He follows the narrow street which leads out of the square towards the west.

Lolita is waiting for him, as arranged, on the green outside the imperious main university building, where he had prowled all those weeks, looking for her. She is wearing the long dark brown coat with jeans. She looks lovely, but tired: there are smudges under her eyes. He knows she has been working beyond what would be the norm for her level of study: the previous day, she had back-to-back shifts.

'Hi.' He kisses her soft mouth, which sends the usual electric current through him.

'Hi.'

'Did you sleep well?'

'I went for a swim after I finished, which was wonderful,' she says. 'Then I cooked some food, and I was in bed by seven in the evening. I slept like a log, a full twelve hours.'

'I'm impressed you had the energy to cook.'

'There's only so much bread and cheese I can eat, Theo.'

He laughs, proffers her the paper bag Rainer has packed for them, and when she peers inside, she blushes, laughing.

'That's so sweet of him.' She pauses, then asks, tentatively: 'Did Rainer not want to come?'

She has asked after his grandfather a few times. She must sense that something has happened. He kisses her again.

'No,' he says.

'I'm even more nervous to meet your parents than I was to meet Rainer.'

'They'll really like you. But we won't see them that much anyway. We've got to be back for your shift on Saturday,' he says, just as he remembers he has packed his manuscript. But he doesn't mention it: she may then ask to read it on their train journey, and for this, he is not ready.

She smiles, squeezes his arm and they set off for the train station. When they board the train, they find that it is packed. They bump into Philip and Lothar, who are with their own entourage of friends, on a similar mission. It is with luck that they find a bench to squeeze onto; many others are sitting on the floor in the corridors. There is a carnival atmosphere at least, which is infectious. He leans across to whisper in her ear:

'Sorry it's so crowded.'

'It's those sheep again.'

'What?'

She blushes. 'Nothing. It's just something you said once...'

The picnic by the lake. She obviously takes more note of what he says than he gives her credit for. And she has intuited his resistance to feel anything collective, to imagine himself as unique, when he is like everyone else. Today, however, if anyone appears out of sync it is Lolita. She looks out of place, as if an onlooker swept up in a tide. Perhaps he should not have suggested she come with him, or perhaps he should simply have stayed away himself. At least with the din and the energy in the compartment, the journey feels shorter. They arrive in Berlin and as his workmates disappear down the street, he sees that Lolita is looking around as if searching for something. But then she catches his eye and smiles.

'I had no idea it was going to be so...' he struggles for the right words.

'Exciting?' But the way she says it, he can see she has noted his ambivalence.

He smiles back at her, abashed. 'I suppose I've become a bit of a recluse, living with Rainer. I've forgotten how to be sociable.'

'That's understandable. You've been immersed in your writing.'

Again, he finds himself disarmed by her perceptiveness, and he wonders if, despite believing himself in her thrall, he has, in fact, done worse and underestimated her.

'Are you okay to be here?' he asks her.

'Are you okay to be here?' she is smiling.

'What do you mean?'

She takes his arm. 'Are you not happy to be back?'

He shakes himself. 'I'm happy,' he says, 'and happy to be here with you.'

They have a short ride on a crowded U-Bahn, and then they are coming into view of his parents' street. It is an area that used to be working-class, but in the last decades has attracted a bohemian community of artists and writers and musicians. There are many disused buildings, but these have been splashed with brightly coloured murals. Empty patches of earth between warehouses have become community gardens, filled with vegetables and flowers. He sees her taking all this in, and now she looks more relaxed, and her eyes are brighter. He is glad to note the absence of crowds, but when the door to his parents' apartment opens, as well as his mother's smiling face in front of them, he sees behind her many others crowded into the living room and kitchen. Hugo and Kurt and Tanja and Irene and Christine and Marina, Hugo's girlfriend, and his parents' friends and colleagues. The atmosphere is buoyant, for there has been talk that the Politburo is at this moment in talks, and there are rumours that they will capitulate.

His parents greet Lolita warmly and they are soon ensconced in the crowd. The table in the kitchen is laid with food, his friends are already filling their plates. Tanja is talking to Lolita and before he can move to her, his mother appears and puts her arms around him.

'I thought you'd like to have everyone round,' she whispers, 'but I can see you don't.'

'No, it's nice,' he kisses her cheek.

'I've got a cake in the oven.'

'When did you become so domestic?'

'I know. I've learned how to cook when my children don't live with us anymore.'

'Typical.'

'I suppose it's because we've barely put anything on in the last couple of years.' She means the theatre company she belongs to, whose numbers have dwindled. He squeezes her hand.

'Is Lili coming?' he asks, but she has moved away already.

Lolita has a plate of food in her hands and Christine is talking to her. The other girls have started chanting at one end of the table, a familiar chant, always ending with their own coda: 'go to sleep old men'. It had always been a point of irritation, that when compared to the Party in Hungary or Poland or even the Soviet Union – the Russians at least had Gorby! – the DDR seemed to be governed by the oldest leaders, all men, nearly half-dead. The atmosphere, orchestrated by the chant, finding a groove, begins to coalesce. He feels his irritation dissipate as they eat and drink and watch television, tuned to a West German channel.

'I got a new satellite dish last month,' his father's voice is now in his ear.

'It's great.'

'How is Rainer?'

'Fine.'

'I know you two had an argument. He called me.'

He glances at his father who does not look particularly perturbed.

'What did he say?'

'Just that it was about something that didn't matter anymore.'

He might be right. But if it doesn't matter now, does that absolve Rainer from something that did matter? His father's eyes are kind, as always.

'He loves you.'

'Everyone loves me.'

His father grins.

'Well,' he says. 'It sounds like it will be a big demonstration tonight.'

'Do you want to come?'

'No,' His father shakes his head. 'No, your mother and I have already talked about it. We want to watch it all on television, like the Wessis.'

He laughs.

'She's nice. Lolita.'

'She is.'

'Hopefully we can talk to her more tomorrow. Anke wants to make crêpes.'

He watches the television, surprised that he wants to fast forward to the morning, when it will be just his parents and Lolita sitting around the table, eating pancakes. Hugo begins to gather the troops, and there is then a hubbub, a long queue for the bathroom: it might be a long night. He takes the opportunity to go to his bedroom and take out his manuscript. Why did he bring it? He sits for a moment on his bed, just as Lolita appears at the doorway.

'Come in.' He stands up and ushers her inside.

'Can I leave my bag in here?' She sounds shy.

'Yes, yes, of course. Sorry I should have said.' He lifts it off her shoulder and places it on his desk. 'Come in.'

He closes the door, and the noise from outside is slightly muted and they are alone for the first time since getting on the train in the morning.

'I didn't know that my parents were going to throw this party.'

'It's nice. I like meeting your friends.'

He thinks she will make a tour of this, his other bedroom, which holds many clues to his younger self, even scrutinise his bookshelves and pictures, but she sits on the bed and he sits next to her. Perhaps she has tired of trying to learn more about him. She touches the brown envelope between them.

'Is this it?'

He nods. She picks it up, almost reverentially, weighing it in her hands like a new-born baby.

'Quite hefty.'

'Probably quite rubbish as well.'

She half-smiles, shaking her head. 'You know that's not true.'

She does not ask to read it, but she holds it for a few moments longer before putting it aside. Then she clasps her hands in her lap, and he can see that the way the day has played out has neither invigorated him nor made her feel very comfortable. He says, on an impulse: 'Shall we just head off? We can watch the protests tomorrow on television.'

She looks at him, biting her lip.

'It's up to you.'

But before he can respond, someone bangs on the door, and it opens to show Kurt and Tanja, grinning from ear to ear.

'Sorry to interrupt,' Kurt says, through a wide toothy smile.

'Kurt—'

'Dude, let's go.'

'We were just—'

'Come on. You can play doctors and nurses later. We've got to get going.'

Lolita laughs uncertainly as Tanja bundles them out. Ahead he can see that Hugo, already rather drunk, is unfurling the banner Irene has made, emblazoned with 'Freiheit' in a variety of colours and sizes. The chanting has stopped, but everyone is in high spirits, except, when he glances back, Lolita, who is now being propelled into the crowd by Kurt. He makes up his mind: he will tell Hugo that he will not be joining them. This sheep is going to break away from the flock. But he has barely waded through the crowd to reach his friend, when Irene is shrieking for quiet and turning up the volume on the television. They see that Schabowski is in a press conference, delivering the decisions made by the Politburo in their meeting. A hush falls and they watch as a journalist probes and then the man declares, perspiring and red-faced, that, yes, they have listened to the people, and, yes, the travel restrictions which have been in place for decades will end tonight.

There is no sound in his head and although the television keeps playing, all he can hear is silence, and in this silence, a faint rustling like leaves in the wind. He finds himself staring at Hugo, whose jaw has dropped open, and he is unable to stop looking at his friend and the new beard he has grown. This beard has been clipped with precision around the cavern of his gaping mouth: Hugo has always been rather vain. He tilts his head slightly to the left, and then to the right as if he is trying to let out the water in his ears, and then, with a rasp like the striking of a match, the silence is punctured by a collective gasp and the party explodes. Everyone is shouting and jumping and cheering. He glimpses Lolita being hugged by Christine and his mother grabs him, before she gropes through the crowd for his father. He sees his parents embracing, his father's face buried in his mother's hair. Everyone is babbling at the same time. Is this for real? Does this mean the gate on Bornholmer Strasse will be open? Is it conceivable that they can just wander into West Berlin? Should they get their exit visas from a police station? Where is the nearest police station? Can one person go and collect exit visas for everyone? But, hang on: why would they need exit visas if travel is no longer restricted?

The consensus is that they will need to go and see for themselves whether this is really true and what exactly they are allowed to do. He only has time to grab his coat, before they all spill out of the house, and as they plunge into the cool, sharp evening, he begins to realise that no matter what he might have envisioned for this night, there is a greater momentum at work, and he will be carried along on its wave. It is a relief to accept this: whatever he had planned with Lolita, there will be tomorrow. He looks around, then, for her, but she is not beside him as he had thought. Neither is she behind him, back in the house. It takes a few seconds before his eyes finally find her. She is standing under a streetlight at the end of the street, talking animatedly, her face bright and happy as it has not been yet on this strange day, and she is talking to Armando.

The last time he saw the man was at the child's birthday party. Armando does not know that he sat in the car outside the factory, and then turned around and left. Lolita must have told him that they were coming to Berlin, and Armando must have also sensed what he has sensed: that whatever is happening in the country, whatever is crystallising, it appears this day will also determine what happens to the three of them.

Tanja is pulling at his sleeve.

'Who's that?'

'A friend.'

'Is he American?'

'No.'

'He's—'

He leaves her mid-sentence and walks over and the two break off their conversation and watch him approach.

Armando is the first to speak: 'Hi, Theo.'

He is smiling, but not widely, and his eyes are not cool, not challenging. He looks different standing on this familiar street. He is wearing a dark grey jacket, buttoned up, and he looks stylish, more like he should be a university student than a factory worker. The strap of his bag is across his broad chest and his hands are in the pockets of his jacket.

'Hi, Armando.'

'I told Armando we were coming down.' Lolita says.

'There's not much to do at the factory. So, I thought I'd come for the day.'

'How—'

'Petra's mother told me where you lived,' Armando says.

'Right.'

'I got here about half an hour ago. I've just been walking up and down your street.'

'Right. Yes. Listen, are you—'

But Hugo has joined them now. And it is Lolita who speaks up, 'This is my friend Armando.'

Hugo's face is a picture: he is clearly impressed by the friends that Theo has amassed up north in the short time he has been away from the city.

'Great, great. Freundschaft,' an expression he has never heard Hugo use before, and which seems incongruous today. And then, 'We should get going.'

He does not expect her to, but she stays by his side rather than Armando's, and the man brings up the rear, flanked by two of the girls. At the station, they bundle themselves into the metro, and again, she sits next to him, while Armando stands at the other end of the car. But this means nothing, for he sees that they exchange many a glance and that when they do, the man's eyes crinkle in a smile, as if it is the most natural thing in the world that he has appeared. No respite can be found when they descend from the train, join the crowds heading up the tunnel to ground level, burst into the cold, dark night, rippling with disbelief and euphoria. All around them, people are chattering excitedly to each other as the news is carried around as if by a spirit flying above. There is a line of policemen standing to one side, as solemn as statues. Is it true they will not be stopped if they try to cross over?

'I'll go and ask,' and Hugo runs over to the policemen. They watch as he talks to them, and then another pair of policemen join them, one of them holding a radio to his ear. Irene and Christine and Marina are bouncing up and down with excitement. Tanja and Kurt have plunged into the crowds without a word and have disappeared. Next to him, Lolita is quiet, her face is pale. When she sees him looking at her, she whispers: 'How are you feeling?'

'What do you mean?'

'Are you happy?'

'I think so.'

She laughs then and squeezes his hand, but he notices her gaze is somewhere else and he sees then that a few feet away from the end of the police line there is a group of men, gathered around a transistor radio set on an upturned wooden crate. Music is blaring from it, with a Latin, tropical beat. Armando is walking over to the group, with that distinctive athletic gait. He shakes their hands, and he stands with them, and from their gestures, it is evident that they are all talking about the developments. He cannot hear which language they are speaking, but he knows it will not be German.

Hugo rushes up, his face contorted with excitement.

'Yes,' he says. 'It's all true. We don't need to show anything other than our IDs.'

'I…'

'Come on!'

There are many people crying around him. Most of them are older than him. The woman in front of him has tears coursing down her cheeks. He knows some people have been separated from partners, even children. People have been shot while trying to climb over. He suddenly feels young. If he lives to be the age of his parents, then a greater portion of his life will have been lived after this night than before. By now, the policemen are dispersing to line up closer to where the gate is open. People are already squeezing through. One policeman hurries past them, and he finds he is catching the man's elbow.

'Can we go through?' he asks.

The man stops and glances at him briefly, and then his eyes rest on Lolita and further behind her, where he sees Armando is now standing, and as if the whole world is in on a cruel joke, the policeman barks: 'DDR citizens only.'

He turns to Lolita. Her eyes are shining, and she takes both of his hands, and he can see that she understands nothing. She is not wholly perceptive, then.

'Theo, you absolutely must go,' she says. 'Go with your friends. Please don't worry about me.'

'I want to stay with you.'

'I won't let you stay,' she says. 'You must go. It's what you've always wanted.'

'I want to stay with you,' he repeats.

'I won't let you stay,' she says again. 'Please don't worry about me.'

'What will you do?' he manages to ask.

'I'll be fine. Please, you have to go. I can't imagine how you must be feeling.'

'I'm not sure how I am feeling.'

'Theo!'

Christine and Hugo are waving madly, already being carried along by a wave of people. Irene runs up and tugs at him. Lolita is laughing now, her eyes glittering, and he looks around at the mayhem.

'What will you do?' he asks again, but now Armando speaks up, and there is no triumph in the man's voice, only warmth, and yes, some sympathy.

'I'll make sure Lolita gets back safely to your parents' house.'

'Theo!'

'Will I see you later?' His voice is urgent and young and desperate.

'Theo!'

He turns back to Lolita, and she reaches up and kisses him on the lips.

'I'm so happy for you,' she says.

So, this will be how it is. Irene grabs his arm, and he lets himself be led away. He only looks back once, and sees that Lolita is still standing there, her eyes brimming with tears, an iridescent smile on her lips. Armando must be nearby, but for some reason all he sees is Lolita, with her wavy black hair pulled back in a ponytail, in her long, dark brown coat.

Many years later, he will be asked, in an interview at a literary festival in Munich, after the publication of his book, which also coincides with the twentieth anniversary of that night, how he felt when the Wall fell: when he was twenty-two-years-old and for the first time in his life he was able to walk into West Berlin, as if the previous twenty-eight years had never happened. He will pause, take a sip from the glass of water on the low table in front of him and reply, with a grin, with perfect comic timing, and to a burst of laughter from the audience: 'I found it really stressful.'

The audience will not know that it is half-truth and half-lie, because that night in early November, as he and his friends walk into the streets of West Berlin, he cannot be sure exactly what he is feeling. He could be stressed or anxious to be making a journey that just days earlier could have been fatal □ or simply, he is already heartbroken. He does not know if he will ever see her again, but he knows he will never be the same again and nothing will ever be the same again.

He is leaving her behind, and he is leaving the DDR behind. Like the dead boy had tried to do, the boy they had found in the sea those months ago, that day when he first met her, when she careened out of her residence and set his soul on fire. There is, he supposes, at least some symmetry in the way that today they have been reunited, Lolita and Armando. That they have each other while he is alone, that they are both witnesses as he makes his own escape to the West.

22

He sees her tumble out of a doorway with a group of others, all German by the look of it, none Theo. She canters down the stairs from the building's entrance and sees him. Her face reflects nothing other than pure astonishment and joy, and his heart soars. Her hair is bouncing behind her, and then she is in his arms, so he can feel her and smell her, Lolita, all too briefly, before she takes a step back, her hands holding his.

'You're here,' she is saying, and her face is lit up like he has never seen it before. 'You're here.'

He bends down and kisses her cheek.

'You look lovely.'

'So do you,' she says, and she tugs the collar of his jacket. 'Very smart.'

She laughs and covers her mouth with her hand. He can see she is now blushing and happy and uncertain.

'How did you get here?'

'It's a long story,' he says, 'I'll tell you later,' and then he winces inwardly at this presumption, as well as at his habit of putting off what he needs to say.

'I hitched a lift,' he says.

'You didn't come with the boys?'

'No, I came alone.'

'And Clara?'

He touches her cheek briefly. 'She's safe and well and I am not going to think about her today.'

Her eyes widen slightly.

'I wasn't sure why you called me,' he says.

'I didn't know why I called you when I was calling you,' she says. 'But now I do. If you know what I mean.'

'I think I do.'

'How did you find us?'

'Petra's mother has seen Theo's mother in a play, and she knew his parents lived opposite the theatre.'

She glances at the theatre he has gestured to, and then her eyes are back on him.

'I can't believe that you...'

She is shaking her head, and he takes the opportunity to drink her in.

'...we could have easily missed you.'

'I was feeling lucky today.'

'But when do you have to get back?'

'I've taken a few days off and I have Joachim's cousin's address. Apparently, she'll put me up.'

'You've arranged everything,' she says in wonder.

'That was Joachim's idea. I have him to thank, as always.'

She says: 'Have you heard that—'

'The border has been opened,' he interrupts her, smiling. 'I was in there,' he points to the shop on the corner, 'when it was announced on the news.'

Now she looks around and they both see that Theo is standing, stock-still, at the other end of the street, watching them. He feels sorry for the boy. This feeling is yet another surprise and only intensifies as he joins this crowd of strangers, with Lolita a beacon among them. He makes easy conversation with the other girls, but he finds it hard to take his eyes off Lolita. It is thrilling to see her, to see how she comports herself with elegance and grace in this large, strange city. Among the crowds, she stands out, so that he is not surprised that when they arrive at Bornholm Strasse, and he makes his way to greet a group of men playing music by André Mingas, after he introduces himself and finds out that they are, indeed, Angolan, that one of them asks, 'Who is that girl?'

'Which one?'

'You know which one I mean. The Indian girl.'

'She's a friend.'

'Only a friend?' The man is laughing. 'Your eyes betray you.'

He can laugh with the man, tonight.

'Have you heard the news?' he asks, although from how they have set up their impromptu music stall, it is evident that they have.

'Indeed, indeed,' one of them says. 'All will change now. For them, and for us.'

Para eles, e para nós.

When the boy is carried away with his friends, he finds himself standing in the swirling crowd with Lolita. He waits quietly by her side: he knows that it will not be easy for her to shrug Theo off. Despite feeling real sympathy for the boy, he also hardens himself against any softening of his purpose. For he has a purpose tonight. He waits for Lolita to make her farewell, and he scans the crowd in case by chance – for it is a night of chance – he finds Petra. He can see there are camera crews and journalists: but none are Petra. She could have herself crossed over and she could be reporting on events from the other side.

'Armando?'

He hears Lolita's voice. She looks small next to him, amongst the crowd. He bends down and places his lips against her ear to ensure she will hear him amidst the clamour.

'What do you want to do?'

'I don't want to stay here,' she says.

He has to take her hand as well as brace himself against her to guide their way through the throngs, and they are travelling against the current. Finally, they break through to the ragged fringes of the crowd, where groups of people are gathered as if in preparation for hurling themselves into the scrum.

'Hey!' someone shouts. 'Are they letting people through?'

'Yes.'

But then he leads Lolita away, so that they skirt the crowd and round a corner to leave the main square. Suddenly it is quiet, and he can look at her. Her eyes are wide, her hair has come out of its ponytail and is now lying around her shoulders, and she looks pale

'I couldn't breathe at one point,' she says.

He takes her hands, and they are like blocks of ice. He rubs them between his, and she smiles.

'Have you eaten?' he asks.

'Yes,' her voice is stronger now. 'Have you?'

He shakes his head. 'I'll pick something up.'

Fortunately, there is a shop at the end of the street. He buys a ham sandwich and two mouldy apples and asks the man behind the counter for a mug of tea.

'I don't sell hot drinks,' the man says.

'Can you boil some water?' he asks. 'I'll pay whatever you charge for the tea bag. It's for my friend here, she's very cold.'

The owner's eyes rest on Lolita and he can see the man is much taken by her. Who wouldn't be?

'It will take a few minutes.'

'Thank you.'

The man moves into the back room before reappearing.

'Have you come from that side?' The man jerks his head westwards.

'Yes.'

'It's true? They've opened up the border?'

'It is, yes.'

The man grimaces. 'You didn't want to cross over?'

'They're only allowing DDR citizens.'

The man shrugs in reply and goes back into the backroom. He comes out with a large mug which he hands over the counter to Lolita.

'For you, Fraülein,' he says, blushing like a schoolboy.

'Thank you,' she says.

'How much do I owe you?' he asks, but the man swats his question away.

They stand under the awning of the shop, so that he can eat his sandwich, and Lolita can drink her tea, and he can see the colour slowly seep back into her cheeks. At one point, she offers him the mug, and he takes a sip. It is a simple meal, but intimate, and he feels that joy inside him, to be sharing a moment with Lolita Devi, after weeks of not seeing her.

With sandwich finished and an apple munched by each, with the tea drunk and the mug restored to the owner, it is time to reassess the situation in hand.

He says: 'I'll take you back.'

'Do you know the way?'

'Yes.'

'I'd like to walk, if you don't mind.'

'It's an hour on foot,' he says.

'I'd like to walk,' she repeats.

They set off, and in these streets, it is as if nothing of note is happening. A girl opens a door to let out a cat, they pass a man smoking a cigarette quietly under a streetlight, another carrying his daughter on his shoulders like he has done so many times with Clara. There is a woman tipping her rubbish into a communal bin. There is an old man talking to himself, while sitting on a bench with a bottle of vodka. At some point, he takes her hand, so that for most of the journey they walk like lovers, speaking in quiet voices and he can think of no better way to savour Lolita's company than to travel in the opposite direction, away from the story that will be told and re-told over the years to come.

'Why did you come on your own?' she asks. 'Didn't Gilberto and the others want to come with you?'

'I didn't ask them, to be honest. I've not really spoken with them for some time.'

'Has something happened?'

He will not tell her of the threatening letters, but he says: 'They're not happy with me.'

'Why on earth not?'

'I've not been great company, Lolita. I've always kept my distance in some way, I'm not sure why. I suppose I've always felt a bit different from them.'

'Why?'

'I'm not sure. They seem to assume that one day we will go back home, be paid all that money we are owed by the government, and everything will be fine. But there is still a civil war going on at home, how can we be so naïve as to trust that our politicians are somehow incorruptible, and what will I do about Clara?' He stops. 'I don't know whether they have the same worries, to be honest. I like to believe I'm different, but it's possible that I'm not.'

'But you are.'

'You think?' He smiles at her.

'I do.'

'How so?'

'You're deep, Armando,' and she might have wished to extol his other virtues, or maybe he wishes to hear these from her lips, but then she says, 'What about Joachim?'

'I suppose he's finding things hard at the moment. It's not been easy. He has all of us to worry about, plus his own future.'

'He's such a nice guy.'

'He likes you a lot.'

'Does he have a girlfriend?

'Not one I've seen. No, I don't think he does.'

'Is he lonely?'

He glances at her and meets her eyes and he feels a flash of envy for Joachim, for eliciting Lolita's obvious concern.

'Probably.'

'There are so many lonely people here. Have you ever thought that, Armando? There was a doctor at the hospital whose wife left him, I mean, she defected from the DDR, and he just seemed so sad and strange. Maybe it's because with the Wall, there has always been something to blame, and always the dream that things must be better on the other side. I hope that now they can go to the other side, they will find that things are better, not that they aren't better, just different.'

She doesn't say it, but she pauses, and so he asks: 'Are you thinking of Theo?'

She gives him a weak smile.

'I suppose so. I hope he finds what he has been looking for over there.' She flicks her fingers behind her. 'I hope he won't be disappointed.'

'Maybe he will do both, Lolita. Find what he is looking for and be disappointed at the same time.'

'Maybe Joachim will meet a lovely woman over there and get married and have lots of kids.'

'Maybe we should stop worrying about our Germans and let them get on with their own lives.'

She bursts out laughing and squeezes his hand and his heart flies again, up high in the night sky, to have her so close, to be so alone with her. They arrive at a wide road which would normally be lined with traffic, but tonight it is empty and they run across it, unhindered. They pass an old fountain, where there are groups of old men sitting on benches, smoking and talking, all of whom break off their conversation to watch them make their progress. They are now on a tree-lined avenue, with old apartment buildings decorated with iron balconies. As in Theo's parents' street, there are many lights on, showing silhouettes of people in gatherings.

'How are your parents, Lolita?'

'Baba and Elisabet are getting married.'

'Is that good news?'

'It is, we're all really happy for them. Even Mummy.'

'It sounds like your parents are still friends?'

'I think they are, although what can I know, really?'

'Where is the wedding?'

'In Manipur. In Baba's family's village.' She laughs. 'He comes from a very humble background, none of his brothers even finished school. And Mummy's family is so upper class. They made an odd couple.'

'Sometimes opposites attract.'

She understands what he means, because she gives him a long look.

'Sometimes they do. Although my parents ended up divorcing, remember?'

'I do remember.' He pretends to look crestfallen, and she laughs again and he grins.

And that is how it goes, this night-time odyssey as, somehow, he leads her down streets and avenues he has not walked along for years, but never erring, never taking the wrong turn, so that their journey is frictionless, oiled. He finds it so easy to talk with her and he can feel that it is mutual. The awkwardness of their last few encounters has vanished; they are, finally, both in step, both simply taking pleasure in each other's company.

He had estimated correctly earlier, for when he glances at his watch, he sees that they have been walking for fifty minutes, and talking for that time as well, but that now they are on Botzowstrasse. She has recognised where they are, for she slows down, and then she sighs, and looks up at the night sky and then once again at the apartment building, which they are approaching, steadily.

But he has already made up his mind and has the speech ready: he intends to call for her in the morning. Any plans she made with Theo would need to be rejigged, anyway, given the night's events. He drops her hand in preparation, but before he can say the words he has been rehearsing, she speaks.

'Do you think Joachim's cousin would mind putting me up tonight?'

He stares.

'I've never met her before,' he says. 'I don't know.'

'I don't want to stay with Theo's parents, not when he's not here.'

She is looking up at him and the expression in her eyes is calm and determined.

'Would you mind?' she asks.

He stirs himself and he can hear the wonder in his voice: 'No, of course, I'd be—'

But she doesn't wait for him to complete his sentence. She only flashes him a smile. 'Wait here. I just need to get my bag.'

He watches as she climbs the stairs to the entrance, and presses a buzzer on the intercom, waits for a few seconds before lifting her hand as a signal. Wait for me. When she disappears into the building, he cannot help but feel that this will be when the gods burst out laughing at him. She will not come back. She will change her mind as she climbs the stairs to the Beckers' apartment, they will refuse to let her go. She will next be spotted at a window, waving a handkerchief, mouthing to him to leave for she is staying put. His heart is racing from all the permutations he can conjure, when the entrance door opens and Lolita reappears. She skips down the stairs and half-runs over to him. He does not know what she has told the parents, and he does not ask her when she joins him. The decision has not been made lightly: he can see that her eyes are glistening.

'They're very nice,' she says. 'They said that they'll let Theo know I'm with you.'

He holds her eyes.

'He might be disappointed,' she says quietly, 'when he gets back. Or he may not even be surprised. I don't know. But,' and now she takes his hand, and she looks at him squarely, 'I'm not going to think about Theo today.'

He squeezes her hand, and she smiles.

'It's far,' he says. 'We can't walk it and anyway I wouldn't know the way. But we can take a tram to Treptow and then we'll have to ask someone.'

Now they are silent, as if Lolita's decision to extend the time together has, conversely, removed the chance for conversation. The tram is quiet but not empty, and he wonders if its passengers know what is happening on the other side of the city. The couple opposite them are bickering, in undertones, about an episode with relatives and a pet. A young man standing by the door is listening to a Walkman, the music of a well-loved punk band filtering from his headphones. No doubt all these people will learn of the changes in the morning – or perhaps they know already but are unmoved.

Treptow is bucolic in contrast to the centre and the night air is fresh and clean and sweet when they descend from the tram. He finds a bottle store still open and asks for directions. It is past eleven o'clock at night, late enough for Martha to be already in bed, but when they approach, he can see there is a light still turned on in the living room. The door opens and a tall woman stands before them, in a dressing gown and with thick, black hair framing her face. She peers at them in the dark, while the news on the television, a West German news channel, sounds behind her. 'People are still climbing,' the presenter is laughing through her words.

'Armando?' she asks.

He holds out his hand and she grips it, tightly.

'I think Joachim might have called you.'

'He did, yes.'

'Uh,' he suddenly feels shy. 'Uh, this is my friend, Lolita Devi.' The woman holds out her hand to Lolita.

'Will you be staying over as well?'

'If you don't mind.' Lolita, too, sounds shy.

'Not at all. Come in.'

The house is blessedly warm, and as they hang their coats, the woman says, 'I've made some soup, if you would like some?'

There is something which runs in the Bechtel family, he cannot help but think, and it is a great fortune that he has crossed paths with them. The soup is heated in minutes, and soon they are both sitting in front of the television with bowls on their laps, and a glass of cognac each, while Martha strokes her cat, which lies sprawled on the arm of her sofa. The programme continues, showing endless queues of young people sitting in rows on top of the Wall, and street parties on either side, while Martha asks after both him and Lolita. It appears she has worked with many students from India and Nigeria in her job as an engineering researcher, but not with any Mozambicans. Her family and Joachim's were particularly close, and the four cousins grew up more like siblings. The other two siblings are now married; only she and Joachim remain unattached.

'It's my choice,' she says, raising her glass to herself, 'but I don't know what it is with Joachim. Maybe he's scared of women.'

They have enjoyed their own dissection of Joachim's love life and so he exchanges a furtive glance with Lolita, who suppresses a smile. When the news begins to repeat itself, Martha yawns and stretches, and it is only after she has given Lolita a towel and pointed her to the bathroom upstairs, while he is washing up the bowls and glasses in the sink, that she says: 'You know, Joachim said to me, if Armando comes alone, he should sleep on the sofa. If he brings the girl with him, he deserves a bedroom.'

His cheeks grow warm as she laughs.

'I have a cabin in the garden outside,' she says, pointing into the dark. 'I put the heater on an hour ago and it will be nice and warm now. You will have more privacy there.'

He gulps. 'I don't know whether Lolita…'

'You haven't asked her yet?' Martha's eyes are dancing.

He clears his throat. 'No.'

'We'll see then,' Martha says, smoothly. 'She can change her mind if she wants.'

They hear Lolita's footfall on the stairs and the woman winks at him.

The bathroom upstairs is filled with plants and a mirror, which has the look of a seventies' nightclub. He stands under the gloriously hot water and scrubs himself vigorously. The morning at the factory, his dash from the city feels like a lifetime ago. When he re-enters the kitchen, there is a pile of bedding on the table, waiting to be carried outside.

'You can both stay in my garden room,' Martha is saying, innocently, and she repeats, 'You'll have more privacy there.'

He ventures a glance at Lolita, but she does not look at him, only follows Martha, who leads them to the end of the garden. It is a lovely wooden chalet, with a foldup bed, and a separate neat room with toilet and sink. He can see that Lolita is now blushing to the roots of her hair, but remains silent. Martha leaves, taking with her the trail of light from her torch.

'I'll sleep on the floor,' he whispers.

'I don't want you to,' she whispers back.

They make up the bed quietly, and the heater glows, warming their legs as they move around each other, politely. When the bed is made, he stands, uncertainly, like a boy, not sure what to do. It is Lolita who sits down on the bed and slips off her boots, then lifts off her jumper. Without looking at him, she unbuttons her jeans, wriggles them down over her hips and slides them off her legs, then stands up and crosses the small space with her clothes balled up at her chest, so he can see the triangle of her cotton underwear, and the long muscles in her thighs. She places her clothes neatly on the floor, her hair falling forward, and then she dives into the bed and under the bedcovers. There is much movement happening, and then one of her arms emerges, a brassiere dangling from it, which she lobs into the air to land precisely on her pile of clothes.

He laughs and she laughs, and pushing the bedcovers down to her hips, she reveals herself, so he can see that Lolita Devi is lying in the bed he will also lie in, with her black hair fanning out on the pillow, wearing a soft grey t-shirt, and not much else now. He strips down to his trunks, trying to attain the same level of matter-of-factness as she did, but very aware that he has an erection, an inevitability, but which he wishes to shield from her view. Then he is slipping into the bed with her, his knees grazing her knees, and they are lying on their sides, facing each other. He cannot stop gazing at her, at her lovely, familiar face, one which he has sketched in his thoughts nearly every night. But he does not touch her, still not sure what he can expect from this extraordinary day.

'I'm dead tired,' she says.

'I'm not surprised. We've walked miles and miles.'

'I really need to close my eyes.'

'Okay.'

'Don't go away.'

'I won't.'

He watches her as her eyelids drop, her eyelashes now curving against her cheek. Her lips are slightly parted, and he can see a flash of white teeth. She is inches from him, but fast asleep.

He replays the events of the day, and then finds he is rewinding further back, much further back, to a night he spent with Petra, in a cabin in the mountains. She had arranged everything, arriving at the factory, with borrowed car: literally and metaphorically in the driving seat. Why has he thought of Petra? He blocks any thoughts that will lead to Clara, for he will not think of his daughter today. He looks on at Lolita. He did not even kiss her goodnight. He stops himself from planting a kiss on her mouth for fear of waking her, and listens to her breathing, as if listening to the swell and ebb of a sea. He does not want to close his own eyes, but he must have fallen asleep, because he wakes to find that he is half on his stomach, and something is brushing against his face. It is her hair and as he rolls over onto his back, he feels her mouth on his and her tongue is tracing his lips.

'Are you asleep?' she is whispering.

She is poised on top of him, like a cat. God, please don't make this a dream. But his hands are already sliding over real, warm flesh, skin like silk, and he can feel her body, which is hot, so hot he feels burned by her heat. And then all that he has wanted to happen all these days, weeks, months, happens, and it is more than he could ever have wished for and afterwards, after they have lain silent, still disbelieving of what the night has witnessed, after they start murmuring to each other, after they begin touching each other, he pulls her close and it all happens again.

INTO THE WIND

23

As she leaves the bed, she feels his fingers catch at her hair. She pads down the hall in her slippers, passing rows of closed doors. The building is half-empty: most of the students are in Berlin, crossing over into the West, as easy as that. The residence porter has been conspicuously absent, his post abandoned, as all over the country, border guards might have abandoned their posts. Travel across fences and gates and walls has, over the space of only a few days, become disquietingly normal.

They had spent the morning after leaving Martha's strolling around the streets of East Berlin like lovers on a weekend break, revisiting some of Armando's old haunts, before making their way to the station to take the train back up north. This time there was no crush, no stampede – their carriage held only a handful of passengers. Yesterday, Saturday, they had gone their separate ways: he for his usual visit with Clara at her grandparents', and she for her shift. The hospital is nearly unrecognisable. The weekly lectures on communism have long been gone, but now scores of medics are similarly absent. Beate has disappeared, as have Maria and Jürgen. The remaining final-year students have been conscripted into active service on the wards to help the remaining clinicians, generating an energising camaraderie. She has been serving as aide-de-camp to an obstetrician, Norbert Wanger, with whom previously she had only exchanged a few words. He, alongside a handful of other Fachärtze, roam the entire hospital, tending to emergencies in any area, not only of their specialism. 'Don't worry, Lolita,' Norbert Wanger has said, 'this madness will not last.'

When she finished her shift, she had found Armando waiting for her on the forecourt, to escort her back to the residence, and, holding onto his arm, she felt like she was walking on air. He had insisted she nap while he concocted a delicious dish from rice, tinned fish and vegetables, in the small kitchen two floors up.

There he laid the table, complete with bottle of Hungarian wine and a candle standing on a saucer in its pool of melted wax. He had also brought up her cassette player, to play the Georgian folk music she so likes. And so, serenaded by the exquisitely mournful tones, they had dined in that unprepossessing kitchen, in the glow of candlelight, and she had felt transported to the most romantic destination imaginable. After the meal, after a few minutes spent in her bedroom, he had taken her hand and led her down the hall.

It was quiet, no one could be seen, but when they reached the showers, he had locked the main door, for there are three shower cubicles. The water had pounded down on them for, sterile and harsh as they may be, the showers in the residence at least have excellent water pressure. The fluorescent lighting was bright, unremitting, as he knelt in front of her, his tongue finding exactly the right place, his hands moulding over her buttocks and thighs, and then he was moving up, up. She could barely stand upright, and then she did not have to, for he was lifting her off her feet, her legs twining around his hips. At one point she remembers that he was holding her up with only one hand, the other was laid flat against the tiles behind her, that was how close he was to her. And when everything was still again, they had remained as they were under the torrent of water for many moments until she realised the thumping of her heart was being echoed by a banging noise on the door.

'Hey! Hey!'

She had stared at him, aghast, but he had only buried his face in her neck, shaking silently with laughter.

'Hey! Open up!'

They had clung to each other, the water still running, until they could hear grumpy footsteps retreat, and then Armando had set her on her feet, and turned off the shower. They had sneaked out of the bathroom, run back to her room, where they had fallen onto the bed in each other's arms, pressing their faces into the pillow to muffle their laughter.

They had shared that intimacy yesterday, and more, but he had spoken little about his visit earlier with Clara. They have, in fact, avoided talking about the little girl, their erstwhile chaperone.

She slips back into her bedroom. He is lying on his side, the bed sheet pushed down to his waist, one of her textbooks in his hands, a study in male beauty. But more: he is intoxicating, he elevates her, he makes her see herself differently. She reaches for her hairbrush and brushes out her hair to slow the pulsing in her veins, aware that Armando will be watching her. Her room has taken on a new significance. The bedroom she has spent nearly five years in, with her revision notes stuck on the walls, the poster of Rajamalai: now she thinks of how the mountain has watched them together.

That first evening back, the Friday, he had inspected her room with great care – to find more of you, he had said. He had immediately picked up the photograph she has of her parents taken at her school-leaving ceremony, not long before she left for the DDR. He had held her chin lightly on his palm, his thumb drawing a line from her cheekbone to her lips.

He had said: 'You get those eyes from your father.'

She had replied: 'I'd love to see a photo of your family.'

'I'll find one, when I go back.'

For they are on an egg-timer: she can visualise the grains of sand falling down the funnel. He will need to go back to the factory, and he has said that it will be later today.

Now he reads out: 'If a patient presents with symptoms, confirmation of Guillain-Barré Syndrome can be found by biomarkers present in the blood.'

She pauses, tilts her head. 'You mean in the cerebrospinal fluid.'

He grins. 'Correct, Dr Devi. I was just testing you.'

She pulls out a pair of jeans and a jumper from the wardrobe.

'Lolita.'

She turns around. His eyes are on her. He marks his place in the book with a finger, as if it were a novel.

'Come here.'

She wobbles slightly on her feet: his voice has that effect on her. She sits on the side of the bed, and strokes his chest, which is smooth and hairless. He tosses the book aside and picks up her hand and brings it to her lips.

'Did you sleep well?'

'I did. Did you?'

'Very well. You were talking in your sleep.'

'Oh God, was I?' She feels her face grow warm. 'What was I saying?'

He strikes a dramatic air: 'Armando, Armando...' But then he laughs at her expression.

'I don't know. Maybe you were speaking your mother's language.'

'I doubt it.' She is embarrassed, for in her dream, they were in the ocean and he had been swimming away from her.

He lifts the bedclothes. 'Come inside.'

She accepts his invitation, and presses her body against him, kisses his mouth while his hands slide onto her. He is smiling.

'How do you do it?'

'Do what?'

'Make these so nice.' He squeezes her buttocks.

She laughs, but she can already feel her body tingling in response. He tumbles her over, so he is lying against her back, his fingers teasing her nipples.

'Tu es tão bonita, Lolita.' His voice is hoarse now and this in turn sends a shiver through her. 'I dreamed of this, you know, when I first saw you.'

She feels the colour rush to her face.

'You don't believe me?'

'I do.' Her own voice is as hoarse as his.

He has slipped off her clothes, while they have been speaking, and his body is suddenly arcing over her as he stretches for the box of condoms and then he is back, so she can feel his nakedness against her nakedness again, feel the heat between their bodies. He is touching her between her legs, and she is melting, and then he is moving inside her, languorously at first, and then more urgently, harder. When everything quietens, when her heartbeat slows, when he releases her hips, she hears his voice in her ear.

'Amo-te.'

He told her there are some things he wants to say to her in Portuguese, and this is one of them. She turns around now in the circle of his arms to face him.

'Amo-te.'

His teeth scrape her neck, and he strokes the small of her back, his index finger dropping into the indentations he has so admired on either side of the base of her spine, and she closes her eyes to feel engulfed by him.

She hears his voice in her ear: 'You must tell me what you like.'

She opens her eyes. 'I like everything about being with you.'

He lifts his head so he can properly look at her and his face breaks into a wide smile.

'Aie,' he pecks her lips. 'Aie, aie. I can go crazy to hear that, Lolita.'

He is still smiling, and he looks happy, nothing else, but that part of her she does not like – which relishes in scratching at her own insecurities – suddenly prickles with annoyance at how hard she has fallen for him. This, teamed with the memory of how he has handled her in a seamless, skilful way, prompts her to ask: 'Who was your first love, Armando?'

His eyes crinkle at the edges.

'Probably you, Lolita.'

'I'm being serious.'

'So am I.'

But he is grinning, widely.

'I mean your first girlfriend?'

He makes a big show of thinking hard, and then says: 'Graciela.'

'That's a pretty name.'

'As pretty as Lolita.'

'Who was she?'

'A school friend. We worked in the same hotel on the beach. Where all the Portuguese and South Africans used to visit.'

'In Xai Xai?'

He touches her nose with his. 'Very good.'

'How old were you?'

'Sixteen, or seventeen. I can't remember.'

'Have you kept in touch?'

By now she knows he will have heard the tinge to her voice.

'A little. I saw her when I was home the last time. She's still working at the hotel, as a manager now. She's married, she has two small children. It's not easy, though, because of the war.'

'And how long were you together?'

'We weren't together. Not like you mean. She was the first girl I slept with. That's what you wanted to know. I've told you now.'

'Then who was your first girlfriend in the way that I mean?'

He hesitates and she can see he is wary.

'She was called Heike.'

'Was that here?'

'Berlin.'

'How long were you together?'

'Two years or so.'

'Two years?'

'Yes.'

She is staring at him, stupefied.

'And you loved her?'

'Maybe. I don't know. Yes, I think so.'

'What did she do?'

'Why are we talking about other people, Lolita?'

She is suddenly livid. 'Just answer the question!'

He does not push her away or snap at her. He says, and his voice is now gentle, 'She also worked in a hotel, but in the reception.'

All the annoyance, all the tension bleeds out of her, at the uncertainty, the lack of complacency in his expression. His hand is still on her back, and he is still stroking her. She wipes her nose with the back of her hand, furious with herself.

'And you, Lolita?' he asks, quietly.

'What do you mean?'

'Your first love.'

She swallows, but her throat is dry.

She says: 'You know about Willy. You know all about that.'

He nods, his eyes still holding hers. She looks away then.

'And Theo?'

His tone is light. She shifts slightly.

'You don't want to answer me?' He grabs her wrists with one hand and pins them above her head. 'I have ways to make you talk.'

She tries to smile, to match his playful tone, but part of her is frozen by the reminder of Theo. She hopes she is overstating what she means to him, just as she admits that she is being disingenuous. He will be hurt, wounded. He will also, most likely, be very, very angry.

Armando is waiting, watching her.

'There was just the one time,' she whispers. 'When I went for dinner at Rainer's.'

His eyes remain on hers.

'Who is Rainer?'

'His grandfather.'

He says nothing, only releases her hands.

'I think I told you he lives with his grandfather. They invited me for dinner and later we were alone, the two of us and there was just the one time,' she repeats. Then, 'I was so lonely.'

Now he lays a palm on her cheek. She closes her eyes, and it is many minutes before he finally speaks again.

'Just the one time. Lolita, you made that boy suffer.'

She opens her eyes and sees there is a small smile on his lips. But his eyes are sad, and the conversation has made her sad too. She thinks about Theo and his green eyes, and she tries to push him away from the happiness which seems elusive now, ephemeral, as easily dispelled as a cloud in the sky.

'I want to show you something,' she says, and she extricates herself from his arms, and walks to her desk. He shifts higher up in the bed, his arm folded now behind his head. She finds the bracelet in the pocket of her bag. His eyes are on her, moving up and down her body rather than the bracelet, but she knows he has seen it: Tommy. She slips back into the bed.

'I didn't throw it away,' she says.

'No, you didn't.'

'It was a lie when I said I had.'

'Yes.'

He is looking into her eyes, but then he takes the bracelet from her and weighs it in his palm, just like Theo had done.

'I suppose I've always wondered whether I could do something about him,' she is careful to use 'I'. 'Something for his family.

Tommy's.'

He closes his hand on the bracelet, and then reaches across her to drop it gently on the floor.

'He wasn't called Tommy, Lolita,' he says. 'He was called Stefan Müller.'

She stares at him and slowly raises herself on her elbow and he does not flinch from her gaze.

'I saw his ID card in that pouch, with all the Deutschmarks. You remember? Maybe Tommy was his father or brother or friend. Or a nickname. Who knows? But he was called Stefan Müller.'

She swallows.

'Why didn't you tell me?'

'The less you knew the better.'

'Better for whom?'

She can hear the anger creeping into her voice, and so has he.

'The border guards wouldn't have mentioned us in any report, it would have made them look too bad. But months later the Stasi started following me,' he says. 'That's what we were arguing about, me and Theo, at Clara's party. I know you saw us. Because all of this happened after you told Theo about the bracelet.'

The anger disappears, and now she feels like her head has been wrapped in cobwebs.

'Theo?'

'He told his grandfather about the bracelet and his grandfather must have told the Stasi.'

She feels cold suddenly.

'Rainer works for the Stasi?'

He touches her cheek, and his voice is gentle.

'I don't know. He could have been questioned by them or he could have volunteered the information. I don't know.'

'But why did they never start intimidating me?'

'Maybe they were there but you didn't notice,' he smiles, weakly.

She falls back on the pillow.

'It's all over now, anyway, Lolita,' Armando's voice is quiet. 'The Stasi released all their prisoners, didn't they? They don't have any power anymore. Everything has changed. It's already all in the past.'

She finds that she is staggered by his generosity. You shouldn't forgive him too easily, Theo had said to her, after lifting Hans Lütwiler's hand off her shoulder. His face shows no fury, but she can imagine the fear he must have felt, of being compromised, of losing Clara. He had asked her to discard the bracelet and through some misplaced sense of loyalty she had kept it, shown it, endangered this man lying next to her. And they could have lost each other.

She blinks, once, twice, and he is still there, waiting for her.

He lifts her hand to his lips, again.

'Would this be a good time to say that I'm hungry?'

She tries to laugh, but it is hard to move on from what each has revealed. They leave the bed. She picks up the bracelet and drops it back into her bag. He dresses in seconds and then sits on her bed, alternately watching her and browsing through her textbooks, and they should have reprised that delicious ease with each other, but there is now a melancholy which is almost tangible.

They go back to the cafeteria in the humanities building, where they have already enjoyed a dinner and breakfast, courtesy of her stash of vouchers. They order coffee and toasted bread and fried eggs and watch the television in the corner, showing scenes from West Berlin. Rivers of people, flowing like treacle along its streets – the Ossis – while on fringes are lined the Wessis. Some of the bystanders are openly gawping, some are taking photos, some are throwing flowers. There is joy and happiness, but perhaps because the sound is turned down so low, the effect is sinister. She finds herself looking for him and then, again, she tries to barricade her thoughts from Theo. The television commands the attention of everyone in the canteen, and they eat and drink in silence, and her eyes keep finding Armando's, but they say nothing and then he stands up and comes to sit on her side of the table, like he had done all those months ago, after they had found the body in the water. He puts an arm around her shoulders and tracks his finger down her jawline.

'Lolita.'

'Do you have to go back today?'

'Yes.'

'I wish you wouldn't.'

'You have a long day tomorrow and you need to get a good night's sleep. And,' he is trying to resume some of their earlier playfulness, 'if I am in your bed, I won't let you sleep.'

'I'd get enough.'

'You wouldn't. You've seen how I can't keep my hands off you.'

'I don't mind.'

'Mm.' He kisses her mouth. 'Your patients might.'

'Are you angry with me?'

He moves his head back, his eyes searching hers.

'For what?'

'For telling Theo. For lying.'

'Yes,' he says, and she feels his hand drop down, so it is gently tugging at the ends of her hair. 'Very angry. I might need to punish you.'

'I'm being serious, Armando.'

He moves back and clasps his hands in his lap.

'No, I'm not angry, Lolita. I'm not angry with Theo, either, or his grandfather. Not anymore. I've always been like this. When I'm happy, I feel like everything is well in the world and I hold no grudges. Petra always says that it shows my lack of ambition,' and then he stops.

She can see that he realises he has misjudged: the mention of Petra is not unwarranted, but it is jarring. She says nothing, only clears the table and takes the tray to the clearing area. And then they walk back through the park, back to the residence, back through the empty entrance hallway. Hours of the day have passed already: time seems to be conspiring against them. She knows that his wages may be docked for every day he spends away from the factory, but the thought of him leaving is unbearable. In her bedroom, he takes her hand and pulls her to him.

They undress quickly and silently. This time it is slow and tender, and she hears every breath he takes, and he seems to breathe her in, kissing her breasts and neck and shoulders, and when she cries out, he covers her mouth with his, before he shifts his weight off her. They lie facing each other, their breath mingling. The melancholy has not shifted, only descended like a cape, over their noses and mouths and bodies. She traces the shape of his mouth with her finger. He smiles, but then brushes at the goosebumps on her shoulder.

'You're getting cold.'

He pulls her closer and drags the covers over them.

'How was it yesterday with Clara?' she whispers.

She has said her name now, the name of the little girl, and a vision of Clara in her bunches, squatting on the sand, in her dress, suddenly appears and squats down on the pillow between them.

'Why do you ask?'

'You seemed preoccupied when you came back.'

'It was strange, because the Mickes are scared by all the changes. I wanted to take Clara out for a walk, they didn't want me to. But I managed to persuade them. We took her bike to the park around the corner.'

'Can she ride now?'

'She's trying to pedal. She gets it wrong sometimes.' He smiles now, at the thought of his daughter, and she feels that familiar flame, a tiny flare of jealousy.

'Did you tell them you were there?'

'No, I didn't.' He pauses. 'I don't know why. But I didn't want to tell them that I hitched a lift to Berlin.'

'Does Clara understand the news?'

'She knows that Petra is working on a story in Berlin and may be gone a few more days.'

'Did you talk to Petra?'

'She called while I was there, yes.' He pauses. 'I'm going to tell Petra about us. I'm not going to hide anything. Clara will tell her everything anyway.'

She touches his cheek.

'How do you think she'll react?'

'I think I've hurt her more by not being honest with her. Anyway,' he curls his hand around her neck, 'we need to think of many things, not just Petra. The residence won't always be this empty. We need to think of how and where we can meet.'

She feels a throb of fear, that the difficulties of old will loom again and he might be thinking the same, for he says, 'Don't worry, Lolita. It won't be like it was before. I don't want to just see you on a Saturday evening in Sonderbar.'

'I don't want you go today.'

He smiles but his eyes are dark now.

'I can't leave Joachim like that, Lolita. There might still be some work to finish.'

'Joachim won't mind.'

'No. Maybe not. But the rest of the guys will.'

Once again, they get dressed, but this time he packs up his bag, gathering his belongings – his toothbrush, his razor, his comb – and with each object being stowed away, her room becomes emptier and chillier and less appealing. He takes her hand as they walk down the stairs, meeting no one, and they leave the building.

They walk in silence back through the park to the junction where she had boarded a bus to Reutershagen on her trek to find him and Clara, all those weeks ago. This time they walk into the centre of the junction to the tram stop. There are few people around, the city seems deserted, as if its entire population has already emigrated, but there are two middle-aged women waiting, an indication that a tram is likely to arrive.

'I'll call you,' he says.

'It might be easier for me to call Joachim?'

'That's true.'

'I'll call you tomorrow.' She hears the tremble in her voice.

'Lolita,' his deep voice floods into her, as he pulls her close, traces her eyebrows, the cusp of her lip with his finger.

'I'm scared.'

'Of what?'

'I don't know. But,' she hesitates, 'this feels like a farewell.'

'No, no,' he is smiling. 'It's a pause. Nothing more.'

'When will I see you again?'

'Let me find out from Joachim what is happening, and I'll let you know.'

'Will it only be next Saturday? I'm not sure I can wait that long.'

She is laying herself bare.

'No, I can't either. Let me see what I can do.'

'I'll find out my shifts tomorrow.'

'Okay.'

He strokes her hair. There is a rattling sound, and the tram appears around the corner.

'Lolita.'

He has cupped her face between his palms, his fingers brushing the tips of her ears and his kiss is achingly tender.

She waits until the tram is out of sight and then exhales. She feels utterly alone. The last three nights and four days have changed her forever, irrevocably, of this she is certain. She spins forcefully on her heel — we will make this work, I can't live without him — and finds that someone is blocking her way. It is Aditya.

Across the street, one of his badminton friends is standing on the pavement, kitbag on shoulder, smiling at her in recognition. There is no sign of Prem, who will be holed up in Prakash's flat with the television set.

'Di...Didi,' Aditya stammers.

She is a year older than him, and for this he affords her with the respectful title of older sister, one she is not fond of.

'Kaun hai ye?'

'Mera dost.'

'Dost?'

His voice is dripping with sarcasm and when she looks at him properly, she sees that it is not from hesitation that he has initially stammered, but from disgust. She steps to one side to pass by, but he catches her arm. Across the street, she sees that his lanky blond friend is no longer smiling.

'You let him touch you? Vo kaala aadame?'

This reduction of all that Armando is to those words — that black man — incenses her so much she finds she cannot breathe, but Aditya is still speaking, and his hand grips her arm.

'Kya tumane use choda?'

She does not deign to reply, only tries to push past him, but he blocks her, hopping from one foot to another like a boxer.

'What of that German boy? I thought you were fucking him.'

'Aditya, let me go.'

'You have no shame…' she sees spittle on the sides of his mouth, he is genuinely revolted. 'You bring shame to your family.'

'You don't know my family.'

'Banaji knows. Banaji knows your mother…'

'It's none of your business, Aditya.'

'You think your mother will feel no shame? Have you forgotten who you are?'

'You don't know who I am.'

She shoves him hard in the chest, and he lets her go. She rushes onto the street, into the path of a man on a motorbike, who roars in anger as he swerves around her. She wants to walk away in a dignified, unrepentant manner, but instead she finds she is stumbling raggedly down the street.

For you and me, this is paradise. She had taunted Armando, then, but it is true. She has been utterly free here, answering to no one, only her heart. This heart is beating in a terrifying percussion: from anger, but also from a generous measure of fear that Aditya can see something she is blinded to.

*

She crosses the river, which is now running full. She remembers the way well enough, even though the last time she had arrived in Theo's car. Darkness is falling, the darkness of a cold autumn evening, with the promise of snow around the corner, and a crunchy white blanket covering the city for weeks on end. Ahead, there are lights on in Rainer's apartment and now she waits, to gather her resolve.

It is over two weeks since she waved Armando off on the tram, and it already feels like years. They have spoken every night, but have managed to meet only twice. The last time he met her from the hospital with Clara and her bike, and after dropping the little girl back at Reutershagen – for Petra has returned and been apprised of the situation – he had come back to her residence. The porter has not rediscovered his previous zeal, and this has allowed her to sneak Armando into her bedroom. They have spent magical evenings sleeping in each other's arms – just the thought of this makes her heart ache with longing. But the students are slowly filtering back into the residence. The weekend of near isolation they enjoyed in the aftermath of the borders opening was a gift, a halcyon time.

Yesterday evening, when she had spoken to Armando, it was to receive the chilling news that the flat below had been set on fire the previous night. Someone had entered the factory complex, broken the downstairs window and hurled an oil-doused, burning rag into the kitchen. The curtains had caught fire, but one of the men had raised the alarm soon enough, so there was limited damage. There is now a nightly patrol, on a rota, to pre-empt a repeat attack. On the phone, Armando had tried to maintain a philosophical tone: she knew he did not want her to worry. But Joachim, who had answered her call, had sounded tenser than she had ever heard him before.

It is not long now before she will be leaving for India, a sojourn for which in normal circumstances she would be counting down the days. But these are not normal circumstances: she does not want to leave Armando, not when there is a real possibility that she will only manage to spend two or three days with him before her departure. She is not going away for long, relative to the rest of their lives, but this separation has arrived at an inopportune moment. Too many unknowns, too much worry: she has barely thought of the implications of her father acquiring a second family. She has already started packing, and she has already decided that she will give something of hers to Armando, as a talisman of hope, of their love. She has wondered whether it should be one of the textbooks he keeps dipping into, but has decided on the cotton dupatta, the multi-coloured shawl with the embroidered mirrors, an impulse purchase from a stall in Imphal the year she left to start her studies, but which now has so much more significance: for he had touched it and admired it that day on the beach.

And now she is outside Rainer's apartment, for he is brokering a meeting with Theo. He had phoned the residence to ask her to come and see him, and to see Theo, who will be back only for a few days, to pack his things – for he is moving back to Berlin.

She does not know if Theo knows she is coming, and so in the pocket of her jacket is a letter she has written, in case he refuses to see her. It is the first letter she has ever written which is not addressed either to her mother or father, and it lies back-to-back with the last letter from Sushilla: *I'm so proud of all the news you have been sending. You sound like a real medic now! Remember to ask Banaji and Shanti if they want you to bring them back anything from home – it's the least we can do for all the help they have given you.* Normally her mother's pride, bursting from the lines, would buoy her spirits, but all she can think about is Armando. The mention of Banaji is also unpleasant: she has not called or visited since that encounter with Aditya, afraid of what might have been relayed. The help they have given you. What help, exactly? She has found her feet in this city in her own way, on her own terms.

It is impossible to tell from the lights how many people are in Rainer's apartment. She is terrified of entering. She will crumple in the face of an ugly confrontation, raised voices, or worse, a disdainful iciness. She will die if either Rainer or Theo hurl any of the words that Aditya had used at her. But she owes Theo an explanation – as much as she can explain the last few months. She was never pretending, she wants to tell him, and she has written as such in the letter. What she felt when she was with him was completely real, completely genuine. Only that when she could be with Armando, it was the only thing she wanted. She has tried to be as eloquent as she can in the letter, in the strange language, and she will fare not much better in person, but if she knows a little of Theo, then she knows that he himself is a complex, sensitive soul, and he may well be better equipped than many to grant her an amnesty. She gathers all her courage and knocks firmly on the door.

She can hear footsteps, before the door opens. It is Rainer, with his bushy white hair and black eyebrows, looking handsome in a heavy, navy-coloured fisherman's jumper. For some reason, she is reminded by this that she is wearing the same outfit – her blue jumper, her denim skirt – that she wore to dinner, those weeks back, before she chides herself for assuming he had even noticed or would notice.

'Lolita,' he says, and his voice is warm and gentle and welcoming. 'Thank you for coming. Please,' he stands aside.

She finds herself hesitating on the porch.

'Theo is not here at the moment, Lolita,' he says.

'Then would you please give him this?'

She pulls out the envelope from her pocket and he smiles, does not take it.

'You can give it to him yourself. He will be back soon. Please, do come inside and have a glass with me. And if you want to leave before he gets back, I won't stop you.'

His eyes are so gentle, and his manner is as courtly as it was before, and she has arrived with the intention to talk to him as well. So, she steps into the house.

'Is it warm enough for you?' he asks, as he takes her coat. 'I have been lazy about building a fire, but I will make one now. Come, come.'

He leads her into a small living room, which is on the same side of the apartment as Theo's bedroom, with windows looking out onto the river. She can see the lights lining the promenade.

'It was an adventure in Berlin, I hear,' he says, as he stacks the logs in the hearth, and crumples old newspaper into balls. He strikes a match.

She settles into an armchair by the side of the fireplace and watches the flames glow. 'Yes,' she says. 'It was.'

'Would you like some vodka? Or would you prefer wine?'

'I'm on my way for the night shift.'

He leans back briefly on his heels. 'Commendable. Then would you like a hot chocolate? Some cookies?'

She smiles. 'Yes, please.'

'You stay here, by the fire. I will not be long.'

She watches the flames. She is tempted to tiptoe into the hall, place her letter to Theo on the table and let herself out. But she wants to talk to Rainer and his living room is very comfortable. Her feet are resting on a thick, soft rug. The room is packed with books. There are pictures on the wall, and on the desk in the corner, she can recognise a photograph of Theo as a young boy, with a mop of floppy brown hair, and she feels her heart contract with guilt. Rainer enters with a tray and places a tall mug next to her on the table, and a plate of round biscuits dusted with icing sugar, then settles in the armchair on the opposite side of the fireplace. He pokes the fire with a stick, while she lifts the mug to her lips. The chocolate is scalding hot and delicious. She dunks one of the biscuits into her mug and then lets the soggy, sugary mass melt on her tongue.

'Would you like something else to eat?'

'No, really,' she says. 'This is lovely, thank you.'

He is reclining, his eyes on the fire. He appears content to allow her to lead the conversation.

'How is Theo?'

He throws a swift smile at her.

'Devastated, of course, Lolita,' he says. 'But,' he holds her eyes, 'he is not angry. At least, that is what he is saying. You'll see for yourself.'

She can feel the colour has rushed into her cheeks.

'It just happened,' she says softly. 'Nothing was planned, it just all worked out like it did.'

Rainer smiles at her again.

'You don't need to explain anything to me. I'm sure you'll be able to explain to him and that you've done a good job in your letter.' He gestures to her pocket.

She had expected to feel some anger when she saw him again, but she does not. She is treading on a very fragile crust, one which might crack at any moment and send her plunging into the depths of a history and a people she has little understanding of. There are other photographs mounted in frames and hung on the far wall, which show previous generations of the Beckers, many of whom, she imagines, may have suffered persecution, many of whom will not have survived the war. There is a pathos in the old man opposite her, who might be witnessing the decline and fall of a world he believed in, or at least an order he lived by. Or perhaps in a long life, and one as full as Rainer's has been, the last few days and weeks, and all the changes, are merely an addition to a long list of disappointments and betrayals and losses. She hardly knows him, and she cannot judge.

But she does not feel so moved by his age and his almost spiritual gentleness to detract from what she intended. She pushes her hand into the pocket of her skirt and withdraws the small package.

'I brought you something,' she says, and leaning forward, hands it over to him.

He doesn't say anything, which makes her suspect that he already knows what is inside, and when he retracts the bracelet – Tommy – he allows a sigh, 'Ah,' before replacing it back into the wrapping, and then he gives her a little bow.

'Elegantly done,' he says.

'It might be the only thing left to give his family. They may never be able to find his body.'

'If he has family.'

'It will be something you can find out.'

'Yes,' he is nodding, still smiling, still gentle. 'That's true.'

'The rope to his board had got twisted on something and so the board had trapped him in place. This might have caused him to drown. He did have a bruise on his forehead so he might have lost consciousness, but I wouldn't rule out hypothermia.'

'I see.'

'From what I could tell, and I am no expert, we found him within twenty-four hours of his death, so he was not out there, all alone, for very, very long.'

'Will you like a report on the mission, once it is completed?'

'No,' she says. 'No, I don't think so.'

'I understand.'

She gets to her feet.

'No,' he says, and while he is no longer smiling, his eyes are still gentle. 'No need to rush off, Lolita. Finish your hot chocolate. You will need some energy for your night shift.'

She sits back down. The fire crackles, the hot chocolate settles her nerves. But then there is a step in the hall, the door closes and there is a pause, as Theo must be observing her coat and boots in the hall. Rainer gets to his feet.

'I'm going to leave you two alone,' and he leaves the room. She can hear them murmuring in the hallway, in low voices, and she gets to her feet, patting down her hair, her heart in her mouth, and then he comes in, with his brown hair falling onto his forehead, looking younger than she remembers.

'Hello, Lolita.'

'Hello, Theo.'

He stands uncertainly, and then closes the door, glancing back at her for approval.

She steps forward, bracing herself and holds out her hands, and to her relief he takes them, and as she reaches upwards to kiss his cheek which is slightly scratchy, he does not pull away from her.

She steps back, dropping his hands.

'I'm sorry for how it all happened, Theo.'

He looks on at her for a long time, and she forces herself to hold his gaze. There is no anger in his eyes, at least none she can discern, but there are depths, many depths, and she knows instantly, with a pang, that the time she has set aside for this conversation will not be enough for him.

'I should say that it's okay and that I understand,' he says finally. 'And that's true. But it's not true at the same time.'

She remains silent.

'I haven't always known where I am with you, Lolita,' he continues. 'But I do know when I've lost.'

She stirs. 'It's not about winning or losing, Theo.'

'I know,' now he looks uncomfortable. 'You're not some prize, I know that.' He pauses. 'But I also have to say that I wish things had gone differently that night.'

She risks a smile.

'At least the Wall fell.'

'The Wall fell,' he repeats, nodding, then smiles, sheepishly.

She smiles back in relief.

'How was it on the other side?'

He runs his hand through his hair.

'Bizarre.' He smiles. 'They've managed to annoy me already. The Wessis.'

'How?'

She hopes that he will relate an amusing tale, and that they will regain somehow the ease with which they kept company all these months. She could intuit that day itself, that the collapse of the border did not fill Theo with joy, that the allure of free movement into the West had dimmed the very moment when it became a reality. He had said to her at the gate: I don't know what I want. She had understood him completely, understood the subtext, and she had been disingenuous when she had proclaimed: I can't let you stay. She had framed it as if it were a selfless act, when it was an act of self-interest: she was desperate to be alone with Armando. If he had not understood then, he has had ample time, and he has ample sensibilities, to understand now. She is not surprised when he refuses to take her bait and does not elaborate on the Wessis, but only says: 'Do you want to sit down?'

She sits on the sofa, opposite the fire, but cannot stop herself glancing at her wrist, before meeting his eyes. He has noticed, and she instinctively covers the face of her watch with her hand, which only makes her look more guilty.

'Don't worry. Rainer told me you're going on shift.' His voice is calm.

'Yes, sorry...'

'No, don't worry.'

But she can see that he is pained, they are both trying too hard, and now they are silent. She finds she is twisting her fingers in her lap, in such an overt display of discomfort that she immediately untangles them, smooths her hand over her jumper and her skirt, which only makes him look at her, look at all of her. Even if Rainer had not, she is somehow sure that Theo has noticed that she is wearing the same clothes she had been wearing that last time, their only time. He had taken the clothes off her body and they had made love on his bed, after which she had closeted herself in the bathroom as a deluge of hot tears had gushed out: tears of shame that she was testing herself with a real-life human being, with his own feelings and doubts, but more than anything, if she is honest, tears for her unconsummated love for Armando. Well, it has since been consummated and Theo is most likely aware of this. He swallows, noticeably, and she feels a wave of sadness and tenderness for him, for how he helped her, more than anyone, finally decide.

'What are you going to do, Theo?'

'Waste away and die, probably.'

But then he smiles. 'I went to a police station the first Monday after the border opened, and applied for a West German passport before anybody could change their minds, and then I went to the Freie Universität to apply for entry.'

She lays a hand on his forearm.

'Theo, that's wonderful.'

Now he hesitates, but then continues, 'And do you remember that short story I gave that guy in Prague? He's been in touch to say that it's being published in an American magazine based in Frankfurt. It's being translated, so it will be published in both English and German.'

'Theo, I'm so happy for you.' She finds that she is filled with joy for him, but also from relief for a weight being lifted off her shoulders: the burden, self-imposed, of ensuring his future happiness.

He grins, places his palms together and points forward.

'I can see my future unfurling before me and the starting blocks are in Berlin, not here.'

She is surprised to feel a sting from his words, so soon after her relief, but it is short-lived, because then he turns to her: 'I suppose you won't come with me?'

He is smiling, but his eyes are dark, and she can see he is completely serious. She shakes her head and finds that she cannot break his gaze, and that by declining his invitation, however flippantly it was made, she has hurt him, again, and even angered him. There is a long, painful silence before he speaks again.

'What will you do?'

His voice is cool and measured but his eyes are tunnelling into her.

'You mean?'

'The two of you. What will you do?'

It is a hard, cold question, but he deserves to ask her, and she knows that he can see that she does not know how to answer. But she allows him to look on at her, unblinking, revealing everything in his gaze: she needs to allow him this. For he is not only asking the question for himself: it is a small act of cruelty, which he may deserve to inflict on her. He is stripping away all the optimism and hope and romance of their situation and forcing her to admit that neither she nor Armando are the sole authors of their future.

'I don't know.'

He nods, saying nothing, and then she looks away, and he looks down at his hands. She gets to her feet.

'I'm going now, Theo,' she says.

He does not rise, only nods again, his head bent. She has the letter she wrote in her pocket, but she does not withdraw it.

'I'll say goodbye, then,' she says, and winces at her shaky delivery.

'Do you want me to walk you to the hospital?'

It is said half-heartedly, but it is at least said, and she answers hurriedly, 'Oh no, please don't worry.'

He nods again, and for want of anything better to do, she holds out her hand. It is in his eye line, and he stares at it for a long time, and she is surprised she can hold it out so steadily. Then he takes it, looks up at her and she can see the tears in his eyes, and some pity: for her, for him. Maybe even for Armando. She presses his hand, and when she tries to withdraw it, he holds on to it, now a slight smile on his lips. But then he releases her and she leaves the room, not looking back.

Rainer reappears in the hallway as she is doing up her boots.

'I'll drive you to the hospital, Lolita,' his voice is soft. 'It's late now and really dark and it's me who asked you to come all this way.'

'I'm happy to walk.'

'But I won't let you.'

He lifts a set of keys off a hook by the door, and pulls on a jacket, then cocks a head in the direction of the living room. It is utterly silent. He opens the door and ushers her outside, and down the path, where he opens the door of his car for her, just as Theo has done so many times before. He is not interested in making small talk, for which she is grateful. Her skin still feels stretched and tight after the encounter, the farewell, with Theo. They drive along the river, further northwards, until they join the ring road, arriving at the hospital from the opposite direction to what she is used to. He waits with his hands folded in his lap, as she unclips the seat belt and gathers her bag.

'Thank you for the lift. You really didn't have to.'

'I wanted to.' He smiles, then shrugs. 'We must learn to live differently. We have become too used to our simple DDR ways, but things are different now. And it's always at this point, the point of change, that we must take greatest care.'

She is not sure what he means: perhaps he is referring to what she has already noticed. A brittleness to the life as they have known it, as if one leg has been removed from a table balancing an orderly array of objects, and these are now suspended in the air for those few seconds, before everything crashes down.

Rainer says, in a low voice: 'I have not mentioned your friend, Armando. Not because I am not thinking of him, but because I feel it would be inappropriate for me to do so. I know things have not been pleasant and I wish him well. And I wish you well, dear Lolita.'

She opens the door, but before she climbs out of the car into the night, she turns back to him.

'Have you any plans, Rainer?' she asks.

He smiles. 'I hope a friend will be visiting from Hungary. Or I may visit her in Budapest. And,' now he grins, 'I promised my daughter that I would baby-sit the children for a week while she and my son-in-law take a holiday in the West together.'

Then he takes her hand and presses it to his lips. 'I'll make sure to look after Theo, Lolita. Please do visit again.'

*

She knows she will not, but there is also a feeling of returning something to a rightful owner, or at least tasking the right people to finish a job. She has tears in her eyes as she leaves the old man, and Theo, and she feels she is not only leaving them, but an era. Armando, Armando, she thinks. She tramps across the forecourt to the hospital entrance and then makes her way to the changing rooms, lost in her thoughts. She brushes her hair out, something she always finds relaxing and then plaits it, and winds the plait into a bun. Because of the changed nature of the hospital's workings, they have been wearing scrubs instead of street clothes under their white coats, and she stows away her coat and jumper and skirt in a locker, before clocking in.

It is quiet in casualty, where she has been asked to start the night, although a party of head injuries, three men in their twenties, arrive at the same time: they were all involved in the same brawl. They sit together, muttering to each other, their argument apparently forgotten. They submit themselves to investigation sheepishly, providing embarrassed responses. One needs stitches, which she attends to, while she orders head scans for the other two. By the time she has finished with them, it is midnight already. Only seven more hours before she will sign off, and sixteen more hours before she will see Armando. She munches on a sandwich, while writing up her notes on the trio of head injuries, making desultory conversation with one of the nurses. The nurses seem to outnumber the doctors – if this hospital is a reflection of the country, fewer nurses have absconded. She sees one of them approaching, as she is finishing her notes, to inform her that she is needed on the maternity ward.

The lift buzzes happily as it rises to the obstetrics department, a triumph of DDR efficiency and quality. Perhaps because so many have wanted to flee the country, the women who are serving to re-populate it are given stellar treatment. Unlike in her mother's clinic in the Western Ghats, she has known some mothers stay on in hospital for eight days after childbirth without complications, simply to rest and recuperate, courtesy of the State. How long will this luxury last, with all the changes on the horizon?

Lena, the supervising nurse, who now sees every pregnant woman as a liability, is at the desk and is looking frazzled. It is a miracle, she has declared, that they have coped, with medical staff dropping out and the hospital running on a skeleton crew: perhaps proof that a significant portion of the general public of the city have also decamped, taking with them their medical conditions.

'Lolita. Thank God.' Lena greets her with a squeeze of her forearm, then nods to the seats in the waiting area. 'We have two.'

'Is Dr Wanger in?' she asks.

'He's on his pager. He's had to go to cardio.'

It has been like this for weeks now. Hence, Norbert Wanger, obstetric-gynaecologist, consulting in the cardiology department. She approaches the pair sitting two seats apart on the plastic chairs. The woman on the left accosts her. She is thirty-four and she is having her third child.

'They both came quickly,' she is saying, of her earlier offspring. 'I decided to come as soon as my waters broke. My husband is at home with the other two. My mother is on her way, could you let her know where I am?'

Her contractions have not started yet, and after a short assessment Lena leads the woman away, babbling happily.

The woman next to her has progressed to thirty-two weeks with her first child. She is more of a girl, eighteen years old, with strawberry blonde hair in ringlets tied away from her face. Her arms are thin, as are her legs, evident in the loose flannel tracksuit she is wearing. She lives with her father, no mother, and the boyfriend has gone down to Berlin to join in the festivities. Her father drove her here, but left to go back to watch one of his favourite shows on television.

Her palm is placed on her belly, in the classic pose of a worried expectant mother.

'Do you have pain in your stomach, Natasha?'

'No.' Then. 'It's here.'

She touches her shoulder, and her face reddens, as if she is ashamed that it is so far from the swell of her belly.

'But it's bad enough to bring you in here?'

'No, it's not so bad,' the girl says, not meeting her eyes.

'Have you eaten something you're not used to today?'

'You think it's indigestion?'

'I don't know. Is that possible?'

'I've not eaten anything different,' the girl's eyes fill with tears, suddenly. 'And my head hurts.'

'You have a headache and a pain in your shoulder?'

Now the girl looks defensive. 'My dad didn't want to bring me here. But I know something is wrong.'

'That's fine. I'll just take some readings and we can talk more.'

The girl leans on her arm, as she leads her to a bed. There is a puffiness to her face, which is noticeable, given how slender she is elsewhere. When she lifts her t-shirt to attach the foetal heart monitor, the belly is voluminous in comparison to the girl's frame. The cuff of the blood pressure machine needs to be wrapped much tighter around the girl's frail arm before it begins to inflate. She takes a reading and inspects the trace and she can feel her head filling with ice-cold clarity, as if with ice-cold water, while her own heart begins to beat slightly faster. The girl has started moaning, softly. She opens the curtains and catches Lena's eye.

'Can we page Dr Wanger immediately, please?' She manages to keep her voice low and steady.

The nurse lifts her eyebrows, but hurries away. She turns back to the girl.

'Do you think you can go to the toilet, Natasha? I'd like to take a urine sample.'

The girl nods as Lena approaches, her face pinched with worry, to whisper: 'He's dealing with an emergency in cardio.'

She glances back at the girl and then at Lena.

'Stay with her. Take another blood pressure reading. And we'll try for a urine sample.'

She walks to the desk and picks up the phone.

'Which Fachärtze are on call?'

'Dr Wanger and Dr Hirschoff.'

'Could you page Dr Hirschoff, please?'

'One moment.'

She counts to ten and then again, to stop her heart from beginning to race.

'Dr Hirschoff is in the operating theatre.'

'Which other doctors are on shift?'

'One moment.'

But then the alarm sounds and she puts the phone down. She sees another nurse is running to respond, and then Lena has pulled the curtains aside, so she can see that the young woman, Natasha, is convulsing. They wheel her into theatre, the anaesthetist arriving and nodding his greeting, as she moves into the adjoining room, where she scrubs her hands and dons an apron, fresh gloves and a mask.

'Dr Wanger?' she asks again.

The nurse shakes her head, presses her lips. She looks at the anaesthetist, who nods his signal. At the head of the table, the girl's face is a white sheet, with eyes which have rolled back into their sockets, and she is taking short, painfully light breaths.

'I have to operate, Natasha,' she says.

There is no response, no sign the girl has heard her or understood her. She moves back to the end of the table, where the surgical instruments have been laid out, and she identifies immediately that the correct instruments are present and which she will use first, and that she can do this sends a surge of adrenaline through her. She marks the site on the swollen belly with a pen, asks for the first instrument and makes the incision, and then inserts her hands and begins to push apart the wall of the uterus.

'I need more light.'

She digs her hands in, her fingers brushing the baby's shoulder, the arm, and then the head, but slipping, slipping, until finally, she gains traction and scoops out the small body, eyes closed, impossible to see if the little boy is breathing. She cuts the cord and hands him to Lena, then plunges her hands back into the womb but the placenta does not give as it should. She stamps down a momentary wave of panic, the perspiration now trickling down her forehead, and begins, slowly, methodically, trying to prise it away. She must have managed to retrieve only a third when the doors swing open. Norbert Wanger appears, and she nearly bursts into tears in relief.

They work quietly, Norbert Wanger giving her instructions in terse, tense sentences. The blood pours out of the young woman's slender body, but then it abates, enough so they can see where the sutures will need to be made. She is infinitesimally grateful that he does not suggest she does them; perhaps he suspects she is close to collapsing. She watches as his fingers dart: Norbert Wanger is well known for his beautiful stitching. But at the end, he hands her the scissors, to snip the end of the thread. She holds his eyes, her heart hammering in her chest.

'Very good work, Lolita.'

THE OTHERS

Later, very early in the morning, they both visit the neo-natal ward, where the baby is in an incubator, and as Norbert Wanger speaks to the nurses, she leans as close as she can to the window and catches a glimpse of a perfectly formed but diminutive hand, miniscule fingernails, and then beneath the swaddling, the signs of a tiny chest rising and falling.

24

They got soaked in the park, for it only rained – the snow has not arrived yet – and when they returned, Petra suggested that Clara have her bath immediately to warm up. This is why he is now kneeling on the floor beside the tub, while Clara is immersed in sweet-smelling froth, settling like snow on her head. She is using her mother's bubble bath, another treat, and recounting the story she learned from her kindergarten, a Norse tale involving birds and trees, which he is finding difficult to follow, partly because it takes effort to dampen his emotions. His heart is full of love for his Clara, her perfectly rounded arms and swan-like neck, the water glistening on her eyelashes. Petra is in the kitchen preparing a meal for them all: he has also been invited to stay for dinner.

He could not have predicted just how much change would ripple from the recent events into his personal life. Petra has returned from Berlin determined to exploit the crest of the wave she is riding: her insightful reports are in demand, even if their rapturous reception is simultaneously maddening. She finds the Wessis patronising and in turns surprisingly ignorant of or indifferent to their sister country, which they regard very much as the backward, defective sibling. They think we've all had cholera and are barely literate, she has told him. They think we should be grateful for everything they are doing for us; they've forgotten that we did it ourselves.

He is amused by her anger, and he is pleased to see her so vibrant and enthused. This has most likely played a part in her generosity when he told her of Lolita: no doubt they will talk more when Clara is tucked away in bed. She has been similarly fired up by the attack on the factory. Earlier this morning, she had arrived with a photographer, to interview Joachim and some of the men. That was when she invited him to accompany her back into the city. Her mother is getting on her nerves, and she wondered if he would be able to take some time off and collect Clara from kindergarten? He swapped his place on the rota with Gilberto and drove back with Petra.

The door to the bathroom opens.

'Will you be much longer? Dinner is ready.'

'Come, filha.'

She stands up in the tub and stretches out her arms and he wraps her in a towel and lifts her out. She is giggling, as if at her own joke.

'She has to practise climbing out herself,' he can hear Petra calling from the kitchen.

He makes a face at Clara and she places a finger on her lips, grinning.

'And she dresses herself now, Armando. Don't help her.'

In her bedroom, his daughter stands on one foot and then the other to pull up her knickers and pushes her arms through her pyjama top correctly. Only her pyjama bottoms get twisted, so she starts again. She shows him the creams and medications she has for Fufu, who requires a much more complicated toilette than she.

'I just need to brush her hair,' delivered as if a harried single mother, which makes him laugh to himself.

'Shall I brush your hair?' he asks her. 'Would you like me to plait it?'

She is awe-struck, Fufu now neglected, while he tries to remember how his sister had shown him how to braid her hair. He does a not bad job of it.

'Do you like it?'

Clara's eyes are wide with appreciation.

'Thank you, Papa,' she says, so solemnly that his heart breaks.

Petra is similarly impressed, cooing over her braids as she serves them at the table. And then they sit, like a family, Fufu occupying the fourth chair, while they each, he and Petra, direct most of their sentences through Clara: 'Show Papa how well you can use your fork.' 'Mami worked very hard so you have to eat all your peas.' When the meal is over, Clara is allowed to scamper off and he stands up to clear the table. Petra lays a hand on his forearm.

'Why don't you stay the night, Armando?' Then laughs at his expression. 'This isn't a seduction,' she says. 'You can sleep on the sofa. I'm too tired to drive.'

'I'll get a tram.'

'You'll get beaten up.'

He laughs. 'I can take care of myself.'

'You don't have to be so macho. My dad is right, you know. It's dangerous. Why take the risk? I'll take you back in the morning. You can call Joachim to let him know.'

He can see that she is utterly sincere.

'And leave the washing up. I'll do it,' she says.

'You did all the cooking,' he says.

'But Clara will love you to put her to bed. I know she will.'

Joachim, on the phone, only reminds him that he is on security detail from eight in the morning. He has tucked his daughter into bed only a handful of times, and the significance of this invitation is not lost on Clara. Rather than the usual litany of questions, she says nothing of his surprise presence in her bedroom, which is cosy and warm, lit by the warm glow of the bedside lamp. In its midst, Clara is a bundle of huge eyes and soft skin.

'We have to make sure Fufu is warm enough,' she says officiously. The doll is wedged next to her under the covers. He kneels on the floor beside her.

'Come up, Papa.'

'Is there space, filha?'

She moves Fufu over by an inch.

'Will I break the bed?'

'Don't be silly, Papa. Come up.'

He climbs obediently onto her bed, feeling like a giant, the doll now squished between them. She smells of mint toothpaste and her cheeks are plump and soft.

'Shall I read you a story?'

'Can you tell me one?'

'Tell you a story?'

'From Mozambique?'

He racks his brains: he cannot remember a single Mozambican children's tale, but he can make one up.

'Era uma vez... he begins.

'What does that mean?'

'It's the same as 'es war einmal'...'

She nods.

'Era uma vez um menino e uma menina...'

He is thinking of himself and his sister, the one whom Clara resembles so strongly. When they were children and their father was in a Portuguese prison, they had one day decided to help their mother by cooking an evening meal of rice and matapa. This dish is a staple and, while delicious, uncomplicated. But he and his sister had agonised over how to boil the cassava leaves, how to crush the peanuts, whether to add shrimp, how much coconut milk would be used. Now he modifies the tale for added jeopardy and comedy, inventing an argument between his sister and him, which entails many mishaps with the recipe. His daughter's eyes are filled with wonder at this narrative of a simply cooked meal. She may have intuited that it is, at least partially, a vignette from her father's childhood.

'And then finally, hours later, the meal was served and everyone enjoyed,' he concludes, to his ears, on an anticlimactic note.

Clara says nothing, only purses her lips and gives him a small smile.

'Did you not enjoy it, filha?'

'I enjoyed it very much, Papa.'

She looks so serious and solemn, and he can see her mind whirring, as if she is memorising all the sentences he has used, and then she holds out her arms and he kisses her cheek.

'Boa noite, Papa.'

'Boa noite, filha.'

He leaves the door slightly ajar as she likes it, and re-enters the living room. Petra is wiping down the surfaces of the kitchenette. The dishes have been washed and cleared away.

'Would you mind taking this downstairs?'

She hands him a bag full of rubbish.

'Of course.'

There are communal bins in the quadrangle, which all the apartments overlook. Outside it is pitch dark, and he waits for his eyes to adjust. There is a shadowy figure by one of the bins, and as he approaches, the figure jumps.

'Who is it?'

'Sorry,' he says. 'I didn't mean to startle you.'

The figure relaxes and he can make out now that it is an old man, short and stout. He is peering at him, and then he says, 'You are Frau Micke's friend?'

'Yes.'

'Clara's father?'

'Yes, sorry. I was just taking out the rubbish.'

'It's so dark, I can barely see anything,' the man complains. 'I've called five times about these lights, but nobody gives a damn.'

'Mm.'

'Nobody seems to be at work.'

'Yes.'

'Where do you work?'

'In a factory in Lütten Klein.'

'Ah, I see.'

He can make out that the man is eyeing him curiously.

'So you're not at work either?' The man's teeth flash in a smile.

He laughs. 'It's slowed down a lot.'

'Yes, yes, I can imagine.' Then, 'Well, there have been stories, you know, about some bad behaviour towards your people. You need to take care.'

Your people. But the sentiment is generous and concerned and so he says, 'Yes, thank you. I will.'

The man shuffles off, and he hurls the rubbish bag into the bin. Everyone seems to be determined to remind him of the attacks. He is not scared, not at all, but he makes sure that there is no one behind him before he opens the door to the entrance hallway. He steps onto the square of stained blue carpet, before climbing the short flight of stairs. He lets himself into the flat, placing the keys on the small table next to the door. Petra is now sitting on the sofa, a glass of wine in her hand and another set on the coffee table. He sits down on the other end of the sofa.

'Prost.'

'Prost.'

They each take a sip from their glasses.

'It's dark downstairs, the lights aren't working,' he says.

'I know, it's hopeless. Everyone is down in Berlin, chipping off pieces of the Wall to take away in a wheelbarrow and sell on the stock market.'

'Have you phoned up to complain?'

'No.'

'Well, you should, Petra.'

'One would think you were worried about me, Armando.'

'You don't need to be so macho,' he says, and she bursts out laughing.

'But seriously. Isn't there anyone at the newspaper who has a contact at the council?'

'Bruno might,' she says. 'I'll ask him.'

'Okay.'

She appears amused by his concern, and she is also watching his reaction. She wants to show him that she does not need him. And she doesn't need him. She has arranged her life independently of him, and of any other man: even this mention of Bruno is unusual. He catches her eye and they smile, and as always, he thinks what a charming smile she has. But then she balances the glass on her knee.

'So how is Lolita?' Her tone is brisk.

He takes another mouthful of wine. 'Fine, I think.'

'You only think? You haven't seen her?'

'I saw her yesterday,' he says.

'She's very pretty.'

He says nothing, only braces himself.

'How old is she?'

'Twenty-three.'

'Mm,' she sips her wine. 'She looks younger.'

Again, he says nothing.

'Or maybe she just makes me feel really old.'

She might be fishing for a response, but he finds that he wants to give her one.

'You're not old, Petra.'

'Do you remember my age, Armando?' Her voice is a tease, but there is an underlying edge and he shifts on the sofa.

'Thirty-four next month.'

She toasts him silently with her glass.

'They didn't like it, everyone, that you were younger than me.'

'I remember.'

'There were many things they didn't like.'

'I remember that too.'

'Hmph.' She curls her legs against the arm of the sofa, then looks across at him, her expression soft. 'I'm happy for you, you know. I can see that she's special.'

'Petra…'

'Don't tell me that I'm special too…' she is grinning, and he cannot bear it.

'You are,' he says. 'You've taught me a lot. And you're terrific at your job. You're a fantastic role model for Clara.'

She toasts him again, and he sees, to his surprise, that there are tears in her eyes. But then she repeats his words, 'You've taught me a lot. Armando, when will you learn that you've taught yourself everything you know? When will you believe in yourself?'

He is silenced, uncertain whether she is paying him a compliment or delivering a criticism. Before he can respond, she gets to her feet. 'I'm taking my glass to my room. Did you bring a book?'

He shakes his head.

'Help yourself to anything,' she says. 'I'll wake you up and we can have breakfast together before I take you back.'

He gets to his feet as well.

'Thank you, Petra.'

'It's for Clara, you know. She adores you.'

'Thank you.'

He hesitates, then bends down and kisses her cheek, which she allows him to do, standing stiff and straight.

'Good night.'

'Good night.'

He finds a detective novel on her shelf which he dips into, sitting on the sofa, while Petra traipses from kitchenette to bathroom and, now in a towelling robe, back to her bedroom. She closes the door. He gets up from the sofa then and tiptoes to Clara's door. He can hear her breathing and he peers into the room. The bedside light glows dimly. She is sleeping on her stomach, like he tends to, but she has her thumb in her mouth. He tiptoes back to the sofa and stretches out. It is lumpy, but comfortable enough.

Now he thinks, as he always does in times of rest, and always with that flutter of anxiety, of Lolita. She is on shift this evening, but he is due to see her again in a couple of days. He has not yet managed to think of a solution to the perennial problem of where they can meet, and he knows that, showing a singular lack of initiative, he is hoping that Joachim might wave a wand. They have declared their love for each other, and he is certain they both believe that it is love. He knows that she does not pine for Theo, and that she has reconciled herself to this truism. Petra no longer presents a forbidding presence. Look where he is tonight: sleeping on her sofa! No, now the obstacles facing them, for it appears that theirs is not a course of true love which will run freely, are grand decisions over borders and nations: who can stay and who cannot.

The work at the factory has in effect halted, and the men are now in limbo, pending discussions on which variables will allow them to stay if they wish, and which will propel them home. Already they have had a meeting with a man from the Party, who has been charged with negotiations about their future. Would they have to serve in the army on their arrival in their homeland? Unlikely: they would simply be asked to use their skills to re-build their country when the war ends. When will it end? It is not possible to give a date. When will they receive all the money that has been transferred to the government in Maputo, but which represents a significant portion of their salary? The papers only need to be processed once they are back. What if one wishes to stay in the DDR? The DDR may not exist in a few months; the talk is of the two nations being unified again as one Germany. What if one wishes to stay in this new, unified Germany? A legitimate reason to remain must be presented and each situation will be considered on a case-by-case basis. What constitutes a legitimate reason? The only option that has been discussed is marriage to a German. If one stayed, would the salary transferred to the government in Maputo be paid in Deutschmarks instead? No, the salary will only be reimbursed on return to Mozambique.

Most of the men have saved enough to buy a home and equip it with modern electrical equipment and furniture, and the prospect of a homecoming is growing in appeal in contrast to their current lot, semi-imprisoned in a cold, damp, dank factory near an unfriendly village. He cannot imagine actually leaving, descending from an aeroplane onto the ravaged tarmac of the airport in Maputo, to – what? – resume the life he was always supposed to have? Few men, as well, and none of Joachim's, have the ties to the DDR that he has: a child, his name on Clara's birth certificate, and Petra's growing acknowledgement of his status as father. But there is no marriage certificate, no wedding on the horizon. If he were to marry Petra – if she would even assent – then he would gain Clara and lose Lolita.

He will admit that he can contemplate a life spent with Petra. He likes her, he admires her, they both love Clara. They shared a chemistry once. But – and this is the crucial point – if he opens his mind a fraction, if he allows Lolita Devi to seep into his thoughts, he cannot consider any life other than one with her.

He turns over on the sofa, tries to find a comfortable position. Where does he picture them, making a home, living the mundane, ordinary life of a couple, where Lolita is stepmother to his Clara? He is not a man without imagination, but it is both disturbing and disappointing that the only place where he can picture them is sitting around the dining table not long vacated, in this soulless new town, in Petra's apartment.

*

This image stays with him over the next few days, unsettling, disconcerting. Lolita is due to depart in days for her father's wedding, and he cannot stomach the thought of being separated from her. She knows of the attacks, the hostility, he has told her of the rapidly reducing options available to him. Petra is uncharacteristically silent on the matter. She has been in charge until now: now she appears to be forcing him to take charge of his own life.

He is becoming more and more unpopular with the men, forever swapping his place on the rota at short notice, and always for a reason that most resent: in order to spend an afternoon or a night with Lolita. He knows they will be discussing their assignations in the crudest terms, he has been questioned by a drunken Paulo for details of their lovemaking, but he does not care. Now that he has tasted what it is like – for Lolita to phone him in the morning and to be able to have her in his arms within hours – he cannot revert to the days of old, that prehistoric period, when they snatched moments together, without touching.

So when she calls in the morning to let him know of her two-day break, and to suggest he meets her later in the afternoon, he sets the wheels in motion. The thought that he could spend the night with her immediately make his legs feel like jelly. He could tag on a morning and see if Petra would let him take Clara out of kindergarten for a few hours and be back at the factory to take on some back-to-back security details. He spends an hour pleading with one compatriot and another, accepting the bruising comments, the crass commentary, wheedling and bargaining and bartering without shame, until he has secured eighteen hours absence from the factory. Next is to present this to Joachim, who will need to fill in scandalous amounts of paperwork, now that the men's movements are so monitored. His departure from the grounds is also not desirable, given the tide of unpleasantness which laps at the shores of the factory gates. Every excursion that Armando makes, Joachim has told him, not only raises the risks he faces for himself, but the risks all the men face.

The other day, Joachim had shared with him what he in turn had heard from an acquaintance: of the chaotic pardon given to political prisoners the previous month, a last-ditch attempt by SED and its Ministry for State Security to assuage the increasingly raucous and forceful demands for change. It is not common knowledge – not yet at least, and certainly Petra has made no mention – but in their haste, the prison officials have discharged several inmates with known histories of violence, hardened criminals, who are now dispersed among the general population, who may even be crossing borders to escape re-detention. The blanket amnesty is now acknowledged, privately, as being rushed and clumsy, a salvo by the State for the years when it subjected the nation to scrutiny and privation. This news only adds to a prevailing unease, even dread, alongside what also prevails: a real sense of optimism and hope. Confusing, unsettling times, and Joachim reminds him of all this again, as he fills in the paperwork himself, as a token of gratitude. But the warnings fall on deaf ears. All these intrigues have no bearing on what is most central to his days: Lolita and how she has captivated him.

Finally, he can leave the factory gates, to walk down the road to the village, from where he will take a tram. Risk, risk, risk, at every corner, but he is confident in his ability to defend himself. He ensures that he remains alert, not allowing himself to indulge in pre-dreams of the evening that lies ahead with Lolita, and it is for this reason, just before he arrives at the village, that he notices, tucked down an alley as if abandoned, the blue Trabant.

It has been a few weeks now since the man stopped following him. By now he has received an official dismissal, for the Stasi face an inquiry into their actions, and there is talk that all the surveillance documentation on DDR citizens will become publicly accessible. But it is definitely the same car. He looks around, but there is no one in sight. Did the man always live here, nearby? Or perhaps he cannot resist what has become a fixation, to keep watch even when ordered not to.

The blue Trabant, relegated to the past along with everything else that has fast become ancient history. This man, who had caused him, Armando, so much fear. It's Tommy, isn't it? He feels a sudden thirst to seek revenge, to deface the car, so that when the man comes back to his vehicle, he will know. What to do? Let down the tyres, scratch the already scruffy paintwork, urinate on the bonnet? He pulls his gloves out from the pockets of his jacket and puts them on, then looks around for a brick or a stone and finds a rock big enough to prop open a gate. There is no one around, no one to witness this act of vandalism, but the man will know. He takes position at the side of the car.

But he finds he cannot summon the anger he believed he would easily resurrect. He tries to relive the anguish: he could have lost Clara! He might not have seen her for years! His own daughter would have forgotten him! While he can list his fears, he cannot evoke the despair and the rage that had felt so entrenched, so consuming. Instead, he feels ridiculous to be exhuming something that has died. Things have moved on. He lets go of the rock and it falls to the ground. He takes a step away. He should be proud that he has reached a state of such forgiveness, but he has a sudden overwhelming feeling that if Petra was here, she would remonstrate with him. She has never used the words, but he knows what she thinks – that he behaves as if a serf, that he is servile – and this thought finally allows him to feel some anger: at her, at this crazy country. He picks up the rock again and smashes it into the windscreen.

It breaks through the glass and falls into the interior of the car, and a series of shockwaves audibly ripple out from the central crater in near-perfect symmetry, like a spider's web. He looks around for another stone. Should he drag it down the bonnet of the car? Scrawl a message? But he finds that his legs are carrying him away, away from the sight of the damaged car, and that his heart is pounding and continues to pound for many minutes, even after he has climbed into the tram and sat down and it is trundling away, removing him from the scene of the crime. He feels sick, his forehead is damp and his hand hurts. He pulls off his glove but sees no cut. He regrets it now. Yes, the man will know it was him, and their reversal of fortunes might be now well understood. But it was strangely unsatisfying, and he feels that it was somehow cowardly. What malign spirit led him to act in that way? He should have stayed true to himself, even if that is a self for whom Petra has little admiration. It is an unfortunate, unpleasant start to his journey to see Lolita, and he has the same sense of foreboding he had that evening when Petra had seen them together on the street: of the day not quite having finished, not quite having had its say.

Yet his spirits lift when she comes out of the residence and crosses the street at a clip, pitches herself into his arms. He laughs, kissing her mouth, his heart thudding. As he holds her to him, he catches the scent of her shampoo.

'Did you wash your hair? You should have let me do that.'

'It's nearly full now,' she says, following his thoughts. 'The residence. We'll have to be as discreet as possible.'

'Did you have a nap?'

'Yes,' she kisses him back. 'Are you hungry?'

'Of course.'

'Potatoes with potatoes at the humanities faculty?'

'Sounds divine.'

She laughs, squeezing his hand and he winces involuntarily.

'What happened?'

'I was mending a machine...'

She removes his glove, and he can see the makings of a bruise developing in his palm. He should tell her about the blue Trabant and his revenge, but he cannot be certain that she will not think badly of him, so he says nothing. She has his hand resting on both of hers and is pressing her thumbs tentatively into his flesh in a series of concentric circles.

'It looks okay...'

'Do all your patients fall in love with you?'

She laughs, releases his hand and slips her arm into his as they start walking. Yet he feels he has been given only a temporary reprieve from his lie, and this lingers as they choose their items from the counter at the canteen and carry their trays to the table. Lolita appears unaware of his strange mood: she looks happy and lovely. She has told him that she feels suited now as never before for the profession. In truth, he had not known of her doubts, so convinced is he of her abilities. He feels the same way about Petra. If he has a type when it comes to women, it must be for those who are far more accomplished than he. As he cuts the grey piece of meat, which lies forlornly next to the mound of potatoes, he is filled with a burning desire that Clara will be able to pursue whatever career she wishes for.

'You're not listening to me,' Lolita says.

He brings himself back. 'Sorry. What were you saying?'

'Nothing terribly interesting. Just that I'm so tired of potatoes.' She smiles. 'I still remember that delicious meal you made.'

'I only remember what happened afterwards,' he says.

She blushes and laughs. 'I remember that too.'

'Mm.' He holds her eyes.

'Have you seen Clara this week?'

He is momentarily taken aback. She is picking at some sauerkraut with her fork.

'I have. Actually,' he dabs at his mouth with a napkin, and then regrets the action, which looks shifty, like he is trying to pass a lie-detector test. 'I stayed over with Petra on Tuesday. I put Clara to bed.'

She smiles back but her eyes have darkened as well.

'That's lovely. Clara must have been so pleased.' Her voice is bright.

'I think she was.'

And then silence falls, and she lowers her eyes and her fork stabs repeatedly at the items on her plate.

'Do you mind that I stayed over?' he asks, quietly.

'If I did, that would make me a pretty ungenerous person,' she replies.

'Which you are not.'

'Why the sudden personality change in Petra?'

He steels himself. She is owed a few moments to digest the information.

'I think it's about Clara, actually.'

'I think it's about me, actually.'

He smiles at her mocking tone, even though he can see there is little humour behind it.

'It might be.'

'Yes, it might be.'

'But,' he says, 'you have nothing to worry about.'

Now she lays down her cutlery and stares at him.

'Of course I have to worry, Armando,' she says, and her tone is low and even. 'Because Petra is your ticket to staying here, not me.'

Nothing is new, nothing is a surprise, nothing is a revelation. Only that, for the first time, it has been articulated, out loud, and by Lolita, the one person whom he did not wish to hear it from. She has not shouted at him, as Petra might have, she has not railed at him that he accepts things too easily, that he is passive, unimaginative. Maybe he deserves to be working in a factory, perhaps even if his country had not been ravaged by war he would have just drifted about, working as much as is needed to ensure good clothes and women and beer. How long can he hide behind the epithet of a 'war-torn' country to explain why he has not been driven enough to mould his own future?

'I'll find a way,' he says, 'to have everything. You, Clara, and fewer potatoes.'

He grins, but she doesn't smile back and her lower lip trembles. He reaches across to take her hand.

'I mean it.'

He is sincere, he can feel the sincerity oozing from his pores, and he means every word he has said. But at the same time, it is on the tip of his tongue to say: I'll speak to Joachim, and then, I'll speak to Petra. He stops himself in time. It's up to him, alone, to find the right way.

After they finish eating, after they have placed the tray in the clean-up area, she slips her hand into his and he presses her close to him.

'How's your hand?' she asks.

'Much better. Fine.'

They stroll along the streets, and he hopes to feel the tension leave her. Looking across at her, she appears tranquil, or perhaps philosophical, and then she catches his eyes and asks: 'What did you do all those weeks when you weren't coming to Sonderbar? What did you do on your Saturday evenings?'

The lost epoch, he has liked to think of it as, bookended by their interrupted embrace on an insalubrious corner of this city, and their reunion weeks and weeks after, in Berlin.

'Not much,' he says. 'I read, played football with the others. Sometimes I went to the bar in the village. Why do you ask?'

'No particular reason. Just trying to fill in the gaps.'

He doesn't ask her to return the favour: he already knows enough and would prefer not to colour in the blank spaces. As well, he admits, he has thought very little, if at all, of that period. There has been no need: Theo vanquished, Lolita gained. He tightens his hold of her, half-ashamed by how he has framed this, even in the privacy of his own mind, and whether reading his thoughts or not, she smiles at him, and he hopes her mood is lightening.

Back in her bedroom, there is a suitcase he has not seen before on the floor next to her wardrobe. She notices his eyes on it, and she says, 'I've started packing whenever I get a spare moment.'

'It will be a nice change of weather for you.'

'Not at the wedding. It will be really cold during the nights, nearly as cold as here. But when I go and see Mummy yes, it will be really hot.'

And then she has flung herself on the bed next to him: her hands are twisting in his shirt, her face is buried in his neck and her body is heaving with sobs.

'Lolita.'

But she continues crying, for a very long time, the tears pour from her, drenching the collar of his shirt, her face is still buried in his neck. Finally, it subsides, so that he can push her gently away to see her face, swollen from the tears.

'Just give me some time,' he says. 'It's down to me to find a solution to everything and I will.'

He tucks her hair away from where it is plastered against her cheeks and kisses her mouth. He does not want what he has said to be a lie, but he feels the enormity of the task to make it a reality. Perhaps now is when he should share with her that he smashed a rock through a windscreen, as if to break with his previous inaction. But, once again, he remains silent.

He sees that she makes a conscious effort to pull herself back: she does not wish to spoil their evening. She says she needs to sort out some of her notes, and this appears to soothe her. He browses through her music collection, playing different songs on her small cassette player, and at times she hums along, looking lighter, happier. Then he scans through her textbooks while she uses the bathroom. It quietens in the hall, and so he takes a chance to pad down the hallway to have a shower, encountering only one distracted student on his way back to Lolita's room. She brushes her hair out and he watches her from the bed. Then she lies down next to him and he strokes her face, and her neck and her shoulders and this sends a thrill through him, but also a throb of unease. He does not wish to spend a night without making love to her, but at the same time there is something amiss, as if an object has not been slotted back into its right place.

'We don't have to do anything,' he whispers. 'We can just talk.'

'Don't you want to?

'Yes, I want to,' he lies.

She kisses him and rolls her body onto his and he feels all the nerve endings in his body come alive from her touch. She looks like a goddess above him, powerful, like a young woman with the world as her oyster: her black hair flowing like rivulets over her naked breasts, her nipples standing stiff and erect, her lovely collarbones and shoulders. He is mesmerised, but neither can he stay in the moment. He keeps slipping away, thinking back to their conversation, back even to the conversation a few days ago with Petra. She brings herself to climax, but her rhythm has been too slow, too sensuous for how he is feeling: he knows he will not follow on from her so easily. And because he does not want her to sense his distraction, because he does not want to explain, he grips her hips and thrusts himself inside her hard and fast and roughly enough so that he ejaculates. She falls to her side on the bed when he is finished, one leg draped across his stomach and kisses his neck – unperturbed, uncritical, unquestioning – which only makes him feel even more uneasy. He thinks she will want to talk now, but she simply turns slightly, and she is breathing regularly in minutes. He manages to remove the condom, and he arranges the bedclothes into less disarray, and then he watches her for some moments. She is trusting and trustful, and there is a strength in her, a resolve, which makes him want to be better than he is, to match her. All these things, he thinks, all this taken together is love.

Finally, he closes his eyes. He falls into a deep dream, of he and his sister preparing that dish of matapa, the story he had related to Clara, and he dreams of the fictitious argument, over who should pound the peanuts before adding them to the greens and the shrimps. His sister is berating him, but she is not speaking in

Portuguese. He realises she is speaking in German and then he realises it is Lolita's voice he can hear, and that the pounding of the peanuts is someone knocking on her bedroom door.

'Fraülein? Fraülein?'

It is the porter. She stares wide-eyed at him.

He scrambles for his trunks, and she pulls a t-shirt over her head. The knocking continues while she is wriggling into pyjama bottoms.

'One moment, please.'

He lies stock-still, hoping to be in shadow and watches as she crosses to the door. She opens it a crack and a shaft of bright light falls into the room.

'Fraülein.'

The porter's voice is almost instantly overtaken by another: more familiar and yet less familiar, for he has never heard it sound so anguished.

'Lolita,' Joachim is saying. 'Something awful has happened to Petra.'

*

He is told that Petra's parents are both at the hospital. Joachim has been asked to bring Armando to the parents' home, where Jessica and her husband are with Clara. His daughter is confused, has been asking for Armando, is convinced that he was sleeping on the sofa. All this is told to him through a fog, not a silent fog, but a fog which has an accompanying soundtrack: of all things, an upbeat Mozambican marrabenta, which was popular in his teens.

Joachim's face is ashen, his black hair is standing up on its ends and under his coat his pyjama shirt is visible. His hands are gripping the steering wheel so tightly that his knuckles show white, but when he lets go of the wheel to help with the seat belt, his friend's hands are steadier than his own. Then Joachim starts the car, and circles around the park towards the southern end of the old town. He could have walked it in twenty minutes, but he is glad to be in the cocoon of the car, the cadences of the marrabenta enclosing them both, but offering no solace, only rising to a crescendo as he hears himself speak:

'Did Petra's parents call you?'

'Yes. To tell me the police were on their way. They came looking for you at the factory.'

'Why?'

'They thought it might have been you.'

He is silenced, imagining the scenario. They must have lost interest in him after questioning Joachim, and it was he who rang Petra's parents, who asked then for Armando.

'When did all this happen?' he asks.

'She was found at around ten o'clock last night. A neighbour called an ambulance.'

Last night. He looks at his watch, it is now two o'clock in the morning. Four hours. The Mickes had not thought to inform him immediately. He looks outside the window, at the shadowy shapes of empty buildings which are still standing, still there, unchanged. He has had time to think, in those awful minutes after the door closed on Lolita's bedroom door, and they were alone and he started packing his belongings and getting dressed. He has had time to arrange events in his head, stretching back to that day they found the body of the young man, Stefan Müller: a stranger, then and now. But he could not stop himself pulling that stranger out of the water at the expense of those he loved, setting off a chain reaction that he thought had ended.

'Is it them?'

'What?'

'Is it them?'

'Who?'

He tries to swallow but finds his throat is too dry.

'The Stasi.'

'No.'

He looks now at his friend, who is shaking his head vigorously, bewildered, eyes still on the road.

'No,' Joachim repeats. 'They're finished, Armando. They have been for months.'

'That man was still sending those letters.'

'He's deluded. He's a loon.'

'Exactly why it could be him.'

'No, Armando. It's very different. Sending anonymous notes and talking big. It's very different to what,' and now his friend bites his lip, hesitates, 'to what has happened to Petra.'

He remains silent, for Joachim does not know that earlier in the day – no, it was yesterday – he had thrown that rock and shattered something which appeared sturdy, robust, but which proved to be brittle as an eggshell. He was more inclined to walk away, but he had forced himself to act, to react. Petra.

'This is not your fault, Armando.'

He closes his eyes. Joachim's words echo what Lolita said to him before he left her, and because of this, he only feels that both, deep down, believe the opposite.

They arrive, but before he gets out of the car, Joachim stops him.

'Wait.' He reaches into the back seat and produces a bag. 'Tiago packed these for you.'

Tiago, his roommate. He has slept next to the man for five years, as long as he shared a room with his older brother. But he knows nothing, really, of Tiago: he has not wanted to, beyond the superficial. He has kept himself apart and now he feels himself apart.

'Be strong, Armando.' Joachim's voice is steady, and his hand is gripping his wrist. 'Call me in the morning.'

He cannot look at his friend, only nods, and somehow unpeels himself from the car seat, the extra bag pressed to his chest, puts one foot in front of the other and knocks softly on the door. It is opened immediately by Jessica, her eyes wild.

'Armando. Thank God. Listen, Mattias is inside. I'm going to the hospital.'

And she pushes past him, struggling with her coat. Mattias appears in the hallway, looking exhausted. 'Come in, Armando.'

He ushers him inside.

'Do you want some coffee?'

'Where is Clara?'

'In Petra's old room. Go and see her. I'll make us some coffee.'

The door is ajar, and the bedside lamp has been left on. His daughter looks tiny in the bigger bed, but is sleeping deeply, her thumb in her mouth, on her stomach, one arm placed protectively around Fufu. He walks back to the kitchen, where Mattias has set out two cups.

'Tell me what happened.'

'She went downstairs to take out the rubbish. The man must have been hanging around, because he entered the building with her. She was found when a neighbour noticed she had left the front door of the apartment swinging open. They went inside and found it empty, other than Clara in her bedroom.'

His stomach clenches.

'They found Petra in the entrance hallway on the ground floor.' Now Mattias blanches. 'She was unconscious, lying on the floor.'

He finds he has been pressing his nails into the palms of his hands, and that these are balled into fists.

'Tell me everything.'

'It was likely sexually motivated. She was naked from the waist down, but all her injuries are around her head and her face. They haven't mentioned anything else, at least not to me. That's all I know, Armando.'

'How is she?'

'They've sedated her. I don't know to be honest. Alice is beside herself, of course.'

'Did Clara see anything?'

'I don't think so. When we came to get her, she was still sleeping and she asked for you, that's all.'

He barely knows Mattias, but he is glad he is speaking to him, rather than Petra's parents.

'Can I see her?'

The man hesitates. 'I'm sure you can. But perhaps we should wait until the morning and figure out things with Clara first.'

'Yes.'

He leaves him then, his coffee untouched, and goes back to Petra's old bedroom. He fashions a bed out of some cushions on the floor next to the bed, and finds a blanket to throw over himself, positions himself so that when his daughter wakes up, she will see him. He cannot close his eyes, for fear that the images that are lurking in the periphery of his vision will parade themselves in monstrous technicolour. Petra lying cold, alone, on that sticky, dirty carpet, one flight of stairs down from the apartment. The apartment door swinging open with Clara tucked in her bed, oblivious, on her stomach. It suddenly overwhelms him. He makes a sound like a sob, like a child, and just makes it to the bathroom, where he retches over the toilet bowl, then hangs onto it as if it is a lifeboat.

When the nausea abates, he forces himself to get to his feet and washes his hands, splashes his face with water. He looks at himself in the mirror and sees that his eyes are red-rimmed from shock and fatigue, but that otherwise he is whole and untouched and smooth-faced. While Petra. He blocks his mouth with his fist. Naked from the waist down. A sob escapes. Most of the injuries. He presses his fist harder against his teeth.

Mama, where are you? I need you. He has never called to his mother in this way, and then he calls for his older brother, his sister, but no one speaks back to him. His mother thought he would become a man if he left her shelter: has he? He stands in front of the mirror but sees nothing until, finally, he can breathe regularly and, eventually, he leaves the bathroom. Mattias is fast asleep, snoring loudly on the sofa in the living room. He lies down again on the cushions on the floor, ashamed that he has a blanket to cover himself when Petra did not.

The porter, who looked shaken by the news, had left them and Joachim had waited downstairs in the car. He had silently pulled on his clothes, finding it hard to button up his jeans. Lolita had watched him, her hand at her throat, only once darting to the sink in the corner and back to hand over his toothbrush. He had scooped the belongings he had dumped on her desk into his bag, and then she had brought him his shoes, placed them on the floor in front of him, as if in obeisance and he remembers he had winced at that thought.

'Thank you.'

'Armando. This isn't your fault. None of this is.'

She had sounded breathless and her voice was laden with concern, and love. He had not looked at her, fearing that if he did, he would not be able to leave the room to face the awfulness that lay ahead.

'I'll try and find out as much as I can myself,' she said.

'Thank you.'

'Armando. Wait. I want to give you something.'

She had opened her wardrobe and had extracted the exquisite, mirrored shawl she had worn on the beach that day, that other life, only months ago.

'To give you strength,' she said. 'To know I'm with you.'

He had taken it, the soft material flowing like water over his wrists, the mirrors twinkling benignly at him like stars, and somehow it had ended up in his bag. Before he left the room, he remembers he kissed her, quickly, and then miraculously his feet had found the treads of the stairs.

It was a gesture of love to give him her shawl as an amulet: it was naïve, it was doomed. He plunges his hand now into his bag and yes, it is there, but he will not take it out. He may never take it out. How can he allow it to billow in the air, like a flag staking territory, proclaiming her existence? How can he press it to his face, to smell her, while Petra lies alone? How can he hope to use it for warmth, when Petra's father could walk in on him, to see him wrapped in another woman's shawl? He scans the room to settle his eyes on something, an object, a photo, something that will give him some respite, a chance to calm, but his eyes keep tracking back to his bag, holding Lolita's shawl. Back and forth, back and forth, and now, when he would appreciate a soundscape – music, the sound of waves, anything – it is total silence in his head. He can't even hear Clara's breathing.

He thinks he will never sleep, but he dips in and out of lurid, nonsensical dreams, to feel Clara patting his cheek. She has joined him on the cushions, and when he opens his eyes, she asks him if he has taken the rubbish downstairs. An early morning light is seeping through the curtains. He shakes his head and presses her palm to his lips. Mami is ill and she is in hospital, he tells her.

'Is Lolita looking after her?'

'Yes,' he replies without thinking, then hopes his daughter does not relay this to Petra's family. Any mention now of Lolita is anathema.

Just before eight in the morning, Jessica returns with her father: Petra's mother is refusing to leave her daughter's side. That is when he asks, 'May I go and see her?' It appears, however, that his duty is to look after Clara, which makes sense, but which leaves him feeling neutered, emasculated. Mattias leaves and Jessica collapses on the sofa, while Petra's father shuffles around bleary-eyed. Neither appear able to withstand an interrogation from him, and Clara is now circulating, with ears pricked up and wide inquisitive eyes.

He takes Clara out with her bike, which will allow Jessica and Richard Micke to sleep, and now there are no misgivings, no mutterings about his safety. Now even worse has happened and he no longer merits any concern. He walks along the street, a dark, tight knot in his stomach, almost willing someone to make a move on him, craving an excuse to explode in retaliation, although he has a real fear that he would be unable to exercise any control. He would not want his daughter to bear witness to the ugliness inside him. He takes Clara to a quiet street outside an empty warehouse, one of the few dilapidated buildings within a half-mile radius of the Micke's house. Here they have been practising with the bike. He adjusts the stabilisers on the bike but after a few attempts, Clara becomes listless: she is missing her mother. A day with a child, however, has its routines: an hour with the bike, another hour with a snack in the playground, back to the house and preparations for lunch. He cooks up a stew in the kitchen, trying to remember how Alice Micke has arranged everything so it can all be replaced exactly. The least he can do is maintain her orderliness and precision. Petra's father and Jessica emerge and the four of them share the meal, a motley crew, but like a family.

Most of the talk, and there is not much, is directed at Clara, and he feels sorry for his daughter, for being a channel for these adults, who have been connected for years, but who only now are recognising the full depth of this connection. After he clears the table and does the washing up, he knocks on Petra's parents' bedroom, where her father, moving heavily around the room, is preparing to return to the hospital. He lowers himself onto the pink and green coverlet on the bed, bearing the distinct hallmark of Alice Micke and her dainty tastes. A mother now keeping vigil over her comatose daughter. He watches as Petra's father collects some items from the dressing table, presumably for his wife.

Finally, he asks: 'What have the police said?'

Richard Micke does not stop his deliberate packing, but his shoulders visibly tense.

'They have a suspect. One of the prisoners released last month, a known offender who should never have been discharged.'

A wave of nausea, like that which overcame him last night, briefly resurfaces, but he can dampen it. He remembers how he had welcomed the news of the amnesty: it spelled the end of his fears that the Stasi would somehow engineer his expulsion from the country. What Richard Micke has revealed only confirms that this is no reprisal for that rock he threw through a windscreen. Yet he feels no exoneration. He has had time to assess his behaviour over the last few days, even months and years, from afar, and the verdict is not in his favour.

He did not press Petra that evening he stayed over: get the lights fixed, take care no one is behind you when you let yourself in, don't go downstairs alone in the dark. He should have chided her for her bravado, begged her to be cautious. But he said nothing. He could have tried to repair the lights himself, he does this all the time at the factory. But he did nothing. While knowing of Petra's fearlessness – and simply investigating the fire in Joachim's factory will have made her enemies – he never tried to ensure that she at least considered her own safety. He has done nothing for her, believing that he has nothing to offer. What kind of man is he?

'They didn't fix the lights,' he says, finally, 'near the bins. It was dark when I was last there.'

'Yes,' Richard Micke says.

'I told her to phone the council.'

'Yes.'

He might be waiting for Richard Micke to offer his forgiveness – this is not your fault, Armando – but Petra's father does not elaborate and, the packing complete, only sits down on the bed. This is when he should tell Richard Micke about the blue Trabant and the rock, even if it is, in the grand scheme, irrelevant. He should say it all out loud, because then it will transform into an admission, an anecdote, a memory. It will not then be this dark knot, which has now moved over the course of the day from his stomach to his chest, where he knows already it will reside forever – for he will never speak of it.

Instead, they sit side by side on the bed, in silence, two men, each with hands clasped between their knees, each consumed by monstrous images.

'Has she woken up yet?' he asks.

'No.' Her father sighs. 'But they expect her to come out of it today.' And then he closes his eyes in agony. 'Mein Kind.'

He wants to put his arm around Richard Micke, but he only sits next to the man, his skin frozen, until her father speaks: 'I know the police came to find you at the factory. I told them they were wasting their time if they thought it was you.'

He holds Richard Micke's eyes.

'I was with a friend,' he says. 'She came to Clara's party, Lolita.'

Her father nods, and his voice is gentle: 'Yes, I know. Joachim told us.'

Then Richard Micke leaves for the hospital, and as he sets Clara up at the kitchen table with her drawing pencils and the pastels, he feels a swoop in his chest: these are a present from Lolita.

The evening arrives and he runs Clara's bath: where has the time gone? He lies down with his daughter on the bed until she falls asleep, and then tidies up the detritus from the day and takes a shower in the family's bathroom, shaves at the sink, all acts that he feels embeds him more and more within the Micke family. He cleans after himself scrupulously, wiping the bathtub down, the sink, running the mop over the bathroom floor so that it is as sparkling as before. Petra's father returns alone. Alice is refusing to leave the hospital until her daughter regains consciousness, which has not yet happened, despite the doctor's predictions.

Her father looks exhausted, a reminder that he is seventy years old, more than ten years older than his wife, but he does his best to relate what little extra information they have gathered. The significant development, although neither gathers much comfort from it, is that a man has been detained, and the police are eager for Petra to formally identify her assailant. More news has trickled down of the scale and type of her injuries, indicating how hard she fought back: at this, Richard Micke's eyes well up with tears. The struggle had been intense, unbelievable that nobody heard anything. A survivor, he thinks. Petra is a survivor. Can I see her? he asks again. But only one visitor at a time is allowed, and Alice Micke will not relinquish her post.

He lies down again on his makeshift bed next to Clara, and stares into the dark. He will not diminish his given role with Clara, but there is once again a barrier placed between him and Petra. And can he blame her family? He has maintained a peripheral presence in their daughter's life. He has instead allowed himself to give his heart elsewhere. Lolita. He clenches his fist. He cannot think of her, and he needs to find a way to avoid thinking of her. But he finds he cannot erase the image of her face as he had left her bedroom, her hand at her throat, her eyes glittering. He could write her a note, he could find some paper and pen and start it now. But he does not move, only finds that he is composing sentences in his head, trying to arrange his thoughts, and these are mostly bitter. I'm not sure why the universe seems to be against us. You are my first love; I was not telling a lie. Even this, though a truth, and only voiced in his heart, feels appallingly disrespectful to Petra. He finds his jaw is clenched, and he knows he will grind his teeth in his sleep. Above him, Clara snuffles suddenly, and her thumb drops out of her mouth to lie on the pillow. He reaches up to adjust the blanket over her shoulder, and gently strokes her hair. His hand is large against her features, even though they seem to be magnified in her sleep, her eye sockets even rounder, her cheeks plumper, her lips fuller. Is Lolita looking after her? she had asked him, on hearing Mami was in hospital. In a way, and it is an odd thought, they share Lolita: she belongs to them both. There is something about her his daughter responds to – or is it simply an instinct for her father's emotions? Can Clara discern his capitulation to Lolita's allure, how happy he is around her? Now he is ashamed, for is he not – even in his subconscious – projecting himself and his daughter into a future which has been rewritten? He lowers himself onto his bed, mulling over his thoughts.

He wakes early and makes some porridge, which Petra's father eats, gratefully, before leaving the house for the hospital. He is beginning to think that Clara might be better off in kindergarten rather than spending another doleful day with him, but no one seems able to mention the kindergarten, metres away from Petra's apartment. The phone rings: Jessica, wondering how Clara is. Then she asks: and you Armando? He is touched by this show of concern. He needs a fresh pair of socks, something Tiago forgot to pack, but he does not mention this to Petra's sister. He has enough money in his wallet to buy these, and Clara might even enjoy the shopping trip. Today is, fortuitously, market day, and the town is bustling despite the icy wind. They loiter, he and Clara, long after the socks have been bought, alongside a strange plaster-of-Paris sculpture for Clara, while he scours the crowds. But there is no sign of her.

On the way back home, Clara asks for her mother in a small voice, and he explains that she is still in hospital.

'Can I make her a get-well card, Papa?'

She has been well-schooled in the kindergarten – why had he not thought of it himself?

'That's an excellent idea, filha. You can do that after lunch.'

Clara's eyes light up. 'Can we visit Mami to give her the card?' she asks.

'We'll see.' His stomach contracts again. 'She may be too tired for visitors.' He glances at his watch. 'Time for lunch.'

Suddenly he is ferrying his daughter around like an ordinary parent, years into fatherhood, years into once a week for a few hours, always on a Saturday. While Clara is making a card – industrious, determined – he goes to the bedroom they have been using. He knows that it has been redecorated since Petra left home, but he looks around, as if paying homage to her. He opens the wardrobe and lets his fingers sift through the dresses and the blouses – none he recognises, all relics from her adolescence – then closes the door. The bookcase holds many of the texts she studied on her degree. On top lies an unopened package, and when he unpeels the seal and peers inside, he sees that it contains the photographs from Clara's birthday party in October, fresh from the developers.

He sits on the bed and goes through them: the puppeteer, the children on the grass, the photo of him and Petra – this he gazes at for some time – the cake. And then: the photo of Lolita and Theo, taken soon after their arrival. Lolita is clutching the present she brought for Clara, Theo is clutching Lolita.

He stares at the photograph. He could have left it there. He was jealous, but he may have recovered. The photograph shows that the boy is in love with her and would do anything for her. But Lolita? There is a sadness in her eyes, and she is not looking directly at the photographer, Jessica, but slightly off-camera, to where he was standing. He re-seals the envelope, keeping hold of the photograph of Lolita and Theo, and stows the picture at the bottom of his bag, under the shawl. Then he sits at the table with Clara and when she finishes her picture, he writes a message that she dictates to Petra, after which she uses a bright orange marker to carefully form the five letters of her name.

'Is it nice, Papa? Will Mami like it?'

He kisses his daughter's head.

'She will love it.'

Now his daughter asks in that same small voice as earlier: 'Is Lolita looking after her?'

His chest tightens.

'Everyone in the hospital is looking after Mami very well, filha.'

Later that night, long after Clara has gone to bed, Alice Micke makes an appearance, finally, white-faced with exhaustion, but with a bright light in her eyes, for there is good news. Petra had regained consciousness earlier in the day and the family had been able to talk with her. This is an excellent development, for the doctors have taken it as a sign that Petra is past the worst and could make a full recovery.

He waits for Richard Micke to settle his wife, before he tells him: 'I'm going to the hospital. I need to see her. I'll be back at six in the morning, I'm sure Clara won't wake up before then.'

It is after ten o'clock at night, a full forty-eight hours since Petra was found.

'But if Clara—'

'I'll be back at six in the morning,' he says. 'I promise.'

He is on the verge of saying, I won't let you down, but stops in time. Petra's father nods his assent, weakly, and he repeats to Richard Micke: 'I promise.'

He makes a final check on Clara, ensures that Fufu is tucked securely under the covers, then leaves the house. He stops at a bar on the next street and asks if he can make a call. Joachim answers after a couple of rings, as if he has been waiting by the phone.

'Armando.' His voice is full of relief.

'I'm sorry I haven't called.'

'That's okay. How is she?'

'I'm on my way to the hospital now to see her. She's woken up, which is a good sign.' He stops, takes a breath. 'Have you talked to Lolita?'

'Yes. She'll be at the hospital now. She's working tonight, on the maternity ward.'

'Okay. Thanks.'

'Armando?'

'Yes?'

'She's leaving early tomorrow. For her father's wedding.'

For some reason, this makes him look at his watch, as if it would show the days rather than the hours.

'Has she changed the dates?' he asks.

Joachim hesitates.

'Yes. She's brought it forward. They let her do it, the airlines and the hospital.'

'Did she tell you why?'

'She thought that she should give you some space and she felt like she could do that better if she were away.'

By the way he is speaking, he can tell that Joachim is repeating what Lolita has said, nearly verbatim.

'Have you seen her?'

'We had dinner together. She called me.'

He looks again at his watch. It is a few minutes before midnight. Lolita might have met Joachim four or six hours earlier, before going on shift. He finds it hard to believe that all of this has been happening while he was ferrying Clara around, while Petra has been lying in the bed. Petra.

'How will she get to the airport?'

'She said that there is an Indian man who will give her a lift.'

The famous Banaji, whom he has never met.

'Armando?'

The sound of Joachim's voice is intensely consoling, but his friend can do nothing for him.

'Armando?'

'Yes?'

'Whatever you decide will be the right decision. I want you to believe that.'

He hangs up and leaves the bar.

The streets are dark, and quiet. This will be when he sees the blue Trabant again, when the man in the tracksuit top with the yellow stripes blocks his path and places a palm against his chest. I saw you, I saw what you did to my car. Or perhaps this is when the ghost will appear, the ghost of the dead boy, larger than he was in real life, with brighter blue eyes: you should have left me. You started it all. The whole country has disintegrated because of you. He sees neither. But, more horrifyingly, a man turns down a side street and he is convinced that it is his older brother, José, sent here to convince him that he should return to his homeland, cut ties with all the sorry people he has become embroiled with. He runs down the alley way, the man scurries ahead: a black man, in this city. José, he calls but the man does not stop. José! Suddenly the man whirls around, fists raised. He sees a young man, decades younger than José, with light brown hair under a black woollen cap and terrified grey eyes. Sorry, my mistake, he mumbles, and the boy hurtles off, zigzagging as if under sniper fire.

He breathes in and out, glances at his watch: it is one o'clock already. Why is he capable of losing so much time, all the time? Clara will awake in five or six hours: he has much to do. He sprints now the rest of the way, back down the alley way, and then across the square and along the new road which leads directly to the hospital. He slows before he reaches the entrance so he can catch his breath, straightens his collar and takes the stairs to the third floor, where at the reception desk, positioned in front of the double doors that lead to the ward, a nurse is scribbling notes into a pad.

'Is Lolita Devi on her shift here?' he asks.

The nurse looks at him curiously.

'You are…?'

'A friend.'

'She's busy now.'

'Will she be having a break at any time?'

The nurse laughs. 'It depends on the three women currently in labour.'

'Could you please tell her that Armando Dos Santos is here? I'd really like to talk to her if she is free at any time. I know she's leaving tomorrow.'

'I'll tell her.'

But it is plain the nurse does not fully grasp the situation.

'I'm visiting a patient, Petra Micke, in Ward 12. Will you please tell Lolita she can find me there until about six in the morning?'

The nurse nods. 'I'll tell her.'

He leaves the ward and has gone down half the flight of stairs before he turns and runs back up.

The same nurse is still at her desk, and she raises her eyebrows.

'Sorry. I'll be in Ward 12 until five-thirty,' he says. 'I need to get back somewhere for six.'

The nurse nods, her eyes twinkling with amusement. 'I'll tell her.'

'Thank you.'

Again, he leaves, not without glancing around. Behind the double doors, somewhere, there will be rooms and beds. He never visited Petra here after she delivered Clara; she didn't want him to. The first time he saw Clara was at Petra's parents' house. How can this be? He has just walked into a hospital and demanded to see Lolita and is now on the way to see Petra. He has allowed himself to be tossed aside, listening to other people's rules, waiting to be given permission. Is it any surprise that Petra has thought so little of him? Has he ever fought for anything? If he didn't fight then, why should she believe that Clara is the most important person in the world for him?

It is pitch dark outside, the early hours, and he has not slept yet. But it is at these moments when things crystallise. The last hours have made him grow into someone he never thought he could be. But, similarly, never could he have imagined that he would be visiting the mother of his child, battered, scarred, and she may even have been raped: he cannot shake off the feeling that he has not been told everything. He approaches the nurse at the desk, steeled for a rebuff, already boiling with a rage at himself, so he fears he will roar if the woman so much as looks at him askance. But she looks up and smiles, sympathetically, reassuringly.

'Is it Armando? Herr Micke rang to say you would be coming.'

Then she looks at the clock, for if Petra's father had rung immediately on his leaving the house, then two hours have elapsed when the walk on foot should have taken only half an hour.

'Yes.'

'Mattias is with her. You heard that she woke up earlier?'

'Yes.'

'She spoke lucidly and clearly. Her signs are good, we are pleased to say.' Now the nurse lowers her voice, as if in respect. 'Do you want to talk to a doctor?'

'If that's possible. But please, can I see her?'

The nurse leads him away without a word, without any further delay, through a similar set of double doors as the maternity ward, and he is so grateful he could kiss her. She is small and blonde and moves quickly like a hare, but she pauses at a door at the end of a corridor.

'She is well,' she says, softly, 'but her injuries are upsetting to see.'

He walks into the dimly lit room, into a bank of screens and tubes, Mattias sleeping with his mouth open in the chair beside the bed, and then there is Petra. She has bandages on her scalp, which has been partially shaved. Her eyes are miraculously unscathed, so that she appears to be peacefully asleep, but then his gaze drops down to her mouth which is swollen, the lips split and tinged with some sticky brown liquid. He tries to focus on every patch of skin which has not been bruised or damaged, and with an effort, he can find Petra's clear, beautiful skin, the tones of which have always evoked for him, pleasantly, the colour of the sheets of paper he used in his school in Xai Xai. It is painful, to see her, but he forces himself to gaze at her, at every wound, at every cut, so that he can absorb the blow that inflicted it. God help her, God heal her. Mattias stirs and then jolts awake seeing Armando, and gestures that they should go outside to talk. He tears his eyes away from her, but notes as he is leaving that there is a bulkiness under the covers. More bandages?

In the corridor, he asks: 'Are her legs injured?'

Mattias rubs his eyes. 'Bruising and cuts yes, but nothing broken.'

'Were you here when she came to?'

'No.' Again he rubs eyes. 'Jessica was, though. First thing she saw was her mum and dad and Jessica, which is what Alice wanted. And she spoke, clearly, so the doctors are hopeful there is no brain damage.'

'Do you know what she said?'

'She asked after Clara. It was the first thing she said – where is Clara? And then after you.'

'What do you mean?'

'She asked – is Armando with Clara? And she looked relieved to hear that you were. That's what Jessica said. She said it made them all feel better, because Petra was obviously comforted by the fact that you were looking after Clara.'

'Did they tell her I would come and see her?

'I don't know. I don't know, Armando. I'm sure they did.'

'I'll stay with her,' he says. 'Get some rest, Mattias. I'll need to leave at half past five so that I'm back when Clara wakes up, but I'll stay with her.'

Mattias nods, touches him briefly on his shoulder. They stand eye to eye, they are near enough the same height, and they are closer in age than he and Petra: Mattias is only a year older than him. He has never really spoken with him, but he has never, either, felt any antipathy. There is instead a shared understanding, of both being men entangled with the Micke daughters.

'I could do with a coffee,' Mattias says. 'Or something.'

'I'll be here until half past five.'

'Thanks, Armando.'

He watches as Mattias walks down the corridor, exchanging some words with the nurse and then he opens the door to go back into the room.

Now they are alone, at last, and he leans over her, hearing her faint breathing and he kisses the top of her head, which feels slightly sticky and smells of antiseptic, but nothing else, not of death or what he imagines to be the odour of a dying body. Petra, Petra. He realises his cheeks are wet with tears. I'm so sorry. I want you to know that I believe, now. I believe in what I can do and what I can do for you. Petra, be well, be well.

There is not much of her that is not covered, and after he has gazed at her, without touching her, he slumps into the chair that Mattias has vacated. Immediately, he feels a wave of exhaustion roll over him, but he must not sleep. He completely understands why Alice Micke refused to budge from Petra's side. If Petra opens her eyes, more than anything in the world at this moment he wants her to see him, to hold his eyes, and then she will understand, he will not need to speak. But he is tired, two days spent with a young child, restless nights. He gets to his feet and stretches his arms as high as possible, feeling all the muscles in his back. He drops to the floor and counts through some press ups, stopping after each interval to make sure that Petra has not woken. She would laugh, at least, to see him performing these exercises: to keep me awake, he will say and laugh along with her. She doesn't wake up, not yet, but he feels reinvigorated.

He resumes his position in the chair, sleep dispelled, and leans forward, touches the tips of her fingers with his. He has known her for years, but how much does he know of her? Put himself in her shoes, and can he even begin to understand what she must think of him? He finds himself rolling back, rolling back to the young man who was called to the entrance of the warehouse, where Joachim introduced her: Petra Micke, she's writing a report for her newspaper. She had looked smart and intelligent and world-wise, and this had attracted him. The night they had tumbled into bed together, however, in her old apartment which she shared with a friend, she had been shy and awkward and it was he who was the more practised. He had known then that she was bowled over by him, he had enjoyed the attention. Young, selfish fool. Petra, Petra, he thinks and then she opens her eyes. He rubs his own, but he is not imagining it, her eyes are staring at him.

'Petra,' he says. 'Can you hear me?'

Her eyelids flutter, her lips open but she does not speak.

'Don't tire yourself,' he puts her hand in his. 'Can you hear me?'

She scratches her nails against his palm. He leans closer, so he can speak softly but she can still hear him, so that they can share this precious moment with no one else.

'I wanted to come earlier but this is the first chance I've got. Clara is fine,' he says. 'She's sleeping in your old room. I'll have to go back in a few hours so I am there when she wakes up.'

A small scratch, her eyes soften.

'She made you this.' He pulls out the card from the breast pocket of his shirt and holds it up so she can see it. Her eyes dart over it and he opens it to show the inscription. 'You see, how much she loves you. Because you are a wonderful mother and she is lucky to have you. And see also how she can already write her name. She gets her brains from you, Petra.'

Her eyes are glistening now.

'You are wonderful and so brave,' he says, 'so brave. My Petra.'

His feels the tiniest scratch of her nails again, but then her eyelids drop down. He blinks away the tears. His heart is hammering in his chest. He was here, she saw him, she heard him. The door opens behind him, and the nurse tiptoes in.

'Everything okay?'

'She opened her eyes. I spoke to her.'

His voice is still choked, and must reveal his joy and relief, everything, for she places a hand on his shoulder.

'Yes, she's doing very well.'

She inspects the monitors and scribbles some notes on the clipboard she is carrying, adjusts the covers at Petra's feet. He glances at his watch and wonders if he is reading it correctly: the hands show that it is twenty-five minutes past five.

As if reading his mind, the nurse says, 'Mattias is back. He said you need to go.'

'Thank you.' He hesitates. 'Did anyone else call for me?'

The nurse looks surprised. 'No. Were you expecting someone?'

'No. No, I wasn't. Thank you.'

And so the night is over. He has kept his vigil, he has flown over vast oceans and he has returned. Petra now seems to be sleeping more deeply than before, her face is beautifully at peace. He kisses the tips of her fingers and opens the door to Mattias.

If he sets off immediately, he will be back at the Mickes' house a few minutes after six o'clock in the morning. He leaves the ward and walks up the stairs, enters the reception of the maternity ward. There is no one on the desk. A plastic sign has been left on top: please ring the bell for assistance. But instead, he pushes against the double doors, which open into a corridor, to one side of which is an office with glass windows – and that is where they all are. It is quite a crowd, it must be the day shift and the night shift converging. Pinned to a corkboard on the far wall is a handwritten sign: Viel Glück, Lolita!

He stands to one side of the window so that he is out of sight but can watch the gathering. There is a transistor radio perched on a desk, tuned to a music station. There are bottles of lemonade on the tables, and there are cartons of pastries lying open. Most of the party are wearing nurses' uniforms and four are in scrubs: three men and Lolita. One of the men, a middle-aged man with a surgical mask tied around his head, pirate style, is dancing with her, a waltz, and she is laughing – and he remembers how he had danced with her that very first time he met her, at a similar party. For this is not a gathering that marks the end of a shift and the start of another, or even her absence for a few weeks: this is a despedida.

He gazes at her. Her hair is hanging loose down her back but is pinned away from her face. She has tucked a flower behind her ear, snipped from the bouquet lying on the table. She is in scrubs, but her white coat is pinned around her shoulder like a cape and she is wearing her stethoscope so that metal disc is not against her chest but at the base of her throat like a jewel. Medical humour. She is laughing and as during that last night they shared, she exudes an aura of power. He searches her face hungrily, and yes, it is possible that he sees a hint of tears in her eyes. The man she is dancing with has also noticed, for he kisses her cheek and says something to her, and then passes her on to one of the nurses who dances clumsily with her, before someone else pushes a plastic cup into her hand. There will be a toast, perhaps a song, to wish her the best, to wish her on her way – a farewell. But he will not wait for it.

He turns away and the marrabenta returns to him, at full volume, drowning out any external sound or thought. She had asked him then for the name of the music, and he had found it hard to speak, he remembers – he was so taken with her, so taken by the feel of her in his arms, taken as never before. Now he reaches the ground floor, leaves the hospital, and steps onto the street into the bitter cold air and the pale early morning light.

CLARA

25

It is not lost on him, the irony, that decades after he turned down the Stasi, in refusal to document the habits and peccadilloes of unsuspecting targets, he has now engaged in a similar pursuit. A pursuit of information, for information is power, as was always the case in the vanished DDR. The start of this project coincides with preparations for his second divorce, which is worse than the first, leaving him grievously wounded, underscoring his suspicion that he is unable to hold on to anyone. It sets him up for a furious delving into his youth, marked unforgettably with the dissolution of his homeland, and the broken connection with many of those who shared it with him. The information-gathering, in his mind, is a stepping-stone to the final decision he needs to make. Whether he will write about those two people who entered his life so briefly, but at the exact point when everything was disappearing, so that, conversely, they left an indelible mark on him.

He acknowledges his ego: he had occasionally wondered, as the more well-known and well-received and celebrated he became, with his novels translated into more than fifty languages and sold all over the world, if, one day, one of them would approach him. A message to his publishers. A like on Twitter. Even, for a time at least, he wondered whether they would appear at a literary festival or a book-reading. Would he recognise either of them? He is certain he would recognise Lolita. He has a sketch in his mind of how a girl like her – with her bone structure and build – would age. Armando, he is less certain of. He cannot fully recall his face. In his defence, he had not met the man many times: a handful of encounters. Each when his own mind and body were churning with emotion: a good reason to rebut the man, rather than commit him to memory. But neither has ever come forward.

Inspired by Tolstoy, he has written Childhood, then Boyhood, which have both been published and received to great acclaim, offering 'a rare glimpse behind the Curtain into the ordinary life of a loving family in what was then East Berlin,' and one that is 'told through the prism of a young boy's gaze'. The young boy being the now middle-aged author, denoted as the voice of a generation, of a lost nation. In every interview he has given about these books, he has insisted, taking his cue from Tolstoy, that these memoirs should be regarded as fictional. He has a sister not a brother; it was his mother who was the actor, not his father; his grandfather was indeed a hero of the French Résistance, but was a scientist, not a poet. What he has not admitted: how he has embraced the caprice of a creator and inflated some to a greater prominence in his life and consigned others to non-existence. In neither book does he make any mention of his cousins, which has offended each to an extraordinary degree, none either of the boy in the fourth year of elementary school who gave him a black eye. He has re-drawn his friendship with Hugo, so that he will arrive in his life much later, in the last of the trilogy –Youth. This last has already garnered much attention. For the book will straddle Die Wende, and 'will, refreshingly, offer a young Ossi's perspective of those last years of the DDR'.

A trawl of Facebook and Twitter and the harnessing of several Internet search engines reveal only that each has namesakes all over the world. Neither has left an obvious clue to their whereabouts on the virtual landscape. That is when he begins his grass-roots level detective work and, this pipeline quickly running dry, he recruits agents across far-flung continents. Since, it has been easier to find her, for she has left a trail of completed medical studies and then residencies in Bangalore, Nainital and Hyderabad. There are hints that she lives a reclusive life: no documented marriages nor divorces, no offspring. However, the last ten years have been harder to fill in, and he suspects the agent is eking out as many man-hours of investigation as possible. He is told that her name appears on some medical research papers as L. Devi-Jacob. He tries to read these papers online and can identify that they focus on the area of neo-natal complications. Yet, despite these publications, the agent produces no concrete, recent information, until eventually, satisfied with his booty, the findings come thick and fast. There is a clinic, in a remote town in the mountains of South India, and this clinic has a website whose banner displays a quotation from its founder, one Sushilla Jacob: *The health of a nation is measured by the health of its most vulnerable.* There is no mention of Lolita, but it is likely this is her place of work. And then, fittingly, on the thirtieth anniversary of when he first stepped across freely into the West, the agent discovers her name on the deeds of an old tea-planter's bungalow. Now he has both a street and a post box address in a hill town, Munnar.

He writes a letter which – impressively, considering how extinct these have become – is delivered and received and read, intact, because weeks later the request he has made within it is granted. He receives a ping on his telephone, like an arrow from his past, a WhatsApp message, and it is in German – *Hallo Theo, ich habe deinen Brief bekommen. Ich hoffe, es geht Ihnen gut, Lolita.* A WhatsApp message which was sent minutes before he read it, so she might still be holding the phone in her palm, and one which, breathtakingly, sports a profile picture of Lolita Devi, standing against the backdrop of a mountain: smiling and natural and unadorned, wearing a scoop-necked, light blue t-shirt, khaki cargo trousers, and walking boots. His sketches of her as middle-aged were in turns accurate and inaccurate. She remains slim, but her face is thinner than he had imagined. Her hair is blacker than he has expected, with only the occasional grey and it is shorter than he had imagined, arranged not in a chignon, but loose and wavy and grazing both her cheekbones and collarbones. She still has lovely collarbones. And she is instantly recognisable, her sudden appearance and this appearance itself sending a tsunami of emotions through him.

So he has her, so to speak, on his phone, but he has not gone the extra mile and called, only sent a message in response: *Schön, wieder in Kontakt zu sein.* He transfers the photo to a computer so he can blow it up, zoom in and out, inspect it forensically: no rings on her fingers and what looks like a dog's lead in one hand. Slender wrists. The hint of her nipples under the t-shirt, is she bra-less? At a cursory glance, an attractive woman in her late forties or fifties. Up close, her beauty is radiant. The photo is taken by someone who loves her, that is clear, and –from its perspective – someone much taller than her. Her father? The nipples, however, point to a lover. Or perhaps a close, not very tall friend, standing on an incline? He has pored over the photograph, and she might be poring over his, in which he is very tanned and lean, with hair fully grey and cut short, wearing a white t-shirt which accentuates his pecs. This is an image taken during a summer in the south of France: taken, unfortunately, by his second ex-wife, but which he now feels he cannot update, not when Lolita has already seen it. Each has the other's message and number. Each might be lurking, waiting for the other to take the plunge, and the onus is on him, having made the first overture. Maybe she has tired of waiting, she might have deleted his contact: it has been more than a year.

Finding him, unexpectedly, has proved much harder, and this may be what is deterring him from calling Lolita. For, if she has not been in touch with the man – and all indications point to her being in India, unmarried, since DDR days – then he would like, at least, to share with her any news he has procured of Armando Dos Santos. If and when he does talk with her. Yes, he admits that finding the man could be a way in with Lolita. It would be a reiteration of his previous role, one which over the passing of time he has articulated in his mind: a lubricant, a go-between, a spare wheel.

No easy road to finding an Armando Dos Santos or a Petra Micke, although the latter is mentioned in several documents and texts from the 1990s, following the court case and trial, all of which he remembers from real time. The newspaper cuttings are filled with outrage at the vicious attack she suffered, anger at the authorities for the errors made, and admiration for her courage in attending the trial as a witness to ensure her assailant's detention. Her career as a journalist of integrity and courage is also detailed, as well as the tragedy of its premature end, for she never returned to her calling. The Wessis – for most cuttings are from West German papers – had, and here he is unsure whether it is his natural disinclination to suspect the worst in them, pounced on the story as exemplary of a nation in disgrace: depraved, dysfunctional, crumbling and chaotic.

THE OTHERS

It is only after he changes tack and searches for the daughter that the floodgates of information open. He does not need to hire anyone to find her, for Clara Dos Santos Micke is an independent fashion designer with a presence on social media, a few mainstream media interviews under her belt and a website, all allowing him to learn about her and subsequently her father. *I was born in what was then East Germany, where my mother was a successful journalist,* she has written on her website. *Later, as a child, I lived in Mozambique, where my father is from. I completed my schooling in Lagos, Portugal, before studying art and design at Universität der Künst in Berlin.*

She goes on to discuss how her designs have been influenced by her many trips back to Africa: not only to Mozambique, but also Ethiopia and South Africa. From what he can gather, she has a modestly successful enterprise. Her proudest moment, she states, was when she won a competition for the honour of designing a dress for Graça Machel, widow of both Samora Machel and Nelson Mandela.

He learns more in those few sentences than he could have hoped, as well as an explanation for his lack of success in finding Armando: the man had not remained in Germany for long, after his marriage to Petra Micke. The family leave no trail until one Armando Dos Santos is listed as being the owner of a restaurant in Lagos, from 1998 until it was sold just a few months ago. His name is also found in an obituary in a German-language newsletter, circulated in the Algarve: *Armando Dos Santos spent thirteen years as a young man in the former DDR. He married the well-known journalist Petra Micke in 1990 during the reunification period and after some years spent in his homeland of Mozambique, the family settled in Lagos in 1996. Armando was the well-respected owner and chef of A sua casa de casa, a Lagos institution which was popular among locals and expats alike. He leaves behind his daughter Clara, his beloved wife having sadly passed away in 2010.*

But then, after all that activity, after all he has found, and probably because of it, what he likes to think of as his melancholy descends. The world closes itself against a pandemic just as he closes himself against his past, to take stock of his chequered present: six critically acclaimed, best-selling books, two failed marriages, zero children. But when it begins to open again, he slowly rediscovers a thirst for his quest, and he sends an email to Clara Dos Santos Micke, care of her website. He balks at contacting her through Twitter.

Dear Clara

I hope you don't mind me getting in touch with you like this out of the blue. I am very sorry to have learned that you have lost both your parents. I remember your father very well from DDR days. I also met your mother once, at your birthday party, when I think you turned four years old.

I am currently working on a book, based on that period of my life, and I would very much like to talk with you. We could organise a video-call, but after a year and more of not meeting people face-to-face, I would very much like to see you in person if you are willing. I'm not sure where you are based at the moment, but I am currently renting a villa in Italy, where I'm working on my book. If you feel comfortable with travelling, then we could meet here? I hope you will let me pay for any travelling expenses and accommodation. It would be the least I can do for taking up your time.

I looked you up and see that you are a fashion designer, which sounds incredibly creative and exciting! I look forward to hearing from you and hopefully talking to you. I have become rather obsessed with the past of late.

Best wishes

Theo Becker

Stresa

She does not curate her website regularly, or perhaps she deliberately avoids responding immediately, but he receives an email from her two weeks later, which he reads, most likely ten times.

Dear Herr Becker

I was astonished to learn that you knew my parents in the DDR. My father read all of your novels. I can say that he was a fan. But he never revealed that you and he were acquaintances. On receiving your email, I got in touch with his long-time friend, Joachim Bechtel, who you may know, and he told me that you and my father did indeed know each other. Forgive me for needing this confirmation, but I am really surprised that Papa never mentioned it.

Thank you for your condolences. My mother died many years ago, and I lost my father early last year. While it is still very raw, I am grateful to have had the most wonderful parents anyone could wish for. I suppose I am now trying to make sense of the rest of my life.

I am writing this from Berlin, where I have spent the last year. I would love to come and see you in Italy, but please don't worry about booking a room or my travelling expenses.

Just let me know which dates would suit you. I am pretty flexible.
Clara

So it is that he is waiting by the lake in Stresa, waiting to meet a woman from his past, but not Lolita Devi: rather, the little girl he met once, dressed in a fluffy dress and sucking her thumb, who will now be thirty-five years of age. He knows it is her as soon as he spots her: as in the photograph on her website, her hair is wrapped in a multi-coloured turban, which emphasises the regal lines of her face. She is dressed in flat-soled, silver sandals and a black, linen jumpsuit which she wears with casual elegance and which, as she draws up, he can see is fringed at the neckline and ankles with a vivid batik. She is very tall, possibly an inch or two taller than he, and statuesque, with wide shoulders and narrow hips, and dark brown eyes, and she slows down as he gets to his feet and stops a metre away from where he is standing.

'Herr Becker?' She has a husky, deep, attractive voice, and he remembers with a jolt her voice was similarly deep as a child.

'Theo, please,' he holds out his fist. 'I think this is how we do it nowadays.'

She smiles and they bump their knuckles against each other.

'Thank you so much for coming.'

'It's my pleasure.'

'I do hope you will change your mind and allow me to cover your expenses.'

She brushes his words away, with a swish of her many-ringed fingers.

'I have some of your novels for you to sign, if you wouldn't mind.'

'Yes, of course. I'd be happy to. Then you must let me at least pay for lunch.'

'That's very kind of you.'

Her German is fluent, but there is something about her accent which makes him ask:

'Are you happy to speak in German?'

'Do you speak Portuguese?' she asks, smiling.

He laughs. 'Not at all. I'm terrible at languages, actually. I can barely speak French, even though I was married to a Frenchwoman.'

She smiles again. She has large white teeth, which are framed by her full lips, and a poise about her which means that if he spied her on the street, he would assume she were a ballet dancer. But she is too tall to be a ballet dancer, and he sees that she has noticed that he has noticed her height. She will be accustomed to men sizing her up, and he hopes she does not misconstrue his gaze. She is eight years younger than his second wife, who was ten years younger than he, and this fact only underlines the enormity of seeing a grown woman in place of a little girl in bunches.

'Do you know Stresa?' he says, with a sweep of his arm, as if he owns the lake.

'No, I've never been.'

She looks at the water and he notes a pair of sunglasses tucked into her neckline: she must have taken them off in politeness and readiness to greet him. He suggests they walk the length of the promenade, so he can show her the funicular, after which they can eat a meal at one of the restaurants in the marina. He has reserved a table. Everything will be outdoors, no need to worry about facemasks and suchlike. She agrees and they begin to walk, exchanging their stories of the pandemic and lockdowns and social distancing, and he notices they walk slowly, as if each is uncertain of the other's natural pace. She comments on the beauty of the lake and the charming town on its shores.

'Yes, it is beautiful. I found I wanted to be here after my divorce went through. It's a good place to lick your wounds.'

She says nothing.

'But it's full of Germans at this time of the year,' he continues.

'It's something that has always happened to me. I believe I am doing something completely original, and then find myself surrounded by Germans.'

She laughs.

'Where we lived in Portugal,' she says, 'in Lagos, there is a sizeable community of Germans.'

'Wessis?'

'Probably, yes.' She crinkles her eyes at him. 'You remind me of how my mother always used to differentiate them from us Ossis.'

It is disarming that she calls herself an Ossi, and more so that she refers to her mother. He holds her eyes.

'I'm so sorry to hear she passed away such a long time ago. She was far too young.'

She gives him a small smile and they take a few more steps in silence. When she begins to speak, her voice is low.

'She never really recovered. You know what happened to her?' She waits for his nod. 'She never found her former strength, which I've only ever been told about. I never saw it. She was frail all through my childhood and young adulthood. So, in a way, even though it was awful, an awful time, we were already prepared.' She pauses. 'It was Papa's death that was completely unexpected.'

She looks at him.

'He had arrhythmia, which we never knew about. It was quick. At least he never suffered like Mami.'

He lays a hand on her forearm.

'I'm so sorry. I'm fortunate to still have my parents. Even though they are both in their eighties now, they are at least in decent health.'

They arrive at the restaurant, and he reminds the staff of his reservation in his halting, rehearsed phrases. But when she speaks to the waiter, it is in excellent Italian, and then much discussion ensues, not only of the dishes, but of the weather and the condition of the lake. No, she has not taken the boat to Switzerland. She has heard of Isola Bella and the white peacocks. The waiter ostentatiously ignores him: the old German with the vivacious young woman. He interrupts at one point to ask if she will have some wine and when she responds in the affirmative, the waiter still does not leave but, like a pest, asks: 'The signora speaks German?'

'Yes.'

'A truly international woman!'

They order the same dish – the linguine with zucchini and calamari, extra fresh chillies on hers – and he orders a bottle of white wine and sparkling water.

'You seem to have inherited your father's prowess as a linguist.'

It is too soon, this direct reference to his knowledge of her father, for her eyes darken and he kicks himself mentally. She might have thought that her parents held no secrets from her, yet he is sitting in front of her, the embodiment of one.

But then she smiles. 'Papa was very good at languages. He picked them up so easily and his customers loved him for it. Thank you for mentioning it.'

Her phone beeps, and she glances at him apologetically.

'Please,' he says, and looks at the lake, while she extracts her phone from her bag and begins to tap rapidly, using her thumbs, absorbed. Messages ricochet back and forth: it is an exchange of some complexity.

It is also an opportunity to take stock, to breathe in and out, to inspect her more, discreetly. He feels instantly drawn to her, not in a sexual way. His feelings are more paternal, and needy: partly because this meeting comes months after an enforced hermitage, partly because meeting her makes him all too aware of how many years have elapsed. They have not shared much yet, but he feels incredibly moved by her. She is an echo from the past, but more coloured in, more substantial, more like an incarnation of everything he lost.

She places her phone back in her bag.

'I'm sorry. I thought I would take advantage of coming down to see you to catch up with a friend in Milan, so we are just making some final arrangements.'

'How will you get to Milan?'

'I'll take the train.'

'I could organise a car to drive you?'

'Please don't worry. My friend said he'd meet me at the station.'

The wine arrives, the waiter opens the bottle and waits for his approval, fills Clara's glass and, then, insolently, hands him the bottle to pour his own. He notices she supresses a smile. They clink glasses and each take a sip. Now it is awkward, now he does not know where to begin.

'You don't have...' he clears his throat, and starts again, 'Do you have siblings?'

'No. No, I'm an only child.'

'And,' he hesitates, 'forgive me, but your mother's death was far too long ago, did your father ever...?'

She acknowledges his discretion with a brief smile.

'No, he never re-married. But he had a companion, Ana Maria. She used to work front-of-house in the restaurant. She's from Angola, so they had that in common as well.' She pauses. 'She's really nice, and she was very good to my father. She's taken his passing away very hard.'

He feels a sudden surge of jealousy of the man who manages to inspire so much love from others, a feeling that is so recognisable, so familiar, that it takes him back to the young man that he was. Will he forever feel envious of Armando, even after the man has died? A man who did not luxuriate in a trouble-free life, by any means. It is a small-minded, mean reaction, but somehow the emotion rejuvenates him, heightens his senses so that his vision becomes sharper, and he is aware now that he can smell the scent that Clara is wearing. He sits up straighter and flexes his shoulders.

'You mentioned that you are recently divorced?' she is saying, speaking as one would to someone much older, tentatively, seemingly unaware of the many years that have dropped away from his age.

'Yes, for the second time.'

He pours more wine into both their glasses.

'After the Wall fell,' he says, 'I went to university in Berlin and ended up marrying the first Wessi girl who didn't irritate me.'

She bursts out laughing and it is nice to see, how her shoulders shake. She is a personable, accomplished, charming young woman and again he feels a spark of jealousy for the man, for raising such a daughter. But Armando Dos Santos is no longer here to enjoy his child's company: it is he, Theo Becker, sitting opposite her on a hot day in front of a lake in Italy.

'Well, the marriage lasted a couple of years, which is a miracle.' He grins at her. 'I talk about my first wife, but we were just kids. It was like playing house. But I managed to get a good novel out of it.'

She continues watching him, no judgement in her eyes, but he is careful to put his wine glass down then. He has no wish to come across as a bitter old goat, even though, he reflects, that might be what he has grown into.

'My second wife, well, she's French and a playwright, you may know her. That was a real marriage and she put up with me for fifteen years, for which she deserves a medal.'

She asks: 'Do you have children?'

'No.'

He feels his cheeks growing warm.

'I have two ex-wives, but no children.'

Has he said that already? Their plates of food arrive and the waiter makes a fuss of Clara, insisting she taste a forkful to gauge the heat from the chillies, then pressing his hand to his chest when she pronounces it perfect.

'You've made a conquest there,' he says, as the waiter moves away.

She raises one eyebrow. 'Have I? I think he's just being friendly.'

Has he said the wrong thing, come across as smarmy? There is a short silence, and he determines to eat at least a quarter of his meal to steady his nerves before he renews his interrogation, but she is so compelling and the situation is so compelling, that he blurts out, after only a few mouthfuls: 'When did you live in Mozambique?'

'Soon after the war there ended.' She is tackling the long strands of pasta efficiently. 'We went late in 1992. I was seven, and I remember my mum was worried about what kind of schooling I would get there. But my dad was finding it hard to get regular work, and Mami wasn't working at all. Papa got in touch with a German NGO which was based in Maputo and he got a job with them as a logistician. We lived in Maputo for three years and I went to the Portuguese school, which was very fancy.'

She smiles slightly to soften her words.

'That must have been nice for you all?'

'It was. I could see even as a child that it was good for my father to be back home. I met all my extended family. And it's just this incredibly beautiful...' her eyes flash and widen as she speaks to accompany the description she is painting, 'landscape of white sand and blue sea and palm trees. There are all these art deco buildings. It's a very charismatic city.' She stops. 'I've been back a few times, so I can't always separate what it was like then from how it is now.' She pauses. 'You may know that in the DDR my father worked in a factory with lots of other Mozambicans?'

He nods. 'In Lütten Klein.'

'Yes, exactly. God, I'm still getting used to the idea that you knew Papa.'

She presses a napkin to her lips and takes a moment to swallow her food, her eyes suddenly brimming with tears. He risks placing a hand on her forearm and she rewards him with a smile and then dabs at her eyes, picks up her fork and twists some more pasta around it. They munch in silence and then she continues.

'I don't know if you know this,' she says, 'but they call themselves 'Madgermanes', because they spent so long in the DDR, formative years, you know? They have fond memories, through rose-tinted glasses, I suppose. But they were on this special contract that the two governments had arranged, where the DDR transferred most of their salaries to the Mozambican government. The deal was the men would get the remainder, a really large amount of money depending on how long they had worked in the DDR, when they went back to Mozambique. But they never have. It was a real blow.'

'That's terrible.'

'Yes. But the DDR no longer exists, and plus they kept their side of the bargain. It's the government in Mozambique. Every week they hold these protests in a park in the centre of Maputo, demanding their money. Of course, when we were there, Papa joined them, in solidarity. But he didn't fit. I remember he would come home really disconsolate. They were cold with him, even hostile, because his job with the NGO paid well and it paid in Deutschmarks and he was the only one with a German wife. But many of his friends were relying on that money to build a life in Mozambique. It was a travesty.'

She paints a good picture, and he remains silent, hoping she will continue, and after a few moments, she does.

'We were living in this apartment block in an area of Maputo where most people were working for NGOs, most were foreigners. They all thought he had it easy, but it wasn't easy for my parents. For one thing, Mami needed regular kidney dialysis, which was impossible in Maputo. We had to go across the border to South Africa every couple of weeks, which was really expensive. Then, the apartment next to ours was burgled, and the guys were armed, and tied up our neighbour in his bathroom. The country was, at that time, awash with guns from the war, and violence, but we had felt relatively safe until then. It was all too much for Mami. She didn't want to live in Maputo any longer. My Oma and Opa wanted us to come back and live near them, but Papa knew Mami would always suffer from terrible memories if we went back to Germany, and also that she would feel like she had failed, when what she had done, as he always told her, was survived.'

Here her voice breaks, and he looks down at his plate, then the lake, to give her time. Eventually, she picks up her glass, and her voice is even: 'So we went to Portugal.'

Where he opens a restaurant, becomes chef-proprietor and a valued member of the community. Both he and Petra became émigrés. And both lost, among other things, their homelands – in different ways, but it might have drawn them to each other, that shared understanding. There is no jealousy now, or at least it is suspended, only a feeling of pathos. Just as he had waited outside the factory gates to convey his apology all those years ago, he feels now that he is outside the gates, watching a crackly film of the narrative of the man's life, as if on an outdoor screen. He has learned much but also not much, not enough.

They did not reignite their love affair, even after Petra's death, when there were at least ten years during which he could have found her. Instead, he chose a companion closer to home, in his own restaurant, another African émigré. Perhaps finding Lolita would have forever felt like a betrayal of Petra's memory, or perhaps they had separated so acrimoniously it was never an option. He has no idea how their final conversations played out: where, when, and whether they made a pact never to contact each other, but rather to pursue their own happinesses, within their own domains. He must have fallen silent for some time, for it is Clara who restarts the conversation.

'Joachim told me that my father met you in a bar, when you were reading out your work.'

He brings himself back to the present, to this table by the lake. But the dimly lit interior of Sonderbar, a bohemian basement bar in the DDR, hovers in his peripheral vision.

'It's true. He was one of the first people ever to hear my writing and he said some nice things to me afterwards. I remember I was heartened by his words.'

She smiles.

'Well, he continued to enjoy your work. He bought all of your novels.'

He feels a pang in his chest.

'In Portuguese?'

'No, he read them in the original. In German.'

He finds his throat is tight.

'That's nice to hear.'

'But he never mentioned that he knew you,' she says.

There is a silence. Armando did not mention many things, and by the sound of it neither has Joachim Bechtel, who might have sworn secrecy. So, by trying to unlock an avenue of opportunity for himself, he is now talking with a young woman who will, depending on how much he shares, find out much about her father that she did not know.

'Why would that be, do you think?' she asks.

'We both loved the same girl,' he says. 'This is before your parents got married, Clara.'

She looks at him for some seconds, and he tries not to look away from her dark brown, solemn stare. She blinks, then spears a prawn with her fork, before laying it down, untouched.

She says: 'After you got in touch, I realised that I have a photograph of you. I found it among some of my father's things.'

She slips her hand into her bag and pulls out a flip case, flicks through and alights on a page, passes it over.

It is the photo of him and Lolita, his arm around her waist, taken at the fourth birthday party of the person sitting opposite him. He is shocked by the rush of tears that prick at his eyelids and the scene becomes blurry: he looks so young, he had so much hair, what was he wearing? And Lolita, in that beautiful dress. Such a lovely young woman.

'That is you, isn't it?' Clara is saying, almost shyly.

'It is. I remember the day. It was your birthday party.'

'Is that her? The girl you both loved?'

'Yes.'

She is watching him, her eyes still solemn and suddenly she looks like that tiny person who had taken her present and thanked them with a surprisingly deep voice: Danke.

'Do you remember her?' he asks.

She shakes her head.

'She's called Lolita. I've recently been in touch with her,' he says. And he takes out his phone from his pocket, swipes at the screen, brings up the picture he has saved. 'Her WhatsApp profile picture.'

She takes his phone.

'Yes, it's her,' she says, as if he were asking her to confirm her identity.

He watches while her eyes move from one photo to the next, to see how the young woman now looks in middle age. Then she puts his phone down on the table, but rests her hand over it, and stares for some minutes at the lake. He does not turn his gaze from her, so he is looking at her when she slides the phone away from her side of the table and meets his eyes.

'What happened?'

'There isn't much to tell,' he lies. 'Lolita preferred your father and who can blame her?'

He grins, but she does not smile back and so he clears his throat.

'I think she had to leave when all the changes started, and then of course your parents got married.'

His words provoke a torrent of questions even to his own ears. Were they happy, your parents? Did Armando overcome his love for Lolita? It took me years and I'm not even sure if I am over her, really. She sits quietly. The same questions could be swirling like a tornado inside her, but she appears calm, at least outwardly, and a little sad.

He decides to say: 'Your father and Lolita took you to a beach near Warnemünde one day. Do you remember that?'

She shakes her head.

'They found the body of a man who was trying to escape to Denmark. We used to call them republikflüchtlinge.' He tries to smile. 'Your father went into the water and pulled the body out.'

She watches him. He has learned that all of this is news to her, Armando has not related any of this, never mentioned his name, nor Rainer's. He swallows at the thought of his late, much loved, grandfather. Nothing has been said either about the bracelet: Tommy. Perhaps Armando had learned that from the DDR, the wisdom of not talking too much. The young woman opposite him has no curiosity about the name Tommy, and who it might have referred to, and it is not even a brilliant story, and so he will not say anything more about it, even though he knows he will write about it.

'He had a bit of a tough time after that, your father.'

'With the Stasi?'

'Yes.'

Her expression does not change, and he has no idea what she is feeling.

'Perhaps,' he finds he needs to clear his throat and starts again, 'perhaps that's why he didn't talk about that period of his life.'

Their plates are empty now, and the waiter arrives to clear them away, again addressing Clara at length, which breaks the spell, so that all the visions that were crowding around him dissipate. They both order an espresso and make, now, desultory conversation, observing the boats, discussing her work and he shares with her more details of the life of a successful author.

It is only when they are retracing their steps on the promenade, from where they will turn off to find the back road leading to the train station, that she says: 'I've never learned how to swim. I used to have these bad dreams about Papa trying to teach me how to swim and not doing very well. I've always been scared of the water. Maybe that's why.'

He accompanies her onto the platform which is hot and exposed, but she seems to delight in the sun, holding her face to catch its warmth, and curling her toes in her sandals with pleasure from the rays. He watches her, transfixed, his heart full.

Then she turns to him and asks: 'What is Lolita doing now?'

'Well, I'm not sure.' He cannot tell her about the private investigator. 'But she qualified as a doctor. I think she works in a clinic in India.'

'You haven't spoken to her?'

'No, not for the last thirty or so years.'

'But you have her contact on your phone.'

'Yes.'

'Is she married?'

'I don't know. I don't think so.'

'I think you should call her,' she says.

'Do you, Clara?' he smiles.

'Well, you could tell her about Papa,' and now she holds his eyes. 'That's why you got in touch with me, isn't it? To find out more about Papa, so you could tell Lolita?'

Again, he sees no judgement in her eyes, although she has every right to judge. He does not respond to her, and the train chugs in. She holds her fist out, and they bump knuckles again, even though he truly wishes to take her in his arms and hold her close, all one hundred and eighty centimetres of her, kiss her forehead like she were his child. She puts her sunglasses on and climbs up into the carriage.

He walks back to the lake, on the way passing a couple he has some acquaintance with: she is American and he is from Munich. They exchange pleasantries. Yes, he's just had lunch with the daughter of an old friend. Yes, he plans to swim tomorrow, he might see them at their favourite spot. He settles on a bench in front of the lake and watches the young people and the couples and older people and families with young children.

Perhaps, he thinks, it will be himself and the character who will be Lolita who find the body in the water. And even though he has no ill-feeling towards the man after so many years, and even though he is moved by his life's journey and particularly by his precious daughter, he does wonder whether, finally, he will be able to enact a small revenge for the defeat, the loss, and elide Armando Dos Santos completely from the story. He considers this, and his motives. It will be his prerogative as a writer, and it will not be underhand, because Armando already knew that was how he did it. He had once asked: how do you know when to diverge from the truth? When writing the truth is more painful than fiction.

He shifts his position and watches a man of his age use the outdoor gym equipment, with the lake as its backdrop. He admits that he is not even sure whether he can bear to write about Lolita. He remembers how he tore up pages and pages into tiny shreds, when he had last tried to write of her, those days after he had seen her but could not find her. Perhaps Lolita will be a young blonde from Leipzig who, like him, is sent to live with an older relative in the north of the country and they happen upon the body of a man in the water and embark on a quest to find his family.

The sun begins to descend, but it remains warm. A breeze cools the back of his neck, which is slightly burned. His phone beeps and on opening the message, he sees on the screen the photograph of Lolita and him at the party from more than thirty years ago, and an accompanying note from Clara: *I completely forgot to ask you to sign the books I brought with me. They were just sitting in my bag, but with all our talk, I ended up forgetting you are the famous Theo Becker! I have a book that Joachim wanted you to sign for him!*

He looks at his watch. It is a bit late now, but he could drive into Milan in the morning. Or perhaps not: he should let her enjoy the rendezvous she has made with her friend. He types his message, laboriously, squinting at the screen: *It gives me a good excuse to get back in touch with you and continue our conversation. When I am back in Berlin, shall we meet up again? It would be an honour to sign however many books you have, just as it was an honour to meet you today.* He presses 'send'.

Clara. She is a good reminder of the present: his present and hers and that of the others.

The lake ahead of him is a vast, bright blue expanse. And he thinks: I will teach her how to swim. The water will hold you up, Clara, I will tell her. You have only to give your body over to its waves and you have nothing to fear.

ACKNOWLEDGEMENTS

My deepest gratitude to Stan, for never giving up, and to my editor Isabelle Kenyon at Fly on the Wall Press for taking a punt on me. Thank you, Isabelle, for your boundless energy and ideas, your passion and for making a difference. My gratitude as well to Sarah-Jayne Kenyon for proofing and corrections.

To friends and family and readers who have supported me over four novels and championed my writing – thank you.

The works of the following were invaluable in my research into the DDR: Maxim Leo, Anna Funder, Ulrike L. Neuendorf, Mark Aaron Keck-Szajbel, and Marcia C. Schenk.

The epigraph is taken from the late Elke Erb's poem Thema Verfelht, published in 'Poet's Corner 3' by Unabhangige Verlagsbuchhandlung, 1991. I use the translation by Judith Urban found in Barbara Mabee's essay in 'Studies in 20th Century Literature', 1997.

My gratitude to colleagues Leonie Gaiser and Eva Schultze-Berndt for helping me confirm the small details that really count, and especially to Tanja Müller for our discussions, her research, and her insights into the lives of the 'Madgermanes'.

Finally, but foremostly, to Bonnie and Ruby, who put up with me, and who fill me with pride every day. And James, for everything, always.

ABOUT THE AUTHOR

Sheena Kalayil is a critically acclaimed Manchester-based author and teacher. 'The Others' is Kalayil\'s fourth novel, continuing her profound examination of untold stories from the crossroads of history and human experience. Her third book, 'The Wild Wind', drew inspiration from her own nomadic upbringing shuttling between India, Zambia, and Zimbabwe. Kalayil's debut novel, 'The Bureau of Second Chances', announced her as a major new literary talent, winning the prestigious Writers' Guild Award for Best First Novel and being shortlisted for the Edward Stanford Prize for Fiction with a Sense of Place. With a lifetime of experiences teaching around the world, from Nepal and Mozambique to Tunisia and Venezuela, Kalayil brings a truly global perspective to her writing. Since 2002, she has called the UK home, now teaching at the University of Manchester while penning rich, immersive narratives that transcend borders.

BOOK CLUB QUESTIONS

1. How do Armando and Theo's reactions and emotions toward the DDR compare? What similarities or differences do you notice?

2. How did finding the body, who Lolita believes to be 'Tommy', change the stakes for Lolita and Armando's budding relationship?

3. What was the significance of Theo separating from Lolita at the wall when travel restrictions were lifted?

4. Do you think Rainer was justified in alerting the state about Armando and Lolita finding 'Tommy'?

5. In what ways are Lolita's relationships with Armando and Theo alike, and how do they differ?

6. How did Petra's attack shift the course of the plot?

7. Why do you think Lolita left Germany without saying goodbye to Armando?

8. What is the significance of Theo reconnecting with Clara years later?

About Fly on the Wall Press

A publisher with a conscience.
Political, Sustainable, Ethical.
Publishing politically-engaged, international fiction, poetry and cross-genre anthologies on pressing issues. Founded in 2018 by founding editor, Isabelle Kenyon.

Some other publications:

The Sound of the Earth Singing to Herself by Ricky Ray

We Saw It All Happen by Julian Bishop

Imperfect Beginnings by Viv Fogel

These Mothers of Gods by Rachel Bower

Sin Is Due To Open In A Room Above Kitty's by Morag Anderson

Snapshots of the Apocalypse by Katy Wimhurst

Demos Rising edited by Isabelle Kenyon

Exposition Ladies by Helen Bowie

Climacteric by Jo Bratten

The State of Us by Charlie Hill

The Unpicking by Donna Moore

The Sleepless by Liam Bell

Lying Perfectly Still by Laura Fish

Social Media:

@fly_press (X) @flyonthewallpress (Instagram)

@flyonthewallpress (Facebook, Bluesky and TikTok)

www.flyonthewallpress.co.uk